TATTOO

For Mike & Pat -
Best wishes on the
"Black Cat"

Blackwell 08

TATTOO

INCIDENT AT THE WEIRS

J.P. Polidoro

To order additional copies of this book, contact:
Xlibris Corporation
1-888-795-4274
www.Xlibris.com
Orders@Xlibris.com
39515

For brother, Tony and nephew, John

Avid motorcycle enthusiasts

Prologue

Legend of Lake Winnipesaukee

Many moons ago on the northern shore of this beautiful lake there lived a great chief, Wonaton, renowned for his great courage in war, and for the beauty of his fair daughter, Mineola. She had many suitors, but refused them all. One day, Adiwando, the young chief of a hostile tribe to the south, hearing so much of the fair Mineola, paddled across the lake and fearlessly entered the village of his enemies. Her father happened to be away at the time, and admiring his courage, the rest of the Indians did not harm him. Before long, he and the Indian maid were desperately in love with each other. Wonaton, on his return was exceedingly wroth to find the chief of the enemy in his camp and a suitor for the hand of his daughter, that he immediately raised his tomahawk to kill him. Mineola, rushing in between them, pleaded with her father for the life of her lover, and finally succeeded in reconciling them. After the wedding ceremony, the whole tribe accompanied the two in their canoes halfway across the lake. The sky when they started was overcast and the waters black, but just as they were about to turn and leave them, the sun came out and the waters sparkled around the canoe of Mineola and Adiwando. "This is a good omen," said Wonaton, "and hereafter these waters shall be called Winnipesaukee, or "Smile of the Great Spirit."

Ref: www.lwhs.us/win-legend.htm

The lake today retains the spirit of the Native-Americans and the early colonists that once traversed the steep mountains and traced the rivers to reach the central part of the pine-laden land. Glaciers carved her valleys and created the incremental ranges of peaks that reach to the sky to the North.

Mt. Washington, the tallest icon in New Hampshire, towers over her lower sister peaks, the Presidential Range that also beckon hikers, sightseers and the masses that wish to communicate with nature and bathe in the clear waters that were conceived by melting snow-pack each Spring. Like nearby bucolic Vermont, the State of New Hampshire has long drawn the city dwellers that need to escape the Boston and New York madness of daily congestion, foul air and confusion. Poets, the likes of Robert Frost, and writers like Mark Twain and musicians, like Aerosmith have sought out the Monadnocks, Sunapee and Lakes Region to inspire their written words and congeal their thoughts in lyrics and poignant verse. Inspirational views command thoughtful prose, even today.

In the 2000's, as in the 1800's, travelers have sought out the ragged granite cliffs to climb, meditate and sit, or seek the porches of cabins on Squam Lake (Golden Pond) and the smaller waterways that allow "Man" to think in solitude while immersed in the local visual aura and music of the birds or other feral animals that forage for survival in the nearby wood.

New Hampshire can be quiet and desolate—the farther north one travels, the more remote the forest exists as pure nature. The protection of the White Mountain National Forest was set in stone years ago, virgin to this day in many acres of yet un-traversed or non-abused grandeur.

Drawn by the vast lupine fields to the north, a collage of purple, red, white and yellow flowers and the natural wildflowers of lilac, mountain laurel and sumac, maple and oak's reds, yellows and purples, wanderers yearn for the quiet beauty of the dense pines that are interspersed with pristine white birch, poplar and wetland flora and cattails that often surround each valley town and village, quintessential homes and white picket fences that remind us of the history of the Colonial era when America was young, fragile and unclaimed, except by the New World squatters from afar.

England could not hold her, this "new land" or their brave adventurers that traveled on behalf of their kings or queens from England or Spain. The men and women of red-skinned hue that befriended the new colonists shared their community without adversity until the white man abused the land and encroached upon their native hunting and fishing grounds—their life blood. Often desecrating the burial grounds of their elders and spirits, the "white man" forced the Natives to back further from their sources of food and water, the same lakes we swim in, boat and fish today—the selfish bastards of the day that raped the land, the people and the resources of human survival as in the water bodies and all tributaries south—that were essential to all life, man and beast.

The moose, bear and deer and lesser game retreated to safe harbor and today are sparse unless one ventures deep into the wood to find their sanctuary. New Hampshire, like Vermont, Maine and upper New York has evolved into a playground for the people that follow the asphalt conduits to the north, making virtually all parts of those States easily accessible in a day's ride or less. Now tourist attractions that bring revenue into the Granite State, and to the pristine forests and jagged cliffs, are the framework of the camera viewfinder possessed by some distant visitors with different colored license plates on their SUV's and family vans.

The once proud and ancient (10,000 yrs.) "Old Man of the Mountain" fell 1,200 feet in time as well, May 3, 2003, with five layers of granite from forehead to chin (40 by 25 feet) that eroded over centuries with the chin letting go one foggy night with a thunderous, cascading roar. The *remainder* of the famous stone face and icon of the State followed by gravity, as layer by layer it descended while sleepy campers and U. S. Park Rangers heard the roar of rocky granite crumble one night in the opaque mist.

Once sighted in 1805, at morning's light, the face was gone forever. Neither wires and heavy clamps and turnbuckle tackle, cement or putty could hold him any longer. It was the fissures of times past, where water froze in winter and secretly waited to expand that caused his demise and with that the loss of its grip in the mountain framework, the grand old face tumbled in seconds toward Profile Lake, like it never existed at all. The State of New Hampshire's official symbol (1945) was mourned and the Native-Americans and early settlers who saw the Old Man in its infancy or for the first time, disappeared with him, forever.

The land and water, and the historic events of mankind that evolved over the last 200 years bind tradition in New Hampshire. Some traditions are winter inspired and some are summer and fall. Maple sugaring, annual fishing derbies of note, historical international sled dog races and ski events of Nordic value, while summer draws the lake crowds and sailing races that are garnered from the white sails and jibs of the competitions on the Big Lake ever circling and traversing the islands, "the broads" and "the witches."

The fishing derby of note in winter draws some 6,000 anglers vying for $60,000 in prizes, a boat and miscellaneous anglers' equipment. Starting in 1980 as the Great Rotary Fishing Derby at Meredith Bay, it has consistently raised some one million dollars for local charities. It can draw some 16,000 visitors increasing the local economy in general by two million dollars. The New Hampshire Fish and Game raise, stock and support tagged trout in eleven lakes in the Lakes Region where the Rotary Club offers $15,000 to the coffer that fosters the tournament, future fish stocking and the annual outdoors events each February.

Fishing licenses in the State increase by 11% in February, a boost for early Fish and Game revenues each new year. A 9.92-pound, 33.13-inch lake trout was caught in Lake Ossipee in 2003 by Cory Ricker of Maine. In 2006, the famed sled dog races and fishing derby coincided the same weekend, February 4-5th potentially fostering more money for the locals but stretching the resources for accommodations and restaurants while congesting the local area beyond expectations. The two events are usually held on separate weekends. With the lack of snow in the winter of 2006, the sled dog races were cancelled anyway, saving hotel rooms for the fishing derby, which did occur.

In winter, snowmobiles aid anglers in reaching remote locations on the small and large lakes. The snowmobile events and trails during the winter months let Lakes Region riders follow the woods and towns all the way to Canada if they desire, with manicured and charted trails maintained by local clubs that find refuge in the occasional huts and villages along the way. The Native-Americans had to walk the same territories just to obtain food and game relegated to them by the "Great Spirits" of their time. Traversing the snow depths, ice packs and accessing frozen lakes at 16-24 inches to find the same species of fish sought today for tournaments, required days and weeks of work by the Native-Americans with their extensive land travel, just to survive.

Of all its history, New Hampshire shines, including the birth and historic homestead of an American President, Franklin Pierce, in Hillsborough, New Hampshire. The Lakes Region in particular set a precedent of how man would live and survive the harsh winters and warm summers of beauty in an untamed forest of green pine, white birch and poplar.

The trades began, with established mills, mines and factories that harbored life's riches and revenue, followed by streetcars and trains that brought people together and easily accessible to one another. Textiles, machinery fabrication and paper mills dominated the area, producers of clothing for World Wars I and II and socks for the common man, knitting machines and trolley and boat production operations infused and married the attributes of the Colonial tradesmen from Europe with the Canadian artisans of old. The Franco-American influence from the north made New Hampshire a thriving community of necessary products and employment opportunities.

The waterways powered the mills, which were to some extent the subject of many years of the contamination of those waterways—their effluent containing unknown toxic products and waste including hydrocarbons, sulfur, dyes and heavy metals (lead, mercury) that would need to be remediated in the decades that followed. Both the water downstream and air to the east would be affected by a normal workday. Prevailing jet-stream winds and tributaries carried the noxious agents to other areas of the State.

Historically, smokestacks of brick and metal were welcomed and meant, "work," prosperity and a booming economy for the locals but by today's standards for air quality, smokestacks mean pollution, something the mill owners and workers were not aware of in the days of the Industrial Revolution and an emerging transportation industry where the internal combustion engine was evolving on rail beds and roadways. Mass transportation was needed for raw materials and for products fabricated in vast brick mill buildings along the rivers.

The harmful biochemical effects on "Man" by their mill trades would not be known until a century later, one in which occupational diseases emerged as the European and North American continents fused and married human workers from distant lands, well trained and idealistic for a new and prosperous life in the Americas. Covered bridges of grandiose design became replaced by steel girders and cross arms, yet numerous old covered bridges exist to this day with spans of over 300 feet, a lasting memory of New England transportation by horse and buggy.

Dirt roads of old became "paved," first by oil sprayed to reduce dust, and then by crushed stone and eventually asphalt / macadam, and vehicles evolved in the 1800's some of which, imported from England and Europe, were either four-wheeled or two-wheeled.

The motorcycle was a transport medium back then albeit in its infancy, but often necessary for travel, sport and for the affluent who wanted to venture out into the countryside on Sundays. Sidecars allowed for the women to accompany the men. Groups and motorcycle social clubs from Boston ventured north for fun, pitting one man's machine against another for speed and sport. They gathered at swank hotels in the New Hampshire mountains and ate and drank together and congealed at the pristine beaches on New Hampshire's lakes, where picnics and political events called them together for socials, annual events and ice cream.

What transpired during that growth was the establishment of one recreational sport that remains today some 83 years and counting—the oldest continuous motorcycle rally and races in the history of the United States. The place where the mechanical fanatics chose to meet and cavort was the Lakes Region i.e. Laconia, Loudon and the Belknap Mountain range establishing road races and hill climbs of historical note and folly today.

Each year, the silent enchanted forest and pastures, sleepy towns and villages of New Hampshire are relegated to accept the noise and masses of some 300-400,000 visitors and 100,000 motorcycles that gather like "swallows returning to Capistrano." The sheer numbers of the Laconia Rally attendees during Father's Day week and weekend in June is a constant, rain or shine. The serene State becomes another vision and aura for nine or more days, a surreal vision that is the antithesis of its daily routine for residents at other times of the year. Somehow, with all its history, New Hampshire welcomes the two-wheeled marauders with open arms for a tradition is just that, a repeated scenario that cannot be broken like a human chain letter of old.

It was reported that bikers had aged over the years. The average age of bikers was now 41. One local newspaper claimed that BMW owners averaged 53-years-old while Harley customers averaged 47. All in all, Laconia drew motorcyclists of all ages.

Chapter 1

In New Jersey, and specifically the town of Metuchen, a large man known as Iceman lifted his right leg to straddle his black leather motorcycle seat. His weight compressed the cowhide, which groaned and squeaked from his sheer presence in the early hours of the morn. His journey north about to commence, he flipped the switch that turned on the lone headlight and then kick-started the massive machine. It rumbled and idled in the dark with a sound that mimicked the "potato, potato, potato" sound of the Harley-Davidson mufflers.

Harleys had a classic sound basically because of their unique engine design. Generally in two-piston engines with opposing cylinders, there is one pin for each cylinder to the connecting rod, 180 degrees apart. One piston fires on each revolution of the crankshaft, the other cylinder fires on the next rotation. In the Harley, *both* pistons connect to the shaft by *one* pin not two, making it unbalanced. The motor also has a "V" engine design of the pistons. One piston fires every 360 degrees instead of every 180 degrees. In essence, a piston fires; the next piston fires at 315 degrees; there is then a 405 degree gap, then a piston fires; the next piston fires at 315 degrees of shaft rotation followed by another 405 degree gap. At idle, Iceman's bike sounded like pop pop-pop pop-pop pop, with intermittent pauses between pop pop. Iceman loved the sound, as did most H-D riders past and present.

Iceman was known locally in New Jersey, but primarily by the local chapters of motorcycle gangs that were often well connected to Italian-American New York and New Jersey groups that stretched from Manhattan to Union and Jersey City, New Jersey. Newark-based clubs were included in the geographical mix.

Greeted by two other riders at a local diner, known as Ma's, they met for a quick breakfast and coffee and were about to embark on a long journey north to New Hampshire. Fellow riders, Joe "Rocco" Spinelli and Joey Bertucci sat in the booth at the far end of the traditional building which resembled a train car of old, almost caboose-like with green painted sides, yellow lettering that read "Good Food and Drink," "Ma's Since 1924" and "Hot Coffee to Go." Joey was known as The Nomad. Inside the diner, the parquet tiled, black and white flooring of old was embellished by a garish stainless steel-paneled facade behind the counter, where milk and coffee dispensers implied by their shininess, that the aging eating establishment was "sterile and clean." The Health Certificate from the Board of Health certified *that* in 2005.

A waitress, seemingly between customers, wiped the stainless panels with a moist rag that in and of itself looked a bit tainted by coffee stains. The false impression remained however, even as one noted on close inspection, that it was merely another "greasy spoon" of traditional Americana, enhanced by neon signs and nostalgic pictures of Elvis, 1957 Chevrolets and a velvet Filipino painting of James Dean. These metallic icons, still strewn across America and especially in the Midwest and in the Heartlands, are the precursors and grandparents of modern day fast-food restaurants like McDonald's, Burger King and Wendy's. All that differed at Ma's was the type of food listed on the Xeroxed weekly menus that touted homemade "this and that," including soups, Ma's peach pie and "blue plate specials" of Swedish meatballs, meatloaf and mashed potatoes, as opposed to paper thin burgers, chicken parts and fries.

Iceman's chain on his belt loop held keys and a knife, making a distinct noise as he slid across the cracked leather seat of the corner booth. Rocco, Joey and Iceman talked low, except when they ordered and then quickly powered down their eggs, sausage, garlic and onion-infused home fries while washing the cholesterol and fat-infused conglomeration down with heavy mugs of coffee.

They seemed anxious to hit the road as the young waitress, Trina tried to refill their cups of java. They waved her off with the sweep of a hand and hinted that they needed the tab in rapid order. She smiled and obliged. Returning behind the counter, she felt intimidated by the three men whose faces were new to her. Were they locals? It really didn't matter. She had seen it all at the diner and at all hours.

"Nice ass on that chick," Iceman commented, callously. The others smiled and joked that she would be quite the addition to their harem of women at the Metuchen club.

"Wouldn't mind rolling her over for a couple rounds," Rocco added. "Reminds me of that video we saw of the ladies that Ron Jeremy starred with years back. 'Believe it was called, '*Scooter Trash.*'"

"She looks like one of those babes, you're right . . . similar T&A. Nice booty," Joey added, in fantasy.

She was happy to see them leave.

Within minutes, the three men had accessed the Jersey Turnpike and were headed north. To the right of them, and off in the distance, was the outline of New York City and the refineries of New Jersey whose only real lights were the yellow flames of the towers that burned off the gaseous byproducts of their crude productions that satisfied the gas and petroleum needs of the eastern portion of the United States. The ride had just begun and the sun was rising as the three men sought the New York Thruway and the Tappan Zee Bridge across the Hudson from eastern New York to Connecticut. It would be a good five and one-half hour ride through Hartford and New England before they would cross the border into New Hampshire. The occasional pit stop to relieve themselves of coffee and the caffeine-induced need to urinate or grab a sandwich along the way was their only detour planned on the entire trip.

They were the common breeds of cat who would inundate and infest Rally Week; a welcomed retreat from northern New Jersey's often criticized polluted air and waterways adjacent to The Meadowlands.

Chapter 2

Laconia, New Hampshire, deemed the City of The Lakes, is a city rich with tradition among all the other settlements north of Manchester, New Hampshire and Lowell, Massachusetts. Nestled between Lake Winnipesaukee and Lake Winnisquam, it is a former mill town, like many New Hampshire towns that border the Winnipesaukee, Pemigewasset and Merrimack Rivers—often starting in the mountains and running south from the Lakes Region of the Granite State to other New England States to the south. The Laconia name, incorporated in 1893, was derived from a group that explored the area in the 1600's. They were called the Laconia Adventurers and named after a region of ancient Greece.

The proximity of the waterways provided the necessary power to mechanically run the "operations"—eventually providing the generation of electricity to run each "factory" in total.

Lake Winnipesaukee, the largest of the watersheds, which egresses by way of Paugus Bay into Lake Opechee, and then descends through Laconia proper to vent into Lake Winnisquam is still the mother load of water—the energy provider. The rivers continue south to Manchester where shoe, sweater and textile mills flourished, and eventually ran east to enter the Atlantic near the coastal towns of the Great Bay and terminating at the ocean ports of Portsmouth, New Hampshire or south to other States.

The Native-American names of the lakes revealed and accented the importance of the Natives' roles in the Northeast territory. They relied on the water for their sustenance, fishing with hand-tied netting and often sourced the lakes' edges for game and food.

Although Colonial settlements evolved into towns, which grew the economy, the fabric mills crafted sweaters, hosiery, and knitting machines and needles becoming the oldest mills in the country, many of which employed the French-Canadian immigrants that migrated south from Montreal. Their *talent* drove the industrialization of the Northeast, post colonization.

The Belknap, Busiel and Clow Mills of Laconia were prominent establishments that made clothing for soldiers, the mills garnering their power from the mighty outflow of the largest lakes in the center of the State of New Hampshire—streams that flow today in the same manner and direction as they did then.

Lakeport Village, originally Folson's Mills, and established in 1766, remains a Laconia community located near the termination of Paugus Bay. A dam separates the bay from Lake Opechee. Paugus Bay harbored mills and shipbuilding centers for steamboat construction. Originally a geographical portion of Gilford, New Hampshire, it became part of Laconia proper in 1855.

The remnants of the train service (primarily freight) that carried raw materials, granite, logs and later passengers in the 1800's from Lakeport to Weirs Beach remains today, ever the reminder of the key transport media during the older days of steam. Yearly motorcyclists of Rally Week frequent the roads that involve Lakeport—both Elm Street and Union Avenue provide conduits and shortcuts to local activities during the festivities.

The railroad shuttle to The Weirs is boarded at that intersection as well, thus Lakeport remains a contributing community to the events of Father's Day week and weekend.

Even today, modern diesel engines pull old Pullman-like passenger railcars during Motorcycle Week allowing the masses of people easy access to The Weirs events of the annual Rally some three miles north of Gilford. Avoiding the congestion of thousands of bikes and cars, the scenic ride by rail takes the traveler along Paugus Bay, the channeled outflow of the Big Lake where some spans of the bay mimic a small lake in their own rite. The ten to fifteen-minute ride along the water's edge was no different in 2006 than it was in 1918 when motorcyclists first gathered together to celebrate the famed annual June tradition.

The stately brick buildings in the center of Laconia remain today, renovated in real time and stored on film in numerous old photographs and glass plates within the archives of the historic Gale Memorial Library downtown. The library is adjacent to the original Laconia train station of slate-covered terra cotta and gray stone stature—a structural fortress that will outlast the next centuries of summer visitors. Blue and white English-made enamel signs (LACONIA) adorn the massive building—traditional RR I.D.s by town and depot.

The city of some 17,000 residents becomes a haven for the summer crowds that vacation in the Lakes Region each year. License plates from Massachusetts, Connecticut, New York, Pennsylvania and New Jersey traverse New Hampshire's I-93 and I-95 accessing the beaches of the coast or the White Mountains to the north of Concord. The White Mountain National Forest begins near Plymouth, just north of Laconia.

Glaciers carved the Lakes Region of New Hampshire, but ten thousand years ago the Penacook tribe first inhabited the area. They were the first visitors to the region, living off the rich land and water.

Historical records in the local Chamber of Commerce cite 1652 as the first recorded visitors to the area, with Laconia being the recreational center of New Hampshire. Geographically, it remains close to the center of the State as well.

After the French and Indian Wars in 1763, settlers from the seacoast communities, primarily farmers, migrated inland. Fertile soil beckoned them. Farming and prosperity led eventually to the "mill industry" in the 19th Century sparking the industrial age in the Lakes Region. Once upon a time, steamships flourished on the lakes, and railroads expanded for freight and passenger service in the 1800's, allowing transportation to Boston, often carrying granite, ice, lumber, textiles and people on the new, big steel rail.

Visitors and vacationers came from around the world and country, and Laconia grew majestically. On the other side of the Big Lake, an older town called Wolfeboro expanded as well making it "the oldest vacation spot in the United States."

Chapter 3

Lake Winnipesaukee and Weirs Beach stand at 504-feet above sea level. Twenty-eight miles long and seventy-two square miles, the lake boasts 283-miles of shoreline. Once uninhabited along its coast, one is hard-pressed today to find any land on the shoreline that has not been developed into residences, including its islands. Its depth is maximized at 170-feet and the body of water has some 274-islands interspersed throughout its vast expanse.

As part of Laconia, the recreational center of the lake is still regarded as the Weirs Beach area. In the summer, it is a playground for the summer crowd often mimicking an amusement park atmosphere and boardwalk. Souvenir shops, pizza, ice cream and video game parlors extend the length of the boardwalk and sidewalks of Lakeside Avenue.

Traditional Victorian buildings line the beach road, a testimony to the days of Colonial times and WWI, and the grandiose hotels which offered vacationers R&R from the war torn years as well as big city life in Boston, Massachusetts. Prominent hotels in the Lakes and Mountain Regions catered to the affluent, especially in the 1800's.

Weirs Beach was inhabited by the Native-Americans, offering both shelter and abundant salmon and other fish.

The word, "Weirs" originated from the fencing used by the Aquedoctans to fish the local waterways and the Big Lake. Prior to 1652, no "white man" most probably had ever stepped on the land, which we know today as Laconia and The Weirs.

The northern-most limit of the Massachusetts Bay Colony Grant was marked by today's Endicott Rock at the mouth of Paugus Bay at Weirs

Beach. Captain Simon Willard, at the request of the Governor of the Massachusetts Bay Colony, John Endicott, left his inscription on a rock there. The granite stone marker is considered one of New England's oldest public monuments, and delineates what the Colonists described as the headway of the Merrimack River. Today, that rock marks the egress of the Big Lake.

In the latter 19th Century, The Weirs became the vacation destination with express trains shuttling Bostonians to the popular vacation hotspot. Today, beachgoers, anglers, boating enthusiasts and sightseers in summer and fall appreciate the Lakes Region and the waters of the pristine lake—Lake "Winni."

In addition to the summer crowds that visit or inhabit The Weirs from Memorial Day until Labor Day, the Weirs Beach community hosts the annual Laconia Motorcycle Rally and Race Week. The Sturgis and Daytona Rallies exceed a tradition for over 83 years, the Laconia Rally only in size, popularity and attendance. The Weirs community fosters the thousands of bikes and encourages commercial tents where vendors hawk tattoos, leather chaps, hats and jackets, motorcycles and parts, T-shirts, massages, XXX-videos, rally pins and patches, doo-rags, evangelists with bibles, food and custom motorcycles of the latest craze or vintage models. Because of the thousands of motorcycles, Lakeside Avenue, along Weirs Beach is restricted to mostly bikes and trikes, with larger four-wheeled vehicles limited to a one-way direction and direct access for nine days.

Chapter 4

Sturgis, in the Black Hills, is a monster motorcycle rally. Twenty-eight percent of the attendees are women. The Sturgis Rally is not held downtown but in an area known as Buffalo Chip, a pasture and geographical area of the plains that is expansive. Sturgis' "Hell on Wheels" is an anything goes, party atmosphere when compared to a milder Laconia. The Full Throttle Saloon at Sturgis serves 30,000 bikers a day with beer and other liquors. Riders who come to Sturgis to get their first tattoo are known as "Sturgis Virgins," the tattoo being their right of passage.

"Cherokee Chuck" is one of the famed personalities in the art of tattooing there. As most artists claim, "Be careful which tattoo *name* you get—'tattoos outlast most relationships.'"

At Sturgis and other rallies, Rhett Rotten rides the Wall of Death, a 1940's wooden circular wall that he circumvents with a 1927 Indian motorcycle, screaming at 40 MPH. A similar Wall of Death comes to Laconia as well.

The Sturgis Rally also hosts major performers like ZZ Top and Kid Rock. Kevin Costner has been seen there on rally rides. Sturgis hosts a "Burn Out" contest where bikes are stationary and scream at high RPM's until the rear tire burns, smokes and pops. The crowd votes for the winner by cheers and volume.

Unlike Laconia Rally Week, "anything goes" at the Buffalo Chip gathering, where thousands of bikers party non-stop, get naked, and show body parts while totally uninhibited. Women "flash" for "beads" comparable to Bourbon Street in New Orleans. Bare breasts are common and photographed by onlookers.

At one time, Laconia had similar uninhibited activities, but in recent years the police have increased their surveillance negating most activities that Sturgis actually supports, encourages and endorses today.

The newest geographical venue for bikers is Angel City / Unadilla in Georgia, 120-miles south of Atlanta off I-75. Their April 2006 Rally drew 17,000 people. With 10 million motorcyclists in the U.S., the organizers at Unadilla aim to mimic Sturgis, Daytona and Laconia with rock concerts, fireworks and assorted biker venues and tents.

They offer cheap beer, Western shoot-outs with actors, and the Iron Angels biker chicks that pose next to customized bikes for calendars and promo photos. The two million dollar Western town in the South is on a 400-acre spread, and is a draw for spring and fall rallies. It is styled after the Sturgis event.

Chapter 5

Every year and during Laconia Bike Week, Lakeside Avenue is transformed into a minimum of four lanes of parked Harleys and rice-rockets, often multi-colored or fur embellished with chrome accoutrements and bathing suit or thong-clad biker chicks that hang on to their leathered riders like taillights on a fender. The appealing sight draws onlookers, mostly men, who gawk and photograph them with their 200-800 X lenses that often capture the peaks and crevices of well-toned bodies. The tanned ladies desire to be Eve reborn in the motorized parade of God's motorcycle Garden of Eden—the annual mid-June land regatta of moving metal and riders each year.

Anticipated at The Weirs this year was Chrissy Becktoft, the "Patch Queen," who uses a 100-year-old sewing machine to secure patches on leather vests and jackets for biker clients. Sixteen hours a day, she sews "Live Free or Die" or the latest Harley patch or Bike Week commemorative logo on a variety of leathers, being careful not to make a mistake. "Punching holes in leather is permanent," she joked in a newspaper article. "Can't screw up."

Aside from Chrissy, who attends most annual rallies around the United States, there are myriad of regulars who attend The Weirs event yearly. "Papa Joe," from Swanzey, New Hampshire is a noted minister who has hosted the annual Bike Week blessing for more than 25 years.

Expected again this 2006 Rally was Kitti Lynxxx, a biker chick that touts her mountainous attributes in the flesh and poses with fans for photos. Body paint merely transforms her skin into cat faces and paws. Beneath the paint is pure human leather, that being real skin and no bra or top.

Mike Skiver, a tattooist, considers himself an artist. He claims that it's the "second oldest art form," since "cave drawings," and prides himself in not making his clients bleed. "Credentials like a doctor," he was once quoted as saying in a news article.

"I'm an artist," he was heard boasting the previous year. He travels up to New Hampshire from Pennsylvania for the Laconia Rally.

"Anyone can tattoo," his said to a newspaper reporter, his Santa Claus-like beard blowing in the wind that day.

The sights and sounds of the human influx for nine days of parties, beer and half-naked women can be photographed with a seven-dollar, cardboard Kodak camera—a tall, wooden tower on the main drag of Lakeside Avenue provides the best view. The cost? Minimal—$3.00 to climb the ladder and shoot either one or a hundred panoramic photographic shots.

The economy of Laconia and the Lake Region gains millions of dollars mostly from "guys who want beer, and women that want healthy food." Some estimate that the State of New Hampshire reaps $100M in revenues that week. Beer tents galore are well observed and monitored by local officials including police from surrounding communities that lend "mutual aid" and oversight all week long. Direct train commutes from Lakeport to the south and Meredith from the north allow for sightseers and bikers from across the country to arrive by rail at The Weirs trouble free, without the hassle of massive traffic jams on Route 3 and Lakeside Avenue. They disembark at the Weirs Beach train depot in close proximity to the M/S Mount Washington cruise ship that remains moored at The Weirs dock / boardwalk and evolves into a "beer party boat" all week, never having to leave its berth.

Chapter 6

The year of the 83rd Laconia Bike Rally was celebrated in 2006. During that week the masses of bikers and race fans inundated the Lakes Region and the central and southern portions of New Hampshire. The dates for the event were June 10-18th and incorporated Father's Day weekend. In addition to The Weirs organized events that were scheduled all week, professional bike races were conducted each year at the New Hampshire International Speedway. The modern track in Loudon, New Hampshire was host to the "Loudon Classic" and the track seated over 100,000 race fans—primarily because it hosts two NASCAR events in July and September each year.

The racetrack is located 11 miles to the south of Laconia proper, directly down Route 106 toward Concord, the State Capital. During Bike Week the two-lane 106 is a massive conduit for bikes from all over the U.S. From I-93, I-293 and I-393, Route 106 ferrets riders to and from the NHIS track to towns and accommodations north and south of the events.

At Weirs Beach, and early in the week, where thousands of bikers *call home* from morning to night, there was already a crisis in progress and "Race Week—2006" hadn't even commenced yet. There had been an unexpected death of a woman, a first, and it was the antithesis of the normally docile gathering each June.

A coroner had been requested and arrived at the base of the wooden pier adjacent to the M/S Mount Washington cruise ship at The Weirs. He had been summoned by the police just minutes before he was to have breakfast. He hurriedly ate the donut and coffee as he drove up Route 106, knowing full well his stomach might not accept anything later in the day.

The windless morning beckoned daybreak—a summer sunrise, while the rippling waters of the Lake Winnipesaukee shoreline were almost tranquil at that hour of the morning. It was 5:30 A.M. at Weirs Beach. Much of the beach area was quiet for it was prior to the official influx for the annual Loudon / Laconia motorcycle conclave on June 10th. Father's Day weekend was over a week away. Bike Week had been a tradition for more than eight glorious decades.

Nearby The Weirs docks and boardwalk was the famed Endicott Rock and a small grassy park—the Rock, an historic Colonial landmark, was the demarcation of the beginning of Paugus Bay and the eventual outflow of the Big Lake—Lake Winni. The Paugus Bay initial egress of rapid water and currents was bordered by land, which housed Thurston's Marina to the right and the famed Naswa Resort to the left. Both were local landmarks of their own and popular hotspots for boating and partying revelers.

The Laconia police had arrived at the boardwalk minutes after a local resident had called them. He seemed to be in a panic with a pallor that was not complimentary to his normal skin tone. His hands shook and his knees were unstable, buckling slightly when the policemen approached him.

The local had just discovered the nude body of a young woman, her identity and age of which were unknown but assumed to be in her twenties or younger. By chance, he had noticed the corpse while walking the boardwalk in the early hours. He rubbed his eyes numerous times to get a clearer view of the unexpected situation, then realizing his eyes were not deceiving him after all. There was a body on the shoreline, unheard of in this small community of ingrained and longstanding year-round beach residents.

Jim Fortier, a well-liked retiree lived in The Weirs area. He was 63 years of age and known to all residents as "Gentle Jim." He often walked the wooden boardwalk that parallels Lakeside Avenue and the train tracks that emanate along the shoreline of Paugus Bay and the public beach at The Weirs. The tracks continued north and meandered through woods and communities toward the town of Meredith, located literally a few short miles from the site of the deceased young woman.

Fortier, white-haired and fit, was an early riser who often walked or jogged the boardwalk, paths and piers to the left of the Endicott Rock landmark. It was a routine part of his morning's exercise and the solitude of the beach and lake at that hour pleased the man, often allowing him time to think and to plan his activities for the day.

Normally therapeutic and serene, today's jaunt was not serene by any stretch of the imagination. Shock took its toll as he became stressed and sickened by the unusual sight, his companion dog, Sparky repetitively barking at the dead woman. A limited number of people arrived at the sight of the police car and stood transfixed trying desperately to assess the gruesome scene below the walkway. Fortier had just picked up his dog the day before, from the Meredith Animal Hospital where Dr. David Almstrom, D.V.M. had neutered the young male Husky the day prior. Dr. Dave had a booming practice, which was due, in large part, to a long-time following of locals and summer visitors. His diagnostic and technical veterinary skills were the best in the area and his prices were fair and competitive often cutting the competition's rates by one-half. His overhead was low having owned his practice some 35 years. Fortier had been a client for years and with many companion animals.

Having just neutered the dog, the vet had recommended exercise and an analgesic for Sparky as a way to aid the dog's rehabilitation. The daily walks helped and the handsome Husky only stopped occasionally to lick his wounds below his tail. The silk sutures had been irritating to the skin and once removed, the irritation would lessen over time. Stiff-legged, the dog was doing his best to keep up with his master's exercise gait when the unexpected scene appeared by the water's edge. Both animal and man stopped abruptly, peering over and through the fence to see what was totally unexpected. The barking dog was repetitive and loud for the early morning hours, surely intent on drawing attention from the neighbors. His bark reverberated off the nearby hills and echoed over the water's surface.

Additional sirens could be heard in the distance. The local Laconia police had been contacted by Fortier using a cell phone.

Chapter 7

The police car of white with blue lettering and trim accents and a second darker colored vehicle were parked above a dock area and eventually drew the attention of many more locals who were now gawking from their porches while wondering what might be so urgent at that hour of the morning. Two of Fortier's neighbors crossed the road and stood by him in dismay. One distraught woman had cupped a hand over her mouth and gasped at the sight below.

Descending the wooden staircase and weathered piers toward the waterline, the coroner and medical examiner, Dr. Ned Blaisdell stepped carefully on the rocks and gravel—they led him to the stony shore, his balance somewhat jeopardized briefly by his unsure footing, and a awkward heavy coroner's bag of investigative instruments and sample jars. He stumbled down the remaining embankment while grasping a branch or two of a wild rose bush, a seemingly overgrown bramble of prickly sticks to the right of the site of the original 1890's Weirs Beach railway depot. The present structure, a newer depot, had replaced the original that had long passed.

The well-experienced doctor and pathologist was somewhat overweight, breathing deeply to catch his breath. He was a rapidly balding man whose forehead revealed his years of grim discoveries in the macabre profession. His job was duel in nature in that he was both coroner and M.E. Generally they were separate positions, the coroner being the investigator of an unnatural death occurrence and the M.E. being the person who would perform the autopsy on a death of unnatural and unexplained etiology.

Somewhat out of breath from the awkward descent, the coroner hesitated briefly at first and then slowly approached the corpse, staring first very deliberately at the morbid scene and then leaning directly over her torso as if it was his first-ever sight of a dead body. It wasn't and as a matter of fact, it was all too familiar in his profession with the insurmountable graphics and positioning of cadavers and body parts generally the norm.

He was in no hurry and studied the early morning landscape, intentionally backing up and moving forward in a predictive, deliberate manner—ever assessing each angle of each view. The investigative portion of a crime scene needed notations that differed from the deceased body characteristics. The report needed to elucidate how, why and where she came from as well as an I.D. What gross clues remained in the general area that would aid him later during the autopsy? He was assessing the position of the torso related to the crime scene, trying to determine if she fell down the banking, fell from a pier or from a passing boat. Was she carried and dumped there . . . what other footprints or evidence were visible at the scene?

He seemed to be evaluating the all-too-familiar scenario, now almost a monthly occurrence of unexplained deaths, it seemed, in different parts of the State. Young or old people, his job was to assess unusual deaths whether a murder, an overdose or an accident. As he bent over her for a clearer view, his car keys fell from his jacket pocket and onto the crushed stone nearby. He was quick to place them back in his pocket, almost never missing a beat in the examination of the surroundings. Murmurs could be heard at street level . . . observers' whispers or the occasional passing vehicle. Dr. Blaisdell was emotionless and his furrowed brow showed his thoughts in real time, a series of well-worn troughs in the skin above his eyes. Frown lines appeared above the bridge of his nose.

He was always saddened by the death of someone young, especially a girl . . . a beautiful girl at that. The Coroner's Office had been short staffed for years, the result of State budget cuts that affected all divisions of the Departments of Health and Human Services or the law enforcement and court divisions and related systems operations. Most departments deemed critical and necessary had cutbacks due to legislative laws limiting the funding and staffing of positions often stressing out the existing staff and forcing them to assume additional responsibilities and double jobs. That forced many employees to give up, resign, move on or seek an alternate career change. The prior governor, Craig Benson, had mandated cutting expenditures, which his party approved in the New Hampshire State House. It was taking its toll on the efficiency of the State-run operations.

Blaisdell's department was feeling that pinch as well. Somehow he moved forward ever hoping for more staffing and an increased budget. He had proven that point the previous year. There would always be deaths of unknown cause and he was needed for each and every one. That was his life's mission and as odd as the job was, he was a critical link in an unpopular appointment. Pathology was a cold profession, literally and figuratively.

His job: To find the answer to a mysterious death! He was a Sherlock Holmes of sorts. Sometimes, unusual deaths all looked the same at this point in his career. He was growing disenchanted and tired. Death was death no matter what.

His training in anatomy, physiology and pathology was extensive. He loved his work for there was value in solving the unknown, a sense of accomplishment in a job well done and complete with substantiated facts and data that needed resolution. Clue upon clue often led to myriad pieces, akin to a jig-saw puzzle, the final picture of which could only be discerned when the pathological jagged pieces were elucidated, intertwined and visual.

The causes of death in each case often took months to resolve. Gross anatomical changes in morphology needed the embellishment of pathology data; clinical chemistries combined with bioanalytical data derived from tissues, blood, fecal and urine samples. Fluids told the doctor a lot. Drugs or chemicals metabolized into forms other than the parent drug, toxin or toxic chemicals that often resulted in morbidity and eventual mortality. Add to that the physical abuse, blunt force, concussions, punctures of the skin or organs that were often detected during gross, X-ray or microscopic evaluations.

The job of a coroner and a medical examiner was intense and stressful, analytical and sometimes inconclusive often requiring later exhumation of a body to look one more time and take more tissues to find the missing link. The Coroner's Office never desired that resumption by disinterment—they wanted *conclusion* so that the deceased and their family had finality with regard to the loss, both mentally and physically.

As an example, and decades later, the untimely death of a young Marilyn Monroe was a case of hidden evidence that may have implicated murder and not suicide of the famed star. The key clue was that certain drugs might have been administered while she was in a stupor, a "hotshot" of sorts in the buttocks that suggested evidence that the original drugs given in excess had never metabolized and remained in their original form in her tissues. The implication that her personal physician and friends like Bobby Kennedy and others were present at the time of the final drug administration; suggested a scenario that may have deliberately terminated her life. *The Last Days of Marilyn Monroe* by Donald Wolfe contains facts and interviews with a key pathologist and others that questioned the cause of her demise long after her death. *Was she about to spill the beans on her relationships with the Kennedy brothers? Could that have affected the election and fate of those men?* the author questioned. The implications of the suspected murder of the starlet would make Bill Clinton's sexual escapades look like child's play. As of 2006, no one knows how Marilyn died and whether she was murdered.

Suicide seems less and less a probability, even today. Celebrity can often circumvent the legal process.

Even President Kennedy was returned to Washington after his fatal gunshot wounds without an autopsy in Dallas. Protocol seemed breached due to his stature as a president for it was a violent death that often mandated an autopsy in the State of the crime—in this case, Texas. To this day, the debate over how he died, how many shots were fired and who was the perpetrator(s), remains unclear after the 1963 assassination and official Warren Report. Celebrity, stardom or politics can foster an enigma or control the fate of ones remains without ever resolving the actual death case at hand.

Not withstanding, a coroner or medical examiner's job sometimes required a crutch, i.e. scotch or something similar at the end of a day's work. It wasn't as if Blaisdell could go hang out in a bar with friends and tell them how his day went, like someone in another profession might do. Dr. Blaisdell had to keep most of his work secret out of respect for confidentiality, the rights of the deceased and their family members who had yet to be informed of the young girl's demise. They couldn't be notified since the blonde girl remained unidentified following her retrieval from the shoreline of the Big Lake.

Chapter 8

Blaisdell was seemingly *on his own* regarding this crime. His closest friends and acquaintances were local funeral directors and morticians that supported his daily needs and agenda. He saw them way too often. They understood the scenario, having to deal with the after-remains.

Protocol ruled. There was the inevitable thorax and ribs that he had to piece back together with autopsy tape once the internal anatomical exam was completed. A mental distance from the subject matter was mandatory for people in the trade. The victims often became a rack of beef in many ways, not so much from a callous perspective but from an honest dissociation from reality in order to get through the necessary evaluation—a quest to discern and confirm a cause of death—accurately and professionally but with respect and compassion.

Lying prone and semi-rigid on the water's edge, the young victim's blonde hair of tangled curls moved in symphony with each casual wave of the Big Lake—"Winni." The frothy bubbles kissed the side of her nose and one cheek. Her buttocks and flowing spine were sculptured, Venus-like and perfect, yet sterile and pale in appearance—somewhat akin to a movie scene from the classic film, *On The Beach.*

• She was someone's child, a daughter of parents that may not know her whereabouts as yet, or the facts related to the cause of her death. They could be living anywhere or in any one of the fifty States, asleep, traveling, working and unaware of the tragedy of this ghastly and unnecessary event of wasted youth.

Who was this child of parents unknown? Who would care if she were living or dead? they wondered. Damn the wastage of a valued human life in someone else's eyes. Blaisdell was a person with two of those compassionate eyes and he cared deeply, often shaking his head from side to side in remorse. Resolution and finality of the scenario would be needed and he was the one who would have to seek and determine the answers.

He looked around briefly, saying little as more people arrived to view the morbid scene in the normally vibrant and fun-filled area of New Hampshire. *Stop gawking*, he screamed in silence, noting the occasional murmur and finger pointing from the crowd above, the hushed conversations that were the background noise of this pristine, early morn. Shaking his head repeatedly, he looked down at her once more and became her self-appointed caretaker in death, her surrogate father for a moment. After all, it wasn't as if she was some old woman who had passed on in her living room chair with the TV on Larry King Live, only to be found by a relative a week later during the monthly visit.

There was no odor of death that mimicked the closed room of an elderly person's demise. In contrast, this was the scene of a young woman who was bathed in the fresh New Hampshire air in June, and the chill of a summer morning by the lake. The young person was not a large mouth bass that had washed up on shore after having had its mouth ripped apart by a Number 6, Eagle Claw hook and then died after it escaped its captor on a bass boat. *This* was a human being that had died tragically, leaving the coroner with a cold feeling of loss and a new case of mortal reality that was either a potential crime or medical anomaly resulting in her death.

Blaisdell's day was beginning early and he did not welcome the event. One so young should not be dead no matter what the cause. *It was someone's daughter!*

Two local patrolmen stood silent and pensive, the girl's legal protectors in death—overseers of the crime scene that was unexpected in the popular resort area of the Lakes Region. The police were normally assigned to monitor the Lakeside Avenue annual parade of motorcycles and the black leather riders who gathered from around the country each year. They could not have expected the annual event to commence in such a somber and tainted way. *What was in store for the rest of the week?* they wondered.

The newspapers would be all over this crime and letters to the editor would scream that the Laconia Rally had become a thing of the past, overshadowed by drugs, the indigent and a suspected murder. *Death* was now part of it, and not just loud bikes and black leather from all walks of life.

The men in blue stood stoically near the site of the discovery and stunning facial features of the corpse, acting professionally and respectful yet intrigued by how beautiful a nude body could be—even in death. There was no idle banter or whispers between them. They knew that the young woman was somehow a *victim*, but a victim of what: foul play, a broken home, a violent adult relationship or just sad misfortune—an accident?

Nothing much was voiced as the medical examiner opened a well-worn leather satchel to don protective, sterile vinyl gloves and then probe the dead woman's arms and legs for needle marks and / or signs of blunt trauma. There were none observed at first glance. The young woman's eyes were still open. They were a dull blue color now, having died purportedly sometime during the previous night. They appeared opaque like that of a fish that had lain on a shoreline for an extended period of time or someone with an exacerbated condition of cataracts.

The exact time and nature of her demise had not as yet been determined, but the M.E. would surely be able to estimate a time of death once he had the chance to examine the external and internal remains in detail. The secrets to her death were in the body's tissues and fluids, blood and other physiological parameters that allowed the examiner to determine the time and cessation of bodily function. Upon gross inspection, nothing was apparent, but the sun was hardly up and the scene of the crime had not even been completely assessed. The coroner allowed no one walk around the immediate area, sensing the potential to contaminate the scene.

"Get those people up top to move on, please," he whispered to one of the cops. "At least—get them out of my view. This obsession with death by people who gawk has always made me ill and we will be bringing her up to the street soon."

One policeman waved the people away and other cops appeared in time to assist in cordoning off the restricted crime area. Stakes of wood and yellow tape were now the demarcation of the shoreline in question.

The coroner went silent and seemed almost cold in demeanor, seemingly unfazed by the immediate death scene by his feet. He commented somewhat in a chilling fashion that, "It's another wasted life of a young person."

He had seen it before and the reality of his job began to set in—a seemingly repetitive cycle. He took notes of the general surroundings, drawing visual scenes and landmarks, the overall landscape relative to the position of the body. He was also whispering into a small hand-held digital recorder, capturing and describing the visual and the visceral gross medical observations at the site. He remained professional and objective in his assessment, documenting everything he viewed, felt, surmised and perceived of value. Time was limited and his experience prevailed.

Once the body was removed, he would lose the perspective of the surroundings and the artistic and photographic composition of the beach scene. Detectives were already on their way and Blaisdell was reminded of the circus that enshrouded the scene of the Laci Peterson murder in the Bay Area of California, where investigators had to maintain the morbid scene for hours before her decapitated torso could be extricated from the rocks and beach.

Blaisdell wanted to be thorough but rapid so that the much-anticipated news media and their helicopters were not focusing their camera lenses on this dead child. He tried to alleviate his own frustration by commenting to the officers,

"This will surely put a damper on the forthcoming motorcycle week," he snickered.

The patrolmen nodded in agreement. "Yah, it's a hell of a way to start, Doc. A hell of a way to start the summer season," an officer repeated.

"This will not be a positive light for the local Chamber of Commerce for sure," added another officer. "Hopefully this is not an indication of some 'nut job' out there preying on young ladies. There will be 400,000 people here in this town very shortly and one-third could be women this girl's age. They're getting younger each year, knowin' there's booze and drugs readily available. We don't need some "psycho" playing Tony Perkins from the movies, either."

Chapter 9

For both the State Coroner's office and Dr. Blaisdell, it was the first non-motorcycle related casualty of the impending 2006 Bike Week—ironically during the much acclaimed and celebrated 83rd year of the Annual Rally and races at NHIS (New Hampshire International Speedway). South of NHIS is the "Capitol City," Concord, some 15 miles away, and the site where the young lady would be examined *post mortem.*

The June week, preceding and including the Saturday and Sunday of Father's Day weekend, attracted thousands of motorcycle riders and enthusiasts, each year increasing in popularity and attendance. Added to those figures was an influx each year of summer beachgoers, vacationers and tourists that love the Lakes Region ambiance as well. They stay until Labor Day or until the leaves change in late October.

The bikers who traditionally hung out at The Weirs were predominately Harley-Davidson owners and riders. Many bikers exhibited their current or vintage Harley-Davidson or Indian motorcycles; some H-D models displayed special designs and logos celebrating the Centennial or 100th year of the Harley. Laconia Rally Week had been in existence for almost as long as the Harley-Davidson Company, shy some 20 years or so.

* * *

When he completed the initial physical and landscape notations, the coroner stood up slowly, his knees cracking in the process—his younger football days at UNH had taken their toll on the cartilage and joints. Groaning from the pain, he scratched his temple with his index finger while asking a nearby patrolman for a blue tarp to cover the young woman in the interim.

One patrolman, hearing of the doctor's pain, asked him if he had played football when he was younger. The coroner replied, "Sure did, son. Ya heard my knees crack, right? A sign of the damn times. There's no cartilage left—it's bone on bone."

The patrolman laughed. "Yup . . . that's why I asked you, doctor. Heard it's a common problem for athletes."

"Old age," the M.E. quipped.

Blaisdell then asked the police about any potential witnesses or other indications that there might have been foul play or a strange occurrence that might help shed some light on the current situation along the shoreline. *There was a dead young lady and someone had to have noticed something,* he thought . . . *anything at all would be beneficial.*

"Who found her?" inquired Blaisdell, changing the subject. Before a patrolman could answer, Jim Fortier stepped forward, his dog tethered to a nearby post on the pier.

"Me, sir."

"Your name?"

"Fortier, sir . . . Jim Fortier. I live here at The Weirs . . . . on Foster Street."

"I'm Dr. Blaisdell, Mr. Fortier. I'm from the Coroner's / Medical Examiner's office in Concord and often wear both hats these days. I live the closest to handle this situation, I guess. I don't have any assistants this week since one person is on vacation and I reside in Canterbury, just south of Laconia. I responded when the call came in."

"Nice to meet you, sir," Fortier replied. "How can I help?"

"Is this where you found her, Jim? I mean, exactly like she is now? And did you notice any other people around at the time?"

"Yes and no, sir . . . I was walking the dog and happened to look over the wooden fencing from up there," he said, pointing to street level. "The dog barked at two ducks that were at the water's edge. That's when I saw her. It's tragic . . . she's so young. But I saw no one else around. The dog and I often walk the boardwalk early," he added for assurance.

"When Jim?" Blaisdell asked, taking copious notes. "What time? Do you remember?"

"Approximately an hour ago . . . 5:30 A.M. or so," the man replied. "I thought . . . at first," he hesitated, "I thought it was a mannequin, ya know—a joke played by some prankster or biker. Some sicko."

The coroner squatted again and looked up at the local resident.

"It's no *mannequin,* Jim. She was a real person. Let's get her covered with a tarp, boys. I need a body bag, officer. Can you get one out of my van up top, please?"

The officer nodded, yes and climbed the weathered pine stairs to the roadway.

Dr. Ned Blaisdell looked back at Jim Fortier who was well tanned for that early in the summer season of New Hampshire. Spring had been wet and cold—the water temperature of the lake, a cool 58-62° F, they guessed. Jim Fortier stared one more time before she was covered with a blue tarp. A black body bag was on its way down the stairs, the officer bounding every other step.

"Mannequin or corpse, Jim, they're often the same color at this stage," he said, with callous sarcasm. Jim Fortier said nothing in response. Their voices were overpowered by the sound of loud pipes, those belonging to three Harley riders passing above the crime scene.

"Jesus Christ. They ride early in the morn," the coroner commented. "Don't those *mothers* ever sleep? The sun's hardly up and I'm standing here over a dead young girl."

"Them sleep, doctor? Not really," said a policeman from Laconia. His partner from Gilford smiled and commented, "Prob'ly been up all night. Perhaps they're on their way *home*, to the motel or local campground. These guys are early for the Rally but some people make it a two-week vacation instead of one. They get 'cranked' on Budweiser or whatever and live their lives like a candle burnin' at both ends."

"They ride all night?" asked the medical examiner. "I'm amazed."

"Some do, especially on Lakeside Avenue and Weirs Boulevard. You can hear them all night long."

"Jesus Christ . . . Have they no respect for the dead?" commented Blaisdell, trying to be witty. No one responded. It was a rhetorical question.

Blaidsell observed a beer can near his foot. The Bud can appeared different to him.

Anheuser-Busch coincidently created 96,000 Budweiser (16 oz.) beer cans with the Laconia Bike Week 2006 logo and for the first time. The rare memorabilia cans, successful at prior Sturgis and Daytona events, were expected to sell out in the first week or two. Those that weren't consumed during Rally Week were expected to be kept as collectibles, or sold on Internet auctions.

Chapter 10

A forensic photographer, who had arrived a bit late, took a few photos and lifted the blue tarp before the black body bag was used for final transport. A folded metal gurney leaned against a fence and off to one side of the steps of the pier.

The girl was beautiful and looked aged 23 to 25 as best the photographer and coroner could estimate. The photographer captured the right profile, which was callously caressed by the occasional wave, and where the sun's rays were about to warm the cold body. The photographer took numerous photographs with a Nikon digital camera—he covered all angles, first close-up and then from a distance, capturing the body's position with respect to local landmarks and the horizon to the east.

Had she fallen? Was she pushed or thrown down the embankment? Was she originally in a boat and fell overboard? No one had the preliminary answers but an autopsy would determine and substantiate any internal trauma or evidence of drowning or foul play. There were no scrapes on the torso from brush or stone, so they felt it was unlikely that she rolled down the steep embankment to her final rest on the shore. The police had scoured the hillside for evidence in and around the rose bushes, tall grass and weeds. Other than the occasional paper cups, broken bottles and sand toys from the beach area, the only evidence out of the ordinary was a stuffed animal—a bear. The Teddy Bear was soaked, its fur matted at the water's edge, some fifteen feet from the body.

It was obvious to the authorities that some youngster had forgotten his or her toy or the bear had fallen off a passing boat. The brown fur toy was placed in a small plastic bag that an officer had been using for collecting evidence at the scene.

The stuffed bear was a product of the The Vermont Teddy Bear Company. The manufacturer was located in nearby Shelburne, Vermont by Lake Champlain but the tag was faded. The Vermont company remains today and continues to offer "all-occasion" bears, especially during the holiday season. This particular bear was small and was dressed in a biker's vest, a bandanna and goggles. The fake leather clothing on the animal was saturated by the lake and appeared soiled from rolling in and out of the water. A recent U.S. Postal Service promotion had offered similar bears with biker clothing adornments.

Leaning over the wooden fence of the boardwalk was another photographer, 36-year-old, Donald Wright from downtown Laconia. Don had a chance to photograph multiple shots using a telephoto lens and before they removed the body and the bear. He surmised that the "Teddy" might have had some significance if it was near the scene. *What child would take a fur Teddy bear to the beach?*

Somehow, the local policemen didn't think it was relevant and assumed that some child had left the bear at the shore. Don felt differently—an odd perception with no substantiation.

Don knew the history of the original "Teddy Bear." He had once read about the origin of the name and this bear seemed to be the only significant piece of evidence near the body. *Had it belonged to the dead girl?* he wondered. *A naked dead woman and a bear seemed incongruous.*

Wright freelanced for a local newspaper and had been asked by the editor of the *Lakes Region Times* to cover the entire span of Rally Week festivities—in particular, the unique biker characters and their related activities, hobbies and places of origin—California, New Jersey, Chicago or elsewhere. Each photo and "character," male or female, had a story to tell.

The photo essay series was to be titled: "Faces of Bike Week." Often Don Wright featured someone who had attended twenty-five or more events of the past, the riders often covered in commemorative pins, tattoos, annual patches and memorabilia from past rallies, including Sturgis in August, or Daytona and Laconia from decades earlier. The pins touted the years of attendance on them.

Females clad in black-leather were targets for photographs by both pros and amateurs; girls that revealed more skin than cowhide and leather halters. Bikers and their chicks frequented the never-ending Weir's Beach motorcycle parade up and down Lakeside Avenue on a daily basis. Some meandered on foot down the mile long street that became a sidewalk of sorts for pedestrians. They congregated in city-sanctioned beer tents and bars, basically avoiding the more formalized races of Japanese-made rice-rockets on Father's Day weekend.

In 2006, and three years prior, the owners had clashed with the AMA factory riders who refused to ride in the rain on Father's Days that were often New England unpredictable. Mat Mladin, Suzuki's finest rider, was considered an "Aussie with an Attitude" and fostered a boycott of the NASCAR track. Mladin and fellow riders became the decision makers instead of the AMA. Dunlop Tire Company had offered the appropriate tire models specifically for rainy day Sunday events, which required postponement to Mondays in the past. The holdout by the AMA factory prima donnas, due to rain on Father's Day, resulted in crowds of fans leaving. The riders wouldn't participate in the historic Loudon Classic, citing safety reasons often decreasing the attendance of serious fans of professional road racing.

With Mladin claiming that the NHIS track "needed a complete facelift," the track owners remain staid in their determination and opinion that the NHIS course was safe for all riders. Substantial money was spent to improve the track. Speedway spokesperson, Ron Meade was quoted as saying, "that Mladin thinks there are no good tracks in the U.S." Mladin desired that a whole new track be built for AMA races jeopardizing the 83-year-old racing event. Adding to the Classic's modification in 2006 was the breaking of ties with the Championship Cup Series (CCS), ClearChannel and Formula-USA, which had replaced the AMA sponsorship in 2001. Organizationally, it was a mess.

The Loudon Road Racing Series (LRRS) kept the Loudon Classic functioning and in 2007 planned to move the start date of Laconia Motorcycle Week Classic one weekend before Father's Day instead of running the races traditionally on that holiday. The 2006-scheduled contests of 8-10 races on Sunday had classes of Grand Prix, Thunderbike and SuperSport heats including Motard contests as well. Overall, 125 laps would be run in the afternoon, weather permitting.

The tourists weren't always there for the races. The men were there to party and chase thongs. Women looked to "hook up." Only die-hard race fans attended the major bike races at the NHIS track in Loudon or the hill climb events at Gunstock and Belknap Mountain. The vintage model bike races in downtown Laconia were scheduled for June 11th as well. They drew local and visiting spectators.

*   *   *

"Hey Don, ya made it just in time," commented a policeman who knew the local photographer from other tragic news events—including morbid car crash scenes and fires.

"You can get closer if you wanna. They're about to black bag her and bring her up. Just show your press pass to the guys down below and keep the photos professional," remarked the cop. "We don't want this young lady featured naked on the cover of tomorrow's edition. We don't even know who she is as yet."

Don promised to take only respectful photos of the deceased woman. He was not an ambulance chaser or one prone to gawk. He always took respectful photos unlike those shown in tabloids or on sick Internet sites. He had a younger sister of his own and he was sensitive to the fact that the scene could be akin to one of her friends. As a professional, he knew the ethical limits of photojournalism. He would not breach the trust of the police and other authorities. He needed them as colleagues in his day job.

Don was daydreaming as he walked down the stairs and wondered about the stuffed Teddy, recalling in passing, its history.

Chapter 11

The origin of the unique "Teddy" name had to do with a U.S. president. In 1902, President Theodore Roosevelt, an avid sportsman, was on a hunting trip in Mississippi. The hunting party had lassoed a small black bear and had even tied it to a tree. Roosevelt, felt compassion for the animal and refused to shoot it. Clifford Barryman of the *Washington Post* created a cartoon (November 16, 1902) of Roosevelt and the bear about to be tied to the tree, and titled, *"Drawing the line in Mississippi."* Following the contrived hunting episode and cartoon publication, a shopkeeper (Morris Michtom) in Brooklyn, New York placed two bears (that his wife, Rose had made) in his novelty store window. After gaining permission from the president himself, Michtom called the stuffed animal, "Teddy's Bears." An icon was born—a popular item with high demand. From the popularity, Michtom expanded his toy business eventually becoming the Ideal Novelty and Toy Corporation.

Simultaneously in Germany, the Steiff Company had also produced bears, offering the first jointed bears in 1902-03. Introduced at the 1903 Leipzig Fair, the Steiff Bears finally made it to the U.S. since an American buyer attending the Fair had thousands shipped to the United States. The Giengen, Germany animal was also called the "Teddy Bear."

Don Wright's initial curiosity concerning the stuffed animal was to have later relevance to the mysterious death.

Roosevelt was a strong willed person, for later in 1913, when he was 54 years of age, had also taken an expedition. After losing the bid for the 1912 presidential election, he embarked on a trip to the Amazon with his son, Kermit, to trace the River of Doubt in Brazil. His son was an avid outdoorsman as well. They encountered the Cinta Larga Indians, unwanted malaria and other medical skin-related injuries (scratches) that festered in the humid environment and almost ended up killing the former president, Roosevelt.

He recovered from his delirium and fever according to the biography by Candice Millard in 2005. Neither his son or the former president was afraid of anything it seemed, perhaps making Roosevelt and his bear an iconic symbol of the New Jersey Rough Riders who were fearless as well.

*   *   *

Bike Week often resulted in an average of four to seven deaths annually, each involving a bike or car-related accident, day or night. Something serious occurred each day and was cited in the local papers, complete with photos of twisted wreckage or other macabre scenes. Route 106 from Concord to Meredith was a well-known two-lane death trap. Head on crashes, incurred while passing other vehicles on blind corners of the road, were most common. Serious fatalities like murder, from gang fights and unrelated to vehicles, were unheard of during Bike Week.

Noted gang members of bike groups were prone to batter one another in isolated cases of contempt, but outright murder was not an issue for Laconia in June. The accidents on narrow roads like 106 North or wide-open highways like 111 East or West were often the result of carelessness, speed or intoxication—basically the result of delayed reaction time to a situation that would be fatal.

Many bikers were unfamiliar with the local roads especially in wooded areas.

Rollercoaster Road had just been repaved and the smooth surface and winding curves mimicked a racetrack in its own right. It was a fatality waiting to happen. Muscle shirts and jeans offered no protection from the hard macadam.

Helmet-less vanity, the coroner referred to it. Dr. Blaisdell knew well of the head-kissed rocks and telephone poles each year—a New Hampshire *granite kiss* of sorts, in a New England State that was basically composed of granite, shale, quartz and marble below the pine-laden surface. Riders and passengers often died from collisions with Nature (trees, rock walls, cliffs) or the passenger on the back survived with broken legs, arms or backs. They could be thrown into fields of grass or slide helplessly down the asphalt subjecting their skin to "road rash" which removed multiple layers of epithelial and dermal tissue. Blood soaked and broken, they sometime were spared the fate of the Grim Reaper.

Helmet laws were and remain State dependent. The State of Florida had shown that during Jeb Bush's gubernatorial term and repeal of the helmet law in 1998, helmet-less deaths had risen from 22 to 250 in 2004. Total motorcycle deaths in Florida rose 67% from 2000 to 2004. By weeks end in New Hampshire, ten riders would be killed during Bike Week, many of whom were without helmets. One death occurred to a man who had removed his helmet once he crossed the New Hampshire line.

Lakes Region General Hospital (LRGH) admitted many accident cases each day. Serious trauma events were often airlifted by helicopter to Dartmouth-Hitchcock Medical Center in Hanover, New Hampshire, which had a more elaborate trauma center and specialists than LRGH. Neurological injuries were often life threatening.

Incidences of multiple lacerations were only surpassed by those of "road rash," an almost comical and appropriate term for severe bloody abrasions to the limbs and buttocks. Scantily dressed woman and men riders with no chaps or blue jeans for protection suffered the most.

* * *

The M.E. still desired additional input or clues from the crowd of onlookers that had gathered at the scene of the tragedy at Weirs Beach.

"Anyone have any info here . . . anyone at all?" asked Dr. Blaisdell. The local police interviewed the crowd near the boardwalk fencing. No one stepped forward or offered any relevant or pertinent information. Apparently no noises had been discerned in the night, at least any that would suggest foul play or an unusual gathering of partiers.

Most residents and passersby had arrived after the fact and were curiosity seekers peering over the wooden railing above the scene of the water's edge. They were aware that it was a young lady that has died but that was about it. The police shared a general description of the deceased in hopes that someone would identify her—they murmured among themselves struggling to link her to a local club, bar or fast food restaurant.

She could have been any one of a number of young women that came to the Rally Week festivities to work the food and T-shirt booths and tents where memorabilia and trinkets were sold and touted by vendors from distant States. Some merchants traveled each year from as far as California, this year hawking food, biker clothing, the Laconia Rally and Race 2006 logo, bike accessories and vintage bike posters and bike parts.

Every other tent on Lakeside and those in the parking area of the Drive-In seemed to hold racks of leather goods, studded wristbands, bracelets and bandannas.

"No one seems to know her, sir or the circumstances," offered a Gilford policeman to the coroner. "We have little to go on at this point. We're hopin' you can figure out who she is and what happened to her. Wonder if she's local? No I.D. eh?" the officer asked. "Ya know, a purse, wallet, jewelry with her name?"

The M.E. indicated that there were no personal items near the body that would provide an identification of or lead to her place of origin. It seemed bizarre but fingerprints from the body or DNA were probably going to be the only means by which the authorities could link the young girl forensically to someone or something.

Blaisdell did mention a women's gold chain but he limited his comments to the fact that it was the only personal item they had recovered at the crime scene. The coroner had alluded to a chain, to an attending officer. It was a simple link and elegant, he had mentioned.

He needed to retain the jewelry as forensic evidence. Perhaps later he would be able to share the specifics of the necklace with the newspapers, a photo of the chain's link that might precipitate a clue relevant to solving her identity.

"A waste of a beautiful woman," the coroner murmured. "A damn waste of a young life and we have little to go on at this point." He sighed.

"A gold cross about her neck hung loosely to a broken chain, 12-inch perhaps and barely touching the sand. It contained no initials," he offered. "It was imprinted with 14K. That's all. Otherwise there was nothing unusual. No rings. No bracelets, etc."

The policeman and a detective made a notation. They would review all evidence at the morgue. For now, the agenda was to get the deceased out of the crime area as soon as possible.

"I will examine her closely at the morgue. She did have a couple of tattoos; a cross on her shoulder and another logo on her lower back—a scroll with a name on it."

"Name?" an officer inquired.

Blaisdell remarked, raising an eyebrow,

"Who's *Vincent?* Anyone know a man named Vincent?" the M.E. asked in general. He did not elaborate but had hoped that someone in the small crowd might know the name.

No one reacted to the inquiry. They murmured to themselves for there could be millions of Vincent's or Vinny's that ride bikes and attend any number of annual motorcycle events.

"Apparently the crime wasn't related to a robbery?" stated the patrolman while writing notes on a clipboard. "The gold chain would have been long gone I would suspect."

The coroner nodded in agreement. Surely the gold could be pawned for cash or drugs. The scene was perplexing.

So what was the motive for this death—and who the hell was *Vincent?*

Chapter 12

Earlier, Donald Wright was allowed near the corpse and photographed a close up of the tattoos—a cross, a simulated chain or bracelet tattoo around her ankle and the one near her lower spine. The detail of the tattoo on the back was almost a Romanesque or Greek icon in symbolism. The tattoo, with an unfamiliar logo, appeared to have been recently applied and was the more elaborate art, which the M.E. had described to the detective. It was applied to her lumbar area, waist high and centered just above the groove in her buttocks. That location was popular on women. Often the tattoos were flowers, roses, a heart or wings, often feminine and colorful. This particular tattoo was none of those commonly seen on other biker women; at least it was unfamiliar to Don.

Don noted no apparent blunt trauma to the body—nothing of note to capture on film. Don Wright wanted the close-ups of the tattoos as photos should they need to be published to help seek her identity. He would need clearance from the coroner in order to release the photographs, however Don had a sense that they might come in handy. There was so little to go on regarding her identity and the physical adornments of art might be of value in the investigation. He felt sorrow at the sight in front of him. *Damn,* he thought to himself, *someone must know this kid.*

The coroner had recorded in a journal all of the tattoos as well as the initial examination of her torso. In Concord, he would focus on the details of each ink pattern. He was not forthright in mentioning them to the local crowd but he knew that one of the tattoos, the scrolled logo and name *Vincent,* was unique. What clues did any of the markings have? The dermal area of the lower spine was raised like a wheal as if still inflamed from the recent application of the elaborate artwork.

Blaisdell concluded that the woman had acquired the tattoo that week, maybe a day or two prior to her demise. They might be able to identify her that way—through police inquiries of the local Laconia tattoo parlors or interviews with artists who had set up tents at Weirs Beach for Bike Week. Blaisdell was not in a position to share his presumptions with the locals. As coroner and M.E., he needed to garner as much information as he could at the scene, and on his own.

Her fingerprints, dental records and general X-rays were sure to help, as well. There was so little to go on at this point that every option was a potential starting point.

The M.E. approached Don Wright to gain a photographer's perspective.

Pointing to the lower back of the victim, he commented. "The tattoo at the base of her spine says, *Vincent*. There's a logo too, below the name. You seen that before?"

"Vincent?" Donald responded, perplexed. "Perhaps it's her boyfriend's name, doctor. Maybe he's got her name on his bicep. Biker couples often do that," remarked the newspaper photographer. "I personally haven't seen that particular logo in the past and I've photographed many tattoos here at The Weirs for years. Hmmn . . . I'll have a close up shot of it for your records."

"Thanks. Could be . . . a boyfriend's name, as you say . . . I've seen hundreds of names before," the coroner concurred, "but this tattoo / logo is different. Never have seen that one before . . . personally."

"It's strange," a patrolman commented, while overhearing the whispers. "Looks like a person or figure above some wings."

"Maybe a Roman or Greek god or goddess or somethin'," someone expressed.

"It's unfamiliar to me," said the medical examiner, "and I've seen lots of tattoos on bodies. Many are one of a kind and this one surely is novel."

Out of respect for the deceased woman, he covered most of her body with the tarp again. Blaisdell asked any unauthorized people nearby to move away from the scene. He wanted to revisit the torso once more to examine all angles of a potential cause of her demise i.e. fingernails for hair or skin, punctures or small knife wounds that might have gone unnoticed in her present position. He only peeled back the tarp in the areas he wished to make direct visual observations. He deliberately kept the rest of her body protected.

The policemen asked everyone to step away and began to stand behind the area cordoned off with yellow tape. It was a crime scene, with or without the body and they needed to protect the physical and geographical area adjacent to the water's edge. Their work had just begun and they would scour the rocks for additional jewelry or personal items after the young lady was removed from the scene. The police had much work ahead of them.

Chapter 13

One person of note had inched his way part way down the steps of the dock. He was elderly and slow to move. He stared intensely at the scene below. A U. S. Veteran's ball cap hid part of his face, but the stubble on his chin was indicative that he had not shaved that morning.

"*Vincent,* you say?" he remarked. No one paid attention to the old man, but Donald Wright, the photographer took note. He eyed the old man carefully.

"Step back up, sir," ordered a policeman, helping the man who had now gone silent.

The gentleman was well along in age and frail. Once he was back on the boardwalk at street level, he slowly crossed the road and headed to a nearby Veterans home building. He was mumbling obscenities under his breath.

Don watched him leave and wanted to interview the man out of curiosity. He eyed to which home he was headed since there were many old Victorian Infantry buildings on the opposite side of the road. They were historical and many had military insignias or connotations. They were from the 1800's or earlier and large in size. Most were clapboard or sided with cedar shakes, each with enormous porches and stairways.

A funeral home director arrived in due time, driving a black hearse from downtown Laconia. The Cadillac was the newest model. The mortician had been summoned by the M.E. to transport the body of the young lady to Concord. The funeral director wore the typical dark suit and meandered down the steps that led to the docks—he then negotiated the steep hill to the water's edge. His black, wingtip shoes were wet from the slippery shore.

He was tall and somber and dressed in a black, two-piece suit, a stereotypical look of respect and the macabre associated with death and corpses. He had an assistant who was equally as serious and quiet. Ever respectful of the situation, their job was to professionally assist the coroner by dealing with the morbid scene as if it was just another day, another person or another crime to be resolved. The funeral director was white haired, tall and thin. They knew the routine—once the coroner was through, they would remove the body taking care to show the victim's remains due respect.

A small crowd had begun to congregate at the top of the embankment at that early hour; some were lined at the street level or leaning on the boardwalk fence that overlooked the tragic scene below. The Mount Washington boat, tagged M/S 0001 NH, and affectionately known as "The Mount," was majestically moored at its dock to the left of the crime scene. The Sophie C. and the Doris E., two smaller, sister cruise ships stood berthed a short distance from The Mount. They were the mail boats and passenger vessels to some of the smaller bays and islands of the Big Lake. Each day, tourists clamored aboard all three of the boats to visit islands or see Wolfeboro, Alton or Meredith Bays.

Today, the crime scene was the focus of many tourists and locals, as opposed to sightseers that would venture out later in the morning to visit other portions of the lake.

Only the two smaller boats would depart The Weirs during Bike Week. The larger boat, The Mount, was tethered at the dock for a week of biker activities and parties.

Additional patrolmen arrived and tried to disperse the gathering crowd of onlookers, while encouraging them to keep moving. Some were persistent pedestrian rubber-neckers of sorts, without vehicles. The police were losing patience with the sensationalists but kept their cool regarding the growing local crowd.

"Nothin' to see here. Move please," they spoke while gesturing gently with their hands. "Move along."

Most people complied and retreated to discuss the situation, especially the elderly locals that stood on balconies across the street from The Weirs docks below. They were gazing as best they could from the historic buildings that were Veterans, Infantry and Calvary structures of note. They peered down on the general area where the tragedy was unfolding, knowing full well that this was *an apparent first* in their recent memory for the famed Weirs event.

The elderly veterans from the early U.S. wars commiserated about their ailments while trying to fathom how a young person could have met her demise directly across the street from their historic buildings of yesteryear. It was still not clear to them if the dead woman had been murdered or had died accidentally—from a drowning, drugs or having fallen precariously from a boat or dock. No one wanted to believe that is was a suicide or murder. Their take was that, although she was nude, she may have been partying nearby and fell overboard from a pier or passing boat. Drunkenness, public or private was sometimes part of the Bike Week aura and a major concern for the local authorities that knew that the altered state of mind could cause injury to the inebriated person or death to others, especially riders at all hours of the night.

Her totally nude body suggested numerous scenarios: skinny-dipping during the night, had fallen off one of the passing party boats after drinking or she had been placed there intentionally after foul play, murder or an altered state of mind. Since the official Bike Week activities had yet to begin, her case leaned more toward foul play, at least in the eyes of the police. *If it was a suicide, why was she naked as well?* they wondered. An official autopsy would be needed to help elucidate the mystery and Dr. Blaisdell was as anxious as anyone to resolve the unanticipated death. This type of tragedy just didn't happen at The Weirs. It was bad karma. It shocked the community and the authorities that were hoping for a peaceful week of activities. A death prior to the main influx of visitors was neither expected nor welcomed by the Chamber of Commerce or the official Laconia Motorcycle Week Association—the LMWA. It would taint the entire event of nine days or more.

Chapter 14

As the coroner was finishing up by making his final notations at the scene, the local Weirs Beach Fire Department and rescue squad attended to the metal gurney for retrieval of the body at the base of the embankment. They assisted the funeral home staff. The body bag containing the deceased woman was removed from the scene for the short trip to the Concord, New Hampshire morgue. The local funeral director, Mr. Hammond, agreed to assist by offering to transport the body after the EMT's brought the corpse up the embankment.

In the meantime, additional policemen arrived to survey and scour the shoreline for evidence near the area of The Weirs docks. A motive or cause for her death was needed.

The local Chamber of Commerce certainly wanted to downplay the unexpected death. The area was about to be infested with thousands of Bike Week tourists and attendees. The last thing that the Chamber and Rally Committees needed was the rumor of a "killer on the loose" prior to the enormous gathering in the Lakes Region. Every official wanted the answer to the young woman's identity and to the cause of her death. They prayed that it was not foul play. As the sun rose over the beach area, the warmth of a new day overshadowed the grim scene that had occurred at the popular tourist attraction and beach.

The month of June drew more than just bikers. It was green and blooming with local flora. The Lakes Region fostered and nourished the vacationers that visited the central portion of New Hampshire all summer long. The visitors added millions of dollars to the local economy and the

Chamber of Commerce did not want to see one unfortunate event tarnish the image of The Weirs or bucolic New Hampshire.

Two detectives from the Laconia police were assigned as regional investigators, both of which would supplement the needs of Chief Dalinger, Captain Bennett and the coroner's investigation. Their role was to help coordinate the interviews of local residents and biker attendees, offering forensic leads to the officials that were to scour the area for additional evidence—specifically the general geographical area by the water's edge and embankment. It was a well-organized team effort.

They were supported by the Laconia Fire Department dive team that was assigned to scan the local waters and dock area for any evidence of the woman's clothing, possessions or artifacts relevant to the impending unresolved case. Divers would be in the water by 9:00 A.M. and they were professionals at recovering missing persons and other items that might provide clues to the mystery.

Their "grid" was the Weirs Beach swimming area and the perimeters and depths beneath the cruise boats that stood silent and secured at their berths. If anything pertinent to the young woman were on the lake bottom, the divers would find it. They seemed to have eagle eyes. Some of the divers were familiar with the general Weirs area. They practiced rescue dives in both the summer and winter months. Landmarks were well known. They used the artifacts from the old steamships that lay on the bottom as "markers."

The romantic names of boats like Maid of the Isles, the James Bell, the Governor Endicott, the Minneola and the Chocorua had as much notoriety and misadventure as the Mount Washington had experienced. In the mid-1800's, a dozen or more steamships graced the Big Lake. Cast iron boilers, metal plates, engine parts and boat cranes lay in that general area, rusted grave markers of prior days of the steam engine and paddlewheel era. Boats and small cruise ships that preceded the original Mount Washington Steamer (1872), lay strewn where the original Mount caught fire in 1939. It could cruise at 20 MPH and had 450 HP engines. A 45-inch piston and ten-foot stroke ran the long ship.

While their upper decks often burned, portions of the hulls and mechanical parts that powered them sank to the bottom for posterity. The side wheels and boilers of numerous boats provided excitement for amateur skin divers as well.

The Lake Winnipesaukee Historical Society Museum is located at The Weirs on Route 3 and harbors memorabilia of the ships, like the Dago, hit by a hurricane and sunk in 1913, including its cargo crane. The Lady of the Lake (1849), constructed in Lakeport by the Winnipesaukee Steamboat Company, lies scuttled from 1895, a 125-foot steamboat that remains in thirty feet of water near Smith Cove in Glendale—the hull and deck intact to this day. The Horseboat ("Hossboat") Barge, possessing two horses on treadmills, was powered by two paddlewheels. It lies in 40-feet of water off Bear Island and became obsolete with the emergence of the modern steam engine—the hull, tools and load of coal lay on the bottom.

The steamship, Belknap, sank in 1841 while towing logs in a stormy gale, giving rise to an island name, Steamship Island. Three other wrecks lie off another—Ships Island, in 10-40 feet of water.

The Minneola and Maid of the Isles vessels were screw-driven steamers replacing the obsolete paddlewheels in the 1870's.

Improved roads and the emergence of the railroad, i.e. the eventual Boston and Maine made commercial lake transport obsolete yet to this day, the new Mount Washington ferrets sightseers to Center Harbor and Moultonborough, Wolfeboro, Alton Bay and Meredith. She winters in Center Harbor while the diesel engines are torn down and refurbished. In May of each year, they perform a shakedown cruise, troubleshooting the mechanics of the large boat.

The divers over the years have sought the underwater sights as treasures like pirate adventurers of the ocean—the Cousteau's of the modern day who retrieve lost fishing gear, snowmobiles that penetrated the thin ice of winter, or boats and motors lost in depths where the owners have no means to recover them easily or didn't care. They often had no way to raise them and recreational divers found a lucrative salvage trade.

Chapter 15

Before departing The Weirs area, Dr. Blaisdell received a message on his pager. He read the alert in the window display: **CALL THE OFFICE— ACCIDENT**.

By mistake, he had left his cell phone in his wife's car. He asked if he could borrow another cell from a local resident. The man willingly obliged.

With one hand on his forehead in fatigue, Blaisdell returned the call to the office while leaning for support against the fender of his vehicle. Somewhat noisy at street level, he placed one finger in the opposite ear in order to hear more clearly. The onlookers were now dissipating, but the noise from vehicles made it difficult to hear the office attendant's voice.

The young woman who died on the shoreline was gone and the stragglers were now dispersing rapidly, primarily at the encouragement of the local police. Murmurs of the tragic event continued among the passersby. The occasional conversation was often interrupted by the sound of loud pipes of arriving motorcyclists looking for food and coffee.

Lakeside Avenue was awake now and an occasional biker cruised the famed road of Bike Week. In a couple days, the masses would inundate the Laconia area. Once again and annually, life would be breathed into the arcades, stores and bars at Weirs Beach. The endless tradition was now over eight decades old with some riders almost approaching that age as well. Many were in their fifties, sixties and seventies.

The phone message from the coroner's office was grim, another sad event—and the day had hardly begun. A biker on a California chopper had crossed the centerline on the two-lane stretch of Parade Road, Route

106 just a few miles north of Laconia's center. The location of the crash was just after the Elm Street intersection and below Severance Road. It was adjacent to the condo and residential complex referred to as South Down Shores. A small, but old cemetery, called Round Bay, was also close to the crash site.

Clearly noticeable, the cemetery sat up on a rise above the road and contained stones in excess of 100-years-old. On one particular notorious curve of the 40 MPH stretch of highway, the rider and the custom bike hit a soft shoulder at a speed in excess of 65 MPH, leaving the highway and hitting a utility pole near the side of the road. The rider was riding solo, but he was thrown clear of the motorcycle and landed like a rag doll on the asphalt of the main road. A streak of crimson blood laced the macadam like a brush stroke that ended in a pool of red by his head.

His buddy, following behind him on a Harley Sportster, ran to his aid, crying out for help as his black boots slapped the pavement. Cars traveling in both directions stopped abruptly while a traveling salesman ran from his Ford Taurus and threw down his sport coat on the rider's broken torso in the road. All through CPR by the Good Samaritan, the injured biker riveted from involuntary spasms that implied spinal cord or severe brain injuries. His jeans were wet from urine, an obvious involuntary reflex of the body from the trauma. The efforts by the businessman were in vain—the trauma to the head was too severe. The fellow rider sat close to the now dead corpse, weeping—his own breath exuding the stale odor of hops and beer. There was nothing he could do for his friend.

Without a helmet, the severely injured rider had died before the ambulance arrived—blunt trauma, blood loss and irreparable injury to the forehead and cortex of the brain had quickly arrested his heart. His long hair was saturated with blood, the patches of missing scalp and crimson-coated bone ever apparent from the severity of the fall. The dead man's jeans, now ripped along a seam from the macadam, revealed a compound fracture of the leg. Someone who had secured a blanket from the trunk quickly covered the unsightly lower torso. The attempted rescue was futile—those at the scene all knew that he died never really gaining consciousness.

No one spoke as the fallen biker lay prone and crumpled like a pretzel, strewn among motorcycle parts—broken mirrors, handlebars and foot pegs that had been ripped off by the impact. A saddlebag of clothes for the week was ripped open scattering some of his belongings on the highway. His custom bike was impaled against the telephone pole and unrecognizable as a two-wheeled machine. The front fork was resting in a nearby field some twenty feet away.

His fellow rider had witnessed the accident and his friend's loss of control in the sandy edge of the turn, propelling him across the road into another lane. There was no way to recover after the front end turned 90°. In the attempt to recover from the unpredictable sand, the rider overcompensated with his handlebars and hit the pole.

The odor of alcohol was evident on the deceased rider as well, but the companion traveler who was close behind had somehow managed to live.

The Laconia and Meredith police arrived at about the same time and were on the scene attempting to console the second rider, having checked and covered the dead biker with a police tarp. The arrival of a Medi-Vac helicopter was futile. The sound of ambulance sirens and also the pulsating drone of the chopper could be heard reverberating off the surface of nearby Lake Opechee. In less than a minute it would arrive at the scene, albeit too late to assist in the obvious fatality.

A flatbed tow truck was summoned from a nearby Mobil station. The Harley remnants would be taken and secured at the Laconia Police Department on Fair Street.

An open stretch of road allowed for the helicopter to land, blocking traffic for miles on 106. At that point, the chopper was more dramatic than useful, other than as a hearse if needed.

Chapter 16

The second rider underwent a field sobriety test once he was composed enough to speak. Able to stand and walk, he failed the initial balance test and was to be taken into custody for potential DWI. They didn't even need a white line to measure his vertical stability—he had none. His own bike impounded, the rider was handcuffed and led to a nearby police cruiser. He shouted obscenities at the police and was bemoaning the loss of his friend, criticizing their insensitivity to his emotions of the moment. He did nothing but complicate the matter and further alienate the cops. They were in no mood for more issues from a drunk.

The police considered him lucky that he was not killed, along with his friend. Having him spend some time in a temporary cell in order to be more civil and lucid was all the cops desired. They were already pained by the unnecessary loss of the other biker.

Traffic was paralyzed on Route 106 for miles, both north toward Meredith and south toward Laconia proper. Meredith Center Road was a diversionary detour for northbound vehicles. It circumvented the accident scene. Southbound traffic was diverted by U-turn and back to Rollercoaster Rd., a long conduit to Weirs Beach and old Route 3 in Gilford, northeast of the center of Laconia.

The crumbled and twisted bike frame next to the telephone pole had California tags. A bumper sticker on the customized and metallic-painted fender read:

HELMET LAWS? NO WAY!
Let the Rider decide!

The coroner, Dr. Blaisdell, left the Weirs and sped up Route 3 north and over Rollercoaster Rd. It was the shortest route to the fatal accident. A police cruiser provided him with an escort to the tragic bike scene, his lights flashing and siren blaring. Blaisdell was at the grim scene of the fatality in six minutes or less. An EMT from the Medi-Vac helicopter stood helplessly nearby awaiting confirmation of the rider's death by the M.E. By now, it was clear that the rider was deceased. The EMT certainly knew that. CPR, intratracheal intubation with oxygen and an intracardial injection of epinephrine had failed to elicit a response. There was no pulse or heartbeat, nothing but a straight line on the monitor.

The morning had already been a busy and intense experience for the coroner and this new biker's death seemed to be a precursor to an anticipated bad week from hell. After confirmation of death, Dr. Blaisdell sanctioned the removal of the fallen rider, which facilitated the ability of the police to restore traffic flow on what was one of the busiest highways in the area. Drivers for miles seemed to sigh with relief as traffic began to move at a slow snail's pace.

The two riders had just come from the new Meredith Harley-Davidson dealership and showroom on Route 3, next to a McDonalds and six or so miles north of the location of the accident.

The Bike Week festivities hadn't even begun in earnest and already there had been another loss of life related to the historic, annual event. Don Wright had arrived before the body was removed. He now had his front-page photo for the next edition of the Laconia paper—the twisted bike frame and pole combination which resembled an incongruous Picasso sculpture of chrome, steel, wood and plastic. Symbolically, a collage of unnatural twisted and jagged bike parts and the telephone pole told the story without the necessity of the gore of a dead rider. Don maintained his photojournalistic code of ethics while being creative in the photo shoot of the macabre scene. The picture that would grace the newspaper was "worth a thousand words."

Chapter 17

A hundred feet from where the dead woman was found at Weirs Beach, a heavyset man with a long white beard and sunglasses sat on his cranberry red, highly chromed, Harley-Davidson Softail. He had parked in an open slot on Lakeside and just above the train tracks, which intersected the roadway and the Weirs beachfront parking lot near Endicott Rock. The side road offered entry into a large parking area to the beach and to the historic stone landmark. Endicott Park bordered the Paugus Bay Channel.

The name on the gas tank read—*The Iceman,* in bold script, complete with accents of skulls, facsimile ice cubes, icicles, iron chains and a chilling airbrushed graphic of death and destruction, with flames among glaciers. It was a piece of art, unusual but professionally airbrushed by a New Jersey artist. The raised lettering on the New Jersey license tag read, ICEMAN in block script that graced the backend fender and was nestled between two saddlebags of jet-black leather fringe and chrome studs.

He was austere in presence and enormous in size, clad in leathers himself, and jeans that hardly retained the excess weight around his midriff. When leaning forward, he had "plumber's butt," a result of low jeans and an uncomely view of the crack in his buttocks. Vanity was not an issue here. His ass hung out and he could have cared less. It was part of the ambiance and aura of Bike Week, risqué but common throughout the week and on Lakeside Avenue, in particular.

On his wrists, he wore wide bands—studded, leather bracelets. His long hair and beard mimicked that of the late, Jerry Garcia—the Grateful Dead look. All that was lacking was a tie-die T-shirt from Haight-Ashbury in San

Francisco. He wore wrap-around sunglasses, even at this early hour, as if the shades were hiding his enormous *presence.*

The vest that covered his bare chest and salt and pepper, black and gray hairs was stenciled on the back with the words: NEW JERSEY ROUGH RIDERS. The date, EST 1955 and the word, METUCHEN Chapter were embroidered below the club's name. The name of the club covered the top half of the embroidered circle and the date and Chapter were embroidered on the lower half thereby completing its circumference.

The logo for the club Chapter was an Adonis in stature, centered and naked, one that mimicked a Roman or Greek god. Gold wings embellished the figure and feathered, golden scrambled egg designs adorned the logo, almost as if the yellow filigree was military in nature, a likeness to the brim of a military officer's hat of high rank.

Shortly after the local authorities and funeral home hearse containing the young woman's body had departed Lakeside Avenue and rounded the famed WEIRS BEACH sign at the intersection of Route 3 and the Weirs Drive-In, Iceman stepped off the seat of his motorcycle and pulled out a black cell phone from his rear pocket. It was attached to a chain that looped and drooped on the back of his jeans, and was secured to the belt loop on his Levi's.

He quickly pressed a preprogrammed telephone number to New Jersey. Holding the phone near his left ear, he lit up a cigarette. Wiping the tobacco ashes from his beard with his right hand, someone at the other end answered the call from New Hampshire.

"Ace?" he said, without expression, "the deed's done . . . she's *spent.*"

The man on the line responded happily, "Good . . . Nicely done."

"I'll keep you posted on what the papers say tomorrow. The hearse just left . . . the local pigs look confused," he laughed with a smoker's cough. Ace joked at the other end, "Better quit those cigs, man."

"No friggin' way," came a response, "I'll die on a bike before I get lung cancer."

"Maybe so," Ace responded, in jest. "Maybe so . . ."

Chapter 18

The conversation was short and to the point, leaving nothing to the imagination or anything about specific details for the phone recipient, Ace. Iceman placed the cell phone back in his pocket and climbed back on the enormous 1200 CC machine. It thundered when started and popped the familiar Harley muffler sound—the uneven cadence of an idling motor with an unusual camshaft design at low speeds. It sounded like "potato-potato-potato" to the common person on a sidewalk.

It was the Harley-Davidson classic sound, a reminder of one hundred years of manufacturing and fame, some of which was infamous and tainted by the influence of Marlon Brando, Steve McQueen and James Dean movies and biker video porn in more modern times.

Brando provided the classic image of the black leather crowd bad boy. Never the less, he was idolized as an actor and icon then and to this day by fans and fellow riders who dislike the DMV's rules and restrictive laws of the road. Brando exuded freedom. Brando's most noted role that followed was in *The Godfather* series, a continuation of the rebellious or Mafia-tainted characterizations that are classic and lasting films of today.

McQueen's *Great Escape* initiated an excitement of motorcycle aerobatics, the unheard of midair *escape* of his bike over a barbed-wire fence at a prisoner camp. We are left today with Hollywood icons, Peter Fonda, Robert DiNiro and Al Pacino's to absorb and manifest the iconic attitude of the Brando and Dean eras. The macho aura of Fonda's classic film, *Easy Rider* was the last relevant biker movie of note—a tribute to the late 60's and early 1970's and beyond. The American flag helmets and bandannas are still worn in modern times—often symbols of patriotic veterans.

Even today, the perpetual aura of nationalism and patriotism is exhibited by the black leather crowd who participate in the *Rolling Thunder Tour*—miles of veterans on bikes heading to Washington, DC each year to honor the fallen soldiers. An emphasis on their Vietnam tours of duty still remains.

Nationalism is not limited to the male rider, but enhanced by women riders in flag-patterned bathing suits, tank tops and headgear. The Harley riders amplify the tradition more than any other motorcycle manufacturer. Indian motorcycle riders have tried, but Harley has led the veterans' image for decades. The recent centennial anniversary of the H-D Company had been celebrated in Michigan and throughout the United States.

*   *   *

Following the telephone call, Iceman headed north on Route 3 to a restaurant, bar and snack bar known for lobsters and seafood. It was also well known for BBQ ribs and pork. During Bike Week, they set up tents outside in the parking area, where food was served all day.

Iceman was hungry with pangs for seafood even though TJ's wasn't serving lunch yet. He settled for a large country breakfast and sat at a nearby picnic table where he chased the enormous meal down with a Budweiser from his saddlebag. His eyes were always on the highway, noting club insignias passing by on bikes that were sometimes friend or foe.

Every once in a while, a biker would pull into TJ's lot and head for a leather shop or other stores nearby. Never letting his guard down, Iceman belched and even farted on occasion as if no one was near. He was not alone at the snack bar, but no one cared and no one objected to his rude behavior. He was huge and intimidating and it was Bike Week—anything was acceptable in public. There were no rules of etiquette. *Raw* was etiquette and Iceman was *raw*.

TJ's was a popular family restaurant year round. It was across from FUNSPOT, a video arcade building for kids, and not far from the Dirty Boot Saloon. A lot of popular spots were north of the famed Weirs Beach sign and the intersection of Rollercoaster Rd. and Endicott Rd. north (Route 3), which harbored plenty of action for the riders, mostly places to eat and drink.

Inside TJ's, the dining room and lobby was packed with customers. People lined up outside waiting for an open table. Lobsters, haddock, clams and assorted New England Atlantic Ocean delicacies were offered during lunch and dinner but breakfast was still in order at this hour of the day.

The bar served Budweiser all day long. Kegs were stored in tandem. The dining room was rustic with old farm tools, horse harnesses and other outdated implements aptly hung on the walls. Adorning the top of each wall was a continuous border of old license plates, some from cars and some from bikes.

Once Iceman felt comfortable outside, devoid of competitor gangs like the Outlaws, Angels and Pharaohs and other popular combatants, he phoned some of his buddies on the other side of the Big Lake to meet him at TJ's. By the time they arrived, lunch would be available and Iceman would be famished again. Some of them were traveling from Wolfeboro and Alton Bay, an hour's ride away or less.

Iceman sat back and leaned his big frame against a picnic table top, arms spread out wide as to not allow others to sit near him—personal space that he often desired. He checked out the women that were on other bikes and walking around the parking lot. He wanted a lady bad. He was horny and the views of skimpy attire aroused him. He lit up a Camel with no filter and blew smoke rings while watching through black, reflective sunglasses, the smoke dissipate into the surrounding air. It was still and the rings hung on for a while.

Once his fellow club members were to arrive, an hour from now, they would suck down lobster, clams and suds and he would update them on what happened on the shoreline of Weirs Beach in the early A.M. Iceman would reiterate and recapitulate his memories of the death scene, laughing at times at the mystery the death was to the local police. He relished in the thought that the crime was virtually unsolvable.

A hardened young lady nearby, decent looking and tattooed, looked historically "well-ridden." She was dressed in a tank top and cutoffs and carrying a tray of food. Solo, she was looking for a place to sit.

"Nice beard," she said, breaking the ice. "Room there for me?"

"Sit down right here young lady . . . there's room if ya want," he coerced her. She smiled and thanked him. Retracting his arm, she sat next to the man.

"Thanks, I'm Bonnie," she said, and set the plate of food down adjacent to him.

"Kind of you to free up some space for me."

He told her his name was Iceman. She smirked and then said, "Nice beard . . . weird name. You were holdin' that space for someone?"

Iceman shifted his butt over a foot or so. She wedged herself in, feeling his thigh against hers.

"Yah. Savin' it for you. A lady as pretty as you? Why, it's only proper to come to the aid of someone in distress," he laughed. "There ain't no other place to sit and eat, 'cept on the grass over there and that would be rude. Have ya a seat, I don't bite."

She smiled cordially and thanked him again and they hit it off in mundane conversation. She was from North Carolina and clearly was looking to "hook up" for the week. Iceman wanted to "hook up" as well, feeling his groin pained from the interaction, his thighs getting twitchy.

"You come here often, sailor?" she teased with an old cliché, and eating her pancakes.

"Not often enough I guess, doll, if I've missed seein' you in the past. I come each year."

Bonnie smiled and admitted this was her second year at the Laconia Rally. Iceman interrupted her briefly between her breakfast bites and told her he was camped out on the other side of the lake with plenty of beer and other candy treats. She was welcome to partake if she wanted. "Our cache is much better than breakfast," he enticed her. She seemed interested but unsure of his large size and demeanor. Large bikers were dominating to her.

"Well . . . I have no place to stay so maybe that might work," she conceded. "Every place is booked. I'll need a place to crash."

"Plenty of room in my tent," he offered. "You here with your ol' man?"

"Nah," she acknowledged, in a condescending way. "We're not an item anymore. He's been gone a month and I ain't seen no booty since," she volunteered. "Horny as a hoot owl after that ride up north. Plan to hook up here . . . get back into dating I guess."

Chapter 19

Iceman smiled and offered to resolve Bonnie's dating needs. She didn't verbalize a yes or no but clearly she was intending on staying that night in his tent. She had no other offers and didn't want to pitch a sleeping bag on the side of the road. The weather was not in her favor with rain predicted. For some odd reason she was attracted to the man.

After a few minutes, he put an arm around her, claiming his stake so to speak and they lit up cigarettes and bonded a bit more. She didn't resist his arm or presumptuous closeness.

From that moment he suspected he was "in," and her body was just what he needed. Desperation must have set in for the girl since Iceman was not attractive and appeared somewhat large and unkempt. Apparently that didn't matter to her in her current state of libido. Some women liked the raw and rough image of black leather riders and Bonnie seemed willing to get acquainted with the Rough Riders bad boy.

"Let's take a walk, little lady. I need to pee."

Iceman managed to convince her to join him in a Porta-potty at the far end of the line of plastic vertical "cans" in an adjacent unoccupied grassy lot. A local company known as The Blow Brothers owned the rental potties. They laughed at the name.

Without much coercion on his part, and to his delight she entered the cramped quarters with him laughing and joking.

"Can I help?" she asked.

"Sure," he responded. She directed the stream while giggling. After he was done, she closed the seat and faced him. The door was locked with a simple slide latch. She then performed fellatio on him complimenting him on the large size of his male organ. Voices could only be heard in the distance. No one was nearby the Porta-Potty but music, loud pipes and laughter was everywhere. She stroked him and teased him caressing his privates with the tip with her tongue. He was erect in seconds and she could hardly handle the size of him. He played with her breasts, her tank top now around her neck exposing both beauties to the stagnant air. Her legs were spread as she sat, her shorts unbuttoned.

Pushing her thong to the side with his fingers, he teased her and digitally massaged her clitoris as she sat writhing in ecstasy, her shorts falling down on the floor around her ankles. She was wet with anticipation and felt him pulsating in her mouth. It was all so quick, both of them in need of a climax.

Oddly and pleasurably breakfast had turned into an impromptu sex fest and it all started with Iceman sitting at a picnic table, holding a seat or two for no one in particular.

How he had fallen into such luck with a willing sexual treat was beyond him. After he ejaculated, she continued to tease him sustaining the erection moments longer. As a reward, he stood her up, naked and aroused and then spread a small mirror out on the toilet seat. As she gathered herself together, embarrassingly covering her breasts, he cut a line or two of cocaine on the glass plate. Her shorts were still around her ankles and her buttocks were still uncovered.

Rolling up a dollar bill into a tight tube, he rewarded her and himself with some nose candy dessert. She wasted no time bending over to snort the white powder. Some "blow" for a blow, he thought. While bent, he spread her legs and inserted himself inside her, his penis still hard and her genitalia still moist from the erotic encounter moments earlier.

Groaning, she felt the enormous size of him inside her—she gyrated wildly back and forth touching herself to enhance her own pleasure. She felt like a dog in heat receiving him from the back and oscillated in a motion that made her climax in less than a minute. He covered her mouth with his hand to quiet the screams that might draw attention to the portable blue toilet. They were sweating profusely and breathing hard. If this was what she was like with cocaine and beer, he couldn't imagine what a little heroin would do for her later that night. She seemed game for anything, anal or otherwise.

She turned and they kissed passionately before regrouping themselves, dressing and exiting the pre-molded plastic commode. The door slammed behind them.

That was the first time they had kissed and it seemed anticlimactic considering what had just transpired in the heat of passion. His arm around her, she leaned into his shoulder.

No one was waiting in line or near the remote portable bathroom in the field. Most customers preferred the restaurant bathrooms anyway and TJ's accommodated as many customers as they could. Iceman and Bonnie walked back to the front of the restaurant only to find some of his biker friends ardently searching for him. They had arrived twenty minutes earlier than expected from Wolfeboro.

"Iceman . . . where the fuck ya been?" asked one of the men, with anger. "We searched all over fuckin' hell for you. Saw your bike and no Iceman in sight."

"I was busy man. What's the issue? Had business in the outhouse out there," he said, pointing. "Meet Bonny . . . she's with me this week." They nodded to her and walked away in disgust.

"Friendly sorts, eh?" she voiced.

"Ah . . . never mind them. They're just jealous cause they don't have any chicks. They drink too much anyway and then pass out. They don't deserve no booty."

The gang members heard him and just shook their heads while heading for the beer tent. Bonny clung to Iceman like a long lost boyfriend she had known for ages. He bought her another beer and then asked her to wait at the picnic table bench for a few minutes.

"I gotz ta chat with the boys in private," he said, nicely. "Now don't you go anywhere little lady," he said, impersonating John Wayne. She laughed at him and sat on the bench. "I'll be right here, healing," she laughed, while raising her eyebrows. "I'm in pain."

"I'm a bit sore myself . . . you're good, lady, damn good."

Iceman headed for the beer tent to meet his fellow Rough Riders, looking back once or twice to make sure she didn't leave. The Metuchen Club rule of sharing chicks was out of the question. Bonnie was his and that was that this week.

Iceman was busy updating the riders. His mind was still on Bonnie and he described what he had seen that morning at Weirs Beach. Iceman passed on to the rest of the club executives Ace's compliments saying, "that 'New Jersey' was pleased in the tradition," a tradition of death that was decades coming. No one but select club members knew the agenda for the beginning of the week. They merely followed orders from the club's hierarchy.

Chapter 20

Iceman couldn't wait to get Bonnie back to Wolfeboro. Bonnie sat where he left her at the wooden table and talked to no one other than a solo biker chick who was eating pancakes. He kept looking over at his concubine, the fantasy encounter still fresh in his mind.

Iceman anticipated not sleeping that night and taking care of what her former "ol' man" down south had tossed away for free. *The fool,* he thought. Her Mariah Carey body was all Iceman would need for the week. In return, she would get hers as well and a bit more of the addiction she brought from the south to the north.

"Bonnie baby" had already scored on her first day in Laconia and Bike Week had hardly begun. Iceman had more rider friends coming and he was anxious to show her off.

After meeting with the boys, he returned to the table and his new woman. They drank some bottled beer, chatting like nothing had occurred out of the norm. Her eyes and smile revealed how wasted she was. Cocaine was her drug of choice and its effects were readily apparent in enhancing her increased libido. She was ready for round two and drugs only mellowed and evened her out mentally.

• "They like me now?" she asked, pouting.

"The boys? Oh yah. For sure. They think you're a piece of ass," he laughed. "I told them we had a Platonic relationship."

"Platonic?" she said, roaring. "Is that what they call Platonic? Getting off in a portable toilet in New Hampshire? Jesus . . . I love *Platonic* then. I wonder if Plato got head."

Iceman smiled and laughed heartily.

"Just wait 'til we get to Wolfeboro," he offered. "We'll have a bit more room to roll around. I have some other Platonic positions to try on you."

"Can't wait," she remarked. "I'm kind of likin' Bike Week already . . . and you, Iceman."

In a matter of minutes, they were on the road and heading to the other side of the Big Lake. Iceman left his companions at TJ's. She rode behind him and held on for dear life. She wore a full-faced helmet but Iceman didn't. He was too macho for a helmet and wouldn't be caught dead in one. Bonnie was a helluva lot smarter than him.

Every once in a while she let him know she was there. She reached around and grabbed his crotch gently, but firmly. His enormous size sheltered her from the wind. She leaned forward and turned her head sideways laying it on the back of his vest. Bonnie noted the logo of the club.

She knew that opposites attract and never would she have imagined bonding with someone like the Iceman. He wasn't even her type and lived in New Jersey. With Iceman living so far from her North Carolina, he would be unawares of her lesbian affinity toward women as well. She was bi. She liked both sexes and this week it was men. She was secretive and mystical but game for open-minded pleasures.

*   *   *

The elderly gentlemen that had witnessed the coroner's scene where the young woman had died at The Weirs ascended a long set of wooden stairs at the nearby Veterans Home, an historic Victorian-style clapboard structure. He held the railing as he placed his cane over his forearm, counting each of the ten steps to the wrap-around porch and fenced-in railing of old. He managed to find an empty wicker rocking chair and turned slowly around to sit facing the road and beachfront below the home.

"Ah," he moaned as he lowered himself, placing the handmade mahogany stained cane against the side of the building. It slid to the floor but he didn't bother with it and left well enough alone.

The elderly gentleman hadn't noticed that Don Wright, the photographer, had studied and fixated upon the location of the man's residence. Each of the neighboring homes looked similar and their external colors were gray, blue or dark green.

From a distance, the statuesque vintage residences were similar in appearance. Most had prominent porches that overlooked the beach area.

The old man planted his feet in front of the rocker and gently began the pendulum motion that seemed comforting to the elderly. It was his favorite chair on the porch and just high enough for him to see the beach area and passing pleasure boats. Observing The Weirs festivities was his favorite pastime. People watching was fun and often entertaining, but today, there was a remorseful sadness in his eyes, knowing that a young person had died near an embankment in front of his home and in full view of his steps to Lakeside Avenue.

His name was Wendell Atkins, aged 90. Wendell had lived in The Weirs area most of his life and he had attended and observed the biker ritual for decades. He was a well-known fixture to the locals. Bikers from around the country often stopped by to visit with him each year, a renewal of friendships with a man of history, both local and national.

Wendell was an icon, not dissimilar from a cigar store Indian of old. Ever present on his porch each year, he was the glue that married the elderly with summer's youth.

The old man had his regulars that sought him out to give him something to look forward to each Laconia Rally year and to reminisce. His tales of the old days and of the Lakes Region appealed to the younger crowd that often saw him as a local, living encyclopedia of prior motorcycle rallies. He had ridden motorcycles in his youth, mostly British bike models from yesteryear. Names long forgotten by today's riders.

He would tell stories from WWI and II. Teddy Roosevelt was once on the same street on which his Veteran's Home was located. President Roosevelt had vacationed there and campaigned in the popular vacation spot as well.

Historic photographs of those occasions were in the Lake Winnipesaukee Museum and local library, and in books showing Teddy waving to a crowd near a monument that honored all Veterans of Foreign Wars. Early photos also revealed the earliest of motorcycles and riders visiting The Weirs area. Motorcycles with sidecars were parked along the lakefront area as early as 1918 and 1919. It was no different today except that the numbers of visitors and bikes had increased by many orders of magnitude.

Wendell coughed and then reached for a linen handkerchief in his side pocket, blowing his nose and removing some phlegm. Age had its way of reminding him that each year brought a new ailment, mostly aching joints and painful arthritis. If it wasn't the heart, it was the bowels or the lungs, added to a fading memory and his normally captive brain cognition. Today, he was bothered by a dry cough and the occasional spells of hacking his way through conversations. Somehow, he tolerated the whole mess of aging.

Chapter 21

Wendell Atkins contemplated the recent death of the young woman. His left hand gripped and rubbed his chin as if in a soothing, contemplative support. He seemed deep in thought while struggling with memories and reminiscing about a similar occurrence years earlier. At least he knew there was something similar. He could not remember the date, but there was a familiarity to the morning's events—a deja vu. Both senior dementia and early Alzheimer's had affected some of his long-term memory, a natural product of his aging and genetic history.

At one time, people did not live as long as today hence early signs of forgetfulness decades earlier were probably an indication of the exacerbated Alzheimer's issue so prominently noted today. No one lived long enough back then to see the disease state evolve into the perilous physical state that robbed the Ronald Reagan's of the world of their memory. The president was cognizant of the disease and memory loss ten years before dying; a disease that also emotionally affected the immediate families and caregivers of victims, adversely and painfully. Those that were relegated to years of medical care were also burdened. Wendell only occasionally lost memory—he still had most faculties intact.

*   *   *

After the crowd dispersed, Don, the local photographer, had noted that the old man had departed as well, meandering slowing across Lakeside with the aid of his cane. Don perceived that the older gentlemen had returned to a home near the death scene. Don wished to chat with Wendell, having later noted that he remained sitting on the porch and rocking with vigilance. He overheard a comment the elderly man had made at the scene of the crime. Don felt it might be relevant and helpful toward the mortal mystery that was unfolding.

Wendell looked up from his pensive mood. He was suddenly startled by the photographer's presence near the porch.

"Hello, sir," Don stated, while climbing the last stair spryly. "Didn't mean to disturb you."

"What'd ya say, sonny?" responded the elderly man.

"Hello," repeated Wright. "My name is Donald and I couldn't help overhearing you say something about the tragedy across the street—the death of the girl. Do you have a moment?"

"Sure. The name's Wendell . . . Wendell Atkins, U.S. Army Infantry, Retired. Yours, son?"

Wright repeated, "Don . . . Don Wright, sir."

Wendell attempted to stand to shake his hand when Donald gestured quickly that he didn't need to get up. He felt bad for the older gentlemen who seemed less mobile.

"No need to stand, sir," Donald commented. "Pleasure to meet you."

"Nice to make your acquaintance, son. You here for the races?"

"Sort of, sir. I do photography for a living."

Wendell smiled and asked Donald to sit down nearby. There was a small bench next to his rocker. "Photography? What can I do for ya, sonny?" he asked, cordially.

"Well . . . sir . . . for starters, I was curious to know about the word, *Vincent* that you acknowledged while we were standing across the street. The tattoo on the young woman said, 'Vincent' and the logo looked to me to be the god, Mercury with wings near his heels."

Wendell hesitated. "Yup." Then he went silent. "Could be."

"Did you recognize that name, sir? Can you associate that with something? I'm lost as to what it means or represents to you."

Wendell looked up and raised his eyebrows. He tilted his head to one side and rubbed his forehead with the fingers on his right hand.

"You'll notice, son . . . that they didn't care what I had to say. No one listens to the old folks today, especially when you're an old *soldier*," he commented. "They think we all got affected by the shell shock of the bombs during the invasions, ya know, Normandy and all. They think we're all loopy," he offered, while smiling.

Donald was cordial and smiled in return. "I'm not that way, sir. I'd be interested in what ya have to say, Mr. Atkins."

"Really? That's a first, son. No one pays me no mind most of the time, especially the neighbors in this house. They say I'm cranky. The young folks usually say with profanity that we're "all screwed up" or some such nonsense, and *spent*," he laughed. "The young people think they know it all and have all the answers. They don't."

He was emphatic and Don assured him that he was not that young to start with and surely did not have all the answers. "I'd be interested in hearing what you think, sir," he repeated.

Don sat down on the porch bench almost at floor level and adjacent to Wendell Atkins. He explained that he was a photographer for a Laconia paper. He was assigned to do a feature on Bike Week "Faces." That meant he would be there all week, each day, seeking unusual biker characters to photograph, either male or female.

"I'm usually here on Lakeside to record the Rally history for 2006," he commented. "Plenty of people watching and photo opportunities," he added, while looking briefly down at the street below. There were numerous bikers and motorcycles that had arrived in tandem, drowning out the conversation between the two men. Wendell didn't seem to mind the noise and waited for the bikes to pass before continuing to listen.

"Normally I take photos of out-of-town bikers who have unusual motorcycles or outfits, ya know shirts, hats and weird apparel."

"T&A, ya mean?" Wendell interjected, smiling. "There used to be lots more tits here," he offered, sadly. "The damn cops have stopped all the good stuff," Wendell said. "They arrest the women who bare too much these days."

Donald laughed out loud and responded in kind. "Yah. They've spoiled the whole thing," he concurred. "There used to be a time that all the women would flash ya if ya screamed, 'Show your tits!' Now you'd be lucky to find *one naked pair* in the entire crowd. The police, State Police, sheriffs and other undercover agents monitor the streets. No more nakedness."

Wendell smirked and then shook his head with disgust. He was remembering his youth. "I loved the old days," he offered with pride. "Chicks were everywhere." He continued with a sigh,

"Hell, I can remember when they had women in the parking lot of the racetrack down in Loudon . . . the 'old' track and dirt parking lot. One chick was there from Massachusetts with a sign on her back. FREE BLOW JOBS. Bikers would line up by her trailer just to have their pipes cleaned—free," Wendell mentioned. "And I don't mean the exhaust and mufflers on their bikes," he laughed.

Donald roared at the old man's humor. "For real?"

"Oh, son . . . for *real*," Wendell added, in a convincing voice.

Don wanted to get back to the reasons why he had stopped by Wendell's home. He sought input on the morning's event.

"So what do you think the name, *Vincent* means to you . . . the tattoo on the young lady's body?" Donald asked, hoping for something enlightening besides the rallies of yesteryear. Wendell was hesitant and went pensive. Don allowed him a quiet moment or two before prodding him further. It wasn't needed.

"Anyone who's older, knows," Wendell retorted, firmly. "She was 'marked,'" he said, with confidence, lowering his voice slightly. He looked around to see who might be passing by and then fanned himself in the early morning heat.

It was some sort of secret, Don felt. He awaited more enlightenment.

"Marked? What do ya mean, 'marked?'" Donald asked, with curiosity.

Wendell was cautious but seemed willfully wishing to share the information on his mind.

"The young people have no clue. They don't know *Vincent* from Vincent," he added, with complexity. "There's a difference."

Don was perplexed. *What was the old man hinting at?*

Chapter 22

Don wondered what the hell the old man was talking about but patiently awaited further information from the 90-year-old man.

"Ya got a fancy computer, son?" asked the old veteran.

"Yes, sir. I do. Why?"

"Well then, son, look up 'Vincent, logo,' the man interjected, as if he was an expert of Google.com. "That and there's your answer. She was 'marked' for death, I tell ya."

The old man tapped his cane to confirm the confidential intelligence. He seemed tired by the conversation but nodded and hinted that the secrets of the morning events were in the history of Rally Week.

Donald asked that if he looked up the information, could he come back and chat some more? Wendell assured him that he'd be around, sitting right there all week, God willing. He had nowhere to go and walking the boardwalk daily was his usual exercise.

"You'll always find me here," he offered with assurance. "If it gets too crowded, I stay on the porch. Early in the morning, there's fewer bikers so I walk sometimes or watch the train drop off visitors from Lakeport or Meredith later in the morn. They come every half-hour or so . . . fun for all."

"Thanks," added Donald, "I'll be back when I check out your mystery words on the Internet."

"You'll be back for sure," remarked Wendell Atkins. "Oh yah, remember the names, Howard Raymond Davies and Philip Vincent," he added. "You're gonna want to know 'bout them. Young people don't have a clue who they were," he mumbled before he rose slowly.

"Bye for now, son," and the screen door slammed shut, not on purpose, but the spring was set too strong. Wendell was smiling as if hiding something.

All Don heard as Wendell disappeared behind the screen was, "Bye, son. Do your research now."

Don acknowledged his good-bye. He was pumped up and anxious to delve into the Internet. Wendell Atkins was baiting Don to pursue the lead.

Don hurriedly wrote down the information on his notepad—*Vincent*, and the names, Howard Davies and Philip Vincent. Don Wright was curious about the old man and his sanity, wondering too if "shell shock" had altered his memory from the World War era. Maybe Wendell was a bit odd and loony after all, Don wondered. Were the names, Davies and Vincent old war heroes, or comrades in arms? Friends? Locals? Resident veterans?

Actually Wendell had gotten up rapidly in order to go to the bathroom. He had chronic enlarged prostate problems, which made him have to urinate often, day and night. The condition, known as Benign Prostatic Hyperplasia—BPH, was a nuisance. Always having to urinate at a given moment was a pain and embarrassing. Don did not hear him reflect his biological needs, but Wendell had politely excused himself anyway.

Don later understood the reason for the abrupt departure of his new friend and confidant. Incontinence was apparent from the mild residual odor of ammonia and the persistent dribble embarrassed Wendell. Surely Wendell seemed in a hurry and would not be so rude as to disappear so abruptly without reason.

The photographer put two and two together. Inflammation of the prostate had affected Don as well, although mildly. He was on Cardura® to alleviate the problem. It relaxed the smooth musculature of the prostate allowing the urethra adequate flow of urine from the bladder without the sense of urgency.

Donald was anxious to get on his home PC. He wanted to understand what the elderly Atkins was alluding to . . . with *Vincent*. He bounded down the steps with renewed vigor, his camera and lens cases flapping on his side.

Chapter 23

In a dark and cold refrigeration drawer at the morgue, laid the remains of the beautiful young woman, her face and body now ashen and her wet and previously matted blonde hair, curled and unkempt from exposure to the shoreline pebbles and water. An autopsy awaited her, although Dr. Blaisdell had yet to arrive in the Capital City of New Hampshire. His planned itinerary for the day was altered and he was diverted in schedule with the death of the biker on Route 106 in Laconia.

The unknown woman, deftly named, "Jane Doe" and affectionately, "Lady of the Lake" until identified, was rigid from *rigor mortis*—a temporary state of the body until dead protein was broken down. Over the next twenty-four hours, her Venus-like features and muscles would relax and soften, a natural pathological event after death.

In darkness and prone on a slab behind the stainless steel drawer door, she lay covered with a white sheet, an I.D. tagged to her large toe. Blaisdell was anxious to begin the investigation both grossly and by histological and toxicological protocol—tests that would require state chemistry labs as well as contract labs on the outside—biochemists that specialized in bioanalytical procedures for chemicals, drugs and histopathological determinations related to organ and blood pathology.

Forensic evaluations were a specialty in their own right, but Blaisdell would have to perform the gross anatomy exam at the onset. He hated the thought of carving up the beautiful torso to assess the potential lesions that could not be seen *in toto*. He had performed so many of these *in situ* procedures on young men and women that he often needed a stiff drink after each depressing, laborious task. As coroner and M.E., he was part of the investigation as well as the key doctor for the assessment of her demise.

His first clue was the unusual tattoo at the base of her spine and typically above the separation of the buttocks. He knew that the raised wheal of skin was important and hinted that the tattoo had been freshly applied over recent days. Inflammation and erythematic swelling was obvious and could be a clue to her last whereabouts and the cause of death. Biopsies of the epidermis and dermis in the tattoo areas would be relevant.

*   *   *

Blaisdell finally left the bike accident scene on 106 and drove south to Concord. His day would be long and arduous and he was already tired from the two morning adventures from hell.

At the same time, Don Wright was back in Laconia center in no time flat. He stopped at home, grabbed a laptop and headed for The Black Cat, a local haunt for coffee and pastries, lunch and dinner or just a cocktail. The popular and trendy coffee shop and café lent itself to one having a cup of latte or mocha while surfing the Internet in a wireless atmosphere. Located in the old granite and stone train station, the historic depot now functioned as the home of a flower shop, café, jewelry shop and Mexican restaurant. It had accommodated the Chamber of Commerce office for some time as well but they had plans to move in 2006.

The Black Cat had recently been updated as a non-smoking facility, with wireless technology and the ambiance of the old railway timbers, supports and intricate bead board ceilings. Stained glass reflections were the perfect setting to his researching key words that Wendell had shared with him. He uploaded on the computer some of his digital shots of the young dead woman and cropped and zoomed in on some of her tattoos and their unique attributes and features. It was clear to him from the high-resolution JPEG's and raised skin, that she had recently received the strange logo tattoo with the Roman god. The skin was elevated as if acting in rebellion to the thousands of needle punctures that it had taken to create the piece of art.

Roger O'Malley, the proprietor and new owner of "The Cat" greeted Don with a brisk hello and smile. He was curious to know what Don was doing. Don explained that he had recently come from The Weirs and an early morning suspicious death case.

"What happened?" asked Roger, with piqued interest. "Hadn't heard about the event."

"Actually," Don explained quietly, "they don't know other than a young woman was found naked and deceased on the shoreline near The Mount and to the left of Weirs Beach. Ya know, the dock area."

"You serious? How sad," remarked Roger, shaking his head in disbelief. He had a police and fire scanner but it was in his pickup truck so he was unaware of the tragedy.

"I'm trying to help the coroner with some photos," volunteered Don. He showed Roger a couple of the more tasteful photos from the crime scene. Roger was mortified and aghast at the fact that a potential death by foul play had happened for no apparent reason. It was not a positive note for the Rally Committee on which Roger played an active role.

The downtown, vintage bike races were always held by the train station and used the station parking lot as a pit stop for the racers' needs. This year's race was scheduled for the 11th of June. The track or racecourse was always through the closed-off downtown area and a fun event for riders and spectators. It was an ancillary event to the road races at NHIS in Loudon. This track resembled Monte Carlo.

There was a phone call for Roger and he excused himself from the tragic conversation. Don wanted to check out the key words that Wendell had suggested on the Internet, and in private. Don knew that there was something of relevance to Wendell Atkins input or at least he felt so. He trusted Wendell. Once Roger left Don's table in the Black Cat alcove, Don began his search on the Net. He became engrossed in the initial links and data that appeared in nanoseconds, and was shocked by what he saw.

He would end up having a pastry or two and more coffee before he left the Café. He now appeared to have something to discuss in detail with Wendell during the next visit to the Veteran's Home on Lakeside Avenue. His eyes were wide with amazement.

Wendell wasn't an old coot after all. He was lucid with memories of Weirs Rallies and their potential relevance to the woman's untimely death.

Chapter 24

The Rough Riders Motorcycle Club of Metuchen, New Jersey, of which Iceman and Ace were prominent members, had a reputation of trouble for decades. They were akin to The Mountain Men, Hell's Angels and the Pharaohs that dominated the Northeast and the expanse of the U.S. as far as Fontana, California.

The noted, Ralph "Sonny" Barger often attended the bike rallies around the country, including the Laconia Classic in New Hampshire. Sonny founded the Hell's Angels in California. He appeared last in New Hampshire signing his autobiographical book (*Hell's Angel*) for fans and was willing to shake hands and have photos taken with book buyers. His health had deteriorated over the years. It was suspected that he had cancer of the throat and larynx; there was a noticeable tracheostomy just below the chin and it was covered with gauze and tape. His voice was raspy when he spoke low and positively. His hand covered the open access to his windpipe when he needed to speak. It was now 2006 and he hadn't been seen at the event for a few years. Harley fans and member of the Hell's Angels wondered how he was doing, health wise. His fans longed to see him again.

The New Jersey Rough Riders were into many offerings that the police disliked and sought out hoping to catch members peddling porn videos on the sly at the Laconia and Weirs events. Many of the Angel's chapters had vendor tents as well, offering their logo on assorted apparel. Underneath one chapter's table were items that were not legal—a whole different stockpile of club items for sale. Not all chapters had the illegal contraband and the police had a hard time ferreting them out—the marketing of porn was mostly by word of mouth.

Videos titled, *Scooter Trash, Debbie does Harley* and *Chicks with Dicks* were common "training films," which highlighted lesbian stars and either Ron Jeremy or "Johnny Wad" Holmes. It was well known that drugs were available from other bikers that may not have been club members of any particular gang. Independent dealers came solo offering cocaine, grass and heroin at premium prices.

Iceman and his club members from New Jersey were somewhat new to the Laconia Rally. It was only the second time Iceman had been there and his motives for arriving early with his buddies were ill defined. Although he was fairly new to New Hampshire, the club had members who had attended the event for decades. His father had attended some rallies in the 1950's and 60's.

Iceman obviously knew of the death of the young blonde and he and others were involved in some manner. His phone call back to the club and to Ace earlier that day was not a "Hi, how goes it?" conversation. He was an informant, newsboy and designated scout for Ace back in New Jersey. The girl's body now discovered and removed, Iceman would inform the other members of the situation. Some twenty others had traveled to Laconia for Rally Week. They were staying in Wolfeboro, a short distance by bike from the daily events at The Weirs. A couple of members had friends in Laconia proper.

Bikers were savvy enough to use the Internet, often using local town libraries like that in Wolfeboro and the Gale Memorial Library in Laconia. Using surreptitious code names and on-line aliases, they communicated with the New Jersey Chapter and other members as needed.

The Internet was free to all in public libraries. Librarians and their assistants were often taken-aback by the scruffy riders that appeared from nowhere and from around the nation. The libraries were not used to seeing them as regulars. Intimidating but cordial, the bikers were well experienced in using the Internet medium for coded drug deals, prostitution and pornography exchanges. The authorities rarely caught them, since public access offered them ambiguity and sanitized protection from the police and FBI.

Iceman and the other members found Wolfeboro on the back side of the Big Lake to be less conspicuous. Wolfeboro, New Hampshire billed itself as the "Oldest Vacation Spot in the U.S." The accolade was hyped, painted and engraved on the signs as one entered the downtown. During Bike Week, it was clearly a different crowd for the town, yet the economy was boosted in towns all around the Lakes Region. Bikers meant revenue and quick cash.

The New Jersey Rough Riders were encamped in the woods a few miles from Wolfeboro center. They conned a farmer into letting them stay there on his private property for $1500. Common tents sufficed for their survival and the farmer was glad to have the needed income, which he could rake in under the table. He never questioned their motives or agenda. Money was money to Ol' Man Jasper and his wife, Sarah, who owned a well-known egg farm for many generations of the Jasper clan.

Jasper's fresh eggs were wholesaled to all local stores. The income from the bikers exceeded, in one week, what the farmer would gross in many weeks of egg production. He left them alone, knowing full well that they would be rowdy and careless with their trash and their comings and goings. *What could they possibly do to his pasture or woods?* Jasper questioned. *He could pick up the beer bottles later,* he thought.

In an effort to minimize his work after the Bike Week shenanigans, Jasper would merely collect and recycle the refuse from the temporary residents. He had even left 55-gallon drums in the field for them to use for trash, bottles and cans. He had mowed the whole area and "put up" his first haying as well, just before the bikers were expected to arrive. The field was neat and pristine for the temporary tent residents and transients. Porta-Potties were rented from the popular Blow Bros. They seemed to have the monopoly on the necessary conveniences.

The loud pipes only disturbed Jasper on occasion, and he and Sarah grew accustomed to the constant noise of the riders and evening parties. It was only for a few days, they justifiably acknowledged. The dollar signs outweighed the temporary aggravation.

Chapter 25

Iceman and the boys were happy that they had the Jasper semi-private refuge to escape to. It was far from the crime scene at The Weirs. They did not want to be implicated in the death of the girl at Weirs Beach. With thousands of bikers arriving daily, who would think of Wolfeboro as the site of the suspected villains? No one. The local police had enough to do, right in Laconia and Gilford proper. If the death was deemed foul play, who was going to explore the 300 mile shoreline circumference and remote towns of the Big Lake for clues?

Iceman and the boys felt secure in the pastures and wooded areas set back from the mainstream highways. The Jaspers had no clue they were accessories to harboring any renegades from New Jersey. Bikers were bikers and green money was green money. Ol' Man Jasper just wanted the cash for the week. His campground had many residents. Not all of them were from the New Jersey club.

After the first night of "tenters," Jasper felt that this year would be mild. No one was drawing attention to himself or herself and evenings were relatively quiet. During the day, the bikers were off on rides and looking for bars and Rally events. Jasper went about his farm work and maintenance of his birds and products. Their hen houses were extensive and often the interior lights glowed well into the night—a photobiology requirement of extended light for hens to lay their daily egg. He collected hundreds of eggs per week, while most of his time was spent keeping the facilities clean and the birds fed. He was no Frank Perdue but he had a good business in poultry and egg production.

Bikers found the farm quiet except for the occasional rooster that reminded them that they were in New England and dawn came early for farmers. Roosters were few but noisy, irritating alarms for bikers who had imbibed all night. If drunk enough, no one heard the roosters' calls anyway.

Chapter 26

Bike Week in Laconia attracted some notables beside Ralph "Sonny" Barger, the founder of the Hell's Angels. The actor, Peter Fonda was known to frequent the event and most years he was the Grand Marshall of the motorcycle parade that preceded the main SuperBike race at NHIS on Sunday, Father's Day at the Loudon track.

The parade always starts in Meredith, traverses Gilford and heads south through Laconia and down Route 106 to Loudon where the feature races are located. Local spectators line the parade route waving at the passing police cars, bikers and celebrants.

The riders wave and toot their horns to the fans and kids, and the virtual "train of machines" is escorted by cruisers and cops on motorcycles.

Fonda, the son of Henry and brother of Jane, starred in the films, *The Wild Angels* and most notably, *Easy Rider*. He has many close friends in the Lakes Region. He was relegated as an icon in biker movies ages ago—the original "Captain America." He bunks for the week at the summer home of C.B. Sullivan, a prominent executive of the Paul Mitchell Hair Products Company, in Gilford. Gilford is a town next to Laconia and CB's house is on the water of the Big Lake.

"Kaptain" Robbie Knievel, son of the noted, daredevil Evel Knievel, also stays at the house. They are all buddies during Bike Week. Robbie is a respected daredevil rider in his own right, 'a bone chip off the old block' so to speak. Evel, the father, over the years had broken virtually all the bones in his body jumping cars, trucks, bikes, canyons and other incredible feats for many decades. In 2006, Evel was fighting a serious form of lung fibrosis and avoiding travel. His daredevil days were over.

Fonda, the son of the famed actor who starred in *On Golden Pond* (Squam Lake) in New Hampshire had been promoting the resurgence of the *new* Indian motorcycle until the deal apparently went sour. He had endorsed the products of Indian and attended many of the Bike Week events around the country.

As a fixture at Laconia each year, Peter Fonda remained a popular attraction at the Laconia/Loudon Classic and Rally Week. Captain America, as he was known in the *Easy Rider* movie, remains philosophical in that he still promotes safety on motorcycles in the "Live Free or Die" State. Although he inspired many "free spirit" cyclists to take up the sport throughout his film career, he remains a cautious rider who focuses his attention on the road at all times. In recent years he had switched to a gold Harley-Davidson, the promotional photo of which made the local papers. Indian was no longer his choice of machines.

Ian Ziering, an actor from the cast of *Beverly Hills, 90210* often attends annually as well and rides with Fonda and C.B. Sullivan on the days preceding the major events of Bike Week. They have climbed Mt. Washington together, the highest mountain in the State and in New England. The peak in winter is unforgiving at 6,288 ft.

In 2006, Jim Bedford, master distiller of the Jack Daniel Distillery in Tennessee attended the Rally. He rides a company logo-encrusted Harley touting the charcoal filtered, toasted oak, vanilla and caramel-infused premiere whiskey.

Usually on the Thursday before race weekend in June, motorcyclists hold the "Ride to the Sky," an ancillary event. The eight-mile Mt. Washington Auto Road opened in 1861 and is deemed the "oldest manmade attraction" in the United States. In conjunction with the Harley Owners Group, HOG #8166, the Mt Washington Valley Chapter riders raise money for many charities in the area. They have raised over $30,000 since the late 1980's. It is a positive attribute to Bike Week, which is usually overshadowed by bad press and the occasional loss of life among the 400,000 annual attendees.

Chapter 27

By far the most infamous attraction at the Rally and Bike Week is the "flashing of flesh" of women that has become more subdued in recent years. It was a common occurrence for years to see signs touting the expression, "Show your Tits" almost everywhere in the Lakes Region. It was the battle call for years and in fact, for decades.

The oversight by the local police however has curtailed the extrasensory kudos and has resulted in arrests that have altered the visual milieu of the annual experience.

Laconia has always been tame compared to Sturgis. In many cases, the loose women were the *stars,* over and above that of Hollywood in L.A. All the amateurs lacked over the many June events were their own "Walk of Fame" at The Weirs.

Mud or Jell-O wrestling and Wet T-shirt contests at specific bars and restaurants had replaced the infamous biker women "flashing," leaving much to the imagination once they were soaked or covered in some odd slime. Cold and wet, the women's nipples still protrude and male bikers still tout and tease the ladies to reveal more.

Each year, the black-leather crowd becomes alcohol-embalmed, testosterone-driven observers of the enhanced libido events. Photographers like Don Wright had covered many of those events in the past. There was a photo history for decades. Sex and lewd behavior was still the normal pulse of the week and always will be. Don had plans to publish a book of the famed photos, which he had accumulated over the years. He was still collecting the "best of the best" before pursuing the book agenda, knowing a few more years were needed to complete the photo portfolio.

Bike Week remains *a classic* in the true sense of the word. Aside from the occasional accidents, fights, drug overdoses, drinking injuries or deaths, the Laconia attendees show remarkable restraint at the event in the new millennium.

Virtually no one had ever died directly at The Weirs; at least no one could remember an event akin to the loss of the young girl. The demise of the beautiful young woman was a shock to all, locals and visitors. Promoters, local endorsement businesses and sponsors of the historic event could not accept that Rally Week was starting off with such a devastating negative impact.

If foul play was involved, it had set a new precedent at The Weirs. Investigators promised to work quickly to resolve the crime. They hoped that the death was from natural causes, congenital or otherwise. It was wishful thinking and possible that it was unrelated to foul play, but most observers and the local authorities suspected the opposite—a murder or suicide. Much would now be dependent on Dr. Blaisdell's autopsy results in the next 48 hours and in the weeks to come.

Someone had to know this person, Blaisdell thought to himself, a man burdened with not only the cause of death, but also the *identity* of the victim. Just who was "The Lady of the Lake?"

*   *   *

Ace sat back in a black leather chair at his home in Metuchen, New Jersey. His massive arms rested on the sides of the chair. The room was dark as he sat clothed only in his boxer underwear and a muscle shirt. His girlfriend had just "gotten him off." She loved oral sex as much as he did. Like a concubine, she gloated at being Ace's best girl. To him, she was a nothing more than a sex slave, with kudos that came with being the Metuchen Chapter club president. He had other female choices if he wanted. There were women who waited in line to be his fantasy. Biker chicks in New Jersey were numerous and available, "putting out" for club members—an expectation if a biker chick wanted to be "recognized" by the membership. Some of the women traded their bodies, often participating in porn films for a quick hit of heroin, a dime bag. The cravings for the next needle overpowered their morality, sensibility and sanity jeopardizing their physical health with potential STD's, HIV and other transmittable microbes from multiple biker sexual encounters. Blowjobs almost guaranteed they were protected to some extend from some of the diseases.

Ace had made sure his current chick, Holly, was clean. He had her checked out at a clinic before adding her to the harem. He preferred her favors since she was totally uninhibited. Anytime, anyplace and any orifice was acceptable to her. It was as if she was a nymphomaniac, an estrogen-loaded machine, mid-cycle and ready to be of service to Ace. She aimed to please the boss man and he had no complaints about her willful compliance.

Ace was rehashing the call from earlier in the day. He was pleased to have the update on the phone by the Iceman. The chick was dead in Laconia and the deed was done, as close to plan as they had envisioned. Ace was sorry to have been absent from the event. He wanted to see the woman lying on the shore and experience the hype of the press, the authorities running around in a tizzy and in confusion, all over the girl's cause of death. He was convinced that no one would ever figure out the reason or the relevance of her tattoo to the commemorative event. It did have meaning, at least to the Metuchen Chapter and only a few people knew that, all of which were New Jersey club members.

"Ace" was born with the given name, Carlos Hernandez. He was originally from Fontana, California and grew up in the California hills. His mother was mulatto and his father Hispanic. Not exactly a model student in school and often a bully of sorts, he had quit school when he turned sixteen and left in junior high on his birthday. Exiting the door of the middle school / junior high, he spit on the ground feeling free of the confinement and regimentation and his forced education by law. He never fit in and had no desire to learn anyway.

Ace thought of himself as a mechanic, having taken apart motors and engines when he was young. That is what he fancied and when motorcycles came into his life, he knew how to take apart and reassemble a carburetor blindfolded.

He pumped gas to earn money to buy his first bike. It was an older Harley-Davidson that needed extensive work and renovation. He sold drugs to buy the needed parts, facilitating his connection to the underworld of sorts after he left California for Central New Jersey. Dealing drugs taught him accounting and business, crude but effective—cash out, cash in. What he bought for less, he sold for more.

Chapter 28

Ace had the gift of mechanics and grease and oil in his blood, able to tear down car or bike engines and transmissions almost without a manual. He did not begin his career in crime in New Jersey, but as a youngster in California selling pot. He sought out the easy ways to make a dollar—over time, many hundreds of deals in illegal operations were conducted involving amphetamines, cocaine, crack and "crystal meth." He had his own "kitchen lab" for a while. California was a breeding ground for that influence on Ace with most drugs coming from Mexico, through the San Diego border and north up to L.A.

Ace was recruited by the local thugs in Fontana and in south L.A. to join a number of California gangs during his teenage years. He was bilingual and trained to move drugs easily from Baja, Mexico to the greater L.A. basin, making more money in his teen years than his fellow students would in the real jobs that they acquired after high school and college graduation. He bought innumerable motorcycles, some vintage European and some newer American made machines. He transcended from British bikes to Harleys.

It was later, at age 20, that he got wrapped up in the New Jersey Rough Riders motorcycle club. The influence of the Big Apple prostitution rings so close to Metuchen expanded his prowess in criminal activities. New York City was his second home and he visited it often. His income increased substantially. Drugs, porn and prostitution were like candy to him, ever available with a strong supply and demand of customers and providers. Women that wanted what he had to offer in drugs satisfied his sexual needs as well.

He managed to extol porn videos to his list of attributes and salacious income-generating vocation. He produced a few movies and marketed them well.

The proximity of New Jersey and the turnpike to New York City fostered the trade with chicks from 42nd Street—they would perform all acts of erotic kindness for heroin.

Ace was now president of the Rough Riders. Their clubhouse was a deserted farm property off Route 287 and near the New Jersey Turnpike. It provided easy access to NYC to the north and the southern venues of Atlantic City and the greater Philadelphia area—the City of Brotherly Love.

The club membership was forty-eight to date with recruits from Livingston, Carteret and Piscataway off the east / west NJ Route 22. The club members were highly protective of their turf, but remained low profile, sometimes participating in charity rides for sick children, a Good Samaritan cover-up for their lucrative day and night illegal operations.

Except for Ace, most biker club members migrated to Laconia each year for Bike Week, a nine-day R&R of drunken debauchery and sexual encounters, interspersed with racing. Some members brought their "Ol' Ladies" for sustenance and their tents. Others trolled The Weirs looking for action and offering surreptitiously to young, nubile female subjects, some thrills and high quality drugs.

Often runaways and emotionally confused young women thought that the annual event was designed for "hooking up," never realizing that they were potential victims of booze, elicit drugs and unprotected sex. Physical and sexual abuse, on occasion, with multiple partners awaited the unsuspecting naïve females. They stood the chance of becoming addicts and sex slaves to the predators who were older and extremely manipulative. The worst of the gangs were controlling and domineering often threatening the young women with harm if they didn't comply with the men's wishes. The girls were too scared to squeal.

Members of the Rough Riders had at least one criterion in their rules in order for new applicants to be inducted. Any chick that was the "lady" of a potential member was at the physical disposal of the other members. She had to agree to "put out" for charter members. Many of the women had no apparent problem with that. It was a shared community and drugs precipitated their services, almost at random. Ace himself had had sex with every member's chick that he desired, often taking on three-somes for fun. No one cared. He was "Bossman," as well as "Ace" and he called the shots.

Ace was in half the porn videos that they made anyway. A huge man, and although Black / Hispanic, he was possessed with a Nordic-like appearance, wearing a helmet on road trips—an austere appearance like that of the once-proud Vikings who conquered land and people.

Ace's tattoos ran up and down his arms and clear down the muscles of his legs. Asian designs i.e. dragons, naked women, skulls and tigers all intertwined in varying inks of blue, red, green and yellow making him an artistic billboard for all to see. He even had his penis tattooed, a rather painful endeavor, which required much alcohol to survive the needle. When aroused, it read, "Ace Hardware," unknown to the popular hardware store or John Madden's endorsement.

No one screwed with Carlos "Ace" Hernandez and few called him Carlos. The local riders respected him and all club members followed his mandates and lead, to the letter. Meetings at the farmhouse were monthly and ad hoc as well. It depended on the needs of the club.

Chapter 29

The Iceman had already done his job and done it well and Ace was proud of him. Iceman was now looking forward to the events of Rally Week. New this year was the added musical events at Meadowbrook Musical Arts Center (Meadowbrook Farms) in Gilford. They scheduled major bands all summer long anyway and the schedule usually ran well into the fall. This jam was different during Bike Week.

The summer performance center had arranged for major bands and events for the 2006 Rally. They were touting it as "Bike Bash." It included demolition derbies, custom bike builders, a Hawaiian Tropic Bikini Pageant with many vendors and a food court similar to nearby Weirs Drive-In events closer to the beach. The Bike Bash was to cater to a 6,500-seat concert venue for premiere performances by major and local bands. Steppenwolf, The Marshall Tucker Band, Quiet Riot, Blue Oyster Cult and Foghat were booked.

Don Wright, the photographer, was to cover that new musical festival as well and in fact looked forward to seeing class A rock bands. It would provide him additional photos for his much-anticipated book he envisioned for future publication

The City Council of Laconia had already perused and discussed a six-pound report of the Motorcycle Week Advisory Committee (MWAC) in an effort to increase local revenue from all Bike Week events. Budgeting $228,500 for police and fire protection as well as other safety measures, made the councilors anxious to recoup all expenses associated with the salaries for emergency services across the State. The report of the MWAC committee outlined "fees" for vendors and events that would help defray costs for ancillary police, EMS and fire oversight. One councilor wanted to charge each attendee a fee for the week. That was not part of the MWAC report and was probably unmanageable. *Who would enforce such a plan in the public sector?* other committee members wondered. It was reasonable to expect that some vendor fees would increase since the crowd each year had grown and more profit was being made. That fact, in and of itself, required more police protection of the race-related public events and roadways.

In 2006, Laconia Bike Week had become a major event nationally, with live Web-Cam video broadcast around the world on the Internet. It had already been ongoing one or two years before with much of the focus on activities on Lakeside Avenue.

Bike associations often had interest in how other rallies were run. Earlier in 2005 and 2006, the executive director of Motorcycle Week in Laconia participated in the 25th Anniversary of the Cycle World International Motorcycle Shows, including shows in Washington, New York, Cleveland, Minneapolis and Chicago where he was exposed to 400,000 people and distributed 50,000 copies of the Laconia Rally News. The promotions included a large exhibit booth and handbills of fliers / collaterals encouraging people to visit Rally Week in New Hampshire. The event followed Daytona's own annual Rally March 6-11th, and the promo shows piggybacked one another for the sake of having bikers visit the Granite State in June as well. The events in Daytona, Sturgis and Laconia have become big business that generates significant revenue for each State, including New Hampshire.

Promotion of the Laconia week is a year-round effort both locally and nationally, causing the Bike Week director to travel almost 5,000 miles in the winter months.

Brochures on travel, lodging and the week's related events are dispersed by the thousands at the national shows to potential attendees for June—all enticing the masses to celebrate New Hampshire's history of motorcycle racing. It is effective and proactive.

Chapter 30

Dr. Blaisdell and an assistant had already initiated the autopsy of the young woman who had died at The Weirs. She lay prone on a stainless steel table, naked and pale. The coolness from the mortuary drawer elicited an almost bluish hue to the smooth skin.

Through perforations in a grid on the stainless top of the autopsy table, a downdraft vacuum system sucked air from the surrounding body and exhausted the odor of death and decay, a welcomed accessory appliance for the doctor during the conduction of any autopsy. Refrigeration had maintained the corpse in proper condition.

Following generalized head and body X-rays for possible broken bones and dental X-rays of the upper and lower jaw for future identification of the woman, the cranial, thoracic and abdominal organ evaluations were mandatory. Procedures were methodical and extremely time consuming. There was no rush since valuable data could be lost in haste. Blaisdell was fastidious during the entire autopsy. The protocol was standard for all violent deaths and for all deaths of unknown origin.

Her body was that of a nymph that now had been opened at the thorax, abdomen and cranium. The skin from the back of her head / neck region was transected across the collar area of her neck allowing for the Medical Examiner to fold it up and over her forehead exposing the skull. That provided access to the entire cranial bone areas. A bone saw had been used to open her skull allowing the removal of the bowl-like cap that sheltered and protected the fragile hemispheres of the brain. The brain was removed, observed by gross examination and weighed like a cabbage. The procedure was cold in technique but necessary. Critical sections of tissue would be used to determine normal or abnormal anatomy of the meninges, cerebral cortex, cerebellum, cerebrum, brainstem and other critical areas of the ventricular system and spinal fluid.

All major organs in her chest and abdomen had been removed one at a time, examined grossly and then weighed. Blaisdell had made specific notations of the organ weights and gross clinical observations of the heart, liver, brain, kidneys and lungs. He had sampled many other tissues and aspirated the now darkened, residual blood from her abdominal aorta and any other questionable blood vessels of note where blood had pooled.

The contents of the various segments of the GI tract were saved as well—probing the stomach, duodenum, ileum, jejunum and colorectal area. Whatever killed her may have been ingested orally and retained, and might provide clues to her death. An abdominal scar indicated that she had had an appendectomy when she was young. No other scars were readily apparent.

Dr. Blaisdell was to have the blood specimens analyzed for drugs or poisons, any of which might have resulted in her demise. Those procedures usually took time and required the outsourcing of the tests to another lab. Bodily tissues were preserved in a formalin fixative and were scheduled to be evaluated by a clinical and forensic pathologist.

A board certified pathologist could observe microscopic damage to the major organs that were normally healthy for a person of that age group. The liver and kidneys were prime suspects for adverse changes in morphology and pathology. Once each tissue was preserved, it would be dehydrated with alcohol and special solvents then embedded in wax and sliced in ultra thin, micron sections. Each section was stained for each specific organ. Normal versus abnormal cells could be discerned under high-powered magnification for cellular integrity, general anatomy and pathological anomalies. Drugs and chemicals had varying effects on the integrity of tissues. The pathologist knew the subtle differences in tissues and blood.

Other microbiological tests would eliminate or confirm if she died of a deadly organism, either bacterial or viral. The cultures and processes were tedious, lengthy and costly for the State, but necessary. Anywhere from one to ten deaths were anticipated during the annual bike event. Historically, there had been precedence for severe injuries and fatalities.

Carefully reviewing the dead girl's skin from head to feet, Blaisdell methodically focused on the dermal areas that were commonly used for drug injections, that being major veins at critical joints like the elbow, back of the hands or major muscle groups in the arms and legs. The veins in the hand and inside elbow area were common sites to note needle punctures. Blaisdell perused all skeletal muscle areas as well—the thighs, buttocks and the upper arms into which intramuscular shots might be administered for sustained drug release. Fatty areas were suspect as well since many drugs found refuge in adipose tissue.

Her reproductive organs, the uterus, fallopian tubes and ovaries appeared normal and unremarkable pathologically. She was not pregnant and a follicle on her ovary suggested that she was near the middle of her menstrual cycle when she died. Blaisdell guessed the date to be between days 11-14. She was apparently not on any progestins / estrogens, i.e. steroidal birth control, since ovarian follicle(s) would have been absent. This lone follicle on the left ovary harbored what was to be her next egg to be ovulated had she survived.

The tattoos on her skin intrigued the medical examiner and his assistant. One tattoo in particular revealed the name, *Vincent* and it was bracketed by a scroll of sorts. Above the name, and under closer inspection, was the statue of a Roman-like god with wings and a spoke wheel; it appeared to be a motorcycle wheel and not one from an automobile. Blaisdell surmised it was the god, Mercury, the wings suggesting lightning speed.

Remarking cautiously to his medical assistant, Blaisdell was sure it was a significant clue in the mystery death. His fortuitous intuition was generated by the fact that it appeared to have been recently applied.

Other smaller tattoos appeared older in their applications. The ink had "bled" somewhat into the surrounding tissues over time. The Mercury tattoo appeared distinct with cleaner outlines and the dermis was "raised" suggesting a recent body reaction to the needles and the inflammatory insult.

"This is bizarre," he commented to the assistant. "I'm at a loss as to how to resolve what this logo is supposed to mean. I know most tattoos can often be Asian designs, cartoons or hearts and flowers, even patriotic or religious, or those dedicated to a female or to a Mother. That's usually what I see here in the morgue." The assistant nodded.

"I've never seen that either," added the assistant. "I suspect that it's her boyfriend. Vincent, Vinnie or Vin . . . could be anybody. The more formal name, Vincent is a mystery though. Haven't seen that one before on a body, living or dead."

"Could be a male friend," retorted the medical examiner. He held a surgical light closer to the tattoo in question. He focused on the Roman god.

"Look at the moderate erythema—the skin is elevated from the procedure. It's swollen as if she had it recently applied—recent days."

It could have been only days old, he thought to himself. "We will need to contact the Lakes Region tattoo artisans to see if she might have acquired their services this week. The locals might remember her. Many bikers wait until Rally Week to get these things, marking some prior anniversary year with the current date of 2006."

"Agreed, doctor," the assistant concurred while examining the artwork with a magnifier and light combination.

"She died before the swelling decreased, for Chrissake. Never even had time to heal," added Blaisdell, pondering the tattoo and leaning against a lab bench, his arms folded.

"Whatever it means, I think it will prove to be important to the investigation. We need to find this *Vincent* guy," added the doctor. "Let's be sure to get close-up photos for the file. Don Wright promised us some close-ups as well and his equipment is a bit better than ours, much higher resolution for future investigation. I'll give him a call after we are done. Perhaps he can email them or print us some copies on professional photo paper. Our own photographer missed some angles that I need."

Chapter 31

Don Wright had decided to drive home for he was anxious to research the names, which Wendell Atkins had given him on the porch steps at the Veterans Home. The Black Cat Café became too confusing and noisy. Don needed to focus on specifics and the distractions at the coffee shop were not favorable to his agenda.

He entered his house off Union Avenue in Laconia. Union Avenue was a major conduit from Laconia Center to Gilford, and then north to Weirs Beach.

Bike noise was apparent and everywhere at that hour. Riders from out of town were seeking out the bars and restaurants for drinks and meals. Union Avenue had a stretch of those providers: KFC, McDonalds, Friendly's, one or two Chinese places and the occasional beer joint with burgers. In between, there were car dealerships, boat distributors and marinas abutting Paugus Bay. The road was always busy.

Small markets and gas stations, Dunkin Donuts, Domino's, Subway and a local pizza joint offered an endless variety of fast food filling the void and hunger pangs of both motorcycles and the human needs for fuel.

Don's main PC was already on and the screen saver showed a picture of the 2004 World Series Red Sox team, intermittently changing to individual players celebrating their win after the final game in October 2004. There were photos of Bud Selig, the Baseball Commissioner, swilling champagne and Damon and Varitek celebrating their accomplishments post game. The memory was all too fresh and Don Wright was a huge Red Sox and baseball fan in general.

Don sat in a large well-worn, brown leather chair and typed the words, Google.com into the search box. The computer opened the search engine—the most popular site and the quickest information on the Net. He typed in the names that Wendell had mentioned. The names, Howard Raymond Davies and Philip Vincent yielded some 595,000 Web sites related to Davies alone. Philip Vincent's name generated some 59,000 Web sites.

It was soon clear to Don that both men were instrumental and influential in the early manufacture of motorcycles, but not just any motorcycle—the *Vincent* HRD motorcycle! He was shocked.

Don focused primarily on historical information and the evolution of the motorbike in England. British and European influences were an integral part of the mechanical marvel that also evolved simultaneously with the internal combustion engine of the automobile.

Don became enthralled with the two men that Wendell had suggested. *How in God's name did Wendell Atkins know of these people and what was their relevance to the deceased woman or anything to do with Bike Week?* The Internet information was the clue for Don and a vast amount of research might emerge for each name searched. It was mind-boggling to the photographer, now a part time investigator.

He knew he would be up much of the night searching for clues. The name Howard Davies led to fascinating information that most modern motorcycle riders had probably not heard of, nor did they care about in 2006. Somehow ol' Wendell was tuned into the details of a motorcycle's relevance to the death of the woman. *How in the hell did he relate the two subjects?* Don wondered.

Chapter 32

As Don researched the Net further, he found out that Howard Davies was born in Birmingham, England in 1895 and later died of cancer in Solihull in 1973 at 88 years. Davies' life had been very productive and interesting. Ironically, his wife died two days after him and they were memorialized together. Don Wright took copious notes of the Davies information and printed out numerous pages of documents at his disposal from various Web sites.

Davies founded HRD Motors Limited, the acronym named after himself. In 1924, he designed the motorcycle that would race at the Isle of Man, the famed Manx Grand Prix. The "hefty" speed of 66 MPH back then was enormously quick for the times.

How did Philip Vincent relate to all this? Don wondered. He soon found out the relevance after a more extensive search of the Vincent name.

The relationship was clear. Philip Vincent bought the rights to HRD Motors and started producing motorbikes in 1928. He had his own designs however, adopting the combined name of Vincent-HRD.

Even today, the Isle of Man motorcycle events are a haven for Vincent motorcycle enthusiasts—all attendees of which are owners of vintage, classic Vincent machines that still operate today.

Don reacted with amazement. He felt as if he was "on a roll" and would have many questions for his new friend, Wendell Atkins.

"Holy crap! Wendell knew his stuff after all," he muttered to himself. "Who would think that the tattoo on the dead girl had to do with motorcycles?" *It was the Vincent motorcycle logo of old,* he surmised. *Not a person's name or boyfriend, but a motorcycle manufacturer's logo. Could it be? Why? Why would it be on this young woman as a tattoo? The obscure motorbike was too old to mean anything to someone in their twenties or younger. Some of today's mature riders hadn't heard of "The Vincent" for God's sake,* Don thought.

Bikers didn't normally attend the annual Laconia Rally riding on Vincent's. Don, in all his years, had never seen one or heard of anyone make mention of the particular bike manufacturer. He surely would have taken the time to photograph the vintage models for his future book, had that been the case.

Don feverishly read more, now possessed and totally fascinated with the history of the historic British bike. The thirties and forties had yielded some incredible machines for the Vincent Company. There was the model, Rapide in 1937 (Series A and B), a 100 MPH bike; the Black Shadow, the Comet and the Black Lightning, which was produced around 1948.

Post the 1945-era, there was the Vincent 1000cc Series—B, C and D, twin-cylinder Rapides, followed by the Black Knight and Black Prince. Many other 500cc smaller models followed in the Vincent production line.

The actual Vincent logo struck Don with amazement. He knew it was the same drawing that was on the lower back of the dead woman. *She was obviously too young to know what a Vincent was,* he felt. *Kids, her age, knew of Harleys and the Japanese bikes,* he thought. *Could Vincent bikes have meant something to her?*

The recent tattoo application meant that there was a question as to why she would have the *Vincent* and the god, Mercury embossed in her skin. Had someone suggested it to her? Was it just an unusual and attractive logo in her mind?

What in the hell did Wendell Atkins know that no one else knew including the police and the coroner? Was this a link to her death? Don asked, over and over again in his mind

Don stood up and grabbed a beer from the refrigerator. He needed a break to ponder the questions. *How was any of this related to what Wendell had foreseen?* he wondered, as he sipped once or twice from the longneck bottle and placed his hand on his forehead as if in painful confusion. He was chronically possessed by the recent occurrences and the Internet information—he felt the strain in his upper neck from an emerging headache. Don tilted his head backward and from side to side in a repetitive movement that seemed to reduce the stress. He needed to revisit Wendell Atkins as soon as possible . . . he would try and reach him in the next day. Wendell could surely help him resolve some of the mystery that was emerging from the case at the beach and the Vincent motorcycle history.

*   *   *

Dr. Blaisdell had one more test to run during the lengthy autopsy procedures. He had to swab the external reproductive tract of the victim to determine if she had experienced sexual intercourse prior to her demise. Evidence of a male's seminal fluid or semen would be an important observation with potential DNA. If present in the vaginal or uterine fluids, the DNA of the male might lead to a suspect in the girl's death. Gross examination of the vulva had suggested some intromission had occurred but the medical examiner had also determined that the dead girl was not on any steroidal oral contraceptives. Her ovaries and reproductive tract were close to mid-cycle and follicular development on one ovary suggested no exogenous contraceptives were in her body. Follicular development would not have been suppressed had that been the case.

The aspiration of evidence from the vaginal environment and microscopic inspection showed residual sperm in the vaginal fluids and Blaisdell noted some injury to the external vulva area and vaginal mucosal lining. Not deemed all that unusual it did however present further evidence of "rough sex." There were minor tears in the epithelium and mucosal membranes, he noted. He saved vaginal fluid samples for DNA analysis.

"Rough sex" was not uncommon with bikers. She had been sodomized as well with evidence of abrasions and the fluids of an ejaculate in the lower intestine near the recto-sigmoid colon. Willingly or not, she had experienced anal intercourse, at least by the current evidence. Dr. Blaisdell was not being judgmental of the young woman but he needed to discern and record all possible clues in the investigation. His role as coroner demanded it. He was aware of sexual trends. Young people were now condoning oral and anal sex as an alternative to intercourse and deterrent to common methods of disease transmission. The trend was on the rise to seek alternate protection beyond the condom. Oral gratification was on the upswing.

Chapter 33

Blaisdell was now finished with the gross examination but still needed to close the cavities of the thorax and abdomen prior to any requirements for an eventual funeral. He had saved numerous histological tissues, blood and fluid samples and related specimens that would hopefully elucidate the exact cause of death. Since the deceased was still unidentified and internment was delayed, the medical examiner would have access to more organ samples / tissues if needed. She would remain in the morgue under refrigeration until someone claimed the body. No one in the Coroner's Office knew the timeframe it would require for an actual I.D. of the victim

Close up photos of the tattoos were documented as well. Blaisdell was still perplexed by the name, *Vincent*. He had not talked to Don Wright and Don was keeping mum on the Vincent motorcycle findings anyway. He had his own investigation ongoing with the help of the aging, Wendell Atkins.

The coroner knew that the police were probably searching for someone with the Vincent name. They had no other leads to work on and that was the only relevant hint in the investigation—the unusual name was at least a start for them.

The body of the unknown young lady was relegated back to the chilled mortuary drawer—number 7, her identity unknown other than the names coined by the local authorities, "Lady of the Lake" or "Jane Doe" in the eyes of the public and police. With potentially 400,000 visitors arriving for Bike Week, how in the hell would they find out who this woman or Vincent was? The task seemed insurmountable to the officials investigating the crime.

Blaisdell thanked his assistant for her help.

"Appreciate your excellent technical assistance, Donna," he complimented her. "Hope we find this young woman's identity."

Donna remarked in kind, "Doctor . . . thank you . . . I couldn't be more sad at the moment. She was around my age. Maybe I'm a few years older but that could have been me just the same. She was so beautiful and young." Donna wiped a tear from the corner of her eye.

"How many of these events do we *see* a year?" he asked, with remorse. "I've seen three others just as young and earlier in 2006. You, Donna don't hang out in the same crowd. Ya see? They get in with the wrong friends or tangled up with drugs, sex gangs and other undesirables. They put themselves at risk in so many ways. This had to be foul play. I'm convinced that there was a strange motive for this."

"I suppose you're right," added the technician, tossing her vinyl surgical gloves in the biohazard waste can. "Still, I can't understand what happened to her. Why would someone abuse her . . . and perhaps, kill her?"

"That's what we'll find out. She had friends I'm sure," he added. "There will be clues and people that knew her or saw her recently might come forward. Bike Week hasn't really begun; someone had to know her. She was here before the mass invasion of visitors arrives in a day or so."

"I'll get these biological samples off to the lab, doctor," Donna voiced, while placing the vials and tubes in a specially insulated Styrofoam container packed with ice. It was just the beginning of the clinical and pathological tests that were needed to supplement the gross anatomical evaluation. The labels on each vial read, "Jane Doe—I.D. unknown" and they were coded with the coroner's own sample numbers and date of preparation.

Blaisdell finally showered and exited the austere building and mortuary. His head was down. He drove home and prayed that his pager would not go off again that day. He was in no mood to see any more deceased individuals. As M.E., he had another colleague that could cover for him if he needed. The colleague was also an M.D. pathologist. They often alternated weekends but during Bike Week, everyone was on call, seven days a week.

Blaisdell was to autopsy the biker from the Route 106 accident the next day. He lay in mortuary drawer number 8. Blaisdell already suspected the primary cause of death of the motorcyclist but the State required an autopsy anyway. It was to confirm the injuries sustained, in detail. Severe head trauma was suspected in addition to a high blood alcohol level. Those bloods were already on their way to a toxicology lab for analyses.

Entering his driveway, Blaisdell knew there was scotch waiting for him in the liquor cabinet. He poured some on ice before relaxing. He sat in a leather sofa in the darkened corner of the study and sipped Chivas Regal over a bed of crushed ice. Blaisdell slowly stirred the drink with his forefinger.

It seemed peacefully quiet and the TV was off for a change. The low buzz of an aquarium oxygen pump could be heard in the room. The freshwater aggregation of tropical fish, some fifteen different species, offered the man a quiet, placid scene of reflection. Some fish schooled. Platys, neons, guppies and orange swordtails paced back and forth behind the glass and between the milfoil-like forest of plants. A yellow bulb cast an amber hue throughout the tank and the artificial background of caves and rocky formations. Small fish darted sporadically avoiding other potential bullies and predators.

He swirled the short glass of liquor in a clockwise manner and pondered the day. His job was depressing some days . . . most days actually, and scotch only accentuated the morose feelings. He thought about how many dead persons he had identified over the years. It started when he was in the medical unit in the Army. Ten years out, the job was still the same, body after body looking the same for the most part.

Of course, there was the occasional case of a person found dead in their home from carbon monoxide exposure or death by accidental fire, gunshot wounds and decapitations at dangerous construction accidents. He could handle most of them without letting his feelings interfere. Death was *death* and final, either in total or in multiple pieces. He had been trained to tune out most emotions, especially those that would affect his performance and job.

It was the children that he had to autopsy that bothered him, small bodies on the autopsy table that occupied only one-third of the table. *Fragile children who were too young to leave the earth,* he thought, with despair. The loss of teenagers in accidents made his eyes well up as if they were his own children. The young lady today had that same effect on his psyche. He was human after all and a precious life had been snuffed out and the nude remains awash on the beach. How callous was "life."

Blaisdell knew the routine—death, certification of expiration by his office professionals and the occasional autopsy required by the State of New Hampshire. He became reflective. *The funeral directors / morticians had the worst of it,* he felt. Bodies that required cleansing, muscle and joints massaged post *rigor mortis,* embalming by way of the carotid and jugular, aspiration of internal fluids, repairs to mutilated torsos, cosmetology and perfumed, temporary appearances in coffins and caskets.

By Godsend, a German chemist in 1867, August Wilhelm von Hofmann, had discovered formaldehyde. Thank God. Blaisdell knew the history of embalming, a bizarre continuum of ancient Egyptian methods of dehydration and bodily preservation. He was a trained pathologist in his own right. The use of arsenic once preceded the application of formaldehyde. Even President Lincoln was embalmed for his train ride home.

Yes, he knew it well—the mortuary procedures after he was done at the autopsy table. The infusions of formaldehyde, methanol, ethanol and solvents; arterial fluids containing germicides, anticoagulants, dyes and perfumes carefully injected to maintain firmness of tissues, but not too firm to bloat. The sealing of eyelids with underlying cups that obliterated retraction of the eyes into the orbits, the sealing of lips with sutures, wires or tissue adhesives and the shaving of male facial hair, all known as, "the setting of features" and all in preparation for appeasing the relatives and mourners. Even the pink lighting over caskets enhanced natural skin tones in death.

Even Blaisdell thought the façade at "viewings" a gross misperception of a human body at peace. He shook his head in disgust as he sipped the chilled, amber liquor. He knew that the next autopsy he had scheduled of the biker that crashed on Route 106 would need more mortician's help than the young woman's situation. There was severe cranial damage and creativity would be needed—artistic repair like "Bondo-ing" a fender in a rusted car.

A six-point injection procedure for embalming would be needed to preserve all of the broken body parts of the motorcyclist. The autopsy disrupted the main circulatory system vasculature for general embalming preservation. The funeral director would need to access the femoral, axillary, carotid and other vessels, as well as the viscera to maintain the tissues if a viewing was planned. Internal organs would be bagged *in toto* in preservative fluids as well, generally *en mass* within the body cavity. He hoped the biker's family would elect to cremate his remains.

Tilting his head back in the soft, leather, headrest of the sofa, he closed his eyes to rest and dissipate what redness and irritation had befallen the whites of his now bloodshot eyes and sockets. Closing them felt good and he eventually fell asleep from exhaustion. He remained there for the night and never made it to his own bedroom or bed. In the morning, he would tackle the next case that needed resolution. The scotch the night before was only a temporary fix—one that only masked reality for a few hours.

Chapter 34

Earlier in the year, particularly in January, the Chief of Police in Laconia, Tom Dalinger, had discovered a disturbing trend in the crime rates in the local area. Might the increase in arrests and offenses have been an actual "downward spiral?" Laconia had not been known for a high crime rate in the past, but illicit drugs were on the rise and were suspected to be at least one probable cause for concern. Laconia was no different than other towns with the same demography—kids, some good and some bad influenced kids.

In 2005, the estimates for the "calls to service" by the police were up some 10% in Laconia. Was that an increase in population talking or was it a stable population behaving badly and getting away with common crime and so to speak, "potential murder?" How much of the increase was influenced by the 2005 Rally Week and by the offenses of outsiders? Little was know that could account with impunity what had happened to the stats for 2005.

Service calls by police went from 17,863 to 19,498 in 2005 and that *excluded* over 8,000 routine traffic violations. Rapes had increased that year from 21 to 28, aggravated assaults from 26 to 38, but drug offense rose substantially from 212 to 293. The increased use of weapons—(knives and guns) in crimes was an indication that the trend was of serious concern. Geographically, Laconia was not a large city, the likes of Boston or New York. Other police detectives had cited the increase in perpetrators and events in what they referred to as, "high risk calls."

What was particularly noticeable was an increase in heroin and crack cocaine use, now readily available to the local population that desired the drugs.

Some stats were down. Protective custody for intoxicated persons numbered at 759, down from 2004, while DWI's went from 196 to 224 in 2005, a particularly disturbing fact.

Thefts decreased substantially in the greater Laconia area, but not simple assaults or burglaries. Methamphetamine use was predicted to increase in the beginning of the 2006 Year. The police chief felt that the cost of drugs was substantial yet their use may have reflected an increase in overall crime in 2005 anyway.

In October 2005, one astute Laconia police officer had stopped a 19-year-old driver for a routine traffic violation. A bottle of tequila was observed on the backseat floor. Officer Assad later found 25 bags of cocaine and $645 dollars in cash, all from a routine stop on Weirs Boulevard. That one example lead to a serious look at the drug infestation in The Weirs area—Assad was awarded a special "Commendation" from the Police Commissioner in January 2006.

Bank robberies were becoming more frequent with a burst in activity in January 2006. It affected the whole Lakes Region and major cities in the central part of the State, Concord included. The authorities were concerned about a growing crime rate in New Hampshire.

The murder rate in Laconia was a single episode in 2005, while the official tally would not be confirmed and available until October 2006. As for the other crimes, the chief expressed concern for the future. Bike Week was always unpredictable.

"We can't increase staff to handle this adequately," Dalinger claimed. "There was a budget cap instituted by voters that will affect police and fire services including EMT responses to medical emergencies," he had emphasized to city councilors. His concern was real and the fear that local youth might be enticed to try drugs and commit offenses to pay for more drugs and habits was foremost on the minds of all police officials. It tended to lead to a domino effect.

If the young "Lady of the Lake" was a victim and early indicator of that growing trend, Dalinger surmised that 2006 would be a banner year for crime. How would the Lakes Region adapt to that pessimistic trend?

Chapter 35

Don Wright phoned the Veterans Home on Lakeside Avenue at The Weirs. The bedside phone in Wendell's room rang repeatedly. He was hoping to touch base with Wendell Atkins and update him with his newfound research on the key words that the elderly man had provided. Don was proud of what he had learned to date but he needed Wendell's insight into the initial implications and findings—Wendell's clues were only the beginning of the mystery, Don thought. There had to be more to the implication of the men and the historic motorcycle history. The phone rang numerous times until someone picked up in his absence.

A gentleman answered and indicated that Wendell was unavailable.

"Can you have him call me, please? This is Donald Wright, the local news photographer. I spoke with him yesterday," Don added, for credibility.

The elderly man responded. "I'm sorry, Mr. Wright but he's in the hospital in Laconia. I'm not sure when he will be home. He had an accident."

"Hospital? Accident? Oh my . . . what happened?" asked Don, with serious concern.

"He had a spell," the man volunteered. "Some dizziness. It had happened before with Wendell but this time he hurt himself when he fell. They took him by ambulance just last night. He had fallen down in his room, a few hours after your visit I guess."

Don was aghast and concerned at the same time. He offered his help, if needed.

"He seemed fine when I saw him and while we chatted on the porch. Will he be okay? I mean he seemed a bit tired . . . that's all," Don inquired. "I surely hope he recovers. Those mishaps are common and can be devastating to the elderly. Bone and hip fractures take so long to heal," he added, with interest and grave concern. "Did he break anything?"

The elderly man who answered the call said, "no" and indicated that he should be fine providing his brain spell wasn't more serious than first thought.

"The doctors were planning an MRI, I hear. That may tell them how bad off ol' Wendell is. He's no spring chicken ya know."

Donald was pensive for a moment and the elderly man on the phone repeated himself. He sounded just as old as Wendell. Their voices were similar.

"The ER doc says he should be okay he thinks. Hardening of the arteries to the brain," he claimed, but did not go beyond that.

Don knew that atherosclerosis of the major vessels to and from the brain; the carotids or jugulars could be devastating, affecting major brain areas of cognitive thought, memory and speech. They often predisposed to ischemic stroke where a blocked vessel deprived the brain of needed nutrients and oxygen. Don had no idea how severe the episode was.

"What hospital is he in?" asked Don, with interest. "Perhaps I can go cheer him up is they will let me in."

"LRGH, ya know—Lakes Region General Hospital up on Jewett Hill. They got some good 'head' people there," responded the acquaintance of Atkins. "They deal with major trauma and all," he said, with assurance and confidence.

"Wonder if he can have visitors?" Don pursued, with caution. He did not want to be overbearing having only met Wendell the day before. He didn't know with whom he was talking.

"Relatives and close friends only, they say. Some of us saw him this morning so a select number of visitors are welcomed I guess. Are you a friend or relative?" he asked Don.

"Friend, I guess," Don volunteered. "Just met him recently and we hit it off real good."

"Wendell is friendly with everyone. Maybe they will allow you in. He'll chat your ear off given the chance ya know, having been at The Weirs for decades. He's seen it all," the man at the home responded. "What's your name again, son?"

"Don Wright, sir . . . Don."

"The guy from the newspaper . . . the photo guy?" he asked, cordially having forgot the earlier conversation.

"Yes, sir . . . that's me. Have we met before, sir?"

"No . . . but you do good stuff, son. 'Seen many of your pictures in the paper. You have a good eye and knack for great photo composition," he complimented Don.

"Thank you, sir. I appreciate the compliment. Positive feedback is few and far between."

The man hesitated and then voiced some additional information about himself, being somewhat coy and humble.

"I was a photographer for years, son. I'm retired now but love the art form. My eyes aren't so good any more. It takes keen eyes to do good work with the lens, or paint a picture for that matter. Composition, light exposure and subject matter . . . actually matter in photography."

"You were a professional?" queried Don. "What format?"

The man was now interested in talking about the subject at hand.

"I did portraits, son . . . portraits with the old style cameras . . . the big ones that looked like black boxes on tripods. Ever hear of Ansel Adams?"

"*The* Ansel Adams? Sure! Why?"

"I'm George Adams—his nephew. We did lots of black and whites together," he volunteered. "He taught me everything I know. He knew composition and light."

"Holy shit. Really? I'm pleased to meet you, sir," exclaimed Don, apologizing for the profanity. He didn't even know the man on the other end of the phone but Don felt comfortable with his interaction.

"Ansel was the best. I'm sure you learned a lot from him," Donald added. "He mastered black and white photography, often working for hours in the darkroom to capture realism, starkness and high resolution. Looking at his originals made you think you were looking at the *real scene,* live, whether it was the Grand Canyon or the Tetons and other National Parks in America.

"I did, son . . . I did learn a lot but one must have talent with which to start and my uncle told me I had talent. Nicest thing he ever said to me," he boasted, proudly.

"That's quite the story, sir. Maybe I can stop by and meet you someday—compare photography stories, photos and notes. I could learn from you," complimented Don. "Perhaps have coffee there where I can see your works if you have them handy."

"Sure, Son . . . let's hook up at some point."

Chapter 36

In just two consecutive days, Don had met two of the most interesting people of his life and by serendipity. The unceremonious death of the young girl had led Don to the discreet lives and obscure attributes of two locals generally unrecognized by the residents of the Lakes Region.

The old man had shown excitement immediately, obviously rejuvenated in part by someone interested in his past accomplishments.

"Be glad to show you 'Rochester at night' . . . that's Rochester, NY you see . . . it can be serene and beautiful at night, if one has the right angle. During the day, it's a different story," laughed Mr. Adams. "A shit hole in some spots."

"I'll bet," responded Don. "I'd love to see that photo and all your shots if they are handy. I want to know your works so we can feature them someday in the paper."

"Be glad to dig some out for you."

Don was anxious to get to the hospital and take his chances on admission to Wendell's room. He also wanted to set up an appointment to visit Mr. Adams, a noteworthy celebrity in his own right most probably.

"Try and visit Wendell if you can, son. I'm sure he'd be pleased to see you," remarked the elderly man. "He needs to know people care about him."

"I will try . . . today, Mr. Adams. Thanks for the pleasant conversation. Talk to you again soon and I hope we can hook up." Adams was certainly amenable to that possibility.

"Come anytime," he offered, with sincerity. I don't venture out too far anymore. You are liable to find me here every day, rockin' on the porch with friends. Boats intrigue me and some older vintage models on the

Big Lake are classics. Love to see them passin' by and still runnin' on all
cylinders."

Don concluded the enjoyable chat with a promise.

"I'll get there this week, sir. I'll come say hi."

After hanging up the phone, Don Wright sat down and pondered the
conversation with Adams. He was anxious but apprehensive about getting
to LRGH to visit Wendell and he also needed to meet with George Adams
at some point, hopefully later that week. Don had no idea how serious
Wendell's medical condition was, but he was aware that a stroke or CVA
could debilitate Wendell potentially eliminating a conversation again about
the history that might solve the death of the girl. Selfishly, he hoped that
Wendell was okay.

Having severe brain damage and a possible broken hip or pelvis
increased the morbidity of disease states in the elderly. Few people at
Wendell's age recovered from such trauma to the fragile body. Fractures
were known to complicate rehabilitation and increased morbidity in the
aged population.

Don was hopeful that George Adams was wrong about the severity of
the fall and Wendell's overall condition. Don feared the worst with cerebral
vascular disease since age often dictated survivability and the return to
cognition and memory. He did not want to lose his newfound friend for
any reason. Wendell was also Don's historian on the history of Lakeside
Avenue and the decades of the motorcycle gatherings in front of his home.
It would be like losing a grandfather—the one Donald never had to be
begin with, and a beloved high school teacher all in one.

Additionally, the young newspaper photographer was enthralled and
excited that he would be meeting the nephew of the famed photographer,
Ansel Adams. Don had viewed some of Ansel's originals at the George
Eastman House—a photography museum in Rochester, New York. The
museum included the history of photography and the most prized array
of early production cameras and lenses in the world. It was located in
the former Eastman home and estate. That Eastman was *the* Eastman of
Eastman-Kodak of yesteryear, a founding father of modern photography
for the masses of picture takers, amateur and professional.

Chapter 37

Don drove hurriedly to the hospital located on a side road off Union Avenue. It was close to downtown. Parking in the busy car lot, he ran to the lobby knowing that visitor's hours were often limited, especially when visiting the infirmed or those under critical intensive care. Once in the main lobby, he inquired at the patient information desk as to which room a Wendell Atkins had been admitted. The receptionist, a white-haired pleasant woman, smiled and checked the computer screen on the extensive reception desk.

There was a moment where she looked up and then back at the screen. Bringing up the name on the monitor and the patient histories of recent admissions, she took off her reading glasses and tilted her head upward. There were instantaneous frown lines of concern and a deep sigh of remorse. She bit her lip gently.

"Wendell Atkins . . . are you a relative, sir?" she asked, cordially.

"No ma'am. A friend. I heard that he was admitted for a broken hip or something. I believe he fell in his home. Is he not listed there on the screen, ma'am? Wrong hospital, perhaps?"

"I'm sorry, sir . . . but confidentially . . . Mr. Atkins, ah . . . *passed away* two hours ago. It was very sudden. I'm so sorry. I didn't know that myself until I called up his name on the screen. I apologize for my surprised expression."

Don stood there in shock. He was silently staring at a picture on the wall. There was no one in line behind him and he stepped to the side to view in disbelief the same screen on the monitor for himself. The word, "deceased" was listed by the name, Atkins.

Don felt sick to his stomach and the woman offered him a cool drink. He thanked her and stood there in perplexed confusion. George Adams had said that Wendell seemed lucid earlier that day. *How could this be?* he wondered. Don repeated the name to the receptionist.

"We are talking about Wendell Atkins from Weirs Beach, ma'am?"

"I'm afraid so, sir. Do you wish to speak with a physician concerning Mr. Atkins or his condition when he arrived? There are no other patients with a name even remotely close to Wendell Atkins. I'm sorry to share this bad news with you."

"No . . . no . . . that's okay, I don't need to speak to the doctor," he stammered. "Thank you very much." Don Wright was stunned.

"I was hoping to boost his spirits. I had no idea how serious his condition was. How sad that I never got to say goodbye to him."

"I'm sorry, sir," she reiterated. "I wish I had better news and more information to share with you. I'm not sure why he passed away."

As Don slowly walked away, the woman said, "Wilkinson-Beane, sir . . . they are handling the arrangements for Mr. Atkins. Maybe they can help a bit. I'm so sorry."

"Thank you. I know of that funeral home on Pleasant Street, ma'am," Don replied. "I'll check the newspaper I work for, or maybe I'll call the funeral home about the impending arrangements or calling hours. Maybe they'll have more information, albeit a recent event."

"Okay, sir. I'm sorry for not being more helpful," she said, biting her lip. She hated telling him the dismal news as much as he hated hearing it. She sensed his pain, Don having gone quiet and into a state of moderate shock. His face was expressionless and rigid as if deep in thought.

Don smiled and thanked her, tipping his head in acknowledgement of her expression of sorrow. He slowly walked out the front door, under the protective overhang and then directly into the hospital parking lot.

Ten steps into the lot, it all sank in for Don Wright. Wendell Atkins was deceased and that was unexpected for sure. George Adams had indicated that Wendell probably would pull through the apparent illness. To Don, the symptoms sounded like a more serious stroke anyway, maybe more than one—like a follow on episode hours before his arrival. Not all that uncommon, the dizziness that Mr. Adams had mentioned and observed of Wendell's medical episode, was of major concern and a poor prognosis for recovery in Don's mind.

Unexpectedly, Wendell Atkins was dead and Don's mentor had left him with a challenge regarding the hopes of helping solve the mystery of the death at The Weirs.

Don was hoping to visit and tell Wendell that he had done his research on Davies and Vincent. Now Don was saddened and dismayed that the mystery of those names could not be easily linked to the crime at the beach. Wendell may have taken all relevant clues to the grave. *How did Wendell's input and knowledge relate to the tattoo and the dead girl?* The answer might never be resolved, Don thought.

Chapter 38

The art of tattooing is centuries old and most interesting. Its intrigue is not only because it is a popular art form today and statement of one's human body embellishment and beliefs, but also a ubiquitous form of art that mimics traditional artistic and paint forms on canvas, paper and sculpture. It is "moving art" as well since the body moves and flexes making the tattoo ever changing, with the mechanical flexure of muscles, joints and limbs of the human body. It also has no boundaries since tattoos have been applied everywhere skin can be penetrated. The pain experienced from tattooing depends on how innervated the tissues are, some areas being more sensitive to needles than others.

Tattoos often make a written and colorful statement whether they tout love, politics, patriotism or the independence of one's thoughts on any subject. Oddly, they can be as simple as a cross, flower, heart or name, or scenic display that follows the curvature or lines of a body from head to toe. Snakes, serpents and dragons can wind around a torso. One guy had his four-year-old daughter's portrait tattooed on his stomach. Skulls and sunflowers can be seen on shoulders and backs.

Don Wright had one applied when he was in college; a girl's name that he later had removed after the relationship went sour. Military men had them applied in the Orient or on Asian tours since the artisans were gifted with steady hands and soldiers often desired a remembrance of their ship's name, their regions of deployment or their artillery divisions, airborne or infantry. It was destined to be a constant reminder of their travels around the world and a lasting memory of their friends, places and women that they pined for years later. Often they regretted the experience because of its permanency.

Bikers were known for brazenly touting tattoos for decades. Masculinity was the motive. From the simple "MOM" in a heart design to snakes that coiled around heads, legs and arms, some bikers' entire bodies were tattooed, with more black ink than white skin. Don had photographed many of the walking art forms over the years—on both men and on women.

The American Academy of Dermatology had run studies on their popularity citing that 36% of Americans between the ages of 18-29 have at least one tattoo. Twenty-four percent of Americans between ages 18 and 50 have been tattooed. The Baltimore Tattoo Museum touts that people without tattoos are now the minority. The Office of Cosmetics and Colors at the FDA have reported that 13% of people tattooed have issues with healing. The "industry" is regulated by local and state officials, but not by the FDA in Washington, DC. There are no agency-approved tattoo pigments and inks.

Over the last few decades, women yearned to be part of the art form as well with simple tattoos on their buns, lower backs, shoulders, biceps, ankles or lower legs. A simple rose, sun or moon was common, along with the name of a child, boyfriend or lover.

Those willing victims of the pulsating needle often agreed to the procedure under the influence of alcohol or drugs, sometimes having them applied on a dare by their peers. Alcohol numbed the pain of the artist's application, the decision to have one applied often made late in the evening after heavy drinking. Tattoo artists discouraged alcohol as an analgesic since bleeding was enhanced.

By morning, the women might wake to find that they were oblivious to the procedure and they were now marked for life—a walking billboard of sorts, much to their chagrin.

The art form today is fraught with error, often leading to lawsuits when the artisan misspells a name, or draws the wrong request by the consumer. Sloppy work can result in legal action as well. The quality of the application depends on the artisan, with word of mouth of the talented tattooist being the main advertisement.

Not easily removed or repaired, lawsuits against the tattoo artist can range in the thousands of dollars for shoddy work, fading, poor quality or misspellings. Laser treatment doesn't always work no matter how experienced the dermatologist is with modern tattoo removal techniques.

Those bikers and fans that were pleased with their first tattoo or repetitive applications of the permanent ink often returned each year to rallies to add to the scenic portrayal of the animal or religious gods that they admired. One animal might lead to a zoo on an arm. Tigers and snakes remain common, serpents and the faces of rock and movie stars, now dead—Jerry Garcia, Jim Morrison, Jimi Hendrix, Marilyn Monroe and Janis Joplin.

The best tattooists can apply celebrity faces from memory. One guy from Shamoken, Pennsylvania had the Pittsburgh Steelers logo tattooed above his right ear. It was applied to the temple bone area in advance of the February 2006 Super Bowl in Detroit. His head was shaved enhancing the logo's colors.

Now he had to live with it. It seemed to be a ridiculous endeavor should he ever relocate and change teams—what then?

The Harley logos, varied iterations and time periods in their 100-year history, were often requested by and applied to the hundreds to dedicated H-D fans and H.O.G. members at annual rallies. Black, white and orange pigments mimicked the Harley colors in bold fashion.

Chapter 39

Even in 2006, the trend of tattooing showed no signs of waning, as bikers walked along Lakeside Avenue and the boardwalk at The Weirs flexing and pumping biceps and triceps making the facsimile "lions roar" and their body art more noticeable. Muscle shirts and bikini and tank tops revealed the variety of tattoos that were as different as the artists that had applied them.

If bikers opted not to go permanent with their art, there was the airbrushing of T-shirts or the application of body paint, especially on women, an alternative that could be removed with water or solvents at the end of the week often leaving their bodies unscathed and unmarked. Women liked the idea of nonpermanent adornment to their fair skin. Temporary, removable transfer tattoos fit the bill.

*   *   *

Don Wright was now on a mission to understand the body art form better. He knew little of the history of tattooing. There seemed to be no government regulatory oversight on their application, inks and usage. That scared him since literally anyone could buy a tattoo machine and experiment or practice on unsuspecting people. The savvy customer was relying on word of mouth and the credibility of known artists. To that fact, Don thought it incredulous and chancy, leaving the fate of one's body in the hands of an unknown person who could mare or disfigure someone in a matter of minutes.

He researched the tattoo field while seeking more clues in the death of the young woman. *Had she been to a tattoo artist who was a relative unknown, transient and not credible?* he pondered. Perhaps someone else possessed the same Vincent logo noted on the dead girl. His eyes wandered and focused on every piece of body art he could find.

He scoured the vendor tent area by the Weirs Drive-In, also the parking lot of FUNSPOT, and the bars and clubs that harbored the bikers from across America, basically in search of the famed god, Mercury with winged feet. His mission was to garner as much information from Wendell's friends and any bikers that had multiple tattoos and the knowledge of who might apply what type of art, stencil or free-hand drawing. Don knew that someone had to have a clue.

Local Laconia artists, of which there were two or three, would be a source of general information for him as well. His day job paralyzed his other mission. His time was limited in his quest to solve the mystery so he ran around silly talking to anyone who seemed experienced or knowledgeable in "tattoo-mania."

Don had obligations to the local newspaper to photograph many events during Bike Week. He was not free from work to pursue a crime like Don Quixote tipping at windmills passing by. Don voluntarily wanted to help with the crime.

He slept little and maxed out the day to accomplish all the tasks for the newspaper deadlines as well as for his own personal agenda. He was bone tired and Bike Week was just beginning. The bags under his eyes were noticeable and dark.

*   *   *

The most recent newspaper editions highlighted the dead woman's plight but relegated the story to the first page of section B, not A. They did not want to dissuade people from coming to the annual event at The Weirs. Even with the attempt to play down the mysterious death, the AP newswire picked up the stories and ran each one around the country, in an effort to identify someone missing or MIA. Parents, friends and other relatives were now concerned especially if they had a close relative that fit the girl's description. If so, their family member might be deceased. The death story spread throughout the Internet as well. Bikers took notice of the limited information that was posted locally. The girl could be anyone, a local or a long distance visitor, there to party for the week. Murmurs of her demise were spreading on the street. Some women were generally concerned for their own safety.

*   *   *

The local police sought her identity through a concerted effort and professional forensic approach. They were having little luck even though there were articles about her in the newspapers. No one had come forward.

With the ongoing week of bike-related activities, other women were cautious and more vigilant knowing that the perpetrator(s), if any, had not been caught or the cause of death revealed by the cops. Visiting biker women, out of fear, broadcast the word to complete strangers just in case they had not heard of the potential issue. The sisterhood of riders and fans depended on one another and they were fastidious in their communication leaving no woman or teenager uninformed. A killer was suspected and was serious business—no one knew if it was a pattern or even a serial killer at large. The women assumed it was some pervert killer and yet that had not been confirmed or denied by the authorities. No one really knew why the girl died or why she was found on the shoreline. Rumors and speculation fueled the theories and most fodder was fabricated or inaccurate in the scenario. Elaborate embellishments of the crime scene expanded the story and the fate of the woman. Most rumors was incorrect and exaggerations.

Chapter 40

Don began his own investigation since Wendell had left him with some clues before his unexpected passing. The photographer wondered if he could successfully advance the ideas related to *Vincent* without Wendell's input. Intrigue kept him focused. It surely would be much easier to pursue relevant connections if Wendell had not become ill and died. The suddenness of it all depressed Don, yet he pursued the history of tattoos with a vengeance.

His first quest was to utilize the Internet. He typed simple phrases into Ask.com or Google.com. Numerous informative sites appeared as a comprehensive list. The art form of ink markings was obviously ancient.

Egyptian mummies from 2000 B.C., and later the Greeks, Germans, Gauls and Britons showed evidence of or mentioned tattoos. Later, the Europeans exposed the American Indians and island peoples to the art. The word was derived from *tattau*, a Tahitian word meaning, "to mark."

Don noted that the real "Iceman" from 3300 B.C. was suspected to have tattoos; perhaps the earliest recorded history of the art. The role of tattoos was decorative, but especially the Romans used them during their reign, for identification of status, slaves or criminals. The Tahitians considered the tattoo, "a right of passage."

Sailors acquired them as souvenirs of their journeys. Don almost had a *second* one applied when he was in the service but thought better of it.

He noted that early methods of application involved pricking of the skin or rubbing of the ink into cuts, scratches or wounds. Soot was added to strings, which were then passed under the skin, leaving a mark behind, like charcoal. Don knew that today's tattoo applications differed drastically.

Hand held machines that magnetically vibrated a needle hundreds of times punctured the skin about one millimeter in depth, leaving ink in the dermal layer of the person's skin.

The epidermis, or outer layer of skin, is not usually affected since it would shed the ink if the skin were dry or become chafed. Ink placed in the dermis would last ones' whole life, he noted.

He observed that the technology had improved over decades.

The newest tattoo machines were similar to a sewing machine with varying sterile needle punctures from 50 to 3,000 times a minute, releasing insoluble, micronized particles of ink from the needle penetration into the lower layer of the skin.

Samuel O'Reilly had patented a tattoo machine in 1891 in the U.S. In 1876, Thomas Edison invented a machine that was for engraving on hard surfaces. Basically, O'Reilly improved on Edison's principles creating a patented tube system and electromagnetic-oscillating device for tattooing. Few people knew that Edison influenced the mechanics of the art, and books in grade school only taught of his invention and evolution of the light bulb and phonograph for the most part.

Don was aware of the role of sterility as a priority in tattooing. Today, needles, cups and other devices are autoclaved at generally 250° F and under ten pounds of pressure for 30 minutes. The disposable tattooing equipment is used only once to prevent infection or the transmission of diseases. The implications could otherwise be devastating.

The "art" of the method focuses on one's eye and hand coordination. Using sterile gloves, expert tattoo artists have to "feel the depth" of the ink application. Tattooing too deep results in pain, while shallow applications will create wavy lines in the drawing.

Generally, they trace a stencil or pre-drawn graphic idea onto the skin. Ink for "outlines" is thinner with much thicker ink reserved for shading and the final art details.

Antiseptic cleansing is important between layers of ink and the varied colors. Residual blood from the needle is wiped away repeatedly and is usually minimal. Antibacterial soap, Bacitracin® ointment and a bandage are usually applied after the tattoo is completed. Ice packs can help to reduce the swelling from the needlework.

It was clear from Don's initial research that the young woman must have been tattooed in recent days. The application could have occurred locally or anywhere else for that matter. He needed to determine if someone local had remembered her, or the distinctive Vincent logo. Because the skin of her tattoo on the lower spine was elevated from natural inflammation, the authorities suspected that it had been applied locally, however there was no proof that she had been in the general area for any period of time. It was supposition on their part. Who would know? She could have flown into Manchester Airport the day before her death, and from anywhere else.

Was she a local or from somewhere else? they wondered. She had to have a given name besides her tentative icons in death, "Jane Doe" or "Lady of the Lake."

Chapter 41

Don was to visit local tattoo parlors first to see if he could move the investigation into her demise further ahead. He possessed a printed photograph of the tattoo on her lower spine and he planned to use it for comparison. If they hadn't applied it, maybe they knew who might have created the Vincent name and Mercury logo. The artwork seemed professionally done and highly detailed. Certain tattooists favored applying specific art that they were most proficient at—skulls, crossbones and Harley logos were the in thing.

Don wondered if she could have died directly from the tattoo application. It seemed unlikely. Sterility being paramount, might she have had sepsis, a blood infection from an unsanitary needle or unsterilized equipment? Was it that simple and would the coroner test for that? Don thought yes.

Could ink have gotten directly into the vascular system causing some side effect or allergic reaction to the dye—anaphylactic shock? He was inquisitive about potential medical possibilities since thousands of tattoos were applied each day around the country. He was not medically trained but he knew that most people had no reaction to the process or to the pigments and inks that had been used in the past.

But what were the inks made of? he wondered. *What regulations applied to that industry? None?*

His research led to many Internet sites that elaborated on the lack of tattoo oversight by the government. It was clear that the FDA did not regulate tattoo inks albeit cosmetics had guidelines and they contained pigments in lipsticks, rouge, powders and eyeliners.

They approved or had guidelines for color additives for foods, drugs and cosmetics but not for tattoo inks. Some ink was known to harbor heavy metals that were toxic. They were contained in their chemical structure. Copper, lead and nickel are sometimes present yet no one had tested the inks for toxicity in the final compositions. Other known pigments contain arsenic. If the recipient of a tattoo thought that all inks had been sanctioned or approved by Federal government review for safety, they were mistaken, Don realized.

Some people had reported allergic reactions to pigments, he noted. Furthermore, burns of the skin had occurred during MRI scans, presumably due to the metals in the ink of tattoo sites. Some tattoo inks have been found in the lungs of patients, obviously traveling through the blood stream after application. Don noted all of the unusual medical events and wondered just how widespread the unknown side effects were. *Did anyone in Washington ever look into the potential hazard of the ancient art form? Did anyone care?*

Don Wright was enthralled by the information.

Two types of ink were mentioned for tattoos, he noted. Pigments could be contained in organic carrier solutions or alternately, acrylic inks were and remain plastics-based. Organic inks are considered safer for application but may fade slightly over time.

Don had noted that the dead woman's tattoo was brilliant in color and he suspected that it might have been acrylic, based on the bright coloration. Local side effects were common with acrylics. Reactions to the "medium" included general swelling, pain and prolonged healing according to one report. The erythema or swelling in the woman's lower back might have been from a combination of the ink and / or the general inflammation of the dermis from the direct insult to the skin—the actual procedure. Don Wright pondered what might have happened i.e. if death was directly related to the tattoo. He needed to converse with the coroner about the possibility of the tattoo being the culprit, for some unknown and obscure reason.

It all seemed so unlikely as a scenario since those same inks, acrylics and procedures had been used for decades without apparent issues. Why was Don suspect of this young girl's tattoo in particular? He shook his head trying to rationalize how it all was related, or not related. *Had he taken his imagination too far?* he wondered. *Perhaps so,* he concluded. It seemed all too farfetched that the ink caused her death.

Chapter 42

The funeral service for Wendell Atkins was conducted with full military honors a few days after his death.

After the Catholic, Requiem High Mass at Sacred Heart Church in Laconia, Wendell Atkins' flag-draped coffin was laid to rest in the New Hampshire Veterans Cemetery some 30 miles from The Weirs—in Boscawen and outside of the Capital City of Concord.

The memorial service at the church was well attended by his Weirs Beach neighbors, friends and veterans of many U.S. wars. He received the respectful 21-gun salute by soldiers who were rigid and methodical in the rich burial tradition. Taps rang out prior to the removal and folding of the flag that covered the casket of cherry wood. The ceremonial military honor guard was representative of the Army National Guard in New Hampshire, based in Concord. Their funeral detail was well trained.

At Wendell's Veterans Home residence on Lakeside Avenue, his friends commemorated his loss by placing a black drape over the doorway of his former home. No one sat in his wicker rocker on the porch. The home was eerily quiet. A piece of rope was strung across the armrests preventing anyone from using the chair on the day of the funeral.

Thoughtfully, a few biker friends of Wendell placed flowers on the steps of his home. Small American flags in honor of his military service lined the steps and porch railing over which he often leaned and watched the beach festivities of summer, weekend fireworks, and Bike Week camaraderie. They already missed his presence during the rapidly growing crowd of arriving motorcyclists for the 2006 Weirs Rally. Some

Rally attendees had their pictures taken annually with the icon—that would be no more.

Don Wright attended and photographed the funeral of Atkins for the Laconia newspaper. He was at the funeral home, in the church and at the burial site standing back behind the friends that knew him well. He took digital shots of the mourners, the elderly dismayed at the loss of their friend, and one or two distant relatives that had flown in from St. Paul, Minnesota, Wendell's birthplace. Although he was a Midwesterner, most of his life had been in New Hampshire. He called Laconia home.

A few bikers were in the funeral procession, each of which wore traditional black armbands, a symbol of the loss of a fellow rider or veteran. To them, Wendell Atkins was an honorary "rider." Many of the bikers wore their Vietnam veteran's caps and insignias of their respective military units, Semper Fi, U.S. Infantry, Army Airborne or Naval ship or carrier names while others on the sidelines and sidewalks waved the stars and stripes at the passing motorcade on its way to the cemetery of soldiers to the south—a cemetery of simple white stones and crosses reminiscent of Arlington National in Virginia.

Everyone seemed to know Wendell Atkins, yet he rarely spent time in the Laconia town center. He did attend Memorial Day events at Veteran's Square where monuments stood stoic and listed by name the recognized soldiers who served or died in the early wars—WWI, WWII, Korea, Vietnam and the Persian Gulf. Eventually, the fallen of the Iraq War and those who died in Afghanistan would be added to the sacred plot of grassy knoll.

The monuments were graced by a serene mist and fountain spray offering a quiet circular pool of highly polished black granite slabs tastefully angling upward toward the sky. The small reflecting pool of sorts offered daily solace to those that wished to visit and study the names engraved on each bronze plaque and granite memorial, lasting memories of those who had sacrificed their lives for the freedom of all others. Wendell's name would eventually grace one of those plaques later in the year.

Wendell attended the occasional Fourth of July celebration, parade and festivities on Main Street but during most of his later years of life he was pretty much confined to his Lakeside Avenue home. In his golden years, it became a level of comfort and refuge for the elderly man.

A fellow female reporter covered the details of the burial of the noted and fondly remembered resident of the Weirs Beach area. Jessica Fielding was new to the newspaper and her article on Wendell showed her professional abilities with the written word, offering an eloquent elegy to a respected mortal fixture of Lakeside Avenue. As a wordsmith, she included interviews with local residents and friends who resided near Wendell. Some colleagues and friends touted him as the "local historian" and wondered who would carry on the tradition and torch and share their memories of prior Bike Week events with the general public. Wendell had observed firsthand so many of those events.

Chapter 43

The loss of Wendell and the memorial services facilitated the chance for Don to see George Adams. He was a close friend of Wendell's and almost the same age, maybe a year or two younger. George had dug out his own camera, to record in black and white his friend's memorial service and Don Wright was thrilled to see George "shooting shots" again. The camera body and antiquated professional lenses were German in origin, the best of the best in the years when George had photographed landscapes, portraits and still life shots. The camera predated the Japanese influence into the photography market, a market that saw the demise of traditional Kodak film in a sad way, and the emergence of digital photography and mega-pixels galore.

"I'm sorry for the loss of your friend, Mr. Adams," Don expressed, sorrowfully. "He was a nice person and I never got to really know him well. I'm sorry for that."

"He was the best, Donald, a true friend. I will surely miss him," he said, with misty eyes. He wiped the tears with the back of his hand and forefinger. A linen handkerchief was at the ready.

"I hope to visit with you again someday and chat about your friend. Maybe, sometime after the funeral. I will cover the Weirs events all week and will be in the area if you are around," Don offered, for prospective timing.

"Anytime, son," Adams replied. "I have no real friends left and nothin' to do," he expressed with remorse. "Wendell and I were buds and hung around together—walks, bingo and the occasional ice cream."

"I'll be glad to be your friend," added Don, with sincerity. "I can take you places where we can photograph the wildlife and people on the beach. It would be my pleasure to get you back into the art that you enjoyed so well, and for so many years. A good eye for 'composition' never disappears."

"That would be nice, Donald. I'd like that . . . I'd really like that," he repeated, becoming more introspective and remorseful.

There was a lull in the graveside service and Adams stepped forward all alone and stared at the coffin of cherry that lay in front of him. He saluted his friend, leaning over and grabbing a rose from the spray of flowers, for posterity. The U.S. flag lay on the casket, folded. A gentle wind passed through the cemetery and the day was hot.

For a moment, George's head drooped and he seemed to wobble from his own instability on the hillside. *Unsure footing at his old age,* he mused to himself. Both Don and a military serviceman noted George Adams wavering and reached out to help him settle into a nearby folding chair. After sitting a while, the funeral director offered George Adams a cool drink of water. He seemed well prepared at attending to the elderly, acting as if the occurrence was commonplace at those types of events. The funeral director spoke quietly to the elderly man and then backed away slowly. George Adams seemed lucid now and thanked the attendant. "Just a spell," he said, with embarrassment—"just a spell."

Don Wright offered to drive George Adams home to The Weirs. He was glad to be of service since it was not out of his way and he lived nearby. Adams was appreciative of the thoughtful gesture. "Thanks, son . . . I'll take you up on it. I'm still feelin' a bit woozy."

Don Wright took the back road from Concord avoiding the I-93 highway traffic. He headed up Route 106 and used the bypass just south of Laconia to quicken the trip.

The car passed the NHIS racetrack, home of NASCAR and the motorcycle events, continuing north from Loudon, through Canterbury, Belmont and eventually into Greater Laconia and the Lakes Region. George Adams was fairly quiet the first half of the ride. He was listening to a CD in the car.

"Who's that?" asked the old man. "Who's singin'?" His thoughts focused on the funeral of his friend, Wendell Atkins. It was a reality check for George knew that he had little time left in his own life. Most of his friends had already passed on, making him the lone soldier standing. He did not fear death and left his fate in the hands of the Almighty.

"Lightfoot . . . Gordon Lightfoot. Ever hear of him?"

"I like it," added George. "It's soothing . . . nice and light. Don't think I have ever heard of him, come to think of it."

"He's the best songwriter in Canada and I think in the U.S. as well," added Don. "Lightfoot is a Canadian singer. Been around a long time . . . twenty something albums of mellow music and soothing tunes for times like this," Don commented. "This song is called, '*Sometimes I wish.*' It's a great tune after you lose someone, a girlfriend, friend or colleague. It's from his new album, *Harmony.*"

"Nice," said George Adams, listening closely to the words.

"Gordon Lightfoot was sick the last two years . . . we almost lost him and his music. Had an abdominal blood vessel burst. Somehow, they saved him."

George looked up and said, "Glad he made it okay . . . unlike my buddy, Wendell . . ." His voice fell off and tears appeared in his eyes. "He's gone now."

Don noted the sorrow. Sensing his remorse and grief, he tried to initiate a conversation to elevate George's mood. He switched to a radio station and passed a car or two on Route 106. The two-lane highway was dangerous but Don was a good driver. George rechecked his seat belt and yanked it tight . . . and they both laughed.

"How long did you know your friend?" Don asked, sympathetically. "Bet you guys were buddies for decades, chasin' women and the like."

George laughed gently. "We had our share of the ladies. We were good dancers. Knew him probably forty or more years, son," he continued, with affection, nodding his head. "We were damn close," offered George. "He was my best friend, ya know. We told each other everything . . . just about everything. Two old men with no secrets—a rarity," he laughed and reflected on the past.

"It's nice to have a confidant like that in your life. Someone that you can tell everything too," Don added, supportively and with interest.

George was pensive and shook his head side to side. "I'll miss the old coot," he volunteered. "Had a wife once, he did. Lost her many years ago. Left him hollow inside," the old man commented. "His life after that consisted basically of his fellow veterans and his neighbors at The Weirs. Those folks always looked out for one another and for me too."

"That's nice . . . friends are everything."

Don Wright could see the sadness in the old man's eyes, sighing involuntarily from time to time. He appeared tired and drained from the trauma of the funeral and the heat of the day's events. One by one, he had watched his closest friends die off and the clock for him was ticking as well.

Adams was a realist. His priorities and daily activities would change in the coming days and weeks. Don was to play a role in helping him cope. He willfully agreed to do that in a subtle way. He knew George Adams was an independent person, not an invalid. Don could revitalize him with respect to their mutual interest in photography. Adams would need a diversion in the coming weeks and the hobby of cameras would help him overcome his grief. It allowed him to be active and creative instead of passive and depressed. Don knew it would be therapeutic for the old man.

"Your friend, Wendell was lucky to have a caring person like yourself as a true friend. You can be assured that he appreciated your friendship and closeness. It's worth more than gold, especially these days when people are less caring."

The old man sighed heavily.

"You're right, son. They say you can count your true friends on one hand . . . in my case, it's on *one finger* . . . just Wendell." The old man reflected on all the years they were together. Now he had to go back to the house where they had been pals for so many decades and years. They were often inseparable on a daily basis. Now George Adams was alone.

Chapter 44

Wendell would no longer be rocking on the porch, or walking the boardwalk and watching the pleasure craft pass through the Weirs Channel to Paugus Bay. Wendell used to watch the Mt. Washington cruise ship arrive and depart, often checking the actual times against the pre-printed annual schedule for tourists. He practically knew the moment when she appeared around the bend of Long and Bear Islands toward the marina for docking and unloading her passengers who had toured Winnipesaukee.

The boat had such a rich history. It traveled to the main ports of Meredith, Alton Bay, Wolfeboro and Center Harbor where she wintered and was overhauled each year. On a clear day from Belknap Point, The Mount would pass in front of her namesake, the grand dame of mountains, Mt. Washington. It was nestled in the foothills of the White Mountains, deep green in summer and appearing each year as a snow-covered mountaintop between two smaller peaks in winter.

When Lake "Winni" thawed in the warm New England Spring, "ice-out" was declared if "The Mount" was able to dock at all ports. Residents often gambled on the actual date each year—a lottery of sorts. It might be April 7th one year and April 19th the next—unpredictable, but a constant.

During the winter months, mechanics disassembled the engines and rebuilt them. The first voyage each spring was always a shakedown cruise where some mechanical issues might pop up, needing tweaking or resolution before passengers enjoyed the daily trips each day during the summer. Unlike the early days of steam and cast iron boilers, The Mount was reliable, rarely needing long-term dry dock or major mechanical repairs.

During Bike Week each year, The Mount sat idle at her Weirs Beach port. Bands usually played and liquor flowed freely at daily boat parties. The bands could be heard across parts of the lake, resounding off the hills and the water's surface. It was like Mardi gras for a week

The day after the young woman was found a mere two hundred feet from its mooring, The Mount was setting up for the forthcoming influx of bikers and tourists. The lower and upper levels would be packed with partiers in a matter of days. There was food and booze to load on the cruise boat. Men were actively wheeling dollies back and forth with cases and kegs, snacks and hotdogs, burgers and other staples for the week. The wooden ramp to the boat access descended from the left side of The Weirs train station to the gangplank on the front of the port side of the hull. Banners advertising a beer company, a tequila company and other local sponsors were strewn across the rails of the historic cruise ship. The draft of the boat would be closer to the water in the coming days—the weight of people would raise the waterline. As tradition ruled, the boat was the place to be for some of the festivities—the sights and sounds drew the crowds.

Chapter 45

Aside from the historic noted Veteran's and Infantry homes of yesteryear, Lakeside Avenue possessed a carnival-like atmosphere daily, especially during Bike Week. Mexican restaurants, clubs, pizza parlors, video arcades, fast food stands of fried dough and dogs and a multitude of souvenir shops dotted the main street opposite the Mt. Washington boat. Ice cream and candy venues, as well as T-shirt shops touted the 2006 logos for Laconia's Bike Week, the Loudon Classic, Weirs Beach and the dominant Harley-Davidson motorcycles parked diagonally along the boulevard.

Vendors set up tents and tables along the sidewalk the week before the onslaught, and many proprietors were anxious to sell logo patches, shirts, leather products and skimpy ladies-wear that mimicked or exceeded in fashion the likes of Fredericks of Hollywood or similar catalogues, tawdry or otherwise. Both women and men were drawn to the sensual items of lesser cloth that revealed more skin.

At the south end of Lakeside Avenue, where the road intersected Route 3 was the Weirs Drive-In movie theater. Inside the parking area were rows of tents and vendors touting more biker leathers and clothing, Native-American turquoise jewelry, fast food, massage therapists, sausage and pepper submarine stands, barbecued pulled pork and a large bandstand for continuous rock entertainment. Local and national bands played all day and night. A regular vendor for decades was "Chicken Man," from North Ft. Myers, Florida. He rode for years and now fabricated and sold "doo-rags," often attracting a crowd of onlookers that admired his chicken outfit from head to toe. A personable man with a loving wife beside him in chicken attire, he was always pleased to be acknowledged by the crowd.

His biker headgear remained popular from year to year—his venue known as "Chicken Man Doo Ragz."

Pre-approved beer tents were licensed to distribute alcohol and fast food for the nine-day event, some even located on Route 3 toward Meredith. Laconia in general profited from the vendor fees, while bouncers and local police manned the front gates checking licenses and legal I.D.s of patrons. Each food and beverage restaurant and lounge was packed and the noise level high by the initial weekend of festivities. All that was missing from the Drive-In venues was a Bruce Springsteen-like appearance or a visit from Steven Tyler from Aerosmith, a well-known fan of the boys from Orange County and the American Chopper TV show, starring Paul Teutel and his son, Paul Jr. They had fabricated a chopper for Tyler and fans wondered if any of those celebs would make a token appearance at the annual event.

Bike Week encompassed, in part, the week that preceded and ended on Sunday, Father's Day. Originally, deemed a three-day weekend event incorporating the Father's Day occasion with racing, it had become an extended two-week fest in more recent years. For many bike enthusiasts, the week before or after was their annual vacation of drunken debauchery and womanizing. The bikers usually came to hang out, drink, get laid and often went home story-less and with blue balls since the men outnumbered the ladies. The ratio was not in the men's favor.

The assorted mass of leather-vested men and women was a photo opportunity for aspiring photographers who caught many riders and their ladies in an array of little or no clothing.

The annual parade of bike riders or cruisers by The Weirs venues were known for shocking the crowds, often removing bras or revealing T-thong underwear for the hell of it. It was expected in the milieu of black leather, skimpy fabric, low cut chaps and black boots. The skimpier the better. That was the summer ambiance for the week, night and day, day or night. Sales of cigarettes and beer increased dramatically at all convenience stores and gas station Mini-Marts. There was quick money to be made and larger food chains like Hannaford, Stop and Shop and DeMoulas thrived on the food and drink needs of the visitors.

One store in particular, The Bean Stalk on Route 106 in Loudon, and near the NHIS racetrack, always made a killing in the nine-day event. They sold gasoline, ice, chips, Styrofoam coolers and all other necessities for race goers and spectators.

For over 83 years, and since 1923, the madness had been a yearly event, each year different but with a propensity for increased attendance if the weather was favorable. In poorer weather, the visitors on two wheels stayed in and drank. Restaurants and bars flourished and encouraged the ongoing frivolity with open arms. Entrepreneurs profited.

For some local shop owners, Bike Week was their "annual income" generating some $140-million dollars worth of revenue for the State of New Hampshire, much of it concentrated in the Lakes Region and Laconia proper. If the local residents complained about traffic and noise, they relished in the increased economy from the transient riders. A week of noise and recklessness was worth the hassle to most local residents. Those locals that objected to the unpredictable camaraderie often left town for the week.

Rain or shine, in darkness or daylight, the sound of motorcycles was an overpowering and constant drone of loud pipes and mufflers. If you had a gimmick or novel product that was bike related, there was money to be made.

Garbage bags were sold piecemeal for the occasional rain showers at $1 each or inexpensive cold drinks and hotdogs were popular. Novel red plastic sleeves that read, "Coke" and fit over beer cans were offered for discreet libation in daylight and in public.

If one needed something, anything at all, there was *someone* who could sell it to you or get it for you, illegal items included. Inexpensive, disposable cameras were popular everywhere so one could remember the experiences of the week, exposed breasts and all.

*   *   *

Don Wright parked in a diagonal parking space across from the Veterans Home on Lakeside Avenue. The long trip from the cemetery was over and George smiled affectionately at his home on the hill. Don assisted him up the flag-draped stairs and looked at the main doorway in front of them. George Adams stopped to look at the black cloth over the entrance, a simple but poignant symbol of mourning. Tears came to his eyes. Don was consoling to the elderly man.

It remained a hot and muggy day in June and the temperature was 84°. The late sun in the afternoon beat down on the tents that were now being erected along the beach roadway. A slight breeze off the water was comforting and refreshing.

Some vendors were already hawking their wears to early biker arrivals. Quality T-shirts were $20.00 or two for $35.00. By Father's Day weekend, they would be half the price, a fire sale of sorts to get rid of the 2006 Laconia-related memorabilia. Many tent workers were foreign born vendors—Indians or Pakistanis looking to capitalize on the quick profit to be made at the T-shirt tents and sidewalk tables.

Rows of glass-enclosed wooden display cases held commemorative pins, bracelets and trinkets. The temporary shops and tents opened early and closed late, maximizing their prospective income over long hours, maybe twelve to sixteen-hour days. Competition was strong and keen since the clothing apparel items were similar in nature and price. In some cases, one could haggle down the price on a shirt. Vendors were anxious to move the stock.

Before entering his home, George stood on the long porch of wide board planks and stared for the moment at Wendell's rocking chair. It was the obligatory silent salute to an unmoved piece of furniture from George's morning departure to the funeral and eventual graveside service in Boscawen. He gazed longingly for a moment as Don extended his arm to help him over to the cane and wicker seat. Don removed the rope that had been tied across the arms of the chair. George turned around and lowered himself slowly into the seat, assisted in part by Donald's hand.

The white paint of the wicker seemed to surround him fitting his body like a glove. He was of the same stature as Wendell. It was comfortable. He rocked ever so slightly and listened intently for the inherent squeak that Wendell said he would ultimately repair. George didn't want the noise to go away—it was Wendell's noise, now and forever. It would remind him of Wendell when he rocked each day.

"You look very relaxed," Don commented, while smiling. "A natural fit."

"Fits well, for sure," George responded. "I'm stakin' my claim," he volunteered with a firm voice. "I think Wendell Atkins would have wanted me to enjoy the view and the damn squeak." Don chuckled. There was some humor after all in the transition of the furniture from Wendell to George. It was the changing of the guard so to speak. Don saluted the old man and his new seat of prominence. George smiled and nodded.

"I'm sure that he wouldn't mind if you took it over," Don concluded. "After all, best friends are best friends and his chair becomes your chair. Right?"

George Adams bit his lip gently and agreed. "You betcha."

Don Wright slid a low, three-foot pine bench across the gray floor and sat next to George Adams. They were silent for the moment and stared down at the tent tops and passing bikes, their mufflers crackling and roaring as they passed. The bike enthusiasts were arriving by droves and soon the street would be severely restricted to pedestrians and the two-wheeled vehicles, not cars and pickups. Most travel would be bikes.

Once The Weirs was inhabited by the masses of two and three-wheeled, high-powered machines, Lakeside Avenue became restricted in 1996 to those motor vehicles only. In 2006, they were more lenient, allowing some four-wheeled vehicles on a portion of Lakeside north.

Emergency, police and fire vehicles were the predominant transportation that could traverse the narrow bike-lined passageway, four rows of side-by-side machines and two middle lanes to cruise. Vendors' trucks were allowed during setup and teardown, or during slow hours when they needed to re-supply. Most four wheeled vehicles were discouraged from the main drag, but allowed when necessary.

Chapter 46

The passenger shuttle trains from Lakeport and Meredith to The Weirs were the only sounds and whistles that surpassed the constant noise of motorcycles. They arrived each half-hour at The Weirs Depot dropping off and picking up Lakeside Avenue and Drive-In vendor area pedestrians and bikers without their motorcycles. Taking the shuttle train was quicker than riding to the Weirs Rally activities. Parking was also at a premium for the hundreds of bikes that dared to traverse the local congested roadways to events.

A multitude and cadre of colorful apparel and unique dress could be observed from the New Hampshire Veterans Home porch high above the roadway. It was carnival like. Motorcycles, pedestrians, striped canvas tents, and tie-dyed T-shirts hung for consumer enticement and the colors merged together like a fusion of dyes and paint stippled by a famed artist, a kaleidoscope or collage of pigmented canvases by Picasso, Renoir or Monet. Squinting, one could see the blurred surrealistic vision of a colorful festival. It was almost artistic with swirling colors of motorcycles changing the landscape minute by minute, only their mufflers the primary sound of music and deterrent of the scenic landscape.

Black leather clothing was "in" and worn throughout the throngs of pedestrians. The heavy leather seemed contradictory to the clothing normally worn during the summer heat of New England with many bikers not wearing shirts under their vests, men and women included.

Beards and mustaches dotted the assembly of riders and pedestrians—an irreverent variety of Cheech and Chong-like walkers and motorcyclists in constant motion and colored bikes. Bandannas and doo-rags were commonplace, many of them knotted on the back of the head and sporting the American flag or the Harley-patterned logos over their sun-drenched brows.

Woman wore bathing suit bikini tops and a variety of pants, sensual cutoffs, shorts or blue jeans. Tattoos were often visible on both men and women, some artwork extending down their arms and legs like a mesh of black lines or spider webs—a moving art form that changed when they walked or rode. Some were aesthetically beautiful and others were faded and grotesque as their skin aged with the owners' bodies. Ages varied and so did the biker's skin, in texture.

There was no age limit to riding the two-wheeled monsters of various makes and models and some men and their ladies were graying and wrinkled. In 2006, the crowd seemed older and more subdued. Missing teeth sometimes graced smiles, the result of either poor hygiene over many years or a tough, physical fight along the roadway of life. Some riders needed a hot shower. Sweat was prevalent and abundant.

The 2006 Bike Week extravaganza was now coming to life. The week was officially open for partying. Each day brought more rally participants and racing enthusiasts.

Some bikers, who lined up like they were at a high school dance, stood by the wrought iron fence and nearby railroad tracks and cat-called and taunted the women on the back of passing motorcycles. They cat-whistled and cheered if a pedestrian or rider passed by in a thong or skimpy outfit. The degree of respect for the women was proportional to the type and amount of clothes that they were wearing.

Basically, the view from behind was always an added attraction for the observer especially when it was a Japanese rice rocket forcing the women to lean forward to hang on to their ol' man—low handlebars made the sidewalk viewing more appealing, their butts and butt floss (thongs) inviting the cheers of horny, testosterone-infused onlookers. Lust was everywhere, and present every day. *Bikes, beers and babes* were protocol.

"Show your tits," screamed one overweight biker near The Weirs train depot. His belly overshadowed his belt and his personal identity protected and semi-hidden by his unkempt hair and dark sunglasses.

The young blonde, dressed in a thong and string bathing suit top smiled at him but saw a cop nearby. She would have flashed him had the police officer not been in clear view.

"Come on, honey . . . let's see those mountains!" the male taunted, yelling loudly with cupped hands. No luck. The girl didn't want to be arrested. She appeared to be stoned and barely hanging on to the lime green, Kawasaki.

"Bitch," he responded to her 'lack of balls,' or 'ovaries' in this case. His friends teased the large man in jest, calling him a "pussy" with no clout.

*   *   *

On the front porch of George Adams' residence, Don finally put his camera, strap and 400X lens on the wide board, wooden floor. He had taken some nice photographs of the most noteworthy and most exposed women and men, some riding their unique custom-painted choppers. One bike was virtually all chrome.

Don wanted to document the daily parade of Japanese, German and American bikes. There were Harleys, Kawasakis, Hondas, Buells, BMWs, Yamahas and vintage Indians from the 1940's. The occasional British bike, mostly Triumph and BSA, passed by infrequently, reminding him of his recent research into the other makes and models like Royal Enfield and Vincent.

A fire engine-red Ducati 999 passed by the Adams home in stark contrast to the usual assortment of HOGs, new and old. Realistically, the Ducati appeared to want to go 160 MPH. Virtually all bikers on Lakeside Avenue wore no helmets. Vanity prevailed. The face shields limited the view of pedestrians by the riders.

Some riders faked it with Prussian or Viking-like helmets or the occasional animal skin, which simulated an authentic Daniel Boone raccoon cap.

Parked bikes varied in custom modifications. Jeff Brown of Georgia combined a Harley and a VW Bug and called the merger, "American Dream." Lane Blais of Danvers, Massachusetts concocted an M&M candy logo-bike that drew much favor from the crowd, especially women. His lady-friend was a *looker* as well.

Miles away from The Weirs, a variety of priceless choppers and vintage machines were being judged at Opechee Park. The votes were close but a Canadian won the event.

Leather bandannas and doo-rags were common, seemingly holding in the sweat of the afternoon heat. Most riders looked like they needed to jump into the water off Weirs Beach for relief; the sweat glistening off their backs and chests on this one particularly warm, June day. Formal showers for hygiene were sometimes few and far between.

Accommodations varied from motels to hotel, campsites and rental homes. Lodging had been booked months in advance and many overnight offerings limited the opportunity for common cleanliness. No one seemed to care. The event was primal and raw so the occasional missed shower seemed to be the "in" thing.

Chapter 47

Don Wright desired more input into his recent research of the Vincent tattoo and varied HRD insignias and logos over the years of British motorcycle production. He felt that George Adams might be able to enlighten him; that is if George was as close to Wendell Atkins as he had stated. As close friends, they had no apparent secrets.

Adams had just returned from the bathroom in his home and stood at the stairwell that overlooked the growing motorcycle crowd below. Don's SUV remained parked at street level—this was the last day he could park at that location of the road. The local ordinance for restricted parking was about to go into effect the next day, limiting the type of vehicles that could remain on Lakeside during the formal days of Rally Week.

George laughed out loud at the ant-like flow of people passing by and he admired the young women in scantily dressed clothes.

"Will ya look at that?" he commented, seeing a bikini pass by on a Yamaha.

"Impressive," added Don. "You want a shot of that?" Don offered, grabbing his Nikon from the floor of the porch.

"Sure!" responded the old man. In a millisecond, Don captured the prized photo and showed George the picture in the digital viewfinder.

"Print that for me . . . will ya?" George requested.

"Consider it done, friend," Don complied, smiling with pride. "I'll bring you an 8X10 glossy tomorrow."

"Thanks," George responded with a similar grin. "I'll add it to my collection. I have hundreds over the years."

Don hesitated and then changed subjects, letting the camera and lens dangle off his chest by a wide strap. He offered to take more photos if George wanted him to. George shook his head, no and asked what else Don wanted to chat about. He sensed that Don was on another mission and needed some information about Wendell and his historic Bike Week knowledge.

"George. When I was chatting with Wendell shortly before he passed on, we talked briefly about the young woman who died the other day on the shoreline . . . the one they found down on the beach," he said, pointing his index finger to the general area now blocked off by pedestrians and bikers.

"Damn shame," George replied. "Too young to lose such a pretty girl. Makes no sense."

Don agreed with him and confirmed that it had been an odd occurrence in the history of The Weirs annual bike event.

"Many kids die on bikes, not on the beach," George iterated. "They don't die here on Lakeside or in the Paugus Bay area. Her death was unusual and unexpected for sure. Did they find the cause?"

"No . . . not yet and I agree that she died young," added Don. "I've never heard of a drowning or a murder at Weirs Beach," he reaffirmed. "The newspapers were suggesting that it had been decades since anyone died in this general area."

One exception that few people were aware of was a Laconia firefighter's death, a dedicated dive team expert who was practice diving in winter and became disoriented under the ice. His tank had limited air. That tragic death was the last episode that anyone could remember. Neither Don nor George mentioned that recent event and it had occurred near the same shore, almost fifty feet out from the water's edge.

George shook his head. "They get her name yet?" he asked, squinting from the sun on the deck.

"No . . . she's a mystery woman as far as I know. Don't know if she's local or from another State. They're workin' on the case as we speak."

"She had a tattoo or two, Wendell had said," George Adams volunteered. "Did you see it—the tattoo?"

"Yah. She had a few but one in particular was on her lower back. It seemed to have been applied recently," Don added. "It was unusual. Not the standard rose or heart or butterfly, but a logo of the Roman god, Mercury with the name *Vincent* scrolled below a motorcycle wheel which had wings or somethin'."

"Wings and the god, Mercury? Ah . . . the old logo of the days gone by. Don't see that much of them anymore. Makes more sense!" Adams offered, rubbing his chin of old stubble and early evening beard growth. "Wendell told me the history of somethin' like that some years back."

Don looked at George with a perplexed expression. His eyes went wide and he leaned forward to hear what George had to say.

"History?" Don asked, with piqued interest. "What history, George? You know of the tattoo that I saw on the girl?"

George Adams seemed to ponder the conversation. He closed his eyes as if he was thinking of Wendell's old story and trying to recall some specifics or details that might be refreshed in his mind.

"Think Wendell said he knew of a girl's death decades ago, the year escapes me. That woman also had a similar tattoo I think. A ritual of sorts. Wish I could remember the year . . . 1926 maybe and another situation in the 50's maybe."

Don's heart was fluttering. He pondered the information that George was sharing from a faded memory but Don did not want to seem overanxious. His heart was pounding *Ritual? 1926? 50's?* The relevance.

"What ritual?" he asked, with eyes opened wide and fixed on George's next sentence to emerge.

"The tattoo had the name, *Vincent* on it, right?" George asked, to confirm.

"Yes. It was encased in a scroll-like symbol or outline."

"Right," George reaffirmed, his memory regaining strength. "It has to do with an old motorbike, I think. One of the oldest," George volunteered. "A brand called, *Vincent*—bikes that go way back in time—a British manufacturer, Wendell had told me—I don't know if that's relevant."

"I'm sure it is. Wendell told me basically the same info about old motorcycles," Don offered. "He actually told me of the men who started the Vincent Company—it made me think that Wendell had a premonition the other day and that I should pursue the Vincent tattoo as a relevant *clue* to the crime."

George seemed to be thinking out loud and mumbling to himself, sounding out words with his lips. Don leaned closer.

George sat down on the stairs and appeared to be falling asleep on occasion. He was tired and seemed unfazed by the noise of motorcycles on the street, mufflers thundering in unison below.

Don knew it was time to go and to let the old man rest. The funeral and ride to the Veterans Cemetery in Boscawen had clearly exhausted George Adams and Don was respectful of the man's need to take a nap.

Startled by a loud bike backfire, George awoke briefly and told Don that he could chat with him another day. He would see if he could find any paperwork about the mystery tattoo and logo. George admitted that he had a spare key to Wendell's apartment and would pursue the clues to the mystery deaths of the past decades of note.

"Wendell wrote down everything in personal journals," he commented, while standing slowly to face the front door. "The journals go way back. He had his own library of notes—his life."

"Really?" replied Don. "What kind of library? His whole life?"

"Sort of. Wendell researched the history of Bike Week all those years, noting just about everything he saw or read in papers. He wrote each day, and each year of the event. Think he wanted to do a compilation or book at some point, but he never got around to it," George said, with sadness. "The notes are probably worthless now and the poor bugger is dead."

"Holy crap," Don remarked abruptly. "They're not worthless. He logged all the Bike Week events—all those years?"

"Most of them," George replied, blinking repeatedly and almost dozing off in a standing position.

Don aided him to the door by placing his arm under that of George's. He was astounded by the revelation and hoped he could peruse some of the annual volumes, notes that potentially covered 70 years that the Laconia Bike Rally had existed. They would be historical annotations and a personal perspective for sure—informative and perhaps relevant to the young woman's death earlier that week. Don saw the journals as the ultimate tool in the investigation. It was clear that Don and George were probably the only ones who knew of the writings of Wendell Atkins. If they were historical, there were ways to transcribe them and perhaps publish them in book form as memoirs of Wendell's life at The Weirs. He was a significant recorder of life on Lakeside Avenue for decades.

Chapter 48

What exactly was the relevance of the Vincent logo and George Adams' reference to a 20's or 50's event from the past? Don wondered. *What had Wendell recorded during either of those periods? What did the Laconia papers have on record as well?* Don was beside himself with the potential mass of information that might exist. He wondered if Wendell's journals could provide some answers.

The police still had no clue as to why the woman had died or if there was a premeditated plot behind her demise. *Was she part of a cult, willingly or unwillingly, an unsuspecting victim of someone's demented plan?* Don pondered.

Don departed George's residence after he had reassured him that he would call and check on him the very next day. He was genuinely concerned for the elderly gentleman, surmising that the funeral had taken its toll on the old man's mental faculties. Depression could result from the loss of a friend.

Selfishly, Don also wanted to know what in God's name Wendell Atkins had recorded all those years that he had penned in his personal writings. Don felt that Wendell was onto something that he wanted Don to eventually know. His last conversation was a teaser of sorts, Don felt, that Wendell hoped he would explore and investigate further. Wendell had no time himself to pursue the correlation if in fact there was one.

His death was untimely in the large scenario of things to come. With Wendell Atkins deceased, Don would do his best to ingratiate Wendell's agenda and to research the events of the past, as well as the sad events from the past couple of days. Just knowing and befriending George Adams, in confidence, might initiate a trust and enhance Don's own research and the personal investigation into "Jane Doe's" bizarre death.

The written clues were apparently in the Veteran's Home and George Adams had direct access to Atkins' journal notations. The two men had to peruse the notes and study them before someone, including a distant relative removed all of Wendell's belongings and personal effects, historical papers or otherwise. Don feared that the invaluable documents could end up in the local dump or be auctioned off to people who collected "old paper" with absolutely no knowledge of their potential relevance to the recent Rally Week death event. The Chamber of Commerce and the local Laconia Motorcycle Rally Committee weren't even aware of Wendell's chronological, historical diaries. The Lake Winnipesaukee Historical Museum might find them noteworthy, but Don wasn't ready to share the secret source with anyone as yet.

The hand-written journals must have been voluminous as well, he thought, having described decades and unique years of Bike Week history—chronologically important and pertinent from a personal perspective. Hopefully they were in good condition, Don prayed, preserved without destructive mold, effects of deleterious moisture or the parasite, the silverfish, which loved feasting off the papers of old.

For Don Wright, it was more than the death of the girl that was at stake, but a living written testimony and memorial of bike history and decades that Wendell would want published as a descriptive reminiscence and addition to the Laconia Museum and Historical Society data files. The ramifications could be most enlightening, both in general facts, and with respect to the deceased, "Lady of the Lake" / "Jane Doe."

Chapter 49

Photographer, Don Wright was also a motorcycle enthusiast. He had ridden for years, especially in college. Aside from his Pathfinder SUV, which he used for work related trips on newspaper assignments, he owned a newer model, Ducati Monster 620. The red bike model was derived from the classic, "Monster" bike which was introduced a decade earlier by the Italian manufacturer.

It was often referred to as the "Original Naked" motorcycle, that accolade being attributed to its exposed engine and bodywork. The essential *street fighter*, it was a stylistic and sport riding combination offering six speeds, 90° L-Twins; a SuperBike trellis frame with fuel injection, a computer engine management system and race-performance brakes as the "icing on the cake."

Considered a bit smaller in size and less powerful than the 1000cc model, the bright red trademark colored machine looked similar to the bikes that raced at NHIS on Father's Day. For Don, the powerful machine was fast enough, and classy—a novelty among other machines of the same caliber.

The bike got much use in the summer since Don enjoyed traveling up north through the White Mountains. He rode the local roads that led to Alton and Wolfeboro or he would ride up to the Mt. Washington summit, the highest peak in New Hampshire. The Kangamagus highway was always the most pleasant ride for Don. It skirted the White Mountain rivers and provided access to the Greater Mt. Washington Valley area while offering twists and turns that challenged any competent rider. Franconia Notch to the north offered a similar attraction to amateur *wanna-be* road racers.

Today, New Hampshire's Mount Washington stands at 6,288 feet. It draws some 250,000 visitors to the summit each year. Some folks travel the popular "Auto Road" and others ride the famed Scenic Cog Railway, an austere trip by coal-driven steam locomotives that chug along an antique track and bridge system to the famed summit.

Know as the "Little Engine That Could," the Cog Railway was the inspiration for the children's book of the same name.

Weather can be unpredictable and access treacherous. Mount Washington has the highest wind speeds ever recorded. The record wind speed has been clocked at 231 MPH, a speed unheard of on any other U.S. peak.

Other unique records concerning the mountain have been set by ardent hikers or environmental prone individuals. One gentleman, in the 1800's, walked to the windy summit and counted the actual steps of the journey. He recorded 16,925 steps to the top of the mountain. A bizarre feat but notable endeavor.

Even today, as in past Rally events associated with Laconia Bike Week, riders congregate early in the week and participate in "The Race to the Clouds." It had become an annual event in which Don Wright had been a willing rider participant. He had little free time to participate in the 2006 year hence 2007 looked more promising. His agenda was more focused on the untimely death at The Weirs, hence he elected to bypass the fun ride with fellow bikers or friends from the area.

Today, he had no specific plans other than to research his quest for more knowledge. He jumped on his Ducati Monster and planned to visit local tattoo parlors.

There were two or three in close proximity of The Weirs and the Greater Laconia area. His mission was to pursue the infamous Vincent logo that had been embossed on the dead woman's lower spine. *Was it a common or an uncommon design for tattoo customers? Were area tattooists even aware of the logo?* he wondered.

Don's agenda was to try and scoop information in support of the coroner's and the local police investigation since there was a prevailing theory in his mind generated by recent input from both Wendell Atkins and George Adams.

Don knew that Wendell Atkins was knowledgeable about the Vincent Motorcycle Company and perhaps prior history related to the Laconia tradition each June. Wendell had died before the mystery could be investigated completely. George Adams could potentially be of assistance and Don was anxious to peruse Wendell's old journals and notes if they were available. Until he had access to those journals, he sought out other details on tattooing and information that might educate him on the art form's history.

Don pulled the Ducati Monster in front of "Tiny's Tattoos." Tiny was the antithesis of *tiny* and his Laconia location off Union Avenue was easily accessible by people desiring his telltale superior artwork. Word of mouth was good and complimentary. It was just before 10 A.M. and Don opened the screen door to enter the small studio. Tiny was sitting on a stool with much of his rear end larger than the seat. He was surrounded with photos and paper sheets on clipboards of popular and unique tattoo designs, some of which were scattered haphazardly on flat surfaces or mounted on the walls about him. Tiny was dressed in cutoff blue jeans and a muscle shirt that read, "I'm an artist, not some fuckin' printer!"

Tiny's stool could not easily accommodate his enormous weight. It squeaked as he shifted his body from side to side. The lacquer finish was worn or scraped off the seat and legs. The name, Tiny, was a misnomer, a name that was given to him in affection when he was younger. He wore dark sunglasses indoors and smoked Camels. A sign on the wall said, NON SMOKING SECTION?—OUTSIDE, ASSHOLE!!

Don hesitated, feeling a slight air of intimidation by the size of the man. No one else was in the shop at the time. Don smiled beckoning some kind of greeting from the big guy. Tiny seemed busy cleaning his nails of grime and ink.

Chapter 50

Don finally spoke, "Hello." Tiny reciprocated with a nod and said, "Hi ya. Anything special ya lookin' for? We got it all," he added. "We got your bikes, babes, tits, butts, sayings, logos . . . you name it! I've done'em all."

"I can see that, Tiny. Looks like ya got it covered," Don offered, feeling somewhat more comfortable with the introduction. Don had no interest in a tattoo, but wanted general conversation for his research. Tiny surely didn't know that but assumed Don desired an imprint of a particular stencil.

"You from around here?" Tiny inquired, looking up briefly. He saw that Don was dressed casually—khakis and a solid-colored, short sleeve shirt. Tiny was used to the jeans and leather crowd, not some college prep dude. He asked if the bike outside was Don's.

"Yah . . . the red one's mine."

"Rice rocket, eh?" Tiny commented, sneering. "Run on fried or white rice wine?" he laughed. "You want a copy of the machine tattooed on your shoulder? That bike style? I can copy it from memory. All Jap bikes look the same."

"Actually Tiny, it's a guinea bike . . . Ducati. Runs on olive oil—extra virgin."

Chucking at Don's humor, Tiny thought this "preppie" was okay. He could take a joke and rebut. He offered Don a seat in a chair and asked him what he had in mind. "What da ya need?"

"Ever heard of a Vincent bike?" Don inquired, hands on his thighs.

Tiny turned slowly on the stool and his butt cheeks spread over the seat in an unattractive manner. He had "plumber's butt" as he learned forward, revealing a large unnecessary cleavage for all to see. One could easily note the crack of his ass . . . much more than Don wanted to experience. Tiny hiked up his jeans as he stood. His large girth was a lasting memory of his beer-drinking days.

"Look up there," Tiny offered, pointing with his forefinger, cigarette held between his thumb and index finger, both of which were tobacco tar stained. "There's two of'em—right there. See'em?"

Don strained to see the logos. They were small. One was VINCENT and HRD, and the other was the *Vincent* logo with the god, Mercury, the famed wings and a single, spoke wheel.

Don's eyes immediately lit up! He took a breath. It was surely the tattoo that had been applied to the woman's backside. Don got the shivers up and down his spine, fearing that Tiny may have imprinted the young woman's back just days before she died. *Was he the artist that they sought for clues related to the crime?*

Before Don could ask, Tiny spoke up.

"Nobody asks for those," Tiny volunteered. "Nobody rides those machines 'round here. Those bikes are old shit and few bikers even remember them. British crap from yesteryear."

"Guess your right. Haven't seen any at Bike Week as yet," offered Don, pretending to be ignorant of the Vincent history that he had studied. "Too old a company, I guess—mid-1920's."

"Sometimes the vintage bike guys will ask for that tattoo. But, not often. The young folks have never heard of the bastard," Tiny said, takin' a drag on the one-inch remnant of his cigarette. It was now about to burn him. He blew smoke up into the air while waiting for Don to decide on whether he wanted the damn tattoo or not.

"Why do you want one of those silly logos?" asked the hefty man, somewhat curious but needing the business that day.

"You got one of those old bikes, besides that red 'I-talian job' out front?"

"No . . . one bike is enough," replied Don. "I like the logo design—always have liked it. It flows . . . and looks good on a woman's ass."

"It sure would, 'specially when you're bonin' the chick from behind," Tiny offered.

"I can put that one there on your arm . . . for a Ben Franklin," Tiny commented. "Would look good," he said, pointing to Don's bicep area, just below the shoulder. "We can give it some good color—water-based or plastic, and your arm is big enough to handle the scrolled name. When ya flex, Mercury will look bigger," he laughed, choking on some smoke. He waved his hand to distribute the noxious smell in front of Don's face.

"Plastic?" Don asked with curiosity. "What da ya mean, plastic?"

Tiny pointed to a series of small vials. "Them there are acrylic inks. Last forever . . . no fading. Newest shit in the tattoo world."

Don was amazed at the vibrant colors in the vials. He knew most tattoo colors were administered in water or alcohol, but had read of the plastic-based inks as well.

Don wanted to get to the point.

"Ya ever put that Vincent logo on anyone? Like this year?" asked Don.

"Nope. No one has ever asked for either one of them in the last 10 years or more, and I've been doin' this shit here for many years. I'm older than dirt," he smiled. "Been doin' it for 25-30 years, total. Lost count. I think I'm older than the Vincent," he coughed, smiling. "Nobody wants that shit . . . just you and a couple of old collectors of vintage machines."

"You don't look that old," Don complimented. "Would have thought you were pretty young."

"Young? You shittin' me? I'm 68 or so. Lost track. I'd call my Ma and ask her, but she's dead," he joked. "This is the only trade I've known. Damn good at it too. Look at the pictures and photos on the wall and in the album . . . all those photos are clients happy with my work."

Don Wright flipped the pages and was amazed at the photo album of past applications. He wondered if anyone was *unhappy* with his prior work. No one would probably complain anyway due to Tiny's size.

There were flags of different countries, and biker babes so realistic that they could make the male observer hard as a rock. He had tattooed many *Vietnam—Never Forget* tattoos as well as MIA logos mimicking the noted, "missing in action" flag of black and white—a prison tower and silhouette of a soldier's head.

Don studied the Vincent tattoo stencils up close while Tiny answered a cell phone call. It rang with the Johnny Cash tune, *A Boy named Sue*. While taking the call, Tiny commented into the receiver with confidence,

"Yah. I can do a dragon . . . sure!" he said, raising his eyebrows. He had probably done a thousand dragons. "You got the money buddy, I'll run the dragon around your body from head to toe. Not all at once, of course," he chuckled, winking at Don. "See ya soon."

Tiny cupped the phone so the caller could not hear. "I'll run the dragon clear out his ass," he whispered.

• Don laughed at the sidebar comment by Tiny. He was closely studying the Vincent logo details. The wings were intricate and the spoke wheel, as well. There was the soft gold color of the logo outlined in black.

After a while, Don stood and was ready to leave. He had the basic information that he had sought. Tiny had not applied the Vincent logo in years. That was probably a failsafe for Tiny in the grand scope of things otherwise he might be a suspect in the mystery crime.

"Hey! Don't go," offered Tiny, covering the phone with his hand. "You're the only customer this morning. I'll do friggin' Vincent and Mercury for $75 . . . that's pretty cheap. Sonny's Tat-2s in Concord can't match my work and those guys in tents ain't no artists. They use shit ink anyway and questionable "carriers" of the color. They use vodka sometimes—as alcohol."

"What do you mean?" asked Don, sitting back down on a second stool. "Alcohol? Vodka?"

Tiny held up his hand as if telling Don he would only be a minute on the call. He then ended the phone conversation having convinced the caller to come in that day. The caller, the dragon seeker, would visit later that afternoon.

"Just what I said, dude. Ya got to be careful where ya get these tattoos. Some guys sterilize the inks. Can ruin the pigment—causes it to fade. Other dudes dilute the pigment with "carriers" or a "vehicle" that they make up themselves. The shit they use is toxic. I use quality stuff," Tiny assured him. "Everything here is above board, Grade A shit."

"What carriers, what vehicles?" asked Don, unfamiliar with the terminology.

"Some use ethanol, Witch Hazel, propylene glycol, formaldehyde, glycerine, Listerine and gluteraldehyde, depending on the ink and color. They carry the color."

"Listerine? Witch Hazel? Formaldehyde? Like embalmers use?" Don questioned, wide eyed and amazed.

"For sure, dude!" Tiny added. "Some of that shit *is* used in embalming. They use toxic pigments too. Take a look at this list in my hand. Some are good and some are bad . . . real bad."

Don leaned over and studied the printed sheet of pigments. It was loaded with chemical names that boggled the mind.

"Are these approved for use?" he asked Tiny.

"Nope. Most of them are untested. Some have been used for medical devices and contact lenses, etc. As for injecting them, few are approved. I could inject you with "soot from a chimney" for "black effects" if I want. Who's gonna stop me? The *skin police*?" he laughed.

"The FDA doesn't give a shit. *The inks ain't drugs and they ain't food!* The pigments can be in cosmetics that go on the skin, but nobody says they can't be injected in Listerine as the carrier. The inks like anything alcohol-based.

"You're shittin' me, right?" Don replied in amazement impressed by the chemistry education he was getting for free.

"Look," Tiny added. "There are 5 million tattoos done each year. Nobody regulates the shit. Tattooists get licenses from each State but not for the products. Most pigments are salts of metals. Some ink manufacturers claim they meet European guidelines—approved as antibacterial, antimicrobial and are safe. They use lots of fancy words. There's some Congress of Europe Resolution on Tattoos that claim that Diabolo Novum products are safe. That Congress in Europe *ain't* the U.S. of A."

"Really?" Don responded, with interest.

"Really!" Tiny said in kind. "Anything goes in this trade—ya gotta stick with the pros."

Chapter 51

Don was aghast at the lack of oversight regarding the tattoo industry and inks in general. Here people were injecting humans with unknown solutions, chemicals and pigments that read like a toxic waste dump. The chemical list was vast and confusing to the layman.

White ink was lead carbonate, titanium dioxide and zinc oxide (a topical sun protector). *Blue* ink was azure blue, cobalt blue and copper thalo-cyanide; *black* was bone black, carbon, logwood or iron oxide. *Violet* was manganese dioxazine or carbazole. *Brown* was ochre, ferric oxide mixed with clay. *Red* was cinnabar, cadmium red, iron oxide or rapthol. *Orange* was diazodiarylide, cadmium seleno-sulfate and *yellow* was cadmium yellow, ochre, curcuma or chrome yellow. *Green* was chromium oxide, malachite (a desert rock), potassium ferrocyanide and ferric ferrocyanide. They were all listed on the tattooist's sheet.

Medically, there were warnings—more big words, which Don found overpowering and intimidating even as an educated man.

Allergenicity to the inks could occur in anyone since none of the chemicals were tested for adverse reactions, immunological or toxicological in effect in humans.

The *reds* were known to cause burning and scarring; often the elements listed as heavy metals in a periodic chart from basic chemistry class—iron and mercury were contained in the colors like cinnabar, causing the apparent adverse burns and scars. Using certain liquid "carriers" enhanced the adverse effects when mixed with the colorant and chemicals. They were untested and potentially toxic potions if not certified as safe.

The acrylic colors were longer lasting, Tiny had mentioned. If the tattooist used alcohol to administer the acrylic color, the small particles aggregated or clumped together under the skin. Undesirable aggregates could occur, distorting or disfiguring a picture on the tattoo. Once injected, they were difficult to correct in the tattoo.

"Ya see, my friend," Tiny volunteered, "*the artist* is critical for a sterilized tattoo procedure, and quality products that have stood the test of time should be used. I trained with the best."

Don nodded in agreement. How could he disagree with the man?

"If you decide on 'Vincent,' come on back. Be glad to set you up before Bike Week is over. It'll take 1-2 hours. I got a customer coming over a little later anyway, the one that called on the phone a few minutes ago. Have to do another damn dragon. Maybe he's a chink or gook," he laughed. "They like that shit."

Don shirked at his bias and racism. Perhaps Tiny had been in Vietnam—those derogatory terms were of that era.

"Thanks, Tiny. I'll keep ya in mind. I gotta think about it. I appreciate the chemistry lesson, ya know, about the inks and stuff. I can't believe some people use lead and cyanide-based colors or liquor or antifreeze as a carrier," he remarked, with raised eyebrows and a smirk. "How stupid is that?"

"Not me," said Tiny. "I *drink* the vodka," Tiny laughed. "Come back and see me. I won't hurt ya," he added. "Get yourself a Harley too . . . college boy!" he teased. "Forget the guinea bikes."

"Okay . . . okay . . . I hear ya, Tiny."

Don left the shop filled with information. Not only did he get educated about tattoos and colors, he realized that Tiny was not the one who had tattooed the young, dead woman. Tiny had yet to tattoo any Vincent motorcycle fanatics this year and her tattoo was obviously a recent application. Her death did not even come up in the conversation.

Chapter 52

Soon, the word on the street was out regarding a girl that had been found dead at The Weirs. Although the Weirs Beach residents had known of the unusual episode, it took a while for the news and fodder to spread throughout other New Hampshire areas in the Lakes Region and beyond. The police were cautious and had held back known information in an attempt to allow the coroner time to evaluate the potential crime scene and deceased body.

The local Chamber of Commerce didn't want to frighten anyone either. If the case were murder, visitors would be dissuaded from attending the official Rally Week. The C of C didn't purposely suppress the information, but merely did not mention it.

The news of her death then spread fast at the various formal events and agendas of Bike Week. "Jane Doe" / "Lady of the Lake" remained in a chilled mortuary drawer in Concord pending personal identification. Newspapers in Laconia, Concord and south of the lakes (Manchester and Nashua) ran articles requesting information on the victim's I.D. It became a public plea.

The local TV stations never got much of a chance to cover the original story that morning. It all seemed hush-hush and protected in distribution by the authorities. The media were hopeful that there might be leads with respect to the identity of a missing person. Someone surely had to recognize the girl's features and descriptive plea for information—a friend, boyfriend, traveling buddy or a local place of employment.

Someone who may have not shown up for work or who didn't call in sick would be a candidate for follow up. There had been no apparent identification left at the scene and someone had to know this young, deceased person, the dedicated police hoped.

The TV and radio stations finally initiated their own investigation, talking with local residents and broadcasting *live* from The Weirs boardwalk and adjacent boat piers. Boaters, employers and vacationers were interviewed at the Naswa Resort and other local marinas and motels like the BayTop and Margate. The Naswa was a popular dockside beach drinking haunt located right on Paugus Bay and just around the corner from the public Weirs Beach. Vacationers frequented The Willows as well.

"Jane Doe's" jewelry and tattoos appeared to be the only clues with which to initiate an investigation into her identity. The newspapers made little connection toward or elusion to the Vincent logo tattoo on her lower spine since they thought it might be a boyfriend's name, current or past. They mentioned the Roman god of speed but did not provide enough details for the public to associate the tattoo with a motorcycle company or brand.

The other tattoos were smaller and nondescript, offering nothing in the way of leads to her I.D. or place of origin. One was a Christian cross, another an inked bracelet of black, and a third on the lower spine. She was like any summer blonde—blue eyed, tanned in the usual spots and about 5'7". She could be anyone's daughter who came to Bike Week and had been tattooed before or during the festivities.

* * *

Dr. Blaisdell, who seemed to live at the Coroner's Office in Concord during Bike Week, awaited the toxicology tests of her blood and tissues. Those results required days or weeks for certain biochemical analyses and tissue pathology, although some initial tests were fairly quick indicators. He had already ruled out drowning, a heart attack or a drug overdose as a causative factor in her demise. The initial bioanalytical tests for recreational drugs were deemed negative, except for residual THC, the active ingredient in marijuana. She apparently had smoked dope within the last month. THC hung around for about 30 days and was detectable in small quantities.

More definitive toxicology tests would elaborate on whether or not she had taken any other drugs like heroin, crack or methamphetamine. There were no apparent needle marks in her arms or legs. Because she was "clean," Blaisdell was stymied by the lack of a direct cause of death, at least from the gross anatomical evaluations during autopsy. He had expected to see finite evidence of physical abuse/trauma, or brain or liver damage. There was no renal damage from dehydration or drug effects. He did not observe or note contusions / hemorrhage from the rough sex that she may have experienced.

Rapid cultures for microbial pathology showed no bacteria or viruses that were life-threatening issues or death-related. Blood smears from the victim revealed normal CBC's –total platelets, white and red cell counts. The heart showed no fibroid or collagen scarring from prior infarcts, common coronary congenital diseases or prior drug use, like cocaine. She was an apparent smoker since there was residual tar, hydrocarbons and black particulate matter embedded in the internal tissues of the lobes of the lungs. She had not smoked for very long since most of the lung tissue appeared pink under gross examination at autopsy.

*   *   *

Don Wright had called Dr. Blaisdell's office to see if anything was apparent in the investigation of her death. Although the case was confidential, Blaisdell knew that Don might have relevant photos from the crime scene and he was forthright with Don about some initial findings *post mortem.* He kept the anatomical observations/ evidence vague and in laymen's terms. Don was sworn to secrecy anyway and there was mutual interest by both parties in the attempt to identify the victim.

Don did not mention his interaction with Wendell Atkins, George Adams or Tiny, the tattooist. Don was sure that Dr. Blaisdell's colleagues in the Coroner's Office would also interview area tattoo artists to see if she had visited any parlors in the past week. The Coroner's Office would not release any of the actual details of the tattoos on the victim, but they surely were interested to know if anyone had tattooed the name, Vincent on a customer in recent days. Tiny's tattoo shop was on their list, as were numerous other tattoo parlors north and south of the Greater Concord, New Hampshire area.

Chapter 53

When Tiny received an initial phone call from Concord, an assistant from the Coroner's Office inquired about the unique name, Vincent. Tiny was paranoid about the obscure name having just talked to Don Wright about a similar tattoo the day before. He was reticent to discuss his tattoo practice other than asking how any of this was related to anything in which he might be implicated. He was clueless concerning the recent death of the girl at the beach in Laconia.

Tiny was surprised and perturbed by the apparent *inquest* in the last two days. First, a guy named Don had chatted with him, and now the medical examiner and Coroner's Office were asking similar questions.

What the hell was going on? he wondered. *It couldn't be coincidental,* he thought.

The coroner's assistant had indicated in her call to the tattoo artist that there had been a death at Weirs Beach and that the dead woman lacked an I.D. such as credit cards or a valid drivers license. She explained to Tiny that a unique tattoo had been applied on the girl's body and that the tattoo appeared to have been applied recently. The assistant also indicated that they were trying to locate any tattoo parlors in New Hampshire that may have inscribed, *Vincent* on this particular victim. The puzzle in Tiny's mind was slowly coming together.

Tiny became defensive on the phone citing his credibility and wanted nothing to do with any investigation of any local crime. His shop had not been implicated in any way. He did not mention that Don Wright had asked the same questions during a recent visit to the tattoo parlor. The last thing Tiny wanted was to be implicated in the death of someone who might have been tattooed in his shop. His shop was "clean" and no one had ever become ill or had died from his work.

"I haven't had a request to tattoo the name, *Vincent* on anyone in decades," he offered. "Hell . . . I've done *Vinnie* a million times. All the New York City bike riders seem to be 'Vinny' or 'Vinnie,'" he voiced, spelling out the differences of both names to the caller. "I did a "Vin" the other day, but no Vincent, ma'am."

The caller assured him that he was not under investigation and thanked Tiny for his time and input. She said that they were pursuing other general inquiries of tattoo parlors from Nashua to Conway. She thanked Tiny for his cooperation, albeit relatively insignificant in the larger scope of things. Based on his feedback, there was no need to visit his tattoo parlor. The caller from the Coroner's Office hadn't even asked if he stocked a stencil for the name, Vincent. Furthermore, she had no knowledge of the Roman god and winged wheel specifically as it might relate to a motorcycle logo.

Tiny finally mentioned to the investigator that a man named, Don had been in his shop just the day before—the questions were similar. The coroner's assistant did not know anyone by that name and assured Tiny that the so-called Don was not an official of the Concord office. She made note of the name anyway.

Now Tiny was more curious. He wanted to talk again to the man on the Italian bike. He didn't know how to reach him. *Would he be able to find him?* He thought he had seen his face before, probably related to the newspaper, but he was unsure of where or when. He felt confident that he would cross paths with Don again, at some point during Bike Week.

Tiny wanted to know what the hell was going on with this coincidental interest in Vincent tattoos, the bike logo or otherwise. He was miffed by the inherent secrecy to date.

The Coroner's Office called two other tattoo parlors in the Nashua area, one downtown and the other at a local mall near Route 3. Neither one had any information that was relevant, but they were cooperative with the M.E.'s needs. They agreed to help where they could.

The Coroner's assistant pursued another shop in Concord and one in Manchester, just off Elm Street. No one had a clue about any Vincent tattoo—both were unaware of the Roman god and wings, each agreeing in principle that it was probably some guy's name and a custom tattoo request. They lacked the knowledge that it might be related to a brand of motorcycle.

The assistant was coming up dry on leads related to local tattoo artists that might have met the dead women during the forthcoming motorcycle gathering. In time, there would be a break in the case, but for now all leads led to nothing relevant. The investigation in Concord seemed stalled.

*   *   *

One area involving accommodations that could not easily be covered by the coroner's team was the RV, tent and campground venues that dotted the State of New Hampshire during Bike Week. They were vast and widespread, some of which were temporary and embedded in the woods, both private and public. The infusion of thousands of bikers into the Lakes Region required early reservations for motels, hotels, cabins and guesthouses. The housing alternatives, which were cost effective and discrete, were campgrounds, which were prevalent and cheap accommodations when compared to the inflated nightly rates at area hotels like the Landmark Inn, Holiday Inn, Red Roof or area B&B's. Bike Week demand often dictated inflated room rates and was lucrative for local providers.

Riders also stayed with relatives and friends who had personal residences throughout the Lakes Region. The authorities knew that there might be *transient* tattoo artists looking to make a quick buck during the week and could be based in some friend's home without anyone's knowledge other than by word of mouth. What did investigators from the police or Coroner's Office know of such operations on the sly? The quality and sterility of the renegade, transient operations would be suspect at best. Were they licensed? It would be virtually impossible to trace their activities with tens of thousands of bikers arriving for a nine-day annual bash.

At any given campground, any number of tattoo artists could set up and work all day and night by Coleman lanterns, if need be. Some of the "artisans" were inexperienced neophytes at the trade, buying tattoo machines and ink supplies off the Internet and operating indiscreetly without formal marketing, but by referrals. They practiced the trade on oranges, a tool that mimicked the consistency and "feel" of human skin under the gun and needle.

The inexperienced tattooist could make a fast buck on the simple tattoo designs that were quick to apply and required less artistic prowess—like names, hearts, a rose or a cross. Their prices were much cheaper than the pros or established, experienced artisans. Trying to identify those charlatans, who might have attempted a more detailed logo like the recent Vincent tattoo on the deceased "Jane Doe," would be nearly impossible. Some bikers might only stay in the Lakes area for a day or two and then depart. The neophyte artisans could blow town within days, leaving no evidence that they or their makeshift parlor in a tent or camper even existed. The challenges for investigators were vast.

* * *

Tiny stepped out of his shop located beneath an old opera house that was used for storage. He locked the door shortly after receiving the telephone call from the Coroner's Office and walked a block or two to a popular convenience store. A Coca-Cola sign touting the name of the store hung over the doorway, swinging casually in the light breeze off Lake Opechee. Lake Opechee received the egress of water from Lake Winni—a dam at the end of Paugus Bay controlling its flow into the 400-acre smaller lake.

The convenience store near Tiny's shop was owned and operated by a man named Kumar who ran the store like any typical 7-ELEVEN. The hours were long for the owner and his family took turns working behind the counter and stocking the shelves.

It was a struggle for the little store to survive most weeks, and competition from the local Case n' Keg store was tough. Case n' Keg was popular, complete with a Video store adjacent to it and an active, repeat clientele for beer, wine and snacks. The personable Morin family ran "The Keg."

The "Keg" ran a competitive operation and offered more variety of household staples and products than a standard convenience store operation could supply. They carried kegs of beer and every brand and cartons of cigarettes that bikers wanted, and at reduced, competitive prices. The "Keg" operated daily by volume discounts and they were very successful in capitalizing on the local market share.

The Indian gentleman also sold the basic staples of life along with cold beer and cigarettes, bread, milk, lottery tickets and the local newspapers.

Tiny grabbed the daily Laconia newspaper, paying his fifty cents and headed back to the tattoo shop without opening a page. His own store window was full of neon enticements and advertisements of tattoo services, as colorful as the line of tattoo inks he carried and applied. A local beauty salon and antique shop were located near his own place of employment.

Sitting on his fragile stool, he lit up a cigarette and exhaled one or two smoke rings high into the air of his small lobby area. The low ceiling captured the mist of blue smoke and spread it evenly across the suspended fiberboard rectangles on the ceiling. The panels above seemed yellowed from smoke and age—having absorbed the noxious byproduct of many expired butts consumed in the past.

Tiny was a typical chain smoker and two ashtrays overflowed with the remnants of the perpetual and addictive, chronic habit. His mother and father had died of lung cancer but he didn't care all that much. He had been smoking since he was 15 years old, creating lines in the skin around his mouth and cheeks from inhaling the noxious cancer-sticks.

His eyes caught the headline of a recent article on the front page—it concerned the dead "Jane Doe" or "Lady of the Lake." The accompanying photographs of the Weirs Beach area, where she had been discovered, were credited to a photographer, who's name was Don Wright. A light bulb went off in his mind. Tiny put on wire-rimmed, reading glasses and recognized the name from prior news photos in the paper. He remembered that the Ducati rider was named, Don.

"Had to be this guy," he murmured, feeling smug and confident. "The shit head that was in here."

He looked on page two of the paper for the masthead of contact information for the paper's management. The office phone number was listed for the Main Street bureau office. He checked his Yellow Book as well. The phone book listed additional numbers for individual newspaper operations, including the "photojournalism" department. The Yellow Book was well worn, with ripped and dog-eared pages and marked with coffee, beer and ink stains from the last year of constant use. The cover was now a faded yellow hue since it had sat in a sun-filled front window most of the time.

"Ah . . . that should do it."

He dialed the number listed in the book . . . only to be rerouted to the front desk anyway. The receptionist patched him through to Don's extension. There was no immediate answer, frustrating Tiny further since he had limited patience anyway. After several rings, Tiny hung up leaving no voice message or call back number. He elected to try again later but the appearance of a customer in the shop relegated him to the task at hand. A dragon was needed and Tiny was ready to spend a couple of hours on the customer.

Chapter 54

Don Wright never knew that Tiny had tried to touch base or that he had called the newspaper office. Tiny had read the recent article on the dead woman. He finally understood why Don had stopped by his tattoo parlor and was pursuing the shop's implication in the woman's demise. He resented being used or potentially branded in the scenario of which he had no involvement to begin with. He considered the intrusion by Don to be an invasion of his privacy. To Tiny, Don had not been forthright with him and that pissed him off immensely. If he ever saw Don again, he would tell him off for sure.

It was clear that Tiny was reading too much into the episode with Don. Don's inquiry was legitimate and of a general nature. He surely did not implicate Tiny in any aspect of the death at The Weirs. The phone call from Concord was unrelated to Don's recent visit and was merely the investigative agenda of the Coroner's Office in their own pursuits.

*   *   *

Close to the far end of Lakeside Avenue at The Weirs, the road gradually rose past the train station to a slope up and into a residential area of historic homes. The Crazy Gringo Mexican restaurant was located on the left side of the incline. Adjacent to the restaurant were stores that sold trinkets and inflatable rafts for the summer crowd. Weirs Beach T-shirts were standard fare. The Paradise Club, a dance venue, was adjacent to the "Gringo." The Paradise drew the night crowd.

One small shop featured Native-American jewelry; displays of beautiful turquoise and silver bracelets, necklaces and rings hand-created by Navajo, Zuni and other Indian artisans from Reservations in the Southwest.

The Crazy Gringo was a popular watering hole, especially during Bike Week. It was a combination bar and restaurant that had changed names numerous times, including being called, "Nothin' Fancy" and more recently, "Rita's." The cooks and food remained the same during most of the transitions. The local crowd was the same as well. Unlike many other venues, the "Gringo" remained open year round.

This year's Rally event was no different. The Crazy Gringo was packed as Iceman entered the front door and turned left to sit in the bar area. Tall stools and tables, as well as booths, cordoned off the smoking area. The general restaurant seating area was to the right of the bar and was physically separated from the bar-flys by a partition of open lattice woodwork. Cigarette smoke filled the bar area and customers were standing room only on both sides of the room.

Iceman ordered a draft Budweiser and sat on the only available stool he could find. A massive man with little patience, he could have utilized two stools to support his hulk of a torso. People to the left and right of him shifted their seats in advance of his presence, making room for his oversized needs.

The TV above the bar was broadcasting a rerun of the previous weekend NASCAR race, and there were eleven laps remaining in the event. The volume on the TV was elevated for bar patrons and NASCAR fans as rookie, Carl Edwards was leading the pack at Pocono International Raceway in Pennsylvania. With a few laps remaining, the "yellow" caution light was on as another prominent racer had "hot brake issues" and slammed against the outside retainer wall of the famed racetrack. In the process, Ryan Newman had hit the wall as well. Dale Jr. was in the back of the pack, his number 8 Budweiser car exhibiting nothing but trouble throughout the race, much to his frustration. Once they were back to "green," the race was over and Dale Jr. had lost a formidable position in the "race for the chase."

"Ya can't win 'em all," he told the TV reporter after the race. "The car had its problems." That was putting it mildly as the car had issues all day long.

"Your crew did a nice job," the reporter remarked. "I'm sure they're as disappointed as well."

"The boys always get me a good car, but today the front left tire went down. I'm appreciative of the Bud team and the other sponsors for DEI Racing," he added. "Maybe next week at Michigan." Dale walked away from the microphone and mumbled an obscenity or two in frustration.

Everyone's eyes at the bar were fixed on the TV interview. Cigarette smoke arose from almost every seat clouding the beer and cocktail glasses that hung above the bar, suspended in tandem and on wooden racks. Patrons would later be served drinks in those inverted glasses.

The crowd was predominately a male audience that had sat through three hours of racing previously taped from a recent Sunday afternoon event. Most of the patrons had already consumed their limit of beer and the bar was crowded with bikers that sought out any available seat that became free. They were few and far between as many patrons remained at the bar for hours.

Iceman listened to Earnhardt, Jr. being interviewed. He was less enamored with his excuses for losing than other Rally patrons.

"The car sucked, Dale? Ya blame the car?" he shouted, with contempt. "Admit it. Your crew sucks since ya changed the team."

A couple of toothless wonders sitting near Iceman agreed with him but were quiet, acknowledging his austere presence in the pecking order of biker etiquette. They had seen his vest imprinted with the name and patches of the Metuchen, New Jersey Rough Riders. Iceman's size dictated his dominance as well.

Iceman was respected no matter what he said—even if people disagreed with him. Challengers were few. One biker chick with large breasts and a skimpy outfit approached Iceman and initiated a casual conversation. His predominant interest was in being with Bonnie, his new lady for the week. He initially played coy and showed little interest in the chick.

The newcomer was babbling about nothing in particular and pressing her breasts against his arm as an enticement. Iceman exhaled slowly after a long draw on his cigarette, blowing smoke up at an angle and toward the ceiling. He basically was in no mood to listen to her wonderfulness and trivial conversation. Her name was Susan and he had no immediate interest in her diatribe.

"Quit jackin' your jaw, bitch," he blurted. "My old lady is back at the campground. I'm set for the week."

She didn't seem to want to take "no" for an answer, still trying desperately to convince Iceman that she was a star and had been in the movie, *Scooter Trash*, a biker flick from decades ago. It was her younger, X-rated actress days.

"Remember 'Split Tail'," she offered with raised eyebrows. "Ever see the movie? I was her protégé."

Iceman perked up, being very familiar with the classic porn film. "I thought I knew you from somewhere," he smiled. "You were in that movie with some Metuchen chicks, right?"

She nodded yes and welcomed his unexpected new response.

"Ron Jeremy was in it too," she acknowledged. "I was the young blonde, a teenager. The dick on that dude was huge."

"Mine's bigger than that jerk," Iceman replied, boasting. "I should have been in that flick, not that hoser, Jeremy."

"Show me," she said, feeling the outside of his jeans with one hand. Iceman laughed as his jeans bulged from her immediate tactile stimulation. "What ya gonna do with that now, Iceman?" she asked, chuckling at the expressions of the nearby patrons to either side of Iceman's stool. He was stiff as a pole.

"How'd ya know my name?"

"Tattoo on your arm."

Iceman snuffed out his cigarette in the crystal ashtray tapping the end a few times in the glass base, which was already overflowing with butts and ashes. He blew out his signature smoke ring and stood up slowly, his crotch extended from the response. He grabbed her hand with authority, almost knocking her off balance and headed for the men's room. Only one or two guys noticed him enter the men's lavatory with "Split Tail's protégé." She seemed to have a propensity for bathrooms and followed his lead.

"In here!" he commanded, pushing her into an open stall marked with biker graffiti and pee stains on the floor from prior missed targets with the toilet bowl. Closing the stall door with one hand, he had her turn around and sit on the toilet seat.

"Here . . . stick this in that jacked jaw," he demanded. He was huge and she looked up as if she couldn't handle the size of his penis. "Jesus!" she said, with surprise. "You're too big."

"I saw the flick you were in. You can handle it," he said, pressing her head firmly against the front of his lower abdomen. He had her hair in his hand and held tight. She coughed once and then relaxed, swallowing the entire organ like the pro that she was in her film days.

"Atta girl. You're fuckin' good, doll," he stated, closing his eyes in ecstasy.

In less than a minute he withdrew his unit from her mouth and christened her face. "Ya christened me, you bastard," she screamed, wiping her eye with the back of her hand. She never even flinched, having experienced the scenario many times in the past. She wiped the Ivory soap-like liquid from her cheek with a handful of crumpled tissues from the toilet roll. Her face glistened as Iceman laughed at her predicament.

"You like that don't you, you bitch," he said, feeling superior and condescending, a role he had perfected all his life as a biker.

"Yah . . . my favorite job," she replied, standing up. "I like pleasin'."

He leaned over and kissed her and fondled her breasts, which he had somehow managed to expose during the blowjob. Susan seemed to enjoy the attention. She was the ultimate servant to Iceman and potentially a new girlfriend for the week. He envisioned having Bonnie back in Wolfeboro and Susan at The Weirs, and at his disposal. Double time was all right with him since this lady was as good or better than his companion at the campsite. After all, he had come to the Rally for the basics—beer, bikes and babes . . . sex was everywhere.

Chapter 55

Back at the bar, Iceman commanded that another biker shift down a seat. The guy was somewhat reluctant and Iceman shoved him off the stool and onto the floor. The guy was shocked by his brazen gesture and left without paying his tab. He had no chance against the larger biker and slipped out the door to Lakeside Avenue before the bartender noticed he was gone.

"Sit down here, Missy," Iceman offered his new friend. "The man on the floor was rude to a lady," he laughed. "Looks like a free seat now," he said, pointing her to the vacant stool where he tapped the seat with his massive hand. "Put that ass right there." She sat down and Iceman ordered her a draft beer.

"Who won the fuckin' race? I can't remember. I missed some of the interviews," he stated to nearby drinkers.

Someone yelled, "Edwards!"

Iceman smirked. "'Spose he did the back flip off the car window edge or roof too?" Iceman added. "He's the new hot rookie."

The men at the bar acknowledged Iceman's comment. "Yah. He flipped all right. He nails it every time."

Iceman laughed. "One of these days he's gonna land on his ass . . . or head. He better keep his helmet on."

Just then Iceman's cell phone rang. Turning away from the other patrons he checked the number on the caller I.D. He knew he had to leave and meet with the club members back in the woods of Wolfeboro. He kissed his new friend, threw down a $20 bill to cover his tab and got up.

"Gotta run, young Split Tail," he said. "Maybe see ya tomorrow."

"Can I come with ya?" she asked.

"Not today, doll . . . business to attend to with the boys. One of our riders had a mishap. Have to see if he's okay or needs bail."

"I'll be here tomorrow," she enticed him. "I'll wait for ya."

Iceman smiled knowing he probably wouldn't be there the next day. He had work to do and people to hook up with. He had a bevy of drugs to unload on the locals—supply and demand was the order of the day. Business was business and a priority to Ace in New Jersey. Women were a secondary agenda to the club members. Drugs were Ace's agenda in New Jersey and the club members knew it.

"Maybe," he replied to her comment, smiling. "I'll look for ya. Save some booty for me. Ya know, that pie-hole you're sittin' on." She smiled and hugged him goodbye.

Moments later, another biker sat down next to her. He had watched the whole scenario at the bar, including the bathroom scenario. He was taking a leak in the same rest room when she was "doin'" Iceman in the stall. The new biker had kept an eye on both of them. He wanted his share of the chick if the big man ever left without her. The timing was perfect and he sensed she was easy.

"Can I buy ya another beer?" he asked with reticence, expecting a rejection.

"Sure, honey. My ol' man just left me," she said, with a smile. "What's your name?"

"Harley," he responded, smiling. "Named after the bike by my ol' man. He wasn't very creative with names," he added, laughing.

"Good, Harley . . . love Harleys, both boys and bikes. Got any 'blow'?" she whispered. "I'm kind to those who have the 'candy,'" she offered sipping on her glass of beer.

With Iceman gone, Harley was her new target. Within the next hour, she would be leaving the bar with her newfound friend. So much for her allegiance to Iceman—besides Iceman would probably never see her again and she needed drugs. Her arms looked like a pincushion anyway, but no one seemed to care that she was an obvious addict. She seemed submissive to anyone who would be a "provider" and enabler of her habit. The new guy had his own stash and had no problem sharing.

Chapter 56

The Winnipesaukee Scenic Railroad traveled the local rails during Bike Week and stopped at The Weirs train depot adjacent to the Mount Washington cruise boat. The depot also sold tickets to the cruise boats that were moored nearby.

One Weirs shuttle train ran the route from Lakeport / Laconia to The Weirs and the other offered roundtrip passage on the half hour, to and from Meredith, New Hampshire to the north. Weirs Beach onlookers, Rally attendees and bikers that wanted to avoid traffic on the local conduits and highways to the Bike Week activities took the train east from Lakeport, along Paugus Bay and into the Weirs Beach general area.

For $10.00 per person / round trip, one could avoid the hassle of backed up traffic on the roads that accessed the Weirs Beach venues, restaurants and events from the south, west and north on Route 3. Old Route 3 was always a pocket of congestion—a zoo from all side roads that led to Lakeside Avenue. The route harbored the motels and hotels, fast food joints, arcades, water slides and summer activities for children and adults. Route 3 traveled the entire State of New Hampshire from north to south, predating the newer U.S. I-93 highway, a high-speed road that avoided all the traditional vacation spots and tourist attractions except for the White Mountains. The historic trains and convenient rail routes allowed for easy access in and out of the heartbeat of the tent areas, daytime entertainment and nighttime fireworks and rock band performances near the Weirs Drive-In. Each year, the shuttle train was a popular alternative to any other mode of transportation—surely faster than most modes of getting around.

Thousands of bikes parked along Lakeside Avenue, a tradition that dated back to the original Gypsy Tour, the origin and infancy stage of the modern Laconia Rally and Races. The trains dropped people off beside the long lines of motorcycles, motorcyclists and sightseeing pedestrians, many of whom lined the metal fence near the tracks and boardwalk as spectators.

*   *   *

Older and historical photographs of the early motorcycle riders and bikes can be researched and visualized at the Gale Memorial Library in the center of Laconia. Many commercial shops downtown tout the history of the Laconia Bike Rally and its associated race and hill climb events. The activities at The Weirs are only part of the aura of Bike Week in total. The race history in the Lakes Region is expansive, intriguing and entertaining. Over eight decades of attendees have witnessed a unique event that is iconic in nature.

The old stone train depot across from the library contains photographs, paintings and memorabilia in the local coffee shop know as The Black Cat. The quaint atmosphere draws locals and bikers galore with outdoor tables and seating where one can watch the entourage of red, black, green, yellow and chrome two-wheeled machines pass by for nine days and then some.

On this one particular day, Don Wright sat at one of the green metal tables outside the popular establishment. The green umbrella above him was partially shading his personal seating area as he relished in the azure blue-sky day and pleasant morning temperature in June. Hanging baskets of flowers and window treatments beckoned the passersby to stop and relax among the ambiance of the small downtown. A gentle breeze seemed to want to turn the pages of the paper Don had in front of him.

He was perusing the headlines in the news and photographing unique, vintage motorcycles that were standing silent on kickstands in the parking area. He sipped a cup of French Roast coffee and ate a cinnamon roll fresh from The Cat bakery. A sign nearby read LIVE ENTERTAINMENT TONIGHT, a billboard similar to the ones in New York that scream: *Eat at Joe's*. The sign touted the local favorite, acoustic guitar player, a talented musician and singer with a 400-song repertoire, many tunes of which were sing-alongs that the locals enjoyed on a Friday or Saturday night.

The heavy brown wooden doors of The Cat were left open for air and people came and went, often carrying coffee, tea or assorted carbonated drinks accompanied by a Danish, muffin or French pastry. The flaky "elephant ear" pastry was a favorite with locals, a large but light Danish that looked like its given name.

Don took a sip of the java and noted that the Concord, New Hampshire newspaper had an update on the dead woman from the beach. It was a low-key article in the back of the paper, almost hidden by other trivial news clips from around the world. The one paragraph synopsis of sorts seemed insignificant, often hyping celebrity trivia related to Ben Affleck and his wife, Tommy Lee and Pamela or Tom and Kate, Courtney Love's latest drug fest or rehab, or the split up of Heather Lochlear and Richie Sambora, a surprise after many years of marriage. He was chasin' Denise Richards as of this particular article. *Best friends usually shared spouses apparently,* Don mused.

The placement of the local death case in the news was designed not to cause attention or fear among the attendees of the Rally. No one wanted to stir up the issue during Bike Week, especially when no one knew if it was foul play or a natural death. This was the week when thousands of people would arrive to party freely and enjoy the Lakes Region bike events. Many women who knew of the death feared that a lunatic killer might be running amuck in the general area of The Weirs, preying on other young blondes in the pristine and serene Granite State—a State in which major crime was the antithesis of murderous events in large cities. Crimes of that nature only happened in metropolitan areas and in Boston, at least 90 miles south. New Hampshire was known as the land of pine trees and serenity, clear, cold running brooks, lakes with loons and wildlife galore—unique flora and fauna. Bike Week was the busiest and loudest week that the whole State experienced in any given year. Mother Nature would frown upon the invasion.

Don noted that the latest blurb did not mention much in the way of news for evidence or the I.D. of the woman for that matter. The toxicology data and forensic reports were still outstanding but due back soon according to the latest press report.

The coroner had apparently been interviewed briefly and commented that, the evidence of possible foul play was in question since there was no apparent direct traumatic injuries to the body of the woman. He cited the lack of knife or bullet wounds or severe skin abrasions/ contusions from external physical blows or abuse. The body appeared to be that of a "healthy" young woman, pending further blood tests by the State Lab in Concord.

He reiterated, "That they were seeking her positive identity and asking the public once again if anyone was known to be missing." No one had come forward to report his or her friend, lover or relative having disappeared in recent days. That seemed odd to the Coroner's Office. The coroner, Dr. Blaisdell, begged for information, any information that might help solve the mystery of the "Lady of the Lake" / "Jane Doe."

Don Wright finished his coffee and folded the newspaper under his arm. He was dismayed that nothing new had been found or reported concerning the dead woman. *Was the coroner hiding or suppressing evidence that was already known?* Don wondered. *He had to have studied the recent Vincent tattoo during the autopsy,* Don thought. The fresh application of ink to the tattoo on her lower back seemed to be the only tie of the woman to the Lakes area. His basic intuition was that it was related to her death. *Might the coroner be on the same investigative path as he?* Don wondered.

The newspaper hardly mentioned any personal effects of the woman or the fact that she possessed a strange tattoo with a *man's* name. If the Coroner's Office were looking to solve the crime, Don would have expected the name to be mentioned in the article. *Did anyone know a person named Vincent? Was there a Vincent at this year's Rally?*

To Don, the question was important and relevant to the inquiry and to the attending bikers from all around the U.S. *Why was the mystery tattoo not being discussed in the papers?*

Chapter 57

Don was anxious to revisit with George Adams at The Weirs, specifically at the Veteran's Home on Lakeside. He had fulfilled his day job requirements and had taken the necessary photos for the next day's edition of the local newspaper—they were taken at The Cat that morning. The "Faces of Bike Week" feature had its daily victim, a well-tattooed biker from Michigan who wore a buffalo skin hat and horns. That, in living color, would suffice for his day's job assignment and unique face for the week. Don had even interviewed the guy relevant to his home of origin and profession. The legend below the photo would mention his trade and small town in Michigan—a brief fifteen minutes of fame for the rider and his home.

The photographer's mind was on Mr. Adams now, the key player who had access to the journals that Wendell had recorded by hand for decades. He surmised that George would be on the porch watching the crowd of young hell-raisers, from Wendell's old rocker. Don called ahead and left a message that he would try and stop by that day. There was no answer but that didn't mean George wasn't around. Don would take his chances and purchased an extra Danish pastry and coffee for his elderly friend.

There were two ways for Don to get to The Weirs from downtown Laconia—the Winnipesaukee Scenic RR Shuttle train from Lakeport, or with his own Ducati Monster. He preferred the bike but knew traffic might be slow and painstaking. He took the chance anyway, somehow managing to straddle the paper bag with Danish and coffee between his legs and fuel tank. One slip and he would burn the family jewels.

Heading north out of Veteran's Square, Don rode North Main Street to contiguous Parade Road from Laconia center and leaned right onto

Rollercoaster Road. some five to six miles from downtown. The popular asphalt conduit across town had just been repaved—a well needed project for many years and potential death trap for cyclists before the facelift. It was a bikers' paradise offering curves and hills that the Ducati's tires could grip tightly through dips, inclines and turns.

The objective was to take the path of least resistance by cutting the corners short which meant crossing into the other oncoming lane of traffic. In that manner, a biker could straighten out the road and save time, mimicking the racers at NHIS, those that leaned into the corners so that their knees kissed the black pavement. It was a must ride for all bikers of the stylistic road racing Japanese and Italian motorcycles or those riders that liked the name, rollercoaster. The ultimate danger from eliminating the curves was the occasional oncoming traffic and Don had a hot coffee for George Adams between his legs—that would not be welcomed, if spilled, and if he screwed up a tight turn. He was extra cautious having seen the death of the woman at The Weirs and that of the Route 106 biker as well. He did not want to be Blaisdell's new corpse for anatomical review and investigation.

At the end of Rollercoaster Road, Don turned right and immediately became part of a line of bikes that were headed south on old Route 3 to The Weirs. All he saw was red taillights ahead of him lined in tandem on the right side of the road, his side. The traffic congestion was already apparent and he still had two miles to go to reach the sign at The Weirs. Every rider that he noticed seemed to be coming south from Meredith, heading to the beach, boardwalk and Lakeside Avenue venue area. Don passed the FUNSPOT arcade building and a man on the right side of the highway carving bears from pine logs while using a premiere Stihl chainsaw, one of the preferred saws of professional loggers. The man was always there, whether it was Bike Week or not. Don had photographed him in the past, especially when the wood chips were flying about him like snow. It was a definite photo op for the talented photographer.

He waited patiently as the line of bikes and traffic first climbed the hill and then descended gently to the other side near the Weirs Drive-In entrance. The tented food court and motorcycle parking area could be seen from the top of the hill. In the distance was The Weirs / Paugus Bay Bridge and the famed Weirs Beach art deco sign—complete with a continual border of light bulbs that graced the perimeter and the large illuminated arrow pointing to Lakeside Avenue. The sign was a classic piece of Laconia history for 50 years and the traditional icon had been recently restored to its original condition. Any souvenir postcards of Weirs Beach always had the directional sign in the photograph. It was akin to popular postcards of the historic "diving horse" of Atlantic City, New Jersey fame. For a half-century, it guided visitors to the beach.

Don pulled into the nearest paid parking lot. He turned right into
the access driveway by the Drive-In and decided to walk the rest of the
way to Lakeside. He passed behind two Hell's Angels' vendor tents and
continued down the avenue toward George's Veterans Home. George,
as Don had hoped and expected, was sitting in Wendell's old rocker and
chatting with another veteran who had lived there for nearly as long as
George and Wendell.

It was amazing to Don that some of these men were still around. Each
day it seemed, the remaining living legends had their own "war stories" to
tell, often embellishing or expanding the events, experiences or tragedies
from their time in the military service. They were trying to outdo each
other in a game of "oneupsmanship."

Neither man ever *won* in the verbal iterations of the past since the
stories got more unbelievable with each embellished episode of details.
It was basically Army vs. Navy in that George was an Army infantryman
and his friend was a Naval water tender. The way the two men recited war
stories one would think they had single-handedly won the conflicts and
all the campaigns in the European Theatre. Forget McArthur, Patton or
Rickover. These men were the apparent heroes that single-handedly won
the war, sadly if only in their own minds.

Lying beside George Adams was a stack of notes and journals in
anticipation of Don's arrival. He expected Don to show up in the early
afternoon and Don was true to form and on time. That pleased George
immensely. The coffee Don brought George was lukewarm from the traffic
he had to encounter prior to the walk to the home. It was still a nice gesture
and George would be grateful.

Chapter 58

Walking up the stairs of the porch to greet George Adams, Don apologized for interrupting the "war games" the two men were having in jest. He noted the journals that were piled to the right of the rocker. The black covers showed their age and history.

They appeared to be quite voluminous and heavy, with firm bindings. It was to be Don's assignment and pleasure to peruse the massive notes recorded by Wendell Atkins—notes of years and years of Gypsy Tours and Laconia Classic annual races and events. Don's heart skipped a beat and he smiled at the daunting task ahead of him. He then greeted both men with a firm handshake. He hugged George out of respect for their friendship. "Hi there, friend. Have a cold coffee. The thought was there."

"Thanks, son, this is Virgil, my friend from the Veterans Home."

Virgil smiled and bowed his head to Don. "Nice ta meet ya. George here told me 'bout you."

"The pleasure's all mine, sir," Don responded, cordially while expressing respect for the two military men. "Glad to know both of you," Don added.

Suddenly, there was a noise down below the porch and on the sidewalk. The bikers were whistling, hooting and hollering—encouraging one young girl to remove her bra-like top. She appeared inebriated and looked left and right to see if there were any cops nearby. There were none within her view.

Untying her spaghetti straps, she unleashed two large breasts for public viewing. The crowd of men taunted her even more and flashes from disposable cameras practically illuminated the street around her. She complied further by mooning the crowd, rotating for all to see, revealing her privates for an instant and sending the male crowd into an enabled frenzy. They groped at her and she became scared as men touched her breasts and encouraged her to show more skin. The men were close and she became claustrophobic. The lechers were too wired by the tease and she panicked. A police whistle blew nearby and just in time. It was an officer who was drawn by the loud attention to her display of lewd conduct.

Two policemen arrived from out of nowhere and escorted her off to the side protecting her from harm and potential additional groping. She appeared to be no more than 18 years of age and Don was reminded of the young girl that had died earlier in the week. The cops had saved this girl from harm and the crowd dispersed as fast as it had gathered around her. There were catcalls in the distance.

George and his neighbor, Virgil Gates had hooted at her as well, both leaning on the railing like schoolboys while overlooking the scene below. Don shot a photo from behind them as the two elderly men chanted with the rest of the bikers during the unexpected melee.

"That's the balls," Virgil said, with a smile. "That's what has kept my blood a pumpin'," he added, smiling at the thought of the nubile performer.

"Mine too," George replied. "Those were nice tits," he agreed. "Perky!"

Don laughed at the old men's reaction but he was reminded that the situation could have gone sour quickly. Don wasn't convinced that she was even 18 years old. *Jailbait,* he thought to himself.

By now, the cops had the young woman discretely dressed and covered; they were lecturing her for her own safety. They grabbed her arms gently and a paddy wagon arrived with lights flashing, much to the rampant boo's of the testosterone-infused crowd of horny men. She would be booked for lewd and lascivious behavior. Local regulations were strict especially after the unsolved crime, which had occurred in the beginning of the week. The cops did not desire to see another dead person at the 2006 Laconia Rally.

"Come with us, ma'am," one officer said, pointing to the van and handcuffing her lightly. "That's a no-no," he said to the young woman who appeared dazed, drunk and thankful for their rescue. She was definitely underage and her driver's license confirmed that upon closer examination. She had acquired alcohol from someone local and also broke a local ordinance regarding lewd and bawdy conduct in public. Too giddy to walk, on her own, she was led away laughing while the crowd gave her an ovation, cheers and many thumbs-up. They clapped appreciatively as she stumbled into the police wagon with solid sides and no obvious windows.

By the time the police vehicle arrived downtown at the Laconia Police Station, she had vomited once or twice in the back of the van. The whole scene was unpleasant for her and for the authorities that were left with the unanticipated and unwarranted clean-up detail.

Don had recorded the arrest on film but decided not to use the photo in the next day's paper. The last thing the young woman needed was to have her face in the press—a walking advertisement for her propensity to remove clothes for men later on in the week. She would be "marked" as one who had "bore all for the boys," making her easy prey for bikers after she was released from custody later in the day. The police encouraged her to go home and not return to The Weirs, for her own safety.

Her parents were contacted by phone and that was embarrassment enough for her to face later. She was released to their personal custody for she was not from out of town, but a local girl from nearby Gilford.

While undressed, numerous digital cameras recorded her lewd behavior. Some people with cell phone cameras had already sent the pictures of her to their friends by Internet. Before she was booked, she was a star in porn Web sites and Bike Week daily update news blogs. In less than a few minutes, the world saw the naked woman in amateur video and in still photos, all the primary subject of related discussion groups.

She was Weirs Beach famous now! Her parents hadn't even bailed her out yet and she was better known on the Internet than in all of Gilford or Laconia. Her graduation from high school was the previous week and her arrest, with her name withheld due to her age, would be in the newspaper. She was not immune from identification on the Internet and her classmates would be aware of her actions on Lakeside Avenue. That was not a promising way to start a college career after high school graduation. The Internet was, after all, *forever*.

Chapter 59

Even today, Weirs Beach retains an impressive history in the context of the Lakes Region in New Hampshire. It has hosted presidential campaigns, memorial services for all wars and offered tourists for decades a getaway from the major cities, rivaling the town of Wolfeboro where summer activities, music festivals and boating draw the masses from the greater Boston and New York areas.

For Laconia, Lakeside Avenue, in particular, extends the entire expanse of the beach and the side roads are elevated over the main thoroughfare offering homes and cabin views of Lake Winnipesaukee and its water egress, Paugus Bay (formerly Lake Paugus on many older maps). The Paugus Channel is wide in some areas leading one to believe that it is a *lake* of sorts, connecting Lakeport Village and The Weirs.

Trains, trolleys and horse or steam-drawn carriages traversed the popular shoreline of Paugus on roads and rail beds that were dirt, steel and tree-lined—many of which became scenic rides with views of the distant White Mountains in autumn. Before that period of time, the Native-Americans lived on reservations that had the distant views of the unspoiled natural wonderland of deep green forests and pristine, potable waterways.

Today, Lakeside Avenue touts the most beautiful buildings of the 1880's and 1890's and later—with less and less now remaining as historical structures. Fires destroyed a multitude of buildings that once thrived there as prominent Veteran's and Infantry buildings and pristine hotels or lodges.

The late, great Hotel Weirs, once an enormous structure on Lakeside, was an elaborate sprawling edifice with 230 rooms and a cadre of amenities that far surpassed the times and eras that followed. Those visitors and vacationers with money, old money, partook of the hospitality and the accommodations that supported the tourist and resort businesses in the Lakes Region.

The Hotel Weirs was originally named the Diamond Island House (circa 1860's) that was eventually disassembled and cut up facilitating the transport of the wooden sections across the ice of the Big Lake to its location on the early rendition of modern day Lakeside Avenue. It became the New Hotel Weirs and flourished as a popular resort until a tragic fire on November 9, 1924 when it was totally destroyed. Twelve other structures in the same geographical area perished, including a church and a famed Music Hall.

The popular Music Hall was the origin of the fire at a time when fire equipment and volunteers were limited in experience and speed and the numerous, multiple infernos impossible to stop with hand-to-hand bucket brigades and inadequate old pumper trucks.

Ironically, the Big Lake "Winni" offered millions of gallons of water to combat the fires of the late 1800's and early 1900's but utilizing the natural lake resource was a challenge for the volunteers who struggled to abate the infernos and prevent the demise of the large structures on the main road. In modern times, fires can be stopped in minutes, often preserving the remaining history of the area.

Surrounded by enormous Calvary and Veterans Association homes, monuments to the war dead, cemeteries and iconic testimonials to the Native-Americans of the time, the New Hotel Weirs embraced the auspicious and occasional visits of political candidates, U.S. Presidents and influential business leaders of the Northeast.

The buildings that lined the road were named, Castle Rest, Clyde's Cottage, Story's Hotel, the 3rd, 5th, 7th, 8th, 11th, and 16th New Hampshire Regiments and Calvary buildings of the 1890's and were elaborate and ornate wooden structures, many of which were destroyed by other individual fires or the infamous hurricane of 1938. One prominent building (Story's Hotel) was destroyed by fire as late as 1991.

Few visiting bikers during the Laconia Rally festivities know of the history of the resort area, even today. They ride by the prominent notorious structures thinking of them as bed and breakfast accommodations or summer homes for the affluent. Some remain in disrepair and are too costly to upgrade while others have been restored to their original prominence of yesteryear. In 2006, one or two more structures underwent new renovations and painting.

Near the renowned New Hampshire Veterans Home on Lakeside was once a monument for all of the fallen soldiers, including young Loammi Bean who died in 1862. He was age 37 when called to duty. After his death, his daughter had a monument erected in 1894 for the 8th Volunteer New

Hampshire Regiment. It can be seen in historic books of The Weirs and on postcards of old from that period of time. As fate would have it, lightning destroyed the metal statue on July 23, 1931.

Until that fateful day, the metal monument was testimony to the veterans of many wars and stood proudly in front of the New Hampshire Veteran's Association Home and New Hotel Weirs at the corner of Calvary and Lakeside until its unexpected demise in the 30's. Only elderly motorcyclists from the earliest of Laconia Rally days would remember the military monument, which was never replaced.

When Theodore Roosevelt visited The Weirs August 28, 1902, the crowds were too large for nearby Veterans Grove, an open and treed area that could accommodate 3,000 people on wooden benches. He had only been President of the United States a short time, having assumed that duty after the assassination of President McKinley in Buffalo, New York. Roosevelt had been vice president in the McKinley administration.

Locals, Frank Bailey and Charles Harvell, a U.S. Marshall and a Laconia police officer, protected the president during his tour of The Weirs. The president arrived at twelve, noon by train and "reviewed" a number of regiments and associations. They stood at attention for their Commander in Chief. He drew some 20,000-40,000 people who came by steamboat, steam vehicles, hay wagons and by foot just to witness his presence—a popular president of the day. The Teddy Bear was his legacy.

He visited the New Hotel Weirs. The historic visit to Laconia was photographed for posterity; some people bringing picnic baskets and bags of food for the lengthy and rare visit by the leader of the country.

The president later went on to visit Pittsfield, Massachusetts as part of a prearranged New England trip. There, in western Massachusetts, and six days later, a trolley hit the landau in which he rode, and the popular president was almost killed. He survived the encounter without serious injury.

Chapter 60

Don Wright had found the presidential visit to New Hampshire of interest. Was there a correlation between the president's visit and the death at The Weirs? He searched the library for clues. Might there be a link from history?

Roosevelt was a dynamic president as is clearly stated in, *The Presidents in American History* by Charles A. Beard, circa 1935, with many revisions over thirty years, later by his son, William Beard. Published by Julian Messner, Inc. in New York, it is uncanny that it was the same publisher for New Hampshire author, Grace Metalious (*Peyton Place,* 1956).

The book by Beard highlights Roosevelt's accomplishments prior to and during his term of office. Born in New York City in 1858, Roosevelt was in office from 1901 to 1909 dying in his sleep in 1919—about the same time the motorcycle rally and tours were invading the New Hampshire lakeside communities. Wright found this coincidental and intriguing.

A graduate of Harvard, Roosevelt was in the New York legislature, a police commissioner, on the civil service commission and Assistant Secretary of the Navy. He welcomed the Spanish War, formed a regiment of "Rough Riders" and became involved in the fray over Cuba, all before he was president. In between appointments, he was Governor of New York as well.

He was elected outright again in 1904, a popular choice for office and continuity. Later, after his term as president, Roosevelt was an avid outdoorsman and hunter, often "roughing it" on a western ranch. He hunted lions in Africa yet he was a proponent of the conservation of "natural resources." He influenced the construction of the Panama Canal. Don Wright found the Roosevelt Rough Riders of particular interest. They had been mentioned in some of Wendell Atkins' journals. Don had seen a motorcycle club jacket with New Jersey Rough Riders embroidered on it as well. Was there a connection to the motorcycle club and the recent death or was it mere coincidence or folly in Don's analytical mind? What else might Wendell's journals have to say?

*   *   *

In the fertile days of Roosevelt's America and the early 1900's, train service to The Weirs expanded the geographical area commercially, especially with the establishment of general stores, industrial trades, ice cream parlors, grocery stores and a post office near the 1893 Concord and Montreal train depot at The Weirs. Following commercial rail service for supplies and the transport of granite, wood and ice throughout Boston and New England, the Concord and Montreal Railroad eventually initiated passenger service between Boston and the White Mountains, allowing vacationers to visit Laconia and the beach areas of many lakeside communities. Towns and cities grew from the invasion of tourists—much of the growth to New Hampshire's benefit.

Today, as a testimony to its superb construction, the Headquarters Building of the NH Veterans Association at Lakeside, Veteran's and Calvary Avenues, remains a central location for the Weirs Rally events. The local police use the building as a dispatch office and point of focus for the administration of safety and medical responses to incidents during the week. The patrolmen come and go at that headquarters much like the soldiers of the early wars. Their duties for Bike Week oversight have similar protective orders for the stability of the populous.

Don Wright made a tour of the Headquarters' Building a must in his overall research. He felt that it might supplement his data on the relevance to Lakeside Avenue history and the death of the unknown woman. Part of the history was reviewing the origin of the early Rallies and bizarre events that may have occurred during those annual get-togethers. Some Rally Weeks had been tumultuous and notable, with riots and National Guardsmen being called up. Motorcycle deaths were always part of each event as well. Might there be a historical link?

Even today, motorcycles line the front of the building as they did in 1916 and at later Gypsy Tour Rallies. The Bay State Cycle Club set the precedent, arriving in June, 1918 with some 300 riders who "cruised" on the Big Lake, feasted at hotel restaurants, enjoyed concerts at the Veteran's Association bandstand and later returned to Boston the following day. The same bandstand of note disappeared in the 1938 hurricane, a noted weather event responsible for the demise of other buildings as well.

Accompanying the riders in 1918 were well-dressed women who rode with their beaus or spouses in sidecars. The later Gypsy Tour Rallies were not restricted to men. Men wore suits, embellished and formalized by white shirts and ties. The dress code back then was the antithesis of today's motorcyclist's attire. Leather and vests were not "in" or fashionable then and the motorcycles were an alternative mode of transportation, primarily for touring, yet later yielding to sport riding and racing events in the later 1900's.

The desire for speed and "wind in one's face" was popular back then. Goggles were the only protection from wind, bugs, dust and grime of the road, often dirt. Surely, no one considered helmets and leather chaps in those days. Leather hats were used in open automobiles for sure. The dress code for motorcycle riding was respectful and formal.

The women in their hoop dresses would never have revealed their flesh to other passersby and tattoos were not to be found as adornments on their skin. Women in carnivals or circuses might have been more forward and marked by ink, but not the touring ladies from proper Boston. Sunday drives were for pleasure and exuded class.

The Laconia Rally and Race history had its inception at the Weirs as well. An annual competitive hill climb with bikes occurred on nearby Tower Street at Weirs Beach. Thus began the tradition, which today surpasses some 400,000 attendees and 100,000 motorcycles each year in June. In the mid-1920's, it is surmised that the British bike invasion accounted for many of the motorcycles that permeated The Weirs and motorcycle social clubs of the day. Among the companies that produced the bikes in England was Vincent, Royal Enfield and other manufactures, a potentially significant clue in the obscure demise of the dead girl, known as the "The Lady of the Lake" or "Jane Doe."

Chapter 61

Don Wright knew that Lakeside Avenue was of historical significance. His research on the Internet and at the library encompassed the local relevance of the buildings along Lakeside with the history of the infamous annual Rally.

Lakeside Avenue was not only a testimony to, and a remembrance of the World Wars and various U.S. Calvary and military regiments, but it was the centerpiece of The Weirs leading from Weirs Boulevard to traditional vacation hotels, groves and beaches. Boston travelers frequented The Weirs landmarks on weekends, enjoying hot summer days after long car and train rides, while visiting to picnic near Endicott Rock. The tradition remains today during and after Bike Week. Bike Week seems to grow in popularity each year with vacationers staying around.

Don had reviewed the history of Laconia and had seen the series of books by Warren D. Huse, a Laconia historian. Arcadia Publishing had published a series of books directly related to Laconia, Lakeport, The Weirs and The Lakes Region, in general. Don read them fervently, trying to understand the relationship of the old resort area at The Weirs and its changes in the modern summer days of 2006. The lake views were the same but the people differed over many decades.

In addition to the classic photos from yesteryear, the text in history books offered many facts about the 1800's. They also offered insight into motorcycle Rally history in the era of the early 1900's and the impact of the Veteran's homes on the community at Weirs Beach.

Don Wright supplemented his knowledge with Internet searches, Wendell's personal handwritten journals and other notations from when he was a young man, researched and recorded observations almost to the day he died. Wendell had, in fact, recorded the visit by Teddy Roosevelt and some of the Rally events by members of the Bay State Cycle Club, offering a perspective that no one else had recorded in history. If ever published in book form, the notes would augment and embellish the value of the Lakes Region in the economic stature and industrial growth of New Hampshire. The impact was significant when factories transitioned from handmade to machine-made products. The early Gypsy Tours witnessed much of the industrial growth and transportation changes in the Granite State.

Don was grateful that George Adams was able to find all of the volumes that Wendell had stored for posterity. Within the journals were hints of information that would help explain the "wherefores and the whys" of the young woman's death. Don was the only person with direct access to that knowledge. Without the written chronology, Wendell might have taken the clues with him to the grave. Don's research to date was shallow compared to what was embedded in the journals. He knew his mission and kept it confidential from George Adams. George was too old to care and found the voluminous recordings of Weirs history to be boring anyway. He was happy to pass on to Don anything that he needed. Don, on the other hand, knew he had fallen on a golden treasure chest of information, one the police and coroner would not have knowledge of or access to without Don sharing.

His mission was to solve the crime at the shoreline and the eventual identity of the dead girl in the mortuary drawer. *Could he achieve it during the nine-day period of the 2006 Rally event?* he wondered. That was a formidable challenge.

Chapter 62

Two bikers on older model Harleys entered a campground off Route 11 in Gilford, New Hampshire, a road that continued to Alton Bay if one desired to roll north. They rode modified bikes that looked as if they had dumped all their money or savings into the machines instead of into a home or clothes for their children. Their leathers were old and cracked and the saddlebags on their bikes were weathered from years of riding in all climatic elements of the Northeast. Their saddlebag contents always remained dry yet the side bags looked like they had seen the last of better days. They were untouched by saddle soap since that would make them un-cool.

The two men had seen a pink neon paper flyer on a telephone pole. It read: "Fuzzy's Tattoos-Cheap."

Following the handmade signs off Route 11, they noted a secluded vine-covered driveway that led to some campsites on a temporary campground, some 200 yards into the woods. The vines were the plant, bittersweet, a climbing, choking parasite that depending on the species, can kill the largest of trees over time. In summer, the leaves are thick and are a natural sound barrier or natural fence, ever spreading each year and often thickening the bushes and landscape in New Hampshire's woods. The bittersweet berries of orange and yellow and their vines are used as autumn wreathes on New England doors of older homes, yet the seeds spread the natural flora everywhere when uncontrolled. Their beauty is only surpassed by the hatred by homeowners who fight the overgrown flora that cannot be easily stopped.

A local farmer who enjoyed the extra revenue leased the pastures and property to bikers each year. Rally Week was a windfall for the aging farmer who struggled year round just to get by.

Generally out of the way and nondescript as a farm property, the opportunity each year to make cash was a quick decision for the Tuttle's and their Tuttle Farm, one that had been in Gilford for centuries and handed down to each generation within the family. Farmer Tuttle cared little about who stayed in the freshly mowed grass as long as they paid in advance and kept the place clean. He pretty much left the transients alone for the week.

Tuttle had arranged for the delivery of numerous Porta-Potties to handle the crowd of bike enthusiasts that resided temporarily on his land. He was a pleasant man, white-haired with sun-drenched, leathered skin from years of planting, mowing, haying fields and milking cows.

Barbecue fires were allowed for cooking and Tuttle had used his trusty old John Deere tractor to make dirt pits that safely contained the charcoal and wood campfires. Most of the short-term residents drank anyway, leaving little room for food in their bodies; therefore, there were plenty of 55-gallon drums available for refuse, beer cans and bottles. Excessive drinking was normal fare for Bike Week, an extended party of revelers from many States in the U.S. Bikers didn't exactly recycle bottles of Bud anyway but the patrons of the Tuttle property seemed to respect him and his fields that normally fed his cattle when the campers were absent. The bikers did not want to leave broken glass for the old man to pick up later or for his cattle to cut their feet on while grazing. They kept the refuse in or around the barrels out of respect for his courtesy and land use. There were few issues for the farmer to deal with. The police were only needed a couple times in the past, times when the hooligans were visitors and not resident campers on site.

Once the majority of bikers left after Father's Day weekend, Tuttle and his two sons would clean up and care for the property that remained well flattened by bikes, foot traffic, tent and camper positions. He would mow the field weeks later and reap the proceeds of late grown, bailed hay. His bails were sold locally to area farmers and to the Agway store, almost doubling the summer revenue for the Tuttle family.

The two black leather riders that had entered the campground were not residents therefore the well-hidden community was new to them. They slowed as the pasture appeared, complete with additional neon-colored paper signs directing them to the tattoo artist in the back row of canvas tents. The numerous tents were evenly spaced and consisted of different styles, domed and traditional, a collage of varying sizes and colors.

Privacy was not an option unless your tent was near the edge of the woods and any free space was sold out in minutes if someone left the Rally Week early. One of Tuttle's sons's collected the proceeds from a lock box on a nearby pole. No one dared steal the cash fearing that Tuttle would never open the campground again in the years to come. It was an honor system that actually worked, even for the hardest of riders. Fifty dollars a week or ten dollars a day was the bill. It was cheap, but adequate housing that provided access to and near The Weirs and to the NHIS racetrack, eleven miles south.

Like most riders, the two men sought inexpensive tattoos that were safely applied.

Artisan, "Fuzzy" Walsh was the transient artist who set up in the back row of tents in the Tuttle pasture. Oddly, Fuzzy had no hair to speak of and was quite thin in stature. His 12'X16'—four-room, olive drab, canvas tent was powered by a small Honda generator capable of running most of the campsite, if needed. He used the power for tent lighting, an autoclave (S/S Stove Top) and his Joe Kaplan tattoo machines. One machine, the BJ-1L was for "outlining" the tattoo and the other, a BJ-2L, was for "shading." Each was handmade of Sheffield steel by Big Joe; Joe even produced a model named after his son, Jason Todd who also made popular ink machines but died young December 6, 1993. All three were popular tattoo machine models ranging from $175-$350 each. There were left and right-handed models and Fuzzy's needs were right-handed.

Fuzzy Walsh had acquired the tattoo machines from an on-line site. He bought his ink supplies from the tattoo supplier as well and traveled the country tattooing attendees at fairs, summer events, and carnivals. Bike events were ancillary to the carnival trade, but easy cash for him.

In his tent suite, he had two cots and two special chairs with armrests that enabled him to tattoo all parts of the body. Women preferred to lay face down on the cots so Fuzzy could tattoo their butts and upper and lower backs in privacy. *He had seen more ass than a toilet seat,* he claimed to some male customers, a universal joke at most tattoo parlors. The other tattoo site favored by women was the shoulder area and lower legs.

Fuzzy's own body was covered with samples of his work, showing off his prowess and a variety of challenges. It was free advertising for him, bold and bright in assorted colors. People then knew that he did professional and challenging work, and at a fair price.

Chapter 63

The bikers who entered the gravel driveway and open pasture followed the arrows and placards to Fuzzy's tent. It was one of the largest tents in the Tuttle pasture. Unbeknownst to Fuzzy, the bikers were actually undercover policemen who dressed the part of the black leather crowd. One rider was a detective and the other a local patrolman. The cop remained on his motorcycle, wearing a bandanna and sunglasses often scouting out the general tent area. It was late afternoon and the sun was warm causing him to wipe his brow with a doo-rag.

The cop outside the tent and on the motorcycle was startled by the moans of a woman in an adjoining tent. She was not being tattooed by Fuzzy. They were obvious moans of pleasure, not pain. *It was still daylight for Chrissake,* he thought. Someone was getting' balled at 4 P.M. The cop merely ignored the erotic moment and opened a road map of the Lakes Region area. He wanted to appear like an out-of-town visitor for the week. Both of the officer's bikes had out of state license plates for cover purposes.

The biker-detective who entered Fuzzy's tent was cordial and struck up a casual conversation that was mundane at best. He asked him how long he had been in business, desiring to appear as an interested future customer. He also inquired as to how many tattoos Fuzzy had applied in the past few days, hoping to elucidate if any women were recent clients. Fuzzy admitted that business had been a bit slow but he expected the clientele to increase in the forthcoming days and week. A few people had visited his tent. Bikers from out of state were just arriving and business was expected to expand.

"What the hell is that moanin'?" asked the detective in the tent. He raised his eyebrows and smiled, clad in a vest and leather chaps. "Is that what I think it is?"

"Oh yah, . . . that's my neighbor and some chick. The two of them haven't been out of the tent all day. Been bonin' her all afternoon. This chick is a nympho, I think. It's hard for me to concentrate with the tattoo gun most days. He's been ballin' her for two days straight."

"Really," said the plainclothesman. He looked around the tent wall and saw hundreds of tattoos and samples. "Music to my ears," the cop said, for continuity.

"What's the most popular tattoo? I don't know what to get," questioned the policeman. "People have favorites?"

Fuzzy sat back and pointed to a few examples. There was no *one* favorite, at least in his mind.

"Today, it was American flags all morning and the "twin towers" in New York. Yesterday, it was MIA logos for the Vietnam crowd. Changes every day, man. It varies. What's your gig? Naked women are always in."

"Oh . . . nothin' special. Ya ever do any motorcycle logos from the older bikes?" the cop asked, rubbing his pant leg. "Ya know, the Moto-Guzzis, Indians and the like?"

"Sure. I can do most of them. The British, German and Italian bikes. Half the bike logos I have, I have probably memorized in both color and shape. No need for a stencil if they're a common bike like Harley or some of the Jap bikes."

"I like the older overseas bikes. What British bike logos have ya done? Triumph, BSA, etc?" the detective asked, trying to make conversation and spark more interest. He was gathering intelligence by being knowledgeable about bike manufacturers.

"Done'em all," Fuzzy replied. "What interests you?" asked the artisan, now sitting on a stool. He lit up a Camel and took a long draw on the cigarette.

"Royal Enfield, Vincent's, the old shit," he responded.

"Done lots of Vincent's, old style logos and new . . . HRD's and all," Fuzzy boasted.

"I'm tryin' to remember the Vincent logo," the cop baited him. "Think one was a god. Ever done the one with Zeus or Mercury and the scroll?" asked the cop. "Ya know, think it had wings or some such thing . . . real pretty one."

"Sure . . . that one?" he said, pointing to a stencil print pinned to the wall of the canvas tent. "Done plenty of those in my day."

"Yah . . . that's the one . . . the one with the Roman god and stuff," remarked the cop. "Appears to be Mercury with wings and a bike wheel."

"Hell. I did one three days ago. Some chick wanted one on her lower back . . . spine area just above the crack of her ass. Sweet young chick . . .

nice ass too," Fuzzy commented, with pride. "She probably didn't know what it was. She was too young to know of those old bikes. Guess she liked the style or the god-like statue."

"Really? That one?" the cop remarked, pointing. He was excited by the revelation.

"Yup. She picked that one out for sure," Fuzzy added, taking it down from the wall for a closer view.

"What was her name? You Remember?" asked the cop, who was now on a roll, and hardly able to contain his excitement. It was as if he had hit gold.

"Ah . . . Tammy, I think . . . ya, Tammy was the chick's name . . . *sweeeeet!* She was with some big dude named, Iceman . . . he was huge. Can't imagine they were an item. He was older and pretty rough lookin'. Can't tell these days though. Some chicks like the big, bad boys. Age don't matter."

"Iceman, huh?" remarked the cop. "He brought her in for the tattoo?"

It was like twenty questions now and the tattoo artist was getting perturbed.

"You lookin' for Tammy or looking for a tattoo? Times money here and I haven't got the time to jack the jaw. Have a seat," ordered Fuzzy. "I can do a *Vincent* for ya in a few minutes or you can pick anything else on the wall."

"Nah . . . thanks," replied the cop. "I think I've found the tattoo of choice and pretty much know where the chick is," he responded, arrogantly. "The chick's dead."

"What? Where? Why'd ya ask? What the hell's this about?" Fuzzy responded with trepidation, and with a snarl. "I don't even know the bitch. If she's dead, don't blame me. I do clean shit, man."

"Laconia Police, Fuzzy," he said, showing his official badge and I.D. "I'm Detective Leonard and this guy outside here is my partner, Officer Snow."

Snow, hearing the conversation, elected to enter the tent and removed his sunglasses. Fuzzy was now visibly shaken and totally in the dark concerning the dead girl. He didn't read newspapers and surely did not know of the investigation in progress.

"Tammy is dead . . . at the morgue in Concord. The tattoo is right where you said it was, at least on this girl. She fits the description you gave and the bike logo is the same," the cop said, hands on his hips.

Fuzzy was aghast. "What the hell do I have ta do with all this?" he responded, scared from the unexpected inquisition.

"Maybe nothing, Fuzzy. Then again, maybe somethin'. We need you to come downtown for a bit. Got some questions that might help us figure out why she died."

The other cop spoke up. "We have a dead girl, sir . . . and a tattoo that you probably applied the other day. Hers was recent and no other tattoo parlors have applied the logo for Vincent. We need to know details . . .

as much as you can remember. Especially this guy, Iceman and any other helpful info on the girl."

"Okay . . . okay. Let me shut things down and I'll go with you. This is bullshit. I'm losin' income by goin' with you and I do clean work here. No issues here. My tattoos don't kill no one," he said, defensively and stammering. "I tell ya—I'm innocent and don't know crap about this chick or the guy, Iceman. They came, paid cash and went. Never saw them before or after," he insisted.

The two cops tried to calm him down but Fuzzy was flustered beyond compare. Fuzzy knew there was no way that he caused someone to die and he resented the implication that his artwork had caused it. He told the police he had to go to the bathroom and they followed him to a portable toilet. Fuzzy pissed and threw a small bag of grass from his pocket into the chemical hopper. The damn bag floated but the cops were in a hurry so he rejoined them as quick as he could. The police stood astride him while on their bikes. They would shadow him down the dirt driveway. He slowly began to walk the short distance.

"We'll have a car waiting for you by the gate to the campground," mentioned one cop. "You can ride in style. We'll see you downtown in a bit. You aren't under arrest. All we need from you is some information. So relax. We'll have you back here before the guy and girl in the tent are finished," the cop added, with a smile.

Just as they were leaving and ready to fire up their bikes, the two cops heard the moans of the girl in the tent next door. She was breathing harder now and screamed, "Oh Jesus . . . Oh Lord . . . harder!" The couple was oblivious to the cops and Fuzzy leaving the campground.

Fuzzy was agitated and stopped for a moment. He turned toward the den of iniquity and said, "*Jesus* can't help ya now, lady. He ain't even hard." He turned and walked toward the gate. The girl in the tent screamed, "Fuck off, buddy Get Lost! Mind your own business."

Fuzzy and the cops laughed and started their Harleys—they followed him closely so that he wouldn't bolt on them. He had no intention of running. Where would he go anyway? Everything that he owned was in the tent.

A blue and white Ford cruiser arrived in no time for Fuzzy, having been requested by the cop who was outside the tent. He had a Laconia-paid chauffeur to the Laconia PD station on Fair Street. Although the Tuttle Farm was in Gilford, Laconia was the central location for Bike Week festivities and potential biker violations. They at least had a lock-up facility, if needed.

The sound of the two departing bikes drowned out the woman and man in their moment of heat and conjugal rights. Fuzzy would deal with them later. He didn't expect the interview downtown to be all that long. He was mistaken.

Chapter 64

Don Wright exited the Planet Fitness facility at the Belknap Mall complex on Route 3 / 11A in Belmont. The Mall, adjacent to Laconia proper, was barely west over the town line and Don tried to get there three to four times a week for exercise. They opened early and the massive exercise room and equipment touted the latest in elliptical machines, treadmills and aerobic bikes for cardio health. Additionally, there were ample numbers of weight machines for upper and lower torso strengthening including free weights and the pulley machines with resistance weights for adding and deleting incremental iron at will. The Body Master machines also included abdominal exercises and the fitness plan allowed one to use the tanning beds and elaborate washroom and shower facilities after workouts.

Don had just finished working out for an hour. He entered the nearby back door Mall entrance by Shaw's Supermarket and picked up a newspaper. It had just been delivered to the store. The front page had one of Don's photos, a biker entering Lakeside Avenue at the site of the Weirs Beach sign. He was the epitome of the black leather rider. The background of the photo was a sea of motorcycles parked on Lakeside Avenue and along the boardwalk. The header in the article read, "THEY'RE BACK," reminiscent of the famous movie and line that young Drew Barrymore had once starred in as a child. The famed Weirs sign was illuminated and celebrating fifty years of existence in the year 2006, an art deco icon of lights.

The local Laconia newspaper touted the official beginning of Bike Week, even though riders had been arriving for days. It listed the major events and times for the next two days, especially the social functions at

The Weirs. The newspaper focused on the annual biker ritual touting a paragraph that was akin to a Jeff Foxworthy "redneck" preamble: *"You know it's bike week in Laconia when you hear the continuous sound of loud pipes, the compelling smell of leather and fried food and the ever-present appeal of loose women and tattooed men in muscle shirts. "*The quote was not meant to be condescending to newspaper readers or leather riders for that matter, but rather an enticement to the locals and visitors to participate in all the officially sanctioned spectator events listed in the paper. That revenue and those vendor fees helped defray the cost of police surveillance, traffic flow monitoring and race safety oversight—a huge drain on the local city budget if out-of-town attendance was low for the week. Any unpredictable bad weather could impact the cash flow as well, if attendance fell off the mark. Generally, the influx of out-of-town riders increased each year and Laconia counted on it for financial purposes. Their goal was to end up in the black, not red.

The events listed included the schedule of races prior to and during Father's Day weekend, including racer time trials and preview biographies of the best professional riders in the competition, those who were competing at NHIS on Father's Day weekend.

The schedule for the forthcoming events always highlighted the annual "hill climb" at Gunstock Ski Area off Route 11A in Gilford; an exciting mountain event for serious racers that loved to challenge fear.

Ancillary activities included the sidebar events such as an impromptu women's Jell-O wrestling contest at a local campground, bikini and wet T-shirt events, a tattoo contest at a popular Weirs Beach restaurant and bar, and the "hairiest back" contest for men. Thank God, there were no similar hair contests for women, the public voiced. All of the events that encompassed the week were designed to appeal to every visitor or resident, race fans or not. One did not have to follow the professional road racing circuit to find something of merit to participate in or watch. Even the "Slowest Bike" race at the train depot was popular. Roy Cole of New Jersey was always slower than Guy St. Cyr of Quebec. Cole had won in previous years as well.

Don Wright passed by the Case n' Keg, the local convenience store, Irwin Marine, an electrical supply store and numerous fast food venues that dotted the road as he headed east toward Gilford. The Laconia Motorcycle Week Association office was off to the right and diagonally across from the Dairy Queen. Don knew the director at LMWA well but he was not in that particular day—the small office of which offered mementos for collectors and sold memorabilia for the previous 2005 and current 2006 Bike Rallies. There were hats, rally pins and patches, CD-ROMs of prior event years, and still photos of unique bike-related subject matter. The commemorative patches and pins were collectibles for both the locals and visitors. Some people had acquired dozens from years past.

Don bought a shirt, pin and ball cap for his friend, George Adams. He was going to be seeing him that day and thought he owed him a present for all his help with Wendell's journals. After leaving the Motorcycle Association gift shop, Don drove his Ducati north after having taken a left at Bayside Cemetery and Jon's Roast Beef. The view of Paugus Bay was beautiful on the left side of the journey.

He passed the King's Grant Inn, the only local venue for exotic dancing. The restrictions of the Gilford selectmen, who didn't want that kind of offering in their town, had made it difficult for the King's Grant to operate their entertainment. The women were never totally naked and there was an ongoing court battle involving "free speech" and the right for the motel owner to have exotic dance offerings for the public. Bike Week applications for semi-nude dancing by the motel owner included a "Ms. Bike Week" contest with audience participation, and an outdoors "Bike Washing" event by women that were scantily dressed. It had been at issue since 2003. The selectmen cited numerous "liquor violations" of the motel operation, which needed to be resolved before the exotic dancing could be approved. It was a stalemate and ongoing battle.

Bikers wanted to see T&A anyway and the King's Grant was the only real venue close to The Weirs. Oddly, one could see more ass at The Weirs or at the racetrack in Loudon, for free. The women who danced at the King's Grant relied on the revenue during Bike Week. They were missing their income—dollars stuffed in the their G-strings or generated from a $20 lap dance. *What's a girl gonna do? Ya gotta make a livin',* Don mused as he passed by the motel complex. *Gilford was so stodgy,* he thought.

Bikes were lined up at the motel late at night, bikers taunting the women to bare it all, but each knowing that there were restrictions on the amount of clothing they could remove. It was the only game in town, so to speak.

The road from Gilford to The Weirs was lined with cottages and motels, one of which was the former Peyton Place Motel owned by author, Grace Metalious, many years earlier. Her writing fame (*Peyton Place*) had briefly gained her wealth and she had purchased the motel and given it the infamous name from her first controversial novel. Having died in 1964, she was now a legend from nearby Gilmanton, New Hampshire and the motel had changed names over the years. Don wasn't sure that he knew which structure it actually was now. Many venues, additions and modifications had occurred over decades and on that road to The Weirs. Most people said it was the Bay Top Motel.

Don slowed down as the traffic became more congested, sometimes stopping on the road north. The closer he got to The Weirs / the Paugus

Bay Bridge, the worse it got—bikes were at a standstill and it was stop and go all the way to Lakeside. He was anxious to see George Adams. He had questions to which only George might have the answers.

Police enforcement was always increased on Lakeside Avenue with support by officers from virtually every town in New Hampshire, including the sheriff departments, the State Police and other local authorities that volunteered officers as part of mutual or community aid.

Chapter 65

This particular June 2006 had started with foul weather, Mother Nature being what she is and unpredictable in the Northeast. The local TV channel in Manchester, New Hampshire had prophesized a mixed bag week, weather-wise. They played down the potential precipitation residents surmised, so that people would not be discouraged from attending Rally Week. The rain of days one and two of the nine-day event had kept the crowd rather subdued and "street legal"—meaning very few incidents and violations were cited on and off the roads. There had only been nine arrests thus far amongst the thousands of attendees that had arrived in the initial two days.

Motorcycle accidents were few, early in the game, and the police and EMS staff was thankful for the lower number of incidents and low severity of injuries. One crash off Route 11 required a helicopter Medi-Vac to the Hanover, New Hampshire trauma unit, the affiliated Mary Hitchcock Hospital of Dartmouth Medical School. The biker lived, thanks to the quick response of the EMS services.

The "Tattoo Contest" on Tuesday of Bike Week was of interest to local authorities and also to Don Wright who was researching the Vincent logo on the dead woman's body. *Might the logo appear again on someone else?* he wondered.

Don arrived early at the bar where the contest was to be held, complete with camera in hand. It was adjacent to the Weirs Drive-In aggregate of tents—a carnival in and of itself. One of the most popular venues each year was a "massage" tent. It was a showstopper for pedestrians in that the massage therapist was a very fit woman dressed in a thong and leather top.

With her back to the onlookers, her lower attire consisted of a skimpy outfit complete with a raccoon tail dangling between her butt cheeks. Virtually every person with a disposable camera captured the sight as the vendor used her hand, arm and leg strength to knead the back of a large biker who was sitting in the preformed, massage chair. The woman, with a ponytail, was steadfast; her feet planted solidly into the sandy soil while pressing her entire weight into the biker's *Latisimus dorsi* muscles on each side of the biker's spine. His "lats" were pronounced and she relaxed the skeletal muscles by pressing her elbows and palms into each muscle layer—first with a circular motion that mimicked someone polishing the hood of a car.

The raccoon tail was swinging with each motion of her upper body—her own thighs and biceps well defined and pronounced as she gave it her all. The client biker was obviously loving ever moment of it, moaning in ecstasy. When she finished, he was like Jell-O.

After an hour with George Adams, Don entered the Broken Spoke Saloon north of The Weirs on Route 3, and where it was apparent that most of the patrons were either tattooed, pierced, enshrouded in or covered with leather and artistic graphics, some inked art pieces covering the majority of their extremities. One biker was a "walking billboard" for the tattoo industry. His neck, shoulders, chest, arms, thighs and calves were myriad of colors and painted scenes of bikes, roads, riders, women, naked body parts, logos, dragons and tigers; every one of the creations seemed to encircle his body and intertwine around his muscular frame.

It was immediately apparent that he had to have spent most of his adult life and savings in tattoo parlors. The biker was bald, revealing more tattoos that adorned his head and neck. Upon first glance he seemed to be a member of a gang or cult, almost Neo-Nazi in appearance and stereotype. Oddly, he was not of those leanings. Don thought at first, that he was a revitalized Mr. Clean, but with sunglasses.

He was akin to a modern day sailor, like "Sailor Jerry," and took that name for his own after one of the most famous tattoo artists in the world. "Sailor Jerry" Collins (1911-1973) was a sailor who operated a well-ascribed tattoo shop in Honolulu. People sought him out for his brilliant color graphics. The original "Sailor Jerry's" memory lives on today, almost as if he was still around.

The Broken Spoke had its own infamous reputation occasionally and was the epitome of a traditional Biker bar. The bar's motto was, "Keep the shiny side up and the rubber side down."

In Laconia, the annual tattoo contest touted awards for many categories: the best black and gray, best portrait, sleeve, color, back piece, overall male, overall female and the best cover-up.

The police had interest in this particular tattoo event in 2006, primarily because of the recent death at The Weirs. Don Wright noted their increased presence and wondered if they were looking for what he was looking for—a Vincent tattoo on somebody . . . anybody. The focus of the police was on all New Hampshire and New England tattoo parlors, special contests and potential biker gang rivalries that might reveal bike manufacturer logos on skin.

Chapter 66

In Portland, Maine, during the previous April 2005, bikers wearing the colors of The Outlaws motorcycle gang had entered a tattoo parlor and shot a Hell's Angels member, not in the abdomen or back, but in the groin. Dennis Towne was seriously injured from the unmitigated accosting.

The Outlaws and Hell's Angels were planning on attending Bike Week in Laconia in 2006. Preliminary intelligence led the police to believe that there would be issues near the Angel's clubhouse at Weirs Beach. It was temporarily located adjacent to The Crazy Gringo Mexican restaurant at the north end of Lakeside Avenue.

In Conway, New Hampshire, a young woman shot and killed a tattoo artist with a .357 magnum in 2005, claiming that she had never held a gun before in her life. The family of the victim was astounded when the young woman was not prosecuted. That crime occurred much earlier than the dates of the 2005 Rally Week and was unrelated to the June event.

Still, the Lakes Region police saw tattoo-related crimes as part of the overall biker world. The loss of the young woman at The Weirs prompted a vigilant lookout for all tattoo-related, social and contestant interactions for 2006. They did not desire a repeat of the previous year's adverse motorcycle gang threats and gun issues. The loss of the young woman might have been gang-related payback—but for what reason, if any?

Don Wright was unaware that the police were also scouting the same bar for unusual tattoos, those that might relate to the Vincent logo. Don had already photographed "Sailor Jerry" for the newspaper's "Faces of Bike Week" segment. He also had a chance to chat briefly with "Jerry."

"Ya gonna win for sure," Don commented. "You got quite the assortment of colors. We're featuring you in tomorrow's paper."

"Cool," remarked the sailor. "I've won a few of these contests. I've come here from California. Met the real "Sailor Jerry" in the earlier seventies when I lived in Hawaii. I live in Venice Beach now. I'm sort of a carryover from the 'flower power' days," he joked, while pointing to a rose on his shoulder and an accompanying San Francisco Golden Gate bridge on his chest. The bridge was covered in peace signs and flowers.

Don was enthralled that the guy actually wanted to chat. He had been warned that "Jerry" was too popular to want to deal with stupid questions from the press.

Don took the opportunity to have the man expand on his tattoos.

"What's you favorite tattoo?" Don asked, with interest. "I've never seen so many."

"This *chick* here," he pointed. "Sailor Jerry did that one for me before he died."

Don was impressed. The young women looked like a Vargas girl from the old Playboy magazine days. Alberto Vargas lived 1896-1982. In 1940, he introduced the Varga Girls, leaving the "s" off the name. The women were on calendars and posters during WWII. The watercolor and symmetrical bodies were almost like an airbrushed photograph. On "Sailor Jerry," was one of the most beautiful tattoos Don had ever seen imprinted on skin with tattoo ink. Playboy and Vargas worked together for 18 years, starting in 1960, creating over 150 different sensual drawings of ladies. "Sailor Jerry" had on one of the classics, right there in front of Don.

"Gorgeous Vargas Girl," he commented. "What about bike logos?" Don asked, as people gathered around the tattooed man to see the variety of natural art pieces.

"Got'em all," he replied, removing his muscle shirt. "Most are Harley logos." Don noted a Vincent logo amongst the Harley and Indian chief profiles. He was surprised to see it, fostering a whole new conversation. The police had not noticed the Vincent image.

"Vincent?" Don continued. "That's an old one."

"Yup . . . ya won't see many of them," remarked the tattooed man. "Nobody gives a shit'bout the old bikes. They were the tradition and these young chicks in this place never rode one of those fuckers," he laughed. "They were cool bikes—the Brits made them, ya know."

"Yah . . . I've seen some of the old ones. Did you own one at one time?" asked Don.

"Ya . . . once upon a time. 'Had a Black Shadow. Sold it years ago."

Don studied the logo closely. The figure of the Roman god, Mercury, was *lifelike*. "Sailor Jerry" was proud of that tattoo and touted the Roman god as manly and virulent.

"Gotta' go," said "Jerry." "The contest's about to start. Nice talkin' to ya."

"I'm Don," he said, shaking hands. "Hope ya win. Either way, you'll be in the morning paper," added Don. "Sailor Jerry" smiled and winked. "I'll win," he offered, arrogantly and with confidence. "Nobody has the shit that I have. They're all pussies—you just watch."

Don intermingled with the crowd. Nothing anyone else had compared to the artwork of "Sailor Jerry's" human billboard torso. He was sure to win the men's division.

Don had photographed a close-up of the Vincent logo on "Sailor." It might just have future relevance to the dead woman's plight. The tattoo, however, was not recent and might just be a coincidence in the overall scheme of things.

Chapter 67

Tattooist, Fuzzy Walsh was shown a picture of the tattoo that was taken of the dead woman's lower body. It was a close-up photograph with decent resolution, one of which he admitted looked like *his* work. Another photo of the girl's face confirmed that he recognized her as the woman who accompanied the Iceman. He was shocked and saddened by the photos wondering why she was dead and how he was being implicated in her demise.

"Tammy, you say?" asked the policeman. "That's the name you recall as her name?"

"Yes," he replied, solemnly. "She was so young and pretty. What could have happened?"

"That's what we hope to find out," added the detective, studying all the expressions of Fuzzy's face. He appeared to detectives to be seriously remorseful and concerned for this early loss of life.

"We think she was the victim of foul play. There was no evidence at the scene that she had been killed, but she was naked and may have been placed there by someone, or tossed from a boat for that matter."

"Why me? What do I have to do with her or this?" asked Fuzzy, readjusting his buttocks in a stiff chair in the police station. He seemed to fidget and was uncomfortable with the line of questioning from the authorities, at times being bombarded with queries in rapid-fire motion. He was shell-shocked, but compliant.

"So . . . it's my tattoo job but I didn't kill this girl. She left with a brute of a man . . . I told you earlier. *Iceman* was his name. Go find him," Fuzzy expressed, with anger. "She was fine when she left my tent."

The detectives empathized with the artist. He didn't seem to be directly involved, however, he might have other evidence that could help the police and the coroner. He was their only real lead to date.

One detective, in a shirt and tie, raked his fingers through his hair as if repeatedly combing it backwards, slowly and methodically. His back was to Fuzzy. Turning around, he continued offering statements and questions that might add clues. He was trying to bait Fuzzy for more info.

"It's apparent that you may have been one of the last to see her alive. You also mention some guy named, 'Iceman.' Do you know the man that was with her? Ever seen him before in the campground or was he a prior customer?"

"No. I have no clue about him. First time I ever saw him, or her, for that matter. He was huge and paid for the girl's tattoo in new bills—fresh twenties as I recall. I figured she was his lady for the week, that's all. They came in on a Harley Softail."

The detective was taking notes on a pad while Fuzzy closed his eye to try and recall more information

"Did you see the license plate? The tag?" asked the cop.

"Not really. It was not an New Hampshire plate, maybe tan in color."

"New Jersey has tan plates, Fuzzy. Might it have been a New Jersey plate?" the detective asked. "Lots of people come up from New York and New Jersey."

Fuzzy looked off in the distance as if he were thinking deeply. He squinted and shook his head as if he couldn't remember. "I really don't know. I see too many bikes and plates."

"Anything else, Mr. Walsh . . . that you can think of?" asked the detective. He was pretty much done with the initial inquiry when Fuzzy perked up. "He had a vest that said, 'Rough Riders' or something. Yah . . . 'Rough Riders' and some town."

"Anything else jog your memory of this guy?"

Fuzzy stood and gestured, pacing nervously.

"Yah . . . come to think of it," he added, snapping his fingers repeatedly, "this guy, Iceman, brought his own black ink bottle."

"What?" the detective asked, stepping closer. "His own ink? Why?"

"Yah. He had a bottle of black ink that he preferred for the girl's tattoo . . . the Vincent tattoo. I didn't care since it seemed like a professional brand I had seen on the Internet."

"Jesus. His own ink? Isn't that unusual? Don't you usually use your own ink and professional brands for tattoo colors, black or whatever?"

"Yes . . . I have my own selection of inks . . . all colors of the rainbow," remarked Fuzzy Walsh. "I wasn't about to argue with the guy. Black ink is *black* ink. They pretty much come from the same distributor anyway."

"That could be an important clue here. Maybe the ink was not professional, was tainted or was some other stuff," spoke the detective. "Do you have the bottle that he gave you, back in your tent?"

Fuzzy was quick to respond. "Hell, no. This guy, the Iceman, took it with him."

"Is there anything remaining from the tattooing? Like the needle or anything with the ink still on it or in it?" he asked, in rapid fire.

"Nah . . . the campsite is cleaned each night. The barrels and any waste are tossed. The needle is gone, the towels and gauze we use during the tattooing are destroyed, burned or autoclaved to maintain sterility. It's considered medical waste and must be removed."

"Shit!" said the detective. "Are you sure there is nothing left?" he said, with desperation. He was pacing and rubbing his forehead with one hand.

"Nothing," Fuzzy replied, looking straight at the man.

"That sucks," he shouted. "We have to find this Iceman dude."

The detective and an assistant asked Fuzzy to stay local and to get in touch with them if the Iceman reappeared. Fuzzy was a potential witness and had known young Tammy only briefly. He might be needed for further questioning in the days to come, especially if the investigation led to some other clues and / or the return of the Iceman.

After the personal interrogation of Mr. Walsh, the police exchanged contact information by way of business cards and drove Fuzzy back to the campsite in Gilford. If he was leaving town, he was to let them know. They wanted to be in touch with him should the Iceman be seen, apprehended and brought in for questioning.

Entering the driveway to the campsite, the police dropped him off near the main road. He wanted to walk the rest of the way to his tent. The cops indicated that they would be in touch.

Outside of the tent, there were two people waiting for tattoos and they were impatient. The note on the tent had said, *Be Right Back . . . Fuzzy.*

Chapter 68

The people waiting for Fuzzy had been there for two hours. Disgruntled was their demeanor at this point. Fuzzy apologized and noted that the motorcycle that was parked at the sex tent next door had left. The nymphomaniac and her lover had disappeared for a while, he surmised. He was sure they would be back when she had the hornies again. That's pretty much the scenario he had witnessed the day before. He knew they needed to come up for air on occasion and get food. Fuzzy had offered her a free tattoo if she "serviced" him. He wasn't that lucky.

She had refused to perform the oral compensation, even though her boyfriend agreed to watch. Fuzzy had tattooed the same guy the year before. The chick had no qualms over her desire for sexual satisfaction. She was merely inhibited about threesomes for some odd reason. Fuzzy found that odd. He was going to trade a $100 rose tattoo for a blowjob. *Fair deal. Her loss,* he thought.

After the police had left him off, Fuzzy fired up the Honda generator and returned to his trade. His first client wanted a commemorative tattoo of the 2006 Bike Week. Fuzzy managed to give him a composite tattoo of the Bike Week logo for $300. He was done in less than an hour, a colorful rendition of The Weirs sign and year of the event. The guy left without admitting to the pain in his upper torso. He wanted it centered on his shaved chest—an area that was sensitive, uncomfortable and high in nerve endings.

The tattooed biker was a weird duck. He also wanted his scrotum pierced with a ring. Fuzzy complied after trying to dissuade the man. He wore two pairs of gloves for that bizarre job. The charge was another $100, much to the chagrin of the biker. Fuzzy added a fee just for the aggravation of the unusual anatomical site. He didn't consider piercings, "art," but he loved the money.

*   *   *

Don Wright had plowed through some of the voluminous notes and journals from Wendell's many years at The Weirs. While hanging out with George Adams on his porch, he perused the pile of journals one by one, seeking specific accounts of prior Bike Week rallies—some of note. Most notations by Wendell were historical accounts of the earliest days when motorcycle "touring" was just emerging as a sport and were weekend social events. They captured the era of the birth of the two-wheeled transportation industry.

One of the earliest notations by Wendell was his recollection of the visit of Howard Davies to the United States and, in particular, a visit to the State of New Hampshire. The late, Wendell Atkins had noted that in 1917, Davies and his partner, E.J. Massey from England, had created prototype motorbikes for the future commercial HRD models of that era. Davies had spent years designing specific bikes, at least conceptually on paper and in his mind.

The early conceptive designs were generated during World War II and after he had been shot down in Europe and captured by the Germans. At that point, Davies had fantasized and envisioned the construction of the *perfect* motorcycle, one that would eventually become the commercial line of Vincents. The Germans could confine him physically, but not capture his mind and imagination. Creativity flowed during his incarceration.

Don was excited about reading the text and the references to Davies. They were locked in his mind and appeared to have relevance to the local photographer's quest for answers.

Was that history of the two men in England pertinent? Perhaps that of which Wendell was alluding to just before he died? Did Davies and the early bikes somehow play a role in the girl's death? Don wondered. *Could it be that Vincent motorbikes were there before the first Rally and races in Laconia? Was that a historical clue to any deaths then, or now for that matter?*

Don read with vigor. Wendell had maintained most of the information in chronological order but some books were out of place. There were numerous boxes to scan to find isolated volumes. Don sighed out of frustration. He paced on the porch flipping pages as he walked.

George Adams watched Don, as he seemed to be impatient with the sourcing of the years. "Slow down, son. They ain't goin' nowhere."

Don apologized to the elderly gentleman for his hastiness and preoccupation with the task at hand. He was excited and overwhelmed all in one fell swoop. He stopped and took a couple of deep breaths. His face was red from bending over the cadre of notes and books. He hardly noticed the women walking down Lakeside, often with little clothing. George Adams, on the other hand, never missed a sight from the road.

Finally, he spoke. He was over the piles of journals on the wide board floor. "What the hell are you doin', son?" he remarked, with laughter. "You're missing many of the notes . . . jumping back and forth like that. You're also missin' the sights down on the sidewalk, son. Take a break. There's eye candy down there. Lots of good shots to take."

Don grabbed his Nikon and took some photos to appease George Adams. Shortly thereafter, he refocused on the pile of journals. He was on a roll, chronologically yet he wanted to be cordial to Adams.

Don sat on the floor again and crossed his legs, Indian style. George merely shook his head and smiled. This kid was dedicated to the mission at hand.

"Damn, I need those missing clues," Don voiced with frustration.

"What the hell for?" interrupted George, squinting and frowning while focusing on the issue. "That's a long time ago."

"I'm lookin' for Wendell's notes that might hint of an anniversary of something—birth of the motorcycle, birth of the founders of Vincent, their deaths . . . anything at all.

George perked up. "'Haste makes waste' . . . slow down." Don scratched his head.

"I know George. There must be something here somewhere, but I wanted to read what Wendell wrote about bike events during the earliest years and some journals are out of sequence. I have a hunch it's important."

George Adams saw no relevance to any particular task Don had going on. He was unaware of Don's thinking—that the quarterly or half-centennial anniversary years of the Vincent history might be a clue to the dead girl's investigation. George wasn't in the loop with Don's way of thinking or quest. George went back to observing the young bikers on the street below.

Don thumbed through many journals and notes and finally found a reference to the year, 1923. The Laconia Rally began then but no anniversary dates jived with his theory.

He was sweating from the stress of not finding a relationship.

The journals were out of order in the grand scheme of things and may have been looked at recently by Wendell. That might explain the chronologically misplaced volumes.

Chapter 69

Wendell may have skimmed many of his books shortly before he died hence the confusion. *If so, why? What was Wendell going to share with Don?* Wright wondered. *Hell, Wendell didn't know he was about to die. Somehow, he was anticipating being part of the puzzle Don was undertaking but fate interrupted the agenda perhaps,* Don mused.

Don sat silently on the porch deck while George picked up his German-made 400 X binoculars and studied the landscape of people on Lakeside. He was focusing on the women on the back of the passing bikes. He stood by the railing and leaned over the rail for support. He slowly scanned the crowd for scantily clad women. After all these years of watching the events, he was a pro at picking out the women of note. Every once in a while, he would comment on a hit.

"Will ya look at those hooters?" he screamed out like a teenager. The old man still had spunk.

Don always acknowledged the comments with a smile. "She'd kill ya, George. Quit lookin' at tits. That stuff is no good for ya. Bad for the heart."

George casually responded, "I could easily handle that babe. Viagra, my man. Viagra!"

Don paid the elder man no mind. His focus was on the journal in front of him, the leather binding still in excellent condition.

He flipped though the journal pages, looking for key words He was dumbstruck by how *interesting* the articles were in content and context, revealing details of the two-wheeled machines that people rode in the 1960's in particular, and earlier.

The Japanese impact on the industry had yet to take hold in America but the Asian countries were well aware of the name, Honda. It was a mode of inexpensive transportation in Japan and Korea.

Wendell had alluded to the impact of the Japanese manufacturers on the motorcycle industry in the 60's. Motorcycles and motorcylists still had the bad image of the black leather, bomber jacket crowd and oil slicks. They portrayed a "dirty" image, Harleys included.

Honda had reservations as to the "market" of their bikes in the U.S. Takeo Fugisawa, Managing Director of Honda, had Kihachiro Kawashima survey Europe, Asia and eventually America for sales potential. *The years, 1956 and 1957 were critical annual goals for expansion to other countries besides Korea.*

Was that the link? The impact of the Japanese on the U.S. motorcycle industry?

2006 was the 50th anniversary of Japan's attempt to market in the States. The problem was that the Japanese needed a few more years to break into North America.

The Japanese were offering the Honda Dream (250-350cc models) and the Benly (125cc) as an alternative to the bicycle for transportation, especially to Asia. Soichiro Honda was directly involved, and the emergence of the Honda 50 (Super Cub) at $250 enticed the U.S. marketplace. It appealed to women, of all things, with its wide front panel preventing skirts from flying up. *Innovative,* Wendell had noted in his comments. He actually had studied their history, Don noticed.

Eventually, Honda broke into America with an office in Los Angeles. By 1961, Honda was saturating the existing American motorcycle market of 50-60,000 units per year. They were advertising with "color" ads in *Life* and on TV, spending $70-80K/ printed ad and $300K for two, 90-second commercials. That was enormous dollars back then.

Thus 1964 was a breakthrough year for Honda and by 1966, 40,000 units were being sold in the U.S., many models of which were the Honda 50. As public demand increased, Honda ventured into larger cc engines / models as well as sport and racing bike offerings. The lull in some sales during the Vietnam War, impacted by some distain for Asians by the U.S., had been surpassed marketwise and Honda grew in spite of it all. Their new bikes were fast and quiet. American made bikes were shuddering at the infringement into their industry. The "rice rockets" had arrived and were here to stay and the 1960's invasion by the Japanese provided no clues to an anniversary of that era. Don Wright was stumped. He now felt that the 1950's were worth investigating. His persistence was to be rewarded.

Chapter 70

Don located various pages in many journals that seemed unusual. They were not hand-written by Wendell like the others that had been recorded, a digression of sorts in his notations. In particular, there were old newspaper clippings that caught Don's attention. They popped up out of the blue and Don observed prior bookmarks on certain pages, or dog-eared folds on others that suggested that someone else had recently reviewed them. *Could Wendell have been scanning them recently?* Don wondered. The indications were there.

Wendell, in some secretive manner, was setting Don up for his own investigation. The newspaper clippings included accounts of some deaths or motor vehicle accidents during many Laconia Rallies.

Select obituaries listed local residents and also out-of-town bikers that had been killed in accidents including Father's Day week and weekend.

Don Wright stood and backed into the nearest seat he could reach, which was Wendell's old rocker. He couldn't read the articles fast enough. He stared at the journals intensely, often looking at George Adams with a blank stare or confusion. *Had one of the deaths occurred fifty years earlier that mimicked the events of the past week?* Don was dumbfounded.

George, noting Don's confusion and bizarre demeanor, asked him what was the matter. "Wad'ya find, son?" Don's brow was furrowed.

"Jesus," Don replied, obvious frown lines, now valleys. "It says here that a young woman died, and was found near the Weirs Beach area. Right here," he added, showing George the clippings from the first of several relevant pages. "But there is no date!"

"Just like the death the other day," says here, he expressed while pointing with his index finger. Don opened the page wider for George to examine and read. George reached for his reading glasses on a side table.

George nodded and rubbed the overnight stubble on his chin. "Sounds familiar."

"Maybe there's a pattern here," Don expressed to George with candor. "Look at this. Says here that she had tattoos on her body—one with the name, *Vincent* in it! That was years ago, for Chrissake, and here we are in 2006 with a dead girl and a tattoo with the same damn name, *Vincent.* Jesus H. Christ!" Don exclaimed, in amazement.

"What the fuck is going on? What year did this happen? Crap!"

George Adams became more alert with the revelation. He bridged his nose with his hands, eyes closing for the moment. Suddenly, he snapped his fingers as if a light bulb went off in his brain. He looked up at the sky and then across the lake, pondering some memory fog that was incomplete. It was age related and the details escaped him for the moment. He waited for his thoughts to clear.

"Come to think of it, son, I remember that event. Give me a minute. Wendell and I had talked about that exact death from years ago. He brought it up earlier in the week and out of the blue . . . and I paid him no mind." George acknowledged, somewhat disgusted by his inability to recollect pieces of yesteryear.

"Wendell said that it was important anyway. Guess I should have listened to him. He wanted me to take notes and I was too busy watchin' the girly show on the street." George was sad. "Now he's gone and I can't remember what the hell he was talkin' about."

"Not to worry, George. Wendell obviously was focused on this coincidence and wanted your input. I think he was looking at this journal last week. The bookmark is a bank slip dated this month, 2006. He was definitely seeking out some clues to the dead girl. Sneaky little guy that he was."

George Adams rested his rear end against the railing on the porch. He was desperately trying to recall what Wendell had told him. His brain was not very forgiving this particular day. Don flipped though more pages. It was all right there in front of him. It was the jumpstart that he needed in the quest to solve the death of the unidentified, young woman. Was it deja vu?

Don, alone, had clues and leads that no one else had—he was on a major track forward. The police and the coroner were not even aware of the death. It was serendipitous that Don Wright had met Wendell and that Wendell's notes might hold the answer everyone was looking for. Don knew he was onto something big.

Don was amazed by the find—the parallel coincidence and, most of all, the reference to the *Vincent* tattoo. He had a pattern perhaps, a plot. He just knew it. He said little more to George and flipped more pages seeking related news stories to the earlier death. Surely, Wendell had kept more critical articles pasted in the journal. Don needed to know the date of the prior death and it was nowhere to be found.

Chapter 71

Don knew that he would need to visit the library. He felt the public resource might have detailed police logs from years ago. He thought of seeking help from the police but decided to pursue his hunch on his own. George could see that Don was possessed by the recent journal information. They hardly spoke, so George decided to initiate some dialogue. "You're under a spell, son."

"Yup," Don grunted. "I apologize but this has me intrigued . . . and mystified."

"Yah, you're in a different world for sure," George Adams responded, out of boredom.

"George . . . Wendell was trying to clue me in, don't you see? That was one day before he died. The two deaths of young women are related, damnit. I can feel it. Can't you see where this information is taking us? Same tattoo, similar agenda and location. My guess is something happened earlier than in the fifties as well, perhaps when Davies and Massey promoted their model motorcycle, the HRD—the predecessor to the Vincent motorcycle. It's speculation on my part but what the hell?"

George watched as Don stood to restack the piles of journals. He needed to get to the library as soon as possible and before they closed for the day. Don planned to research the early 1900's and determine if there had been a death at The Weirs that somehow related to motorcycles, and, in particular, the HRD and Vincent inventors. It was a long shot. George Adams was ambivalent to the theory.

Don could not be more excited. If his premonition was correct, there appeared to be a ritual that may have occurred every twenty-five, forty or fifty years and it could be related to Vincent motorcycles. The two dead women were somehow unwilling victims of an unknown, suspected ritual that Don has conjured up in his own mind. A rock had been turned over with the assorted journals but the actual dates were needed to confirm the theory—and all kinds of thing were about to crawl out. It gave Don the creeps.

Chapter 72

The New Jersey club member, Iceman and some of his disciples from the New Jersey Rough Riders had been cruising the area much of the day, back and forth on Lakeside at The Weirs and around the Lakes Region, in general. It was the thing to do. Iceman had Bonnie on the back of the bike having promised her a ride in return for "riding him" for an hour that morning.

They were hot and sweaty in their leathers and their campsite in Wolfeboro had no real shower facilities. Bikers often relied on the local lakes to cool off and clean up.

The entourage of Iceman followers pulled off the Elm Street area in Lakeport and rode down the hill near the old mill and dam at the end of Paugus Bay. A new hotel had been completed since their last visit to New Hampshire. It was called the Inn at Lake Opechee and was located next to a conference center that had been converted from a prior historic mill. To the right of the hotel were the dam and some partial woods. The water from Paugus and the Big Lake flowed into Lake Opechee at the site of the dam, an elevation of some twelve to fifteen feet above the level of Opechee. That rocky area below the dam opened up into a rapid flowing pool where kids generally swam and fished in the rapids. The egress of Paugus Bay into Opechee was deep at that point.

It's also a favorite fishing spot in the summer, a peninsula-like jetty where teenagers hung out, smoked and drank in seclusion. The water was conducive for the larger species of fish, offering safe haven for largemouth bass, trout and the occasional eel or cusk. They hibernated in winter there amongst the tall weeds, especially when their metabolism was low.

In summer, the rapids also provided oxygen and food for the fry of the natural fish population, particularly in the deepest end of Opechee. Not far from shore, the depths could run some 60 feet. Most of Opechee proper was in the 22-25 foot depth range. By July and August, the small lake was warmed by the sun and boaters and skiers often dropped anchor to relax and enjoy the warm water in the middle of the lake.

It was near dusk when the bikers arrived. The Rough Riders decided to strip down to their underwear and take a swim. Not all that unusual, it was as close to a bath as they could find . . . for free. Iceman dove in first and the others followed, leaving their leathers and worldly possessions on the shoreline and near a large rock on the peninsula. A continuum of motorcyclists passed on the bridge above while roaring down Elm Street, a well-traveled conduit that allowed access from Parade Road and Route 106 to Union Avenue in Lakeport.

All main roads in the area were crowded with bikes and cars, providing consumers who increased revenues for the local Case n' Keg convenience store, Fratello's Ristorante, McDonalds, KFC, Dairy Queen, Friendly's and a host of other eating establishments in the greater Laconia area.

After rinsing off for fifteen minutes in refreshing Lake Opechee, Iceman, Bonnie and friends dressed, broke open some beers from their saddle bags and relaxed on the shore. Within an hour of their swim, they were headed to a side road that eventually led to Route 11, a direct route to their campground in Wolfeboro. They had a long way home, which they easily accessed by way of Gilford, Alton Bay and then Wolfeboro proper. The ride would be no less than an hour due to the local traffic that dominated the two-lane narrow roads.

Iceman didn't care much about the masses of bikes. He had been drinking Bud most of the day and was following the lines in the road much of the way home.

Don Wright was riding his Ducati when he noticed a vest that touted the New Jersey Rough Riders' semi-circular insignia and club name lettered in gold. He was on his way home from George Adams' lakeside home. A red light prevented him from following the group of bikes that had turned left toward Route 11. The light by Brooks Pharmacy was inordinately long and he had no idea where the bikers were going. Frustrated, he jumped the light ahead of on-coming traffic, almost causing an accident. Loud horns from passing cars and two bikes resounded in protest of his unanticipated actions. A couple of solitary "middle fingers" went up as well. Don could have cared less. By the time he was at the Route 11 intersection, he had no clue which way they had gone—straight ahead or north or south on Route 11 proper.

"Damn," he shouted from behind his full-faced bike helmet. "Where the hell did they go?" Frustrated, he rode straight ahead toward Gunstock

Ski Area. He spotted no members of the group. They had probably taken a left onto Route 11 toward Alton Bay.

At the next intersection near old Gilford Village and the local library, he stopped and pounded his handlebars with both gloved fists. They were the motorcycle club he had been seeking. His only recourse was to hope to see them in the forthcoming days.

Chapter 73

Once Iceman and his colleagues arrived back in Wolfeboro, they planned to meet and discuss the recent events that had been reported in the newspapers. They knew that the Laconia police were trying to identify the dead woman at The Weirs. Iceman figured that his Rough Riders club would be back on the road to New Jersey at week's end. That gave the authorities little time to identify the girl or to try and figure out what had happened to her. His arrogance was only surpassed by the determination of the local police.

Iceman had no clue that the police had been interacting daily with the coroner and had also interviewed Fuzzy Walsh, the tattoo artist in Gilford. Iceman was also unaware that Don Wright, the local photographer for a Laconia newspaper, was pursuing a theory of a possible historical ritual that might be related to the Laconia Rallies of the past, and the Vincent motorcycle, iconic Mercury logo history.

The serendipitous theory of the Vincent logo being related to the deaths of two or more women was a one-in-a-million chance, since no one but Don Wright had ever met up with Wendell Atkins or George Adams at the Veteran's Home on Lakeside Avenue.

The coroner and police who had investigated the crime scene on the beach that week had avoided Wendell when he had expressed some knowledge of the Vincent artwork on her lower back. Wendell's input was basically overlooked at the scene and he returned to his home in disgust. It was Don Wright that had noted his verbal comment and followed up with Wendell Atkins appropriately.

The police visit to Fuzzy's tattoo tent had elucidated during their investigation, that the girl's name was Tammy. Don was unaware that the police had clues of a partial I.D., one that he did not have. Don had no knowledge of the campground tattooist or the Iceman and girl's visit to the Gilford tattooist.

No one interviewed during Rally and Bike Week could even relate to the remote death of a "Tammy" someone. With Bike Week events now in full swing, few people seemed to care. Some chick had died and that was that—the majority of bikers read few news updates of the crime. They were preoccupied.

Weirs Beach was buzzing with an infusion of thousands of visitors to the entire Lakes Region. They shared Laconia, Loudon, Meredith and The Weirs in a continuous parade of bikes and pedestrians, virtually rambling about with no agenda, 24-hours-a-day. By three or four o'clock in the morning, the crowd had settled down to a few hundred stragglers, until daybreak broke again and the process of a contiguous flow of bikes began around breakfast. That's when the local Paugus and Tilt'n Diners opened and catered to the masses who were hung over and hungry for rapid food. The Tilt'n Diner grabbed the crowd at Exit 20 off I-93 while other fast food venues capitalized on the hungry visitors riding all the way to Laconia and Gilford. Some motorcycle riders took advantage of Route 140 straight to Gilmanton and to the NHIS racetrack in Loudon. It was a short cut to Route 106 from Exit 20 as well. The Route 106 crowd fed off of Honey Dew Donuts, the Egg Shell Restaurant and M&J's Restaurant. The police had checked each restaurant for waitress names. They did not restrict themselves to The Weirs area in the search of the girl's I.D. They sought the name, "Tammy" in every conceivable place, north to south and east to west.

*   *   *

Iceman had conspicuously hid the bottle of black ink quite well. Fuzzy had not used all of it and the artist returned the container to Iceman after the Vincent logo had been applied to Tammy's lower spine. Fuzzy Walsh had told the police that it was early evening when he had applied the tattoo. He really couldn't remember the exact time. Days became nights and nights became days when he was busy. The interrogation at the police station had yielded an approximate time and firm date of the visit.

Before Tammy and Iceman had departed, she had noted a funny feeling in her toes and ears. She paid it little mind thinking the toes were tingling from the position that she had assumed during the tattoo process. The sensation did seem odd to her however, because she had other tattoos that had not manifested that bizarre feeling.

"Is it supposed to tingle?" she had asked.

"Usually, there's a bit of pain but the cream I put on them should numb it a bit."

"Can I see it?" she asked. Iceman seemed in a hurry to go. He became frustrated when Fuzzy held up a mirror for her to view the logo.

"Ain't no time for that shit," Iceman voiced, with distain. "We gotta roll."

Tammy had a quick glance at the work on her lower back and smiled at Fuzzy's artwork with approval.

"Nice job, Fuzzy. You're the best."

Iceman took her hand and they departed the canvas studio. He had paid Fuzzy in advance for the "tramp stamp," a common street term for the location of the tattoo on the girl. Iceman had studied the girl's ass while Fuzzy was stenciling the logo just above her buttocks and he now had the urge to have his way with the little blonde anyway. He was anxious to "christen" the logo from behind. The impulse was dog-like and primal.

Fuzzy had not noticed anything unusual in the girl's response to his tattoo application . . . a tingling sensation was not uncommon. It was all in a night's work. Pretty much everyone reacted in some strange way to some limited pain and / or discomfort.

The majority of the tattoo was the black ink from Iceman's personal cache—it was the typical outlining and shadowing for the majority of the Vincent logo. A gold / amber color was used as a *filler color* for some shading on the statue of Mercury.

Iceman and Tammy didn't leave the campground right away. Tammy was a bit horned herself. He escorted the girl into the nearby woods stumbling in the limited light of dusk. They found an area that was out of the way, with numerous scrub white pines and blueberry shrubs. Iceman found a smooth rock to bend her over, and out of the view of the tented area of the open campground. The Vincent "tramp stamp" was visible to the large man. The thought of violating Tammy had him erect before he unzipped. There was no foreplay involved. She allowed him to enter her and was pained by his lack of preparation and his size. She was dry and it hurt.

When he finally ejaculated he had withdrawn in advance and made sure the fluids of his passion covered the new tattoo. It seemed bizarre to her but she was relieved to have him outside of her. He demanded she turn around and wash him off orally. She knelt in submission, cushioned by pine needles and moss. He was too huge to fight off so Tammy complied with the order. He grabbed her curly blonde hair and pressed her up against his groin, tilting his head back in domineering pleasure. She had just experienced the ultimate barbaric biker, something she had desired only when stoned with weed. It was ironic that she was neither stoned or under the influence of alcohol. She felt cheapened by the episode and said little before they left on the motorcycle.

Minutes later and without much conversation they departed the campground on Iceman's bike. Everything below her waist hurt Tammy but she said nothing to the Iceman. She still had the same tingling sensation that she experienced after she had been tattooed. It was weird and uncomfortable and persistent. She felt woozy on the back of his machine and held on to his waist out of fear of falling off. The Iceman sensed that she was uncomfortable and unsteady. He smiled as they rode up Route 11 North.

Chapter 74

Fuzzy had already been working on another client as the Iceman and Tammy rolled out the campground driveway entrance. The buzzing of the tattoo gun and generator that powered the lights and equipment continued well into the night. One drunken biker after another saw the pink flyer from the road and stopped to see if he was open in the evening. He was. That was when he made the most money.

* * *

Initial results of the autopsy concluded that "Jane Doe" or "The Lady of the Lake" had died of asphyxia; the definitive anatomical cause was however still unknown. Further blood tests would take a few days to weeks to analyze for the precise cause of death. Asphyxia could have resulted from smothering, although there was no physical evidence of a struggle or choking—or skin or hair under the nails suggesting a fight or physical resistance to an attacker. There were no obvious marks on the extremities or torso either.

A newspaper article, three days after the death of the girl, had indicated that Dr. Blaisdell, the coroner in Concord, would have further updates on the autopsy results as they presented themselves. His prime interest now was in the identification of the victim.

Blaisdell was considering all the autopsy data to date. Lack of oxygen could have explained a lot of causes for death. Aside from smothering, unknown drugs, prescriptions, a poison, or carbon monoxide, any host of chemicals might have resulted in the cessation of breathing and low oxygen concentration in her body.

Examination of the GI tract showed no evidence of drug capsules or tablet remnants in the lumen. Her stomach fluids were normal in color and the pH was within clinical parameters. Her blood seemed unaltered in clinical chemistry except for the lack of oxygen common to asphyxia, or low blood hemoglobin. He needed the ancillary toxicology tests to help discern the causes that precipitated the data that he had accumulated from the gross exam. Many of those tests had been farmed out to commercial biomedical labs.

Chapter 75

Don Wright tried to piece together some of the details from the Wendell Atkins journals, the coroner's intermediary findings, news articles and the suspected implication of the *Vincent* tattoo that Wendell suggested as valuable input.

Nothing to date made sense to Don since he was not trained in forensic medicine, pathology or clinical chemistry. He didn't believe that she died from choking or some violent event leading to asphyxia. His own camera had photographed the body and nothing was evident of a struggle . . . in any of the digital photos. Enlarging each photo led to nothing remarkable for marks or bruises on her body.

Although unaware of the police efforts to link Iceman and "Tammy" X to the bizarre scenario, Don had information that seemed to add a historical perspective to a potentially odd ritual; one that somehow related to the iconic Vincent motorcycle history or a bizarre tradition of older Rally Weeks at the Weirs. Don was not ready to share his theories with anyone.

Don had also speculated from the coroner's information in the newspapers that asphyxia or insufficient air to the lungs could have been the result of tattooing, albeit a stretch of one's imagination. His visit to the Lakeport tattoo parlor had enlightened him about the various inks that were used in the technique.

To Don, the acrylic-based pigments were suspect and known to travel from an injection site if they entered the bloodstream by error—a tattoo application that might have been applied too deep. Only microscopic evaluation of tissues (histology) would show if migration of an ink color was in other organs beside skin . . . i.e. the lungs.

The brightness of the black in the recent tattoo led him to believe that it might have been acrylic ink.

In Don's mind, if sufficient material was injected into the blood, the black ink might mimic tar and hydrocarbon particles normally associated with the long-term smoking of cigarettes. The initial coroner's report had revealed that she was a smoker and that gross examination of the hypoxic lungs showed black particles. Her first and second fingers on one hand showed a yellow stain on the skin. That was indicative of cigarette tar and other byproducts during the inspiration of tobacco smoke.

Could it be that acrylic plastic had entered the lungs in sufficient quantity to cause the lungs to fail? The coroner would not know microscopically until the pathology report was complete on all tissues, including the lobes of the lungs. It is unlikely that the coroner would suspect the acrylic pigments in the vascular system anyway. He was admittedly unaware of the detailed mechanics of tattoo application or the probable new inks involved.

Since Don didn't know the time, place or nature of the tattoo application, his theory was subjective but a credible medical concept . . . at least in his own mind. He was analytical in thought.

Was the tattoo water-based, alcohol-based or acrylic? His photos from the crime scene could not discern the enigma other than the subjective appearance of brightness, indicative of acrylic inks that usually stayed localized.

In contrast, the police were working on another approach, which based on Fuzzy's input led to the names, Iceman and Tammy. They had the knowledge of the date of the application and the campground tattoo artist as well. The two independent approaches to solving the crime might eventually merge—a common benefit—that is if Don shared his theory with the cops. He seemed to approach the mystery as a lone wolf and had yet to know that a Fuzzy Walsh was a key player in the scenario.

Don Wright had little reason to travel the road on which Fuzzy's sign was posted. It was later to be serendipity that he would ride on Route 11 when his editor at the newspaper recommended that he photograph some of the campsites and their participants in the Lakes Region. The photos were to accompany a feature on Bike Week accommodations—hotels, motels, campgrounds and rented homes.

Chapter 76

Ace, the leader of the Metuchen, New Jersey Rough Riders Motorcycle Club had visited much of North and South America. He was basically a well-traveled drug fiend and linked to a prominent cartel in Costa Rica, Brazil and the South American Amazon Basin. Cocaine, heroin and recreational drugs like cannabis were at his disposal and he had a long history of distributing those addictive products to locals. His connections allowed for the importation of his monthly stockpile primarily from across the Mexican border. Both, Tijuana, Mexico and towns near El Paso were points of entry into the United States by way of San Diego and Texas.

His journeys took him from Mexico on to South America usually by motorcycle. Occasionally he flew Air Mexico to access the southern parts of the backcountry in quick fashion. He would vacation in Baja, Mexico, Mexico City or Cancun and other areas that offered him local access to conduct business dealings while traveling outside of the United States. No one traced his operations from those locations and he paid off many Mexican runners that stuffed their vehicles with the contraband in hidden compartments, often customizing the doors and trunk spaces. Customs agents at the U.S. borders caught few of the professional transporters. Other routes of the trade included dirt tunnels from Mexico to the U.S. The long border was impossible to monitor and tunnel construction was continuous at night. It was a conduit medium for both drugs and illegal immigrants into America on a daily basis. Ace was a smaller fish in the larger pond of illegal operations. It was a "sea" of drug infestation. There were essentially many "Aces" along the southern border of the United States. Each profited from the cartel of traffickers.

Ace was basically a quiet person, often portraying himself as an auto mechanic and bike repair shop owner in central New Jersey. It was a front for his lucrative drug operation. He remained low-key in the community, bothering no one and maintaining a hidden profile daily. The motorcycle club monthly activities were his real passion. Meetings were often held in secret and varied in location. The covert drug deals were well hidden.

Few people knew that he was once a mercenary and a hit man for hire. His connections to the South American cartel began after he had been hired on numerous occasions to help overturn some local governments and officials that were opponents of the poppy-growing fields and the cannabis pastures of dark green. By eliminating certain officials through assassination or by physical threats, the mercenaries assured the continuous flow of illegal drugs by maintaining continuity of all trafficking outside of South America. Ace was once *the brain* of the operation speaking fluent Spanish and traveling incognito when needed.

Chapter 77

Iceman and his fellow bikers attended numerous rallies each year for the purpose of hanging out and selling grass and cocaine to junkies and young addicts. They were the disciples for Ace's agenda and were successful with promoting his quota of record-breaking revenue. There was obviously money to be made for Ace and the Rough Riders' club by the men attending Laconia, Daytona and Sturgis each rally year.

The Iceman's brotherhood at the Wolfeboro campsite kept a low profile during Laconia Bike Week. Subtle drug deals by individual motorcycle gang members were being accomplished at motels, campgrounds and state parks where some Bike Week visitors were buying recreational drugs with little knowledge or oversight of the local authorities. The police surveillance missed most of the transactions. New Hampshire was vast in scope.

With hundreds of thousands of people attending the rally events and races, the police focused primarily on highway patrols and surveillance of the open crowds for alcoholic beverage infractions, like open container violations and illegal drinking in local parks or parking lots. The police had a good handle on Weirs Beach activities and the known biker bars, hangouts, haunts and social clubs.

Marijuana-related offenses were less of a potential problem than fist or knife fights between motorcycles clubs where rumors had it that they advertised their desire to seek each other out in the advanced news reports and press. It had been rumored that the Hell's Angels and the Outlaws were adversaries and planning to rumble during the 2006 week. The local authorities were on the lookout for any indication of trouble. Drinking infractions always surpassed drug use anyway and motorcycle accidents were more prevalent therefore occupying the attention of the police with other civil disobedience misdemeanors. The hard-core drug trade, if any, was hidden and tough to identify and prosecute.

*   *   *

In 2003 and 2004, Ace had made several trips to South America to meet with his cartel contacts. Aside from his normal interaction and deals with the coke and heroin dealers, he wanted to acquire a unique drug that could pass for the perfect crime—a drug that was not normally screened for by the DEA or the police.

Ace was brought by his personal contacts to many small villages where he studied South American Indian and Native culture and tradition. Three years earlier, he had a plan for 2006 that required something unique and contrived, an agenda out of the norm. The jungle and rain forests harbored traditions and cultures that most people had never heard of in the United States.

One particular tribe had been recommended to Ace.

The Mocousji Indians were a proud people that had survived nature, disease and the deleterious influences of modern man since time immortal. They literally lived off the land, seeking and acquiring the knowledge of many medicinal plants as therapeutics for illnesses as well as local animals and edible plants for food sources. They were resourceful and intelligent. They knew the difference between poisonous and innocuous plants, often teaching their young progeny the specifics of native flora—leaves and various plant species in the rain forest and jungle. Just like one who is cautious in picking mushrooms, the Indians in South America could differentiate between those plants that could be harmful and those that were edible or drinkable as steeped teas.

The indigenous tribes were expert hunters who utilized bamboo dart guns and darts with gummy toxic substances that could paralyze wildlife for capture and food.

They knew of *Chrondrodendron tomentosum* that was a native plant that had a unique utility in hunting. It is a heart-shaped leafy plant that roots in the rain forest, the leaves of which have a hairy white appearance on the ventral surface. The green-white flowers yield an oval fleshy fruit. It is not the fruit that the Indians sought and still seek, but the unique leaves.

The 4" X 8" leaves, when crushed and boiled, undergo a physical reduction into a sticky black mass of goop. The Natives often combine the tar of the plant with aqueous or oily extracts from venomous ants, snakes and strychnos, creating a paralyzing drug combination that is used for hunting and the incapacitation of animals.

The transcontinental travels of Sir Walter Raleigh and later, that of Alexander von Humboldt in 1807, provided the inquisitive Europeans with insight into how drugs were prepared by the South American peoples. The use of plant extracts was not limited to hunting game and the European explorers noted and studied the cultures of the Natives.

The Indians used the drugs in oral form, for madness, edema, as diuretics, relief from swelling and kidney stones. They were not toxic when taken orally due to poor absorption but when they directly entered the bloodstream, they could be deadly—as was the case with blow darts. Birds would die within two minutes, while small mammals would succumb in ten. Larger mammals could die in twenty minutes.

*   *   *

Ace arrived, clad in shorts, leather boots and a T-shirt wrapped about his waist. He was bare-chested and the Natives were impressed with his enormous size and sunburn-tainted white flesh. He was God-like to them—an austere presence that commanded respect. They were dark skinned, the result of heredity and / or the direct sun over centuries. Ace stood among the four or five short-stature people. His dominant presence intrigued them and he was enamored by them as well—a unique clash of cultures with a common bond and agenda. They had seen his black leather clothing that he had left at their camp and fondled the supple cow grain with interest and amazement. They knew it was from an animal yet few of them had ever seen or heard of a cow.

"What is this black tar?" Ace asked his local contact and guide.

The man was straightforward in his response.

"Curare . . . tubocurarine," he responded. "A drug . . . in its raw form. The Indians coat the tip of their arrows and darts with it and use it for hunting."

"As a weapon?" asked Ace, observing a freshly prepared arrow tip with caution.

"No. They are not fighters. They are expert hunters—many with perfect aim. When they hunt, they kill their animal prey with it, not humans. Ya know, they paralyze the prey so it will fall from a tree or drop into a clearing in the forest," commented the guide.

The Native guide smiled as he described how the hunters blew the dart into the muscles or body of a monkey or other mammals of similar size. He summoned a Native hunter to his side and spoke to him in his own lingual tongue. The hunter studied the nearby trees with a keen eye. He moved slowly and methodically, like an African cat that stalked a grazing gazelle. He stopped and listened.

There was a small primate in a nearby tree. Ace studied the now chattering monkey whose vocalizations exuded fear—a warning signal to his own and other species. Ace cupped his face with his hands to block the penetrating sun in his eyes and then focused on the monkey who was animated and bellicose at the transient invading humans. His teeth snapped in a chatter-like vibrato as he vocalized a warning to the others nearby. He was the alpha protector of sorts and persistent, becoming more vocal as the hunter eyed his inevitable prey.

The tribal man who responded to the guide's request was sparsely dressed in a loincloth—stepping forward and studying the monkey's playful, anxious antics in the tree limbs. The branches and leaves of the gum tree shook from the monkey's rebellious attitude and behavior. He was asserting his territorial rights, at least posturing himself that way.

Focusing on the monkey's position and visibility between branches, the tribesman smiled and then placed the handcrafted bamboo tube in his mouth. It appeared almost child-like, a peashooter, and was well polished on the surface from prior use and frequent handling. He aimed the dart gun toward the largest limb—the one with the primate on his haunches. With lightning speed, the dart traversed the air like a silent rocket, hitting the monkey in the right thigh. There was a painful screech by the primate and the monkey rubbed the wounded area with his hand—the muscle had been penetrated with the poisonous dart. The dart hung precariously from the puncture and its contents entered the muscle and blood stream. The monkey's response to the mechanical insult was like that of a human response to a bee sting. First there was pain, then confusion. The monkey could not shoot back and the unfair attack seemed to intoxicate Ace's interest in the differences between man and animals. For a single, brief moment, he thought the scenario unfair.

Chapter 78

Ace watched in amazement as the monkey grabbed tree limbs with difficulty, shifted back and forth like a child's Weeble, while confounded by what had just happened to his body. He wobbled for a moment leaning against the trunk, eyes blinking repeatedly and head occasionally drooping with instability and nap-jerks. He grabbed one large limb and seemed to sink backwards hoping to find a foothold between the trunk and limb. Overpowered by confusion and drowsiness, the flaccid monkey finally dropped to the ground in less than a few minutes. The process seemed endless and cruel to Ace. His eyes never left the defenseless monkey or the visual surroundings as the forest seemed to go silent for a moment.

"Holy shit," Ace reacted, with amazement. "That shit is powerful and fast acting."

"Oh . . . yes, sir," responded the guide with a Hispanic accent. "Very potent by dart gun and . . . lethal."

Ace wanted to know more. He approached the listless primate that lay in a lump on the ground; his arms and legs sprawled across some dead leaves in an unorthodox and unattractive contorted position. The eyes were dilated and fixed in a gaze, the color rapidly fading and his breathing shallow or non-existent at this point. Muscles contracted involuntarily until they stopped completely.

"Glad we are among friends," Ace expressed, sarcastically, while watching the tribesman pick up the monkey by one arm and callously throwing it over his shoulder. He left to "dress" the animal, the head and legs swinging like a rag doll. It all seemed so inhumane, yet it was akin to putting a dog to sleep at the veterinary clinic.

"Yes . . . it could be trouble if you piss off one of the Natives," the guide joked while raising his eyebrows in humor. Ace shuddered at the thought of being "darted" however there were enemies of the Rough Riders that could use the same fate, he thought. Biker clashes between various New York and New Jersey motorcycle clubs were frequent. Territorial rights were the rules of the masses in the Greater New York area.

The accuracy of the hunter and speed of the drug in paralyzing the animal had Ace looking over his shoulder, repeatedly. He felt uneasy in the natural tribal territory, unsure as to whether there was a renegade tribesman that would shoot his butt for fun. Ace wondered if monkeys were their only source of meat, or if the natives enjoyed *Homo sapiens* as well. Were they cannibals? He didn't care to find out.

The guide explained that the chemical, curare, poisoned the nervous system by eventually shutting down the respiratory control of the chest, resulting in the eventual death of the animal from a lack of oxygen. He seemed intelligent in the medical aspects.

"How do they know if the mixture is potent enough or if it's *stable* over time? Each batch of tar must be different," inquired Ace. He was concerned that the potency might be reduced or completely wane on the return trip home; that is if he could get his hands on some of the concentrated tar in the first place.

"They test each batch," the guide replied, "by pricking a frog with the tar and seeing how many times it leaps. It's an age-old test that works well. The less leaps by the amphibian, the more potent the mixture."

"Does it cause a heart attack too?" asked Ace. He figured it must cause the heart to stop as well.

"No. Strangely enough, the heart sometimes beats for a while and a pulse remains. The effects on the heart have been observed in tribal wars when men have been shot at with this goop."

"They use it in war? I thought you said they don't fight," inquired Ace, somewhat apprehensive and unsure of his safety.

"Not often, my friend. They are a quiet tribe who fight only if threatened. The early British visitors wanted to use the curare tar back home in England. The chemical and plants were scarce and too expensive to maintain. The British expeditions who traveled here were impressed with the rapid action of the drug but eventually decided against it in the 1700's and 1800's. What they wanted it for, no one is sure. They say that a man named Brodie noted that the heart was still beating after the drug stopped a person from breathing. That was around 1811."

"It works fast," Ace repeated. "I can't believe how fast the shit works. That little bastard fell out of that tree in no time."

"Oh yes, my friend . . . it is fast and a horrible way to die, by curare. Because the heart still beats, the person or animal watches itself as it suffocates. That is why he staggered in the tree."

Ace was curious. "That shit's been known for a long time then. Can I get some paste to take back home? I think I may have a utility for it." He was smiling.

"Sure, my friend . . . I can get you some . . . a small amount. You are my best *customer* and I will not charge you, sir." The guide spoke the native language to a hunter standing nearby and asked a man for a small amount of the dark, sticky material. He spoke in a bizarre language foreign to Ace. The Native nodded and quickly obliged. Ace had him carefully place the ball of tar in a small plastic Kodak 35mm film container. He wanted no part of handling the stuff himself.

Chapter 79

When Ace returned to the United States from his South American trip, he researched the curare drug on the Internet, merely because he was inquisitive and perplexed by its actions. Numerous Web sites appeared before him on the monitor. He chose the first one.

Curare, it turned out, was a common skeletal neuromuscular blocking agent, sometimes used to this day in small doses as a muscle relaxant during surgery, where the patient needed to remain still during delicate microsurgical operations.

The history of its use was centuries old according to one site. It may have first been noted in 1693, the records indicated. The biological action was already known. It is often used in modern times to block the neurotransmitter, acetylcholine, the active neural communicator between nerve and skeletal muscle cells i.e. the movement of legs, arms and the respiratory muscles in the chest.

Paralysis of those muscles by the drug first occurs in the extremities like the arms and legs, then in the eyes, ears and muscles of the neck. Eventually, the intercostal muscles of the chest are affected adversely, rendering the subject unable to breath and the animal or human dies of asphyxia. It would take large doses or an injection into the blood to achieve the deadly side effects. The Web site confirmed what he was told in South America.

How convenient, thought Ace. It was the perfect scenario for his plan as he had a devious plot in mind for 2006. This drug was just what he needed it seemed and the small Kodak container was stored in his refrigerator.

He was ecstatic that he had access to something nasty; something that few people knew about or could easily trace in the body. If a dead body was eventually embalmed, the killer agent virtually disappeared or could not be analyzed very easily. Standard autopsies might not allow the coroner or medical examiner to pick up the deadly culprit in an unknown crime.

Ace continued to read about the fate of curare in the body. He smiled as he read.

The trick to its unscrupulous use was that *it had to enter the blood stream* to be effective. The detoxifying organ of the body, the liver, removes 60% of the toxic agent and the kidney about 40% if administered to someone in small doses for surgery. At larger dosages, the liver and kidney are ineffective in cleansing the drug from the body. A person usually dies before the drug is removed from the tissues and blood. Physicians control the dose carefully to eliminate those unwanted side effects . . . like *death*.

Ace was satisfied with the potential use of the novel poison. At the vary least he would try it out on some local cat in the Metuchen neighborhood. That was to be his guinea pig. Feral cats always wandered near his auto repair shop. A bowl of milk or plate of leftovers would get him his victim. Ace hated cats anyway. He was evil in that regard. They were too damn independent. They came when there was food, and not when an owner called them, he mused.

When he was a kid, Ace and his friends would put kerosene on some cat's ass and let them run around moaning and draggin' their butts on the grass to remove the irritant, a stinging chemical. It burned their bottom bad. His friends found the show entertaining. Ace preferred to use the cats as target practice with .22 shorts. He had been thrown out of high school because of his leanings toward animal cruelty. The only legitimate classes he took in school were in the automotive and the Vocational / Technical areas. Lacking a high school diploma, he taught himself how to strip down a car engine to each nut and bolt and reassemble it back together in rapid fashion. To do that, he even stole a few cars with friends to take apart. He was considered *a bad ass* from New Jersey, even in his youth.

His wayward actions caused his mother to go to Catholic Mass every Sunday and sometimes daily, mostly to pray for the repose of his soul *on earth*. 'There weren't enough prayers by his mother to correct his behavior,' a priest had once told her. Ace's mother did what she could to get him some kudos with the Man upstairs. In her mind, it might help if he died young. Many a novena was said for Ace.

Chapter 80

Iceman walked along the boardwalk of The Weirs with two or three of the Rough Riders' members. The silver chain attached to his wallet rattled as it hung loosely from his hip pocket. A cigarette dangled between the first and second fingers of his right hand and his belly overlapped his belt and T-shirt. Every once in a while he took a drag on the butt and exhaled the blue-white smoke into the air—it lingered behind him like a small cloud. It seemed that all bikers smoked and Iceman went through at least two packs a day. His hacking cough was evidence of serious respiratory problems, yet he never quit the habit.

The boys had been at the north end of Lakeside Avenue where they passed the Laconia Hell's Angels temporary clubhouse near Club Paradise, a local dance club. Many Angels members who anticipated trouble with the rival group—the Outlaws, their annual nemesis, stood guard outside the clubhouse front door. The threat of a potential rumble had been in the wind all day with the local authorities fully aware of the impending interaction. Some Angels stood guard on *both* sides of the street, akin to sentinels. Many local police officers kept their eyes peeled for potential confrontations that might arise in the general area. The police included members of the University of New Hampshire campus squad as well as State Police, local town sheriffs, and Gilford, Meredith and Laconia police forces. They were visible on motorcycles, mountain bikes, patrol cars and vans often walking the beat in twos while stationed temporarily at the historic New Hampshire Veterans Calvary Home / Rally Week headquarters across from the Weirs Beach train station.

Some 1,200 bikes were parked on Lakeside, a misty day no less, lining both sides of the boulevard and the center portion of the beach road. A temporary mobile van for the police, a paddy wagon of sorts, was adjacent to the Veteran's Home where Wendell Atkins once resided and George Adams still called his abode. To the right of the train depot was the general dock area where "Tammy" X's body had been found earlier in the week. A minority of the thousands of bikers knew of the girl's loss, having arrived after the tragic event. Bikes streamed up Lakeside in slow motion, bikers often using their outstretched legs and feet to balance. The speed was often slower than they wanted due to congestion and the gawking at young ladies in limited apparel.

Occasionally, someone in a bar would mention that a person had died before the Rally had begun. No one seemed to care, but the few that did murmured about her fate and lack of identity. Like most crimes of violence or of unknown cause, visitors paid little mind to the fact that the death meant anything to them directly—there were always some deaths at the annual Daytona, Sturgis or Laconia events. Not *everyone* who arrived *alive* went home *alive* on their bike—some went home in a hearse.

The locals viewed the girl's tragedy differently and so did the police. Transients, especially young, attractive women, were often hired part time for the nine days of social events. They made good money.

Residents and Bike Week officials were speculating that she might be one of the young women hired to promote free "shots" of booze in restaurants sponsored by the Jack Daniels, Wild Turkey or Southern Comfort whiskey companies. The enticement of free samples of liquor and the servers' skimpy outfits brought people into local bars—a company "loss leader" for potential binge drinkers whose end-of-the-day tabs would pay for the seemingly *something for nothing* enticement of free booze.

The young women hired were some of the best "lookers" during Bike Week. They appeared to be barely 21 years-of-age. Innocent and naïve, "Tammy" X may have been someone who had arrived to make some quick cash and then, through fate, may have hooked up by chance with the Iceman. *Had she been a runaway to begin with?* No one knew. Don Wright surmised that it might be the case as he continually pursued her unknown identity, solo.

The police were suspecting that a girl that might have served complimentary drinks could have been targeted, abducted or coerced by money and / or free drugs to follow a gang member's offer. Prostitution was not ruled out either. More money could be made by "hosin'" some of the *boys* than handin' out drinks on behalf of a name-brand whiskey company at Lakeside Avenue bars or any one of the social venues near the Drive-In complex.

Iceman and the boys noted other biker emblems on jackets and vests. There were the Dominions from New York City, Milford and Company from southern New Hampshire and various iterations of the Saints and the Mountain Men from up north in the Great North Woods. Most other Harley riders had black leather jackets promoting Harley gear and the 100th anniversary of the company, which had occurred a couple of years earlier.

Once Iceman sauntered past the railway depot and the Mount Washington cruise boat, he peered over the fence and down the steps that provided accessed to a local public bathroom facility with real toilets. He had to pee bad and thought his eyes would turn yellow if he didn't relieve himself then and there. There were only two guys ahead of him in line for the men's room. The ladies line extended up the steps to the level of the street, a notorious sign of insufficient restroom stalls and the need for women to sit instead of stand, like their male counterparts who might opt for an empty beer can.

When the other men in line saw his austere presence and size, they let him cut the line and go first—a sort of pecking order and sign of respect. He had that aura about him and he laughed as he nodded like he was the king rooster among the young flock of riders. Iceman stood at the urinal and farted like most men who seem to enjoy the combination of relief from two orifices of the body. It was a guy thing!

Above the urinal were words that had been scratched into the walls or penned with Magic Markers. Phone numbers and crude phrases were inscribed during Bike Week. Things like "Charlie peed here in '06" or "Nancy blows horses." None of the graffiti humored Iceman. He shook his private unit once or twice, zipped up and left the public facility without even washing his hands. His friends awaited his return at the top of the wooden stairway.

The water below was calm near the wooden platform / stairwell outside the men's room. Two mallards were swimming in a nearby pool of the shoreline. Wild roses of pink and white dominated the hillside leading to the stony beach below the boardwalk and The Weirs docks. The fragrance from the flowers in full bloom was almost akin to that of a funeral home, somewhat apropos in that the body of "Tammy" X had lain there just days earlier surrounded by stale cigarette butts and paper trash that had been carelessly thrown or blown over the heavy wooden fencing from above. Refuse from boats was sometimes seen along the beach shore area as well. Used plastic water bottles and the occasional paper cup kissed the shoreline on windy days. Plastic white or pink tampon applicators were seen as well, thrown from boats that accessed The Weirs Channel into Paugus Bay. The shore was not garbage infested by any stretch of the imagination, however light paper trash occasionally blew from the masses of people and road above and settled near the cruise boat moorings.

Chapter 81

Iceman smiled behind his shades as he looked over the fence at the former crime scene, a view that now had no residual physical evidence of a body, people gawking or a police investigation. It was as if nothing had happened at that site and most of the bike crowd on Lakeside were unaware of the location of the actual death anyway. It seemed like the perfect crime to Iceman.

Iceman's thoughts were interrupted by the sound of a loud train whistle. The Winnipesaukee Scenic Railroad from Meredith to The Weirs was shuttling in visitors in front of The Weirs depot, dispensing another load of sightseers / bikers on the half-hour, every hour of the afternoon and evening. It was right on time. The railroad cars were heavily patronized and active even on this misty afternoon. Bikers that wanted to avoid riding on inclement days used the passenger train to get to the Lakeside Avenue and Drive-In venue tents and hotspots.

A member of a rival gang and motorcycle club descended the stairs to the public bathroom. There was no line now and like the Iceman he had to void just as bad. Beer often caused that effect. He would have peed in a lavatory sink if he had too. Like Iceman, he didn't care much about protocol or hygiene for that matter. He flushed and left without washing, zipping up his pants virtually in the public doorway and in front of women. Crudeness was not limited to the New Jersey Rough Riders.

Iceman hesitated before climbing the last few steps of the wooden stairway. The open area half way up gave him a perspective in daylight as to exactly where he had placed the young girl's body. It was dark and ill lit when he had left her there days earlier. His friends were beckoning from above but he took his time avoiding their impatient catcalls. There was no remorse in what he had done.

He stared over his shoulder at the Mount Washington boat where people were already partying. Iceman had never been on the boat. There were whiskey and Coors Light banners that covered the side of the classic white cruise ship. They enticed people to come aboard. Loud rock music played and could be heard emanating from the downstairs stage and dance floor. Beer flowed like water it seemed. Some empty kegs could be seen in the aft section of the boat where the waterline appeared higher and the draft seemed lower due to the weight of the people on board.

Upstairs and outside of the train depot, Iceman purchased a T-shirt for $14.95. There was a selection of colorful Laconia 2006 Bike Week commemorative logo tees. There were 2006 logo pins and patches for ones' leathers as well. The merchants would sew the patch onto your outerwear for free.

Shedding his leather jacket, Iceman wanted to try on his T-shirt. It was a 3XL shirt, one of the largest sold that week. On him, it seemed to fit okay. His gut hung out over his belt as he tried it on. One or two passersby pointed at his enormous, rotund and half-naked torso. His arms and neck were now exposed, revealing tattoos from years of prior rallies. The tattoos included his club logo, a Teddy Bear and women's names. On each lower arm was the tattoo of his own name, *Iceman* inked in script. The name, Iceman, was "boxed in" by a scroll and each tattoo had ice cubes imprinted around his moniker. They appeared to be dripping, a facsimile of melting ice. The ice cubes were so real in appearance that they seemed to be *cold*. As he exposed the tattoo, a nearby policeman on the boardwalk took notice. The "word was out" for the authorities to look for anyone with the word, Iceman on their bike license plate, jacket, fuel tank, or body / tattoos. No one had spotted his motorcycle as yet.

"Hey Joe," said Paul to his partner, "There's the biker name we've been lookin' for. Over there . . . see?" He pointed in the general direction. Paul's eyes were fixed on the arms of the brute of a man.

Joe responded quickly and stood closer to Paul. Both officers placed their hand on their holsters and Joe could actually feel his heart pounding and his pulse racing. They were cautious among the mass of people, easing forward slowly toward the Iceman.

They walked over to the T-shirt table where he was in the midst of paying the dark-skinned cashier from India. When Iceman turned, he was face to face with two cops who stood silent and stoic behind their official aviator sunglasses. Iceman said nothing to them and slowly put his leather vest back on. It partially covered the new shirt.

"Hold it, sir," Paul spoke firmly. "Can I see those arms?"

Iceman froze, looking around for his friends who seemed to have disappeared into the crowd.

"Sure," he replied, looking off in the distance at a parade of bikes on the road. "What's the problem, officers?" Iceman said, seemingly acting cool and collected under the circumstances. Under his armpits he was sweating rapidly. His new T-shirt became saturated by the surprise surveillance of the two police officers, up front and personal.

Joe and Paul stood silent while looking at the biceps and then the forearms of Iceman. They noted the elaborate jewelry and gold chains around his neck. Blue-collar working bikers didn't usually wear such heavy pieces of hardware in 18K gold. Drug dealers did.

"Nothing's wrong really, sir," said Paul, the cop. "We like tattoos and noticed yours. Pretty impressive artwork."

"Thanks," remarked Iceman. "I'm pretty proud of them myself. Have had 'em for years."

Officer Joe added his two cents. "Must have had a few woman in your life," he commented, while smiling. "I see a lot of ladies' names crossed out there," Joe commented, while Paul laughed almost simultaneously.

"Yah. Suppose I have . . . way too many," remarked Iceman, casually. "They come and go," he chuckled. "Ya win some and ya lose some," he smirked, while admitting to a moment of failure in many relationships.

"You the 'Iceman'?" asked Joe, while studying his arms. "We assume so since ya got two name plates on your arms." Joe hesitated, "Why two of the same?"

"There are two just in case one or the other thaws," Iceman said, somewhat sarcastically and uncomfortable with the inquiry. The policeman did not laugh either. Iceman sensed that they were onto something yet neither cop had said anything that might lead to an extensive street interview. Then the bomb dropped.

"We'd like to chat with ya a bit, Iceman—that is, if you have time."

Iceman froze. He indicated that he was late in meeting up with friends and had to leave. The two policemen gently informed him that his appointment would have to wait.

"You have a bike here, sir?" one patrolman asked. "Like nearby?"

Iceman nodded, yes. "It's at the other end of Lakeside," he pointed with a cigarette tar-stained index finger.

"What's the tag on the bike, sir?"

"My name—ICEMAN. The New Jersey tag is the same as my name."

"Okay," added one cop.

There was a brief moment of silence.

Iceman then asked, "What's this all about, officers?"

"We're not sure yet," added Paul. "Perhaps you can help us with some answers to an issue earlier this week."

"Issue? What issue? I just got to town today," offered the man in question. "How can I help?"

"Follow us, sir . . . please."

Chapter 82

After Iceman described the bike and color, they began to walk. One patrolman turned and called in the information on a hand-held radio and requested that two other policemen seek out the bike in the direction of Lakeside Avenue south, near the Drive-In. In less than two minutes, Iceman's bike had been located and impounded.

The attention then focused on Iceman as two more policemen arrived from across the road opposite the T-shirt table. They were back-ups and nearby, if needed.

"You'll have to follow us over here," stated Officer Joe, pointing at headquarters. "We have a mobile police office right there," he said, pointing west. Iceman looked across the street with apprehension. His brow was now wet and a crowd began to gather around the rotund man. Iceman was uneasy having the spotlight of the cops directly on him and with no friends to help. They had disappeared like ghosts into the masses.

"What's this 'bout, officer?" he asked again. "I ain't done nothin'—no drinkin', no misbehavin' in any way. Just got to town. I'm clean."

"We have an interest in that name on your arms, that's all. The name, *Iceman.* Need to chat with ya a bit."

"What the fuck for?" asked Iceman, now losing his cool. He stood like a Marine, legs spread at a 45-degree angle and arms crossed on his chest in defiance. The stance increased his bicep size.

Two of his Rough Riders buddies had disappeared into the crowd and stood on the other side of the waiting train while peering through two connecting passenger cars. Their New Jersey club logos could be seen in the distance. The two policemen had all they could do to contain Iceman. He soon became more belligerent as a crowd of onlookers began to congregate, encouraging him and chanting obscenities or catcalls at the police.

Iceman raised his hand to stop the crowd. He didn't need that shit or any more attention from bystanders, even if they were trying to assist him. They responded to his command, murmuring among themselves.

The two patrolmen assisted Iceman arm in arm without handcuffs. He was not under arrest, at least not yet. The police wanted the journey across Lakeside to be as low profile as possible.

The gathering crowd of men and women thought otherwise taunting and chiding the police just as Iceman was led away. As they approached the main street to cross, a loud bike could be heard among the other dual pipes that lined up at the pedestrian crosswalk.

The bike, with its engine racing, quickly sped to the side of the mass of pedestrians and other bikers sitting on cement barricades at the intersection of the New Hampshire Veterans Home and the railway depot. It screeched to a slow roll causing the two policemen to be startled, jumping out of the way of the crazed and dangerous rider. They were surely going to be hit if they remained where they were.

Iceman overpowered both patrolmen who had dragged him to the side as well for his own safety. There were scraped knees on the policemen who were wearing summertime attire—blue shorts. To the cheers of the crowd and in the moment of confusion, Iceman stood like a cat and hopped on the back of the waiting motorcycle. The driver was forced to lay forward to accommodate the hulk; His chest was on the tank.

The driver had on a darkened full-faced helmet and no jacket with anything identifiable as an affiliation. His T-shirt was pure white and he wore standard jeans. It could have been anyone on that motorcycle.

Grabbing for his side arm, a .38 caliper pistol, Officer Joe lay stunned and aimed in the direction of the escaping duo. Pedestrians screamed at the sight of the gun. He could not fire without the possibility of hitting someone else in the crowd—an innocent bystander perhaps. There were dozens of people in the way, potential victims if he fired. Joe grabbed his scraped knee with his free hand and was cursing and screaming, "Halt." Blood oozed from the dermal "road rash" and small laceration. He was in visible pain as another cop arrived to assist him. His partner seemed dazed as well. He also had been knocked down. Both patrolmen were embarrassed more than anything. The Iceman had fled.

An EMT had been summoned from the nearby police mobile headquarters. He was carrying a white plastic First-Aid kit and was dressed in an orange jumpsuit with off-white reflective tape for night work. The EMT glowed in the daylight sun.

The motorcycle headed north on Lakeside Avenue and screamed left onto another side road that was north of Tower Rd.—it had quickly traversed through a residential area and finally accessed Route 3 north, one half mile from the departure scene.

The license plates were beige in color for the State of New Jersey but the tag was unreadable. It had been lightly sanded to appear worn. The letters were not visible. In actuality, it read, NOMAD.

The police congregated by the depot and radioed ahead but had no identifiable tag number to pass on to other authorities that were staked out on other highways.

Two police vans gave chase but traffic on Lakeside, as well as the side roads, made it impossible to maneuver. The bike was long gone, having cut in and out of the massive crowd of people and machines. Police sirens meant little with hundreds of Harleys revving and traversing the street—a continual parade of slow moving motorcycles on Lakeside. The police were afraid to increase their speed of pursuit in an overall effort not harm any pedestrians. They lost sight of the bike, and valuable time.

There were pedestrians in the street that walked the whole of Lakeside to visit the cadre of tents. Some 600 vendors lined the main drag and remote parking lots at the south end of that main road. The congestion was too overwhelming for the police to pursue the perpetrators.

Chapter 83

Iceman's colleague and motorcyclist, the Nomad, from the New Jersey club pulled a double back toward the north end of Lakeside Avenue. He traversed an elevated wooden bridge that crossed the railroad tracks on Centenary Road. On the other side of the bridge was an overhead, hand-painted sign that read, "Methodist Circle." The bike quickly disappeared into a semicircle of historic homes that were built in the 1870's. They once were part of a campground area for religious services and were staggered as a half-moon setting around a pavilion that accommodated the sermons and prayer sessions. It was waterfront religion during that era.

The tightly packed semicircle of houses were built by religious elders and laymen of various groups—for the purpose of housing those attending specialized weeks of preaching at The Weirs campground in the 1870's.

Thousands of people attended the services, sermons and lectures. Some builders were prominent Methodist deacons, church officials and reverends from as far away as Franklin, Warren and Plymouth, New Hampshire.

The campground was originally laid out for hundreds of tents, and later replaced by small homes that remain today. They distinctively had prominent roofline accents of detailed architecture and woodwork. The wood filigree accents on the homes made them appear as distinct little cottages, each one unique. The wood used in construction of the homes was brought in by train and offloaded at the same campground in the 1800's, specifically for the fabrication of each cottage. The railway tracks were nearby and construction materials were available to complete the operation.

As a semicircle of camps, they surrounded a centrally located pavilion for religious services. The historic area on the shoreline of Winnipesaukee remains today and is tucked away from the main street near the train depot. The railroad tracks separated the little village from Lakeside Ave. A footbridge and a bridge for automobiles remain the main conduits between the two areas of The Weirs. In many ways, the old campground that once harbored many tents of parishioners, allowed for tent replacements by one or two stick-built cottages at a time—they encircled the main meetinghouse and pavilion. Even today, the original top of the renovated pavilion, a cupola, remains as evidence of yesteryear and the devout Christian movement of the 1870's.

The renegade motorcycle pulled into a nearby garage at home #5 in the Methodist residential community off Weeks and Baker Streets. The police had lost track of the motorcycle's whereabouts.

The 1870's home of refuge was built in a less than two weeks by a gentleman known as Jeremiah Jewett, a man of many talents and deep religious faith. He surveyed the original home sites, coordinated some of the construction and work crews, and eventually pounded many of the nails himself.

Jewett once owned much land in Laconia and Warren and donated, for a small sum, the land in downtown Laconia for the original construction of the current hospital.

Chapter 84

The motorcyclist and Iceman jumped off the bike in quick fashion. The rescuer and fellow club member had relatives in the Methodist Circle area and knew every road and potential escape route. He had entered the garage behind the #5 home and closed the overhead door behind the motorcycle. There were neighbors who kept to themselves and a line of pines on each side of the house that assured privacy from the public's wandering eyes. Few people were home anyway, with most families working during the day. Bikes and noise were everywhere and nothing seemed amiss in the neighborhood, especially for the two escape artists. They looked the part of everyday Bike Week.

The neighborhood kids were in school, at least most of them. Occasionally, one of the teenagers played hooky, enticing other friends to cop out or call in sick as well. It was often reminiscent of the movie, *Ferris Bueller's Day Off.* They usually went swimming at Weirs Beach or below the pavilion at Methodist Circle where no one checked for truancy in that remote shoreline area. The police hardly ever patrolled the area on the far side of the wooden bridge.

The bridge, which spanned the tracks, offered pedestrian access to the Lakeside festivities, bars and restaurants. The Methodist Circle crowd could walk to the popular venues.

Immediately after closing the garage, the Nomad, changed the license plates to stolen Massachusetts tags. They had been garnered from another bike that was parked by a popular bar in the middle of the night. The owner probably didn't even know they were missing. The motorcycle in the garage was a nondescript bike in that it was a common Harley model that seemed to be prevalent during the Bike Week Rally each year. It was black in color.

Tracing the bike would be nearly impossible, especially with the long lead-time that both men had with their disappearance.

Iceman entered the house through an enclosed, wood-paneled breezeway. He passed an old couch and TV resting on a wooden box. The window shades had been drawn in the entryway and a small refrigerator overflowed with a stockpile of beer. He stopped long enough to grab two Bud longneck bottles—swilling them down in rapid fashion. His rescuer grabbed a beer and began laughing hysterically. Iceman wasn't quite as jovial but thankful for the novel escape. He now knew that the police were on to something, yet he didn't know how.

"Thanks, Nomad. Ya saved my bloody ass. Those pricks almost had me."

"That's what the brotherhood's for, dude. You were about to go down with the pigs."

"No shit," Iceman retorted. "The fuckers know me now. They noticed my tattoos."

"Which tattoos?" asked the rider, taking a long draw on his beer, "the ones on your arms?"

Iceman hesitated. "Yah, they noticed the name and ice cubes like they had been lookin' for me. Rat bastards must be on to somethin' like the death of that Tammy chick."

"That's not possible. How the fuck would they know that you were, or we were, part of the plan?"

"Don't know, dude . . . but they zeroed in on the tattoos on my arm like they were lookin' for the name."

Iceman sat on the couch, placed his boots on a tattered ottoman and flipped on the TV with a remote. A local access cable channel had live coverage/ Web Cam of the Lakeside area, especially for Rally Week. Things looked normal with pedestrians walking back and forth along the boardwalk. The train was again departing to Lakeport as well. Iceman grabbed another beer, making his consumption of three in a short, fifteen minutes.

"We safe here?" he asked his colleague from New Jersey. "Who the fuck's place is this anyway . . . it's convenient."

The fellow rider responded smiling, "It belongs to a distant relative of mine. He goes away during Bike Week. Can't stand the fucking traffic, I guess. Takes his kids on vacation. He's divorced. That's why the place looks like it does . . . crap everywhere and rust-stained toilets!"

"Who cares about the toilets anyway," Iceman joked. "Ya only crap and pee in them."

"Or throw up in them," the rider added. Both men laughed.

Iceman commented, "We don't stay in Martha Stewart places anyway. It cramps our style and I don't need that shit. Are we stayin' here tonight?"

"Nah . . . I'll get you back to the Wolfeboro campsite in a few hours. Have some beers and relax. We're safe here and the cops should settle down in a couple hours."

Chapter 85

Later that night they would ride back to Wolfeboro, on the other side of the lake, by way of Alton Bay—the campground remained the club headquarters for the New Jersey riders and was securely back in the woods and well away from The Weirs. They knew they would be safe there. Iceman had his newfound friend, "Bonnie" service his needs and he was randy after the harrowing but successful escape. She needed a bit of a ride herself and Bonnie was the one to oblige.

*   *   *

The close call for Iceman at the depot had other Rough Riders antsy. They quizzed Iceman about the dialogue with the police and why he had been targeted. *What did the police know? Why was Iceman picked out of a crowd of hundreds near the depot and the Mount Washington boat?* They discussed leaving their leather vests at the campsite in the future. No one wanted to have the police scoping out the club logo on their leathers or on their backs when they rode or walked.

The club colors and name were direct links to Iceman and to them for sure. No one wanted to take a chance of going back to The Weirs and getting sidetracked by pissed off cops. They knew the police were on a manhunt for their leader in New Hampshire.

Iceman's tent was some distance from the other riders from New Jersey. He managed to have sex with Bonnie a couple of times again degrading her with carnal acts in virtually every orifice. She didn't seem to mind and knew the big man was stressed. He needed relief and she was the one to be of service. Submissiveness was her life, having grown up in a broken home and been taught to "trick" at a young age. She knew she was sitting on a goldmine, quite literally. She serviced Iceman for free but had quite a different role back home—exotic dancer and sometimes hooker.

After a couple of rounds on the makeshift mattress, Iceman went straight to sleep. He was snoring loudly and lying on his back, which accentuated the vibration of his sleep apnea. The roar was deafening primarily due to his large size and thick neck of adipose tissue.

Bonnie sought out a nearby stream with a flashlight. She bathed in the direct view of some of the other riders in the club. They were jealous of Iceman's good fortune but had no intention of ridin' Iceman's woman behind his back. Iceman didn't share his women even though other members were encouraged to donate their ladies to him and Ace—a universally known club code.

He was known to seriously harm people that encroached upon his ever-changing harem. He had killed at least one other biker—a violator of his trust as well. Any girl who strayed, didn't fair too well either. He dumped boiling water on their live, naked bodies in a remote town in northern New Jersey. In no way would they ever be desirable again in the future. They were scarred from face to butt and the deformities from the burns were devastating. Appearing more like freaks, no one desired their bodies again. Marked by the Iceman for posterity, they could never squeal on him for fear of being maimed further or being killed.

Iceman was merciless when he needed to be—no one crossed him any more than they would cross Ace. Iceman was number one in line for the throne in the New Jersey Rough Riders club.

When Iceman awoke from his hormone-induced, post-sex nap, he called Ace in New Jersey by cell phone. He explained the situation to his boss and Ace was in no mood to hear of the crap that Iceman had experienced at The Weirs. Ace was disturbed and gravely concerned that his "number one" confidant and "number two" club leader, Iceman, was now a *liability* to the overall plan. To Ace, the police had a bead on the man and he was *marked.*

Ace was calculating—and told Iceman that he thought he should hit the road for home in the morning—the sooner, the better. If the cops knew that Iceman was linked to the death of the young "Jane Doe," the whole Club had an issue in New Hampshire and in New Jersey.

"Why boss?" he retorted, "the week ain't over. They won't find me and there's deals to be done. I've got some deals in progress that will move that new contraband, South American Viagra. The biker customers are buying it like crazy and the shit looks like the same thing Pfizer makes. The color is identical—blue.

"Can't take a chance havin' you in that State. They grab you, and the whole clan up there of your brothers will be nabbed as accomplices. Can't you see the danger?"

"I suppose," Iceman bowed, in verbal submission. "I can head out soon. I'll change plates along the way, perhaps a couple of times on some loaner bike. The other boys can stay behind and move the drugs as needed."

"That's my take as well," Ace said, coldly. "Get outta Dodge soon! But hey, you don't have your bike . . . wasn't it confiscated during the escape?"

"Shit . . . yes," voiced Iceman, with embarrassment. "Crap . . . they have my bike."

"Not good," remarked Ace, while lighting a cigarette at the other end of the line. "Not good."

Iceman reeled from the lecture from Ace. He overcompensated with more conversation.

"I'll get out first thing tomorrow morning. I'll borrow another machine and change the plates tonight. The boys have other registrations and tags from Massachusetts stashed in their saddlebags. See ya soon boss—it's a six hour ride."

"See ya soon, Iceman. Stay low tonight." Ace said, pacing, for he had another call to make. He was antsy, but full of conviction.

"No Problemo," cited the Iceman. "I'll be here in Wolfeboro and not head for The Weirs with the other guys. "There's beer here and a broad I found that will keep me busy."

"Good," remarked Ace in New Jersey. "You do that. Enjoy your time in New Hampshire and bone the chick once for me! Wish I was there."

Chapter 86

With a somewhat chilling ending to the call, they both hung up and Iceman leaned back on a pillow staring at the tent above him. He knew that Ace was pissed over the police situation and Iceman's controversial escape from Lakeside to a nearby side street. Anyone could have videotaped his daring escape.

He was a large man on the back of a smaller bike for Chrissake, Ace thought, with concern. *Someone had to have seen him and could identify him later.*

Cameras were everywhere during the altercation and eventual great escape. Iceman and his buddy were like the actor, Steve McQueen for a small moment in time.

If the police saw any of the photography or video, it would be easy for them to apprehend the Iceman and his accomplice in no time at all. They already had Iceman's bike, which he left behind, parked on the south end of Lakeside Avenue. They impounded the bike back in Laconia at the police station. It was maintained for evidence of a potential crime.

If Iceman were "clean," he would come back for the bike, the police thought. If he were involved in the girl's death, he would be on the run and never claim the Harley. They could chase and trace him back to New Jersey and have the New Jersey Highway Patrol apprehend him in that State. He might run, but he couldn't hide for very long.

*   *   *

The two policemen at the Weirs felt embarrassed by the escape of their potential witness and radioed ahead to the local contingent of officers located strategically to the north, south, west and east of The Weirs. The dispatcher had the description of the bike and at least one of the perpetrators named, Iceman. The police now had a bead on a suspect related to the "Tammy" X investigation. No other officers had seen the name, Iceman on anyone or any clothing.

At the far end of a parking lot, near the Drive-In, a fellow club member had wanted to remove the license plate from Iceman's New Jersey bike. Another rider was to ride Iceman's machine back to Wolfeboro but the police had preempted the plan by removing the bike before the Rough Riders could come to the aid of Iceman.

*   *   *

The police had an all-points-bulletin out for any bikes with New Jersey tags or riders with Rough Riders Motorcycle Club vests on. The New Jersey police had confirmed that the impounded bike had been registered with the name, Iceman for years. The bike and rider resided in Metuchen. All toll takers on New Hampshire Route I-93, the State Police and local authorities were on the lookout for plates and riders from that area. It was almost impossible to scope out all E-Z Pass lanes in Hooksett or lanes that required change. There were thousands of motorcyclists traversing the toll lanes daily.

Chapter 87

At 3 A.M., two bikes left the campsite in Wolfeboro where Iceman was staying with Bonnie. She was still asleep when he departed. One biker was Iceman and the other a fellow rider who had borrowed another bike for the large man to get him to Jersey. The rider was to escort Iceman and be his bodyguard from Wolfeboro to I-93 South.

At that early hour, the back roads and the bypass to Laconia were the least traveled roads around the Big Lake in the area, especially around Alton Bay. "Tiny Tim," another club member, who was also larger than life like the Iceman, rode behind his colleague, his headlights focused on the bright taillights of Iceman's motorcycle. He continually checked his rear view mirror for cops and traffic on the Route 11 bypass to Route 3. That was one of the shortest routes to the Interstate. The other was an approach from Route 140 West.

There were no other headlights coming at them or from behind. Near the Route 106 exit in south Laconia, Tiny Tim suddenly revved up and quickly approached Iceman on his left side. His high beams were illuminated somewhat blinding Iceman's vision in his rear view mirror. He smiled and waved at him since they were buddies. Was he passing him?

As Iceman waved his left hand, encouraging his fellow rider to pass, Tiny Tim veered closer and closer and abruptly grabbed Iceman's hand as a farewell gesture. He didn't want to race at all. Tiny Tim was on another mission from Ace in New Jersey. He was the club member that Ace had called after the depressing chat with the Iceman.

Iceman smiled and then felt Tiny Tim press his hand hard against the handlebar of his bike. Tiny Tim leaned right and shoved the bike off balance almost losing his own machine from the natural recoil to the left. Iceman's headlights and his bike veered suddenly to the right and down a steep embankment. Caught off guard, he didn't even have time to scream—rather he desperately attempted to save himself from the impending woods and brush. He was out of control at a high rate of speed, unstable on the seat and frozen to the handlebars. He had no helmet on, leaving his mark like Sonny Bono on a large pine.

The bike was twisted and broken from the impact. Iceman had flown off the machine and traveled full force into a giant white pine, one that was old growth of some 50 years. The front wheel was crushed as the bike's oil smoked from the devastating crash. Almost the entire frame was twisted and severed from under the seat. The Iceman was slumped on the ground some distance from the bike. There was no movement other than the occasional twitch of involuntary skeletal muscles in the arms and legs. The Iceman was dead.

Tiny Tim never looked back after the unscrupulous deed and proceeded solo to the end of the Route 11 bypass. He made a sharp right and followed the edge of Lake Winnisquam into Laconia. He passed the lake and train tracks to Tilton on his left. After two miles, he mingled with the early risers in Laconia. He grabbed breakfast at the Dunkin Donuts across from Vista Foods near downtown, and headed back to Wolfeboro by way of Gilmanton and Route 140 east, a short journey to Alton and then Wolfeboro. He had no remorse for the deed he had done. The command from New Jersey was not negotiable. Tiny Tim obeyed his master of the club—Ace, in Metuchen.

Chapter 88

In the early A.M. around dawn on Thursday of Bike Week, a passing truck driver in a semi noticed from his high perch, a bike crashed in the woods off the Route 11 bypass. He jammed on his brakes and veered right and onto the shoulder. The grass was high where he stopped, the result of recent frequent rains in the Granite State. Using a cell phone, he immediately notified 9-1-1 and waited for the EMS and police to arrive. The truck driver managed his way through the tall brush and vines of bittersweet observing recent skid marks in the dirt and gravel, a number of parts were strewn in the area of the decimated motorcycle. He happened on the remains of the Iceman and almost threw up from the visual impact of the bodily damage. Blood and tissues were everywhere.

There was little left of the Iceman's head. Dirt and grass and dried blood were caked among his bodily tissues. What clothes that he had on, jeans and a dark jacket, were torn to shreds. His limbs were twisted in different directions suggesting a compound fracture of at least one leg. A foot faced backwards on that leg.

The truck driver stood silent as he heard the sound of sirens. He headed back up the hill to the cab of the tractor-trailer. He leaned against the fender of the massive rig and wept. He had never seen such devastation to a human body. All he could assume was that someone crashed at a very high rate of speed. *Why did he have to find the accident?*

Moments later, the Laconia Fire and Rescue van arrived. Police cars, a fire truck, a trooper and a local ambulance company, all of which were unaware of the carnage they were about to see.

The medical teams were not needed. A hearse and a tow truck were the vehicles of choice now. Iceman had been dead for at least three hours. With traffic snarled during the morning commute and passing rubberneckers in cars checking out the scene of rescue vehicles and red and blue flashing lights, volunteers and policemen scoured the woods and brush for motorcycle parts. They were strewn everywhere.

An assistant to the coroner was summoned and released the body to the funeral director for transport to Concord. An autopsy was planned because of the violent circumstances of death. It would be hours before the morning traffic flow could be reestablished. Route 11 was a major conduit between the town of Belmont and The Weirs area. Bikers used it as a shortcut to Gilford.

The question arose as to whether the dead biker had been traveling alone? No one knew for sure but the tattoos on the body were evidence of the fact that it was the Iceman that the police had been looking for, for the past day.

Had he been riding drunk or was there an issue with his motorcycle? The police knew that his own motorcycle was in Laconia stored behind a mesh-fenced cage having been impounded after the escape at The Weirs. Detectives also knew that he was the man with the clues to the girl's death. Now he lay silent, in broken anatomical shambles and unable to help the investigation.

What clues to the crime were now lost by his death? The Iceman had been a key witness at Fuzzy Walsh's tattoo tent, and a direct link to the unknown "Tammy" X victim at The Weirs beachfront. Their key suspect, Iceman, was of no help now.

*   *   *

Word was received back at The Weirs mobile police headquarters that Iceman had perished in an early morning accident. The now famed tattoos on his arms provided the clue to his infamous identity. His head was so mangled from the incident that he was not identifiable except for a blood soaked beard that was matted from the dried red protein.

Initially, the local police downtown and at the scene had suggested that he had lost control of the motorcycle in the early morning, albeit the road being clear and dry conditions. The skid marks revealed a rapid turn to the right immediately after some guardrails. There was nothing to stop him. The rubber on the roadway showed that he had locked his back breaks and then the front. At any normal speed on that road, he would have flipped after locking the front pads. Momentum would next carry him over the hill and uncontrollably into the woods. The cops measured the tire skid marks with accuracy.

The body would be checked for alcohol and drugs and any other toxicological entities that might be evidence or have contributed to his demise. Because Iceman was wanted by the authorities, the investigation at the scene was to be meticulous. It could impact the other death case and the Laconia police would work closely with the New Jersey detectives in tandem. They surmised that New Jersey authorities had a torrid history on the man.

Chapter 89

Tiny Tim had called Ace in New Jersey after the set up of the Iceman. After he returned to Wolfeboro, he said little to his fellow riders. Ace wanted to announce the loss of the Iceman himself and would lie about what had happened. Tiny Tim would ultimately boast.

"The deed's done, Ace. He's toast!"

"Good job. We couldn't have the Iceman putting the locals, State cops and Feds on us. Let me know when you hear more or see something in the newspaper or on TV."

"Sure boss . . . no problem."

"I'll chat with you in a while," Ace confirmed. "I've got stuff to do here and I'm sure the local New Jersey police will want to have a little chat with me. I need to plan for any questions before they show up and wonder what happened to a fellow club member in New Hampshire. I will play dumb and appear shocked by the news. Better than that, I may blow town."

The Weirs police were pissed. They needed Iceman to confess to some aspect of the "Tammy" X crime. He was the man they surmised took her to Fuzzy Walsh's tent for the Vincent tattoo. Now they had two people for whom they could not explain the tragedies—the girl and the Iceman. At least they knew *his* I.D.

Iceman was the one that had probably killed her and also knew her real name. A saddlebag from the Iceman's now crumpled bike contained his worldly possessions for the trip back to New Jersey. There was also in his possession the infamous black ink that Fuzzy had utilized in the tattoo process. Procurement of the saddlebag would aid the police in their investigation and Ace, in New Jersey, would not know of the pertinent evidence that was now in the hands of the authorities. Ace had verbally told Iceman to burn the remainder of the bottle in a campfire, or dispose of it ASAP. The Iceman never completed the mission hence the remainder of the ink was critical to the police investigation.

The members of the Rough Riders, holed up in Wolfeboro, arose to hear of the demise of the Iceman. Not all members were privy to the reasons for his death, only the top echelon. Only two or three council members knew of Ace's plan in New Jersey to "ice" the Iceman. There was a strict code of silence among the hierarchy and Tiny Tim did not share with others his plan to accompany the Iceman to the Interstate. He was back in Wolfeboro before most of the other riders were even awake.

Bonnie lay sobbing in the Iceman's tent. She had been made aware of the death of her Bike Week lover. She hugged a Rally Week Teddy Bear to her cheek and sobbed. It was similar to the one found at the death scene of "Tammy" X.

Bonnie had grown close to the Iceman and wanted to follow him back to New Jersey leaving her roots down south behind. It was not to be. By the end of the morning, she would be back at The Weirs roaming the street and hanging out in the beer tents. She was to drown herself in sorrow.

The Rough Riders wanted nothing to do with her now. She may have known about the details of the "Tammy" X death. A designated biker that dropped her off at the Weirs Beach area told her that she was to *say nothing* of any conversations she ever had with the Iceman in his tent. She was sworn to secrecy. If she said anything about the New Jersey group or her lover, they would hunt her down and kill her—decapitate her, they assured her. Obviously, she feared for her life.

She got off the back of the bike near the Drive-In and never looked back. Neither did the member of the gang that gave her the ride. Clutching a backpack with her clothing and bear inside, she walked away and immediately mingled with the crowd of Bike Week participants. She did not want to be the next victim since Iceman, in a drunken stupor one night, had told her of the dead girl's tradition—not in substantial detail, but in principle.

Don Wright had heard of the crash on a police scanner in the early morning. He arrived at the scene and briefly questioning his friends from the police department. He took the necessary photos for the newspaper headlines and then departed. He was well aware of the fact that the police were onto something with this particular death. He overheard a patrolmen chatting about the Iceman and his possible roll in the death of the girl at The Weirs.

Don was now piecing together a relationship between Wendell's notes and the role of the Iceman in the complex scenario. Each day revealed new data in the investigation and Don knew he could solve this crime, almost solo.

Chapter 90

That afternoon, the two detectives who had visited Fuzzy in the past, pulled a police car in front of his tent. He was anxious once again, emerging from the tent with a Bud in his hand. "Not again boys!" he stammered, half in the bag.

"Sad news, Fuzzy," said one of the cops. "Your buddy Iceman had an accident. He's spent."

"What?" replied the tattoo artist, "what da ya mean?"

"The dude that brought "Tammy" in here for the Vincent tattoo went off the road in the early morn . . . he's history."

"Jesus Christ. What the fuck happened?" he asked, in disbelief. "Accident?"

"Dunno," added the cop. "Maybe . . . or . . . maybe not. You ever get other New Jersey Rough Riders in here for tattoos—like this week?"

"No," Fuzzy volunteered. "Why?"

"Okay. But we'll need to chat with you again and get a description of your recent clientele. Can we go inside the tent?"

"Sure. I don't have any customers at the moment and your cop car will keep any potential clients away."

"Sorry dude, but this is necessary."

"Wanna beer?"

"No thanks . . . we're on duty."

The police showed Fuzzy a photo of the deceased Iceman. He confirmed that what was left of the face was indeed the guy who had brought the young girl to his tent for the Vincent logo tattoo. Fuzzy Walsh had seen the Iceman's tattoos on his arms, the day that he had brought in "Tammy." He had actually complimented him on the artwork.

After a while, the police left Fuzzy's tent and departed the campsite area of the large farmer's field. Many other bikers were curious to know what was up with Fuzzy and the police. They had been there to visit him on at least two occasions and the other black leather riders in the campground were antsy over the cops scoping out the field and facilities. If there were issues, they wanted Fuzzy to move out for the remainder of the week. No one wanted the cops back there again.

"What's the deal with you and the 'fuzz,' Fuzzy? You got some issues we don't know about? We don't like them snoopin' around here," stated one camper bluntly.

Fuzzy felt uneasy by the inquiry of his peers but assured the bikers that all was okay.

"They had some questions about one of my tattoos. That's all," he touted. "They wondered if I tattooed some chick that had been arrested," he lied. "Not to worry boys . . . not to worry. They won't be back."

"They better not," one biker commented. "If the pigs start ramblin' through our tents for some damn reason—you're dead meat."

"Not to worry," Fuzzy said, now shaking, "they won't be back." Five other bikers from the campground now surrounded him. He really didn't know if the cops would return again.

The latest news was widespread at The Weirs—a tattooed girl had been found dead, a girl with the name, Vincent on her lower back. People were aware that the police were trying to identify who she was. Fuzzy didn't know if the other campers had heard the news. He was not about to share any info about the girl or the death of the Iceman with anyone. He did not want to be known as a "rat."

That night, he hardly slept for fear of repercussions by his fellow campers.

Chapter 91

Don Wright rode to Gilford Village after having been at the scene of the Iceman's death; the old section of historic Gilford played a significant role in the earlier days of the original Laconia Bike Rallies. The town was only a few miles from his home in Laconia and directly on the way to Gunstock Ski Area—the site of the Bike Week hill climbs and Belknap Mountain Motorpark of yesteryear. The little Cape-style wooden library building stood pristine and white. It was directly across from a convenience store that locals frequented for the morning paper, milk, bread and other household staples. Bikers often bought beer, deli sandwiches and cigarettes there.

The structure of the library was that of a traditional Cape, modified and expanded to incorporate numerous volumes of books over the years. The town was growing in population. A new library was being planned for the future. Gilford had outgrown its literary storage, and space was now limited. Still, because of the expense and an anticipated increase in taxes, the town folks were debating whether they would fund a new building to accommodate the expanded literary collection.

It was no different than any other New Hampshire town it seemed, in that any suggestions to build new public service buildings were always met with resistance—i.e. new schools, police or fire stations, libraries or EMS services. Residents knew of and appreciated the eventual need for increased accommodations for town services including the educational needs of schools and libraries, but no one wanted to fund the necessary revenues to accomplish the upgrades or expansions that would alleviate the problems.

For many residents whose children had grown up and moved away, paying for the younger children's needs of newer residents was an issue. The longtime or elderly residents never complained when their own children needed increased facilities or additional staff and teachers. It was hypocritical but a tradition in most New Hampshire towns to avoid increasing taxes even if the need was justified for new infrastructure or improvements. Shortcuts seemed common and Band-Aid solutions in nature.

The Gilford Public Library was in that same quandary. Increased population needs demanded change to support the influx of newer transplants. Town meetings were often volatile and political.

In contrast, the opponents were always the first to complain if police protection or fire department responses were not adequate when needed—i.e. Bike Week protection from the transient influx of riders who might encroach upon their land or become rowdy with wild parties and excessive drinking. It was the smaller towns that had to provide self-protection and community aid ancillary to the bike events, including the annual Hill Climb event at a nearby Gilford mountain. Those unanticipated needs for revenue strained the town's budget because the total expenses were never known until the end of the nine-day event. Laconia faced similar revenue crunches and sought to offset the deficit with increased vendor fees.

The increase in visitors, to the tune of a few hundred thousand, strained the coffers in all Lakes Region towns. The costs were exorbitant to the little communities that already possessed reduced or "lean" budgets for police and fire protection for the entire year. Much of their annual allocations could be drained in one week of Rally activities.

Don entered the attractive library foyer and was primarily interested in researching a portion of the famed motorcycle gatherings of the past. In particular, he wanted to focus on the mid-1900's. He had previously been told that the 1940's and 1950's were very active years with problematic issues, and that the 1960's were a memorable, tumultuous time for the Gypsy Tour events as well.

Motorcyclists were rambunctious back then and police surveillance was limited in number and scope. Don knew of a special edition feature of the *Weirs Times* newspaper that highlighted the 75th anniversary of the motorcycle rallies focusing on, in part, their inception in 1916-1918, as well as the continuum of events from 1923 through the late 1990's.

The library had an extra copy of the 1998 issue of the *Weirs Times,* which he obtained and could remove from the stacks to study at home, if need be. But today, he was happy to ease into a couch in an alcove on the first floor of the library in relative peace and quiet. It was serenely warm and private as he placed his feet upon a nearby hassock and settled into the deep cushions of the sofa. He feared he would go to sleep.

The librarian, Ms. Foster, asked if he needed anything else on the subject and he thanked her for her offer. He had already perused many older photos of Bike Week by a noted, local photographer, Judith Rothemund. She had attended most Laconia Rallies for years, sometimes shooting some fifty rolls of film; they were mostly artistic photographs of the annual Rally attendees for historical purposes—unique bikes, men, women, and children. Each black and white memory conjured up a story, which Don could only imagine in his mind. Rothemund often exhibited her collection in a gallery at the historic Belknap Mill in downtown Laconia. The Bike Week annual exhibit drew large crowds.

The Belknap Mill remains today the oldest continuously operating brick textile mill in America and is listed on the National Historical Register of famous places. Oddly, in the mid-1950's, it was almost razed for a much needed urban renewal of the downtown Laconia area.

Today, in the new millennium, it hosts the likes of Rotary or Kiwanis events, concerts and speeches and political gatherings by modern-day presidential candidates every four years, much like Teddy Roosevelt who spoke in Laconia after his ascension to the presidency. The Weirs Beach event in the Veterans Grove was an auspicious occasion in 1902.

The newspaper was spread across his lap as he read each page of history concerning the Gypsy Tour. The pages had yellowed a bit but the articles and photos were a testimony to the historical perspective of the Laconia races, including the prominent founders of note and the biker racers of a long-gone era.

George Adams had mentioned to Don, and even Wendell Atkins had recorded in his journal, about the 1960's events in mid-June each year.

The highlight was the year 1965 when "all hell broke loose" on Lakeside Avenue.

"They were otta control," George had mentioned. "The bikers trashed The Weirs and injured the police, burned cars and buildings causing a major riot."

Don read about the 1965 event with passion. The paper had news accounts and local input by residents, as well as features by motorcyclists that had attended the events that year, some from long distances. Their accounts were informative and enlightening to Don—as to how serious the riots were and why they erupted in the first place.

Chapter 92

For the longest time, the blame was erroneously attributed to the Hell's Angels, for the flare up in 1965. It may, have however been initiated by a renegade group (bandit riders) from Connecticut, and not the Angels after all. During those Rally gatherings at The Weirs, bikers often hung out or camped in the Veterans Grove behind the Infantry Headquarters building on Lakeside. There was heavy drinking all day and night and bikers would walk the streets with illegal alcoholic beverages in hand. Public drinking was a violation. The bikers from out of town may have wanted respect, or perhaps the issue started over the blockage of the main road by a few cars that wanted to drag race.

In any event, it was clear that tempers flared and cars were rocked until they were turned over and later set afire. Stones were thrown at bystanders and at the local authorities who tried to calm the situation. It was purported that one biker climbed a telephone pole and hung a Nazi flag, screaming "Heil Hitler" or "Sieg Heil" in an apparent inebriated state.

The conglomeration of irate bikers had taken over the evening of June 21, 1965.

Don read more, and was amazed at the confrontation of the bikers with the local residents. There was distain and disrespect for the cops who had no choice but to let the event proceed until reinforcements were brought in at the State of New Hampshire level.

One account said that it started at 7:30 P.M. while another said it initiated later at 9:45 P.M. The riot did not end until 3:30 A.M. the next morning with 4,000 rioters of the 15,000 attendees at The Weirs revolting against the norm.

Apparently starting for no particular reason that was justifiable, the infamous event resulted in the calling up of 200 National Guardsmen (out of 600 on alert with some from as far away as Maine) donning bayonets, tear gas, protective face shields and riot guns with birdshot. There were numerous local police, sixty State Police, and riot squads, armed to the hilt. It was like a war with the authorities confiscating purported weapons the likes of meat cleavers, knives, bullwhips and chains from the rioters.

Then local Police Chief, Harold Knowlton; Mayor, Peter Lessard and Governor, John King responded to the melee. As one eyewitness told reporters, "Rioters with beer and babes in hand were tossing bottles at cars." They started at the "grassy knoll" of The Weirs and moved to Lakeside. Don thought of the infamous "grassy knoll" in Dallas where JFK was shot and that was two years earlier, in 1963.

The librarian sensing Don's intense research offered him a cup of coffee from her office. He gladly accepted and thanked her for her generosity.

"Please let me know if you need more reference material," she added, politely.

He sipped the coffee and stared out a nearby window taking a break from the research. His eyes finally cast down again on the paper. There was much more to the story as he would soon find out.

The riotous crowd that fateful evening had responded by throwing stones, beer bottles and any other object that was potentially harmful. Dangerous items were tossed at passing cars as well. Sixty-eight people were injured and about 40 were arrested in the melee, many of whom were taken to LRGH—the Lakes Region General Hospital. The nearby Half Moon Motel, a bowling alley and a restaurant were set afire and burned along with a portion of the Weirs Beach wooden boardwalk.

Due to the massive crowds, firemen were prevented from accessing the motel fire, the boardwalk or the flaming car, further fueling the inebriated crowds to continue the carnage and rampage.

The June event in 1965 was a permanent *black mark* on the annual Rally, virtually assuring a discontinuation of the event in the future, at least at the time. Laconia had had it with the rabble-rousers and desired to shut down future Rallies.

Don could not believe what he was reading. He was engrossed in the newspaper articles from the past. During the 1965 event, a helicopter was summoned that swooped down on the rioters and dropped tear gas from the open side door. The lack of wind kept the smoke localized in the area of the perpetrators that had already amassed near the burning car.

The State Police then formed a wedge of cops to disperse the crowd. Don had visions of the racial riots in the South and the need for the authorities to assert control.

A man with a camera in the crowd, Bob St. Louis, captured a photograph of the burning automobile on the infamous night in 1965. It eventually appeared in *Life* magazine and he received royalties of $1,400.00 for the classic shot. A flash bulb from St. Louis' camera also alerted the police to his location where they thought it was the flash from a gun barrel. They fired at him injuring the innocent bystander with birdshot, some of which remains embedded in his body today, the article stated.

Don Wright thought of his own prowess with a camera and wondered if riots would ever be instigated again at The Weirs. He thought not. He knew that the Hell's Angels and another gang had been at odds for years, fostering the spark that could result in another episode at the 2006 event. The increase in security over forty years at The Weirs almost assured that a 1965-like adverse event could never happen again.

Much had changed since the 60's anyway and Charlie St. Clair, the Executive Director of the Motorcycle Rally and Race Week Association, had petitioned local businesses and the mayor to revitalize the image of the Bike Week events. Charlie was a member of the Lakeside Sharks Motorcycle Club as well. His efforts helped restore a more positive image of the annual gathering.

Chapter 93

Through the efforts of the merchants and city officials, Don knew that the annual event was a huge income generator for the Lakes Region—a one-hundred-million-dollar plus boost to the local economy each year.

Recent years had ameliorated the past infringements of the bikers long gone. The City of Laconia had become hardened by the past events causing noted motorcycle enthusiast, Keith Bryar (Belknap Sports Park founder and expert sled dog racer) to move the annual events south of Laconia proper to Loudon, New Hampshire. He renamed the Laconia Classic, the "Loudon Classic" in defiance of the political constituents of the larger town to the north. The racecourse was called the Bryar Motorsport Park.

The late 1965 movement of the major Rally events ten miles south benefited Loudon and the surrounding small towns. The 1.6-mile motorcycle track was a favorite in the 1970's complete with a tent complex in the woods known as "Animal Hill." Campers drank, had sex and burned cars for fun or set afire the portable commodes of wood. Don Wright had attended those events when 10,000 people were the total crowd in the wooden grandstands. Today, the racetrack at Loudon is remarkably different.

Bob Bahre acquired the track from Mr. Bryar in 1989 and the modern NASCAR facility now holds up to 110,000 fans. The road races continue at the new venue but the vintage aura of years past, is gone forever. No mischief is allowed at the new facility.

It's a far cry from the AMA race of 1938, when Eddie Kretz, #28 from Pomona, California won the 181-lap, four hour and 41-minute feature race. The modern track in Loudon begs for the days of old.

Gone also are the 1980's winners like Fred Merkel, Wayne Rainey and Bubba Shobert, all race champions in their own right. Don Wright had seen them race in 1986 when Rainey took first place in the featured race that Sunday in June.

What remains today in Gilford however is the hill climb that takes place each year on the out run of the 70-meter ski jump at Belknap Mountain. Fritzie Baer, a Springfield, Massachusetts Indian motorcycle dealer, racing official and announcer, was credited with bringing racing to Laconia and Gilford, the AMA sanctioned events in 1938. Baer eventually moved to New Hampshire. He ran the Belknap Mountain Recreational Area from 1950-59. Brad Andres and Joe Leonard were top motorcycle racers back then in 1954 and 1955.

Baer put the annual event on the national map. He and his wife later owned and ran a Christmas Gift Shop at the Paugus Bay Bridge near The Weirs. The bridge allowed traffic to flow over the Paugus Bay Channel, much as it does today.

*   *   *

The research on motorcycle week at Laconia was vast and comprehensive in the library. There were many aspects of its history that might provide clues to the death of the young woman at the Weirs. With a busy day job, Don was overwhelmed with trying to study the library articles at both Laconia and Gilford and the journals that Wendell Atkins had written for posterity. Part of the key to "Jane Doe's" demise may have been related to the logo for the classic Vincent motorbikes. Then again, it was speculation on Don's part.

Don Wright studied the Vincent logo that he had photographed on the dead girl. He could see enough of the details to discern that the logo included the statue of the god, Mercury.

Vincent motorcycles had two or three renditions of the Vincent name embraced in scrolls. Some logos were emblazoned with the words, *The Vincent*, others said, *Vincent* with the letters *HRD* underneath and the neatest one of all was far more elaborate which showed the *Mercury god above the Vincent scroll* followed by the words, *The Vincent, H.R.D. Co., Ltd, Stevenage, Herts.*

The graceful logo was gold and outlined in black with the Vincent name in white letters. Don knew that the logo design reflected some sort of history and he was anxious to know more about each rendition.

Don was also intrigued by how the logo for the motorcycle came to be so ornate. Other motorcycle logos were impressive, but the Vincent design seemed more European in style and detail. Nothing that he had researched to date in Wendell's personal records elaborated on the initial concept of the design.

Don Wright found information that indicated that the Mercury logo was a decal designed for the side of the gas tank. It represented the "*speed and prestige of the Vincent brand.*"

It was clear that Stevenage, Hertfordshire was an historic town east of London and located in the south of England. The town was predominately known for its agricultural, mining, manufacturing and construction trades in its earliest days. In the early 1900's, it claimed a population of some 4,000 residents. In the early 2000's, it had grown to more than 80,000, a huge immigration of people in less than a century.

In the 1950's, the Vincent 1000 cc model, a V-twin, was produced in Stevenage, Herts, UK where today, many Vincent Owners Club (VOC) members meet at annual rallies dedicated to Vincent bikes, their heritage and the company's unique models.

It made perfect sense to Don, that the god, Mercury was appropriate in the design. Mercury was the Roman god equivalent to Hermes, the Greek god, and son of Zeus and nymph, Maia.

In essence, they were one in the same person. Mercury (Hermes) was the god of merchants and *land travel*. He was the messenger of the gods, *often flying with speed* and skill. Even today, he is sometimes shown with a winged cap and additional wings on his sandals—his swiftness lent to his credit for foot racing. To the Romans and to some extent the Greeks,

Mercury was the *god of the Winds* or "The Winged One," credited again in astrology with the planet, Mercury.

Mercury was precocious in mythology. At six days old, he stole cattle from Apollo, invented the flute and played the lyre. He was later known as the *god of Fertility*, a phallic god who touted good fortune and love often having numerous affairs with nymphs, goddesses and mortals. His offspring included the famed, Hermaphroditus.

Obviously, his presence on the Vincent-HRD logo was to *honor speed and swiftness*, symbolized by his winged feet. Those attributes were ascribed to the fast Vincent models of yesteryear.

Chapter 94

The tattoo on the dead "Jane Doe" or "Lady of the Lake" may not only have been limited to the tradition of Mercury's speed, but some fertility right. Don was mystified that there were many possibilities that might lead to the reasons for her death, or perhaps the cause. The mystery became more of an enigma and obsession for the photographer. *What in God's name did the specific tattoo and the motorcycle have to do with this woman's death? Wendell's records that were outlined in his journals might help in that regard.*

*   *   *

Don headed home on his Ducati. The voluminous reference material he had uncovered in Gilford exasperated him. Except for saying goodbye to the librarian, he had spoken to no one else. There were only two other patrons in the library at that time—two elderly persons reading current magazines.

He stopped to pick up the newspaper at the Laconia Spa convenience store on Church Street and to read of the police "lead" in the newspaper, based on the death of Iceman.

It was finally revealed in the press that the dead woman had been tattooed with a logo of a motorcycle company and that an unidentified Bike Week tattoo artist had applied the logo. The police said that details were sketchy since the investigation was ongoing. That was the standard line they used when the police didn't want to share information that they already knew was critical.

Linked to the woman and tattoo was the death of a man referred to as, Iceman. He was New Jersey-based according to the authorities interviewed in the article.

The police still assumed that the rider had drifted off the road early that morning and died upon impact—particularly from severe trauma to the head and torso. They were interested to know if he had been under the influence of some drugs or chemical, but the police did not inform the press of their suspicions. A full toxicology report would be needed first and that took time to analyze and prepare, and water down for the public layperson.

The police knew nothing of the connection of Iceman to Tiny Tim or the ill-fated ride in the middle of the night on Route 11 toward Belmont. There was no evidence that there was any other passenger or rider accompanying the dead man. Additionally, they had no inkling that Ace in New Jersey had arranged for the demise of the Rough Riders' number two, club member. Ace was number one, top dog so to speak and *Numero uno*.

In essence, Don Wright with the help of Wendell's journals and George Adams' input, as well as the expanded police info in the local papers, was on a different evidence track related to the death of the young girl. Dr. Blaisdell's autopsy of "Jane Doe" was the third link to the mystery. The recent details of those anatomical findings were confidential and Don was not yet in the loop.

The police were onto the tattoo artist, Fuzzy Walsh who was a star witness but Don had the inkling that it might involve a "historical ritual" regarding the motive for the girl's death. The police knew nothing of the Wendell Atkins journals or the fact that Wendell had alluded to a prior death of someone years earlier—a person with a similar tattoo and fate. The sad fact was that Wendell Atkins took his knowledge and secrets to his grave before he could reveal to Don Wright what he remembered from decades earlier.

Chapter 95

Being a newspaper photographer, Don Wright was in close company with the local police, a select group of officers his own age. They knew that he covered stories for the newspaper—locally related accident scenes, public political events and human-interest stories.

Don had coerced a local officer into confiding in him as to who had applied the Vincent tattoo to the dead girl. The policeman merely told Don that the tattoo artist was a transient artisan at a campground in Gilford. The name and location of the tattooist wasn't shared but Don was told that he was in the area for the nine days of the Rally and then would be moving to other race events or fairs around the country. He was a gypsy of sorts, Don had been told.

"Does the guy have a name?" asked Don of his confidant.

"Yah . . . but I can't tell his real name other than his nickname is 'Fuzzy' or somethin' like that. Not real sure. Some of our detectives have talked to him."

"Fuzzy?" Don repeated. "Fuzzy . . . a rather odd name."

"Yah," replied the cop, "Strange . . . since he has no hair!" Both men laughed.

"Supposedly, there is a sign out on Route 11 that will guide you to Fuzzy's tattoo place . . . some tent in the woods," the detective said.

"Thanks for the tip," Don added. "I owe ya one."

"You got it buddy . . . good luck findin' Fuzzy. There are probably fifty people with the name Fuzzy, here this week. Remember, you didn't hear anything from me."

Don nodded in the affirmative—he promised he wouldn't share any information with anyone.

Don, astride his Ducati Monster, headed east toward Route 11 in Gilford as if going to Alton Bay. He had to find this "Fuzzy" guy before the artisan departed the area.

The police had told Fuzzy Walsh to stick around awhile for they might have additional questions for him. For that reason alone, Fuzzy stayed. He wanted to escape the investigation but did not chance leaving town without repercussions. He was in a quandary as to when he could actually leave New Hampshire. He was trying to run his business but knew that he was under constant watch by the local police. Undercover detectives had already approached him twice before. *Might they pull that nonsense again?* he wondered.

He hardly slept at night knowing full well that the detectives might roust him up at any hour if they had more evidence to discuss.

Don Wright was now on a mission to add another piece of data to the infamous puzzle. Time was short and Motorcycle Week only had a few days left—ending with Father's Day. The relationship of the tattoo on the woman and the relevance of Iceman were unknown just like the role of the tattoo artist. Was he merely a pawn of the Rough Riders' agenda, or was he a key player in the death scenario as well? Don had no real clue and surmised that the tattooist was probably not a willing accessory.

By serendipity, Don had become the local Perry Mason through default. His day job at the newspaper was busy enough yet he was now inundated with, and possessed by, the death of the young woman.

Someone, somewhere was missing a daughter or relative. It was unlikely that her relatives even knew that "Tammy" X was deceased. Don could only imagine what that must be like for the girl's closest relatives. That is, if they ever found out she was missing to begin with and now dead.

*   *   *

Bonnie, the biker chick who had become Iceman's physical folly and concubine for the week, roamed The Weirs and vendor area. Overcome with mourning, she was "high" and in a stupor concerning the death of her newfound acquaintance. She would never see him again but she had her own secrets stored from the week of interaction with the man.

Oddly, Iceman had confided in her when drunk or after they had gone "a round or two" in the tent. The sex had been intense but she enjoyed being used and dominated. Like the song by the Dixie Chicks, she and Iceman had done their own "mattress dancing" and often. She was now alone and confused, distraught by the loss of the burly man from New Jersey.

After awhile, she tired of walking the Lakeside strip and entered another beer tent to further drown her sorrows. Having smoked a joint, she was hungry and thirsty. Budweiser and shots of 100% pure tequila were in order. She had planned on drinking alone but that would change. Inside the beer tent, she lit up a cigarette and ordered a drink.

Chapter 96

Dr. Blaisdell finished the autopsy on Iceman. His enormous body lay silent and austere on the stainless steel table, his private parts covered with a sheet. He had been examined from "asshole to aperture"—an expression of completeness by bikers. The pallor of his skin was surreal. His large abdomen, acquired from years of beer drinking, seemed less prominent, a testimony to the autopsy procedure that readjusted his organs and other internal anatomical morphology.

A wide band of cloth suture now closed and held intact his rib cage, thoracic cavity and abdomen. The gross exam had been thorough. Iceman's liver was enlarged and twice the weight of someone with a normal liver of his age. He was a heavy drinker and cirrhosis was evident to the medical examiner from the appearance of white scar tissue on the normally bright red organ. The organ that detoxifies the body, especially after alcohol or drug abuse had been challenged, trying hard to respond to and tolerate the insult from his many years of drunken debauchery and partying. He may have had hepatitis as well and tissue and blood cultures would confirm that later. Drugs and indiscriminate sex enabled that disease.

• Samples of the liver were taken for histology and further evaluations. It was inconsequential that his liver was enlarged other than his hepatic system and spleen had been ruptured from the accident. They were fragile organs in texture and easily damaged in violent accidents.

The immediate conclusion of the medical examiner was that Iceman had succumbed to none other than massive blunt trauma and the resultant irreversible and irrefutable brain damage exposing the gray matter of the brain through the cranium—a protective barrier of bone that had been breached to the open air on one side of his head.

He was killed instantly according to the summary conclusions on the medical examiner's official forms for State of New Hampshire. Blaisdell figured he had been dead three hours. Had he survived the impact, he would have been in a vegetative state. A portion of his head had been removed by the impact with the pine tree. Critical tissue areas of the cortex and cerebellum were missing. *Post mortem* X-rays showed other fractures of the neck and cervical vertebrate.

A portion of the bark from the tree had been embedded in his brain as well—the direct effect of having not worn a full-face, AMA-approved motorcycle helmet.

Iceman almost always wore no helmet. "Only assholes that rode Jap bikes wore helmets," he had said, repeatedly. It wasn't cool to have one on. If he did wear one on occasion, it was a unique, non-protective Prussian-type helmet or some piece of Nazi memorabilia sans the white swastika. The Prussian helmet had a sharp metal point on the top and was more for show than for his protection. It was a status symbol and novelty item all in one, making for popular spectator photography.

It seemed that none of his normal bike attire offered protection for him either. All riders of motorcycles tempted and defied fate. Iceman seemed oblivious to protective clothing or to the precautions or warnings. The non-sanctioned helmets were especially common to motorcycle gang members, often ceremonial or designed for vanity and tourists. Iceman liked to draw attention to himself with unique regalia. He surely did after he died. He was front-page news!

Iceman had once worn another helmet covered in polar bear fur. It had shock value since polar bears were a protected species. It merely reaffirmed his image as "cold" and "ice-like"—like the famed white bears in the Arctic. Other riders had their own identity and karma, often wearing buffalo skins and horns, fox fur or deerskin helmets like the Adonis' of the world.

One rider's bike was covered completely in buffalo hide. He showed up each year at The Weirs, the focus of women's ogling and other bikers who wanted to be photographed on his Harley with him.

June was not a month for animal hides as embellishments on bikes. The daily temperatures were not conducive to sitting on fur, and it naturally soaked up perspiration. If it rained as it did during this particular week, the fur would become matted and wet.

Many of the annual black leather crowd wore leather aviator caps from yesteryear or Model T dust goggles and black leathers. They were conversation pieces at best and emphasized their individuality. Since the unusual apparel and accessories were for show, there was no protection from the accidental motor vehicle encounters that frequently took lives. Don Wright had a file of Weirs Beach biker photos from prior years—each with their own story and message to the world. They were captured on film for posterity.

*   *   *

"This was one of the worst accidents in a while," Blaisdell commented to Donna, his assistant before leaving. She was finishing up the necessary legal paperwork as Blaisdell reflected on the blood and other fluid samples that would be sent out for forensic evaluation and toxicological-pathology.

"You're right, doctor. There's no way anyone could have survived that kind of impact. The funeral director in New Jersey will have to do *magic* to make this guy look normal. Half of his head will have to be recreated with plastic for sure."

"It's always the same, each year," Blaisdell reflected, with remorse. "Four hundred thousand people come here each Rally Week and some six or seven of those folks go home early . . . in caskets. I doubt that we will ever have a year of zero mortality. They take too many chances with bikes and booze."

Blaisdell seemed sadly reflective. He merely wanted to go home and chill out with a scotch on ice—an imported single malt liquor from a famed Scottish manufacturer. That would have to wait until after the paperwork was in order for the State of New Hampshire and the local police authorities in Laconia and Metuchen, New Jersey.

Chapter 97

Iceman's demise in the early morn had opened up another mystery for the police. He was closely linked to "Jane Doe" or "Tammy" as Fuzzy Walsh had heard Iceman refer to her, and no one really knew anything more about her—either her real name, her home of origin, her reason for being in Laconia or why she was with the Iceman the day of her Vincent tattooing in the first place.

Her body remained in a chilled mortuary drawer and next to the temporary slot for the Iceman. Partners in some ways in life, they were now partners in death in a Concord, New Hampshire cooler at the State Coroner's and Medical Examiner's Office.

Post autopsy, a local funeral home was to embalm the Iceman for shipment south to New Jersey the next day. A family member from New Jersey was expected to arrive at the Manchester Airport the next morning from Newark Airport—an airfield now deemed "Liberty Field" after 9/11. The identify the body was required since no Rough Riders members emerged to verify his identity—they remained conspicuously absent from any agenda of the police and wore nothing that identified them as the New Jersey Rough Riders Motorcycle Club. Ace demanded that they go incognito for the remainder of Rally Week.

With Iceman's fatality deemed to be an accident by authorities, the local police desired to interview other members of the gang from New Jersey, if they could only find them. They now had the daunting task of trying to locate any of the members, even one, and where they might be encamped for the week.

The fellow gang members were riding without their vests, which would have identified their club. Most members now wore Bike Week 2006 logo T-shirts making their affiliation with the New Jersey gang impossible to spot or identify. The command from Ace was to have them make themselves virtually scarce since the death of the Iceman.

Bonnie, on the other hand, surmised that Iceman had been targeted, "marked" by his own colleagues—she had an eerie sense that he had become dispensable in order to protect the club in New Jersey. The "heat" was too great after The Weirs escape on the back of the Nomad's bike.

Iceman had mentioned to her that his life was on the line ever since the escape on the bike. Iceman's name had been in the paper, a Mafia-like death sentence for any member being targeted or traced to a criminal investigation of that magnitude. The Rough Riders had house rules that assured their anonymity. Iceman *suspected his fate* long before he headed home to New Jersey. His conversation with Ace was cold and he knew he was doomed. He just didn't know who the "hit man" would be. He assumed wrongly that it would be the club leader, Ace himself, who would either grant him dispensation or a death sentence. No *individual member* was important, only the motorcycle club's survival.

*   *   *

On a mission for the newspaper deadline, Don Wright observed the brightly colored, neon poster on Route 11 north. He squealed to a stop. It said nothing but "Fuzzy's Tattoos—Cheap!"

"Holy shit," he said to himself. *Who in their right mind would be tattooing in the pasture? Could that be the 'Fuzzy' he had been told about and the photo he needed for the next* Faces of Bike Week*?*

He turned his Ducati Monster into the dirt driveway and followed the hand-made signs to the tent in the back of the local farmer's field. It was mid-day and most of the campsites were vacant. Most riders who were camped there had gone off on bike runs or were drinking at some local bar or beer tent. There was the Weirs Rally events and rock concerts, and time trials in Loudon. Fuzzy was one of the few people who remained in his tent. Time was money and the weekend was going to be his busiest time for customers. Revenue from Father's Day weekend surpassed all the money he had earned from the previous seven days.

Fuzzy had made a killing at the March 2006 Daytona, Florida Bike Week. He hoped to surpass that income in Laconia and the revenue target was close. The IRS never knew what income he generated anyway—most money was kept under the table. It was gravy.

How would the IRS trace him anyway? He was an automobile mechanic back home—his day job. Tattooing was heaven-sent, revenue-wise each year and was most profitable at each of the Daytona, Sturgis and Laconia events. County fairs in the fall were another means of making a quick buck. They were spread all over the Northeast and Midwest.

Chapter 98

Bike Week was comprised of more than just a congregation of thousands of motorcycle enthusiasts gathered in Laconia and at Weirs Beach. By Saturday, the long expected arrival of the Outlaws from Alfred, Maine rolled into Alton Bay, some distance from The Weirs festivities. The police were aware of their rivalry with the Hell's Angels and were adequately prepared to deal with any type of adversity. The Outlaws desired breakfast and lunch at a popular restaurant in Alton Bay. They had even called ahead to make sure that the restaurant would handle them in large numbers. They expected an aggregate of some 300-350 biker members in New Hampshire during the entire Rally Week.

The police had anticipated that they might head down Route 11 South to Weirs Beach. They had at least one helicopter in the air circling the Alton Bay area as surveillance. Other officers had radioed ahead in case the Outlaws were on the move. It had been less than a month since a Hell's Angels member had been attacked by a suspected Outlaw and shot in the leg in a tattoo parlor in Portland, Maine. His Angels' logo on his leathers had sparked the apparent incident.

This year it appeared that the Outlaws were not migrating south from Alton. They did promise to visit Laconia, New Hampshire in the future.

The official bike races that were the focus of the week for the non-Harley crowd were conducted in Gilford, downtown Laconia and in Loudon, ten miles south of Laconia's center. Route 106 was a straight shot to NHIS, a multimillion dollar, renovated speedway used for motorcycle road racing events and NASCAR / NEXTEL events twice a year. The track, which had originally seated a few thousand in the days of wooden slat grandstands, now accommodated ten times more people for NASCAR. Bob Bahre had invested millions into the first class arena, drawing NASCAR revenues from all over the United States. The NASCAR cult followed their favorite drivers like Jeff Gordon, Rusty Wallace, Dale, Jr. and forty or more other drivers. Both July and September drew the fans to the two NASCAR/ NEXTEL Cup events.

Motorcycle racing was present more than once a year but the annual Loudon Classic was the main draw. The track, even with renovations, was deemed unsafe by many bikers and sponsors—the shallow banking of the racecourse corners and uneven surface of the macadam were criticized in the past. Bob Bahre had put much cash into fixing those issues.

Foul weather made the track even more unacceptable with rain or moisture a precursor for potential tragedy. In recent years, Bike Week had its share of rainy weather in New Hampshire and main events on Father's Day sometimes had to be delayed or postponed to Monday.

In 2005, the AMA organization with famed international riders decided to talk to the track owners about a return to the facility in 2006. They had boycotted the track in recent years leaving the major Father's Day SuperBike and SuperSport races filled with local New England riders, not international stars. They were great riders but not of the class that had dominated the noted races in the recent past. Attendance by race fans dropped off when the likes of riders such as Duhamel no longer were "on the bill."

Nevertheless, ardent race fans always returned to the track to see who might win. In 2005, the major race on Father's Day touted Mansfield, Massachusetts' Eric and Jeff Wood and the likes of New Hampshire's Scott Greenwood. Eric Wood was defending champion and no one had won the event two years in a row since Duhamel—Eric was favored. The Wood-Suzuki team was expected to take top prize since Eric was the only rider supported by Formula USA, a distinct advantage over the other racers. His # 9 bike was unbeatable. For one thing, Wood had a backup of four to six other bikes that were ready to go. A trailer of parts followed the team. If they had to, they could probably build two more bikes from scratch. The resources seemed endless for the Suzuki-supported rider.

Greenwood, riding a Kawasaki 636 was "one man, one bike," and at a distinct disadvantage if something went wrong with his ride. The 636 model was a backup bike since his new Kawasaki 600 was back home in his shop with transmission issues. He was hoping to have the K-600 repaired and picked up in Massachusetts and ready by race time.

The 1.6-mile serpentine course at NHIS was awaiting both challengers for the main race in 2006. The fans supported both men.

Other events had already taken place. The annual Hill Climb was an old event with respect to the featured race on Sunday. Each year, the Laconia race committee prepared the 70-meter ski jump at Gunstock Ski Area in Gilford for the event. The vertical ride up the "outrun" of the ski jump landing area was a distinct challenge with winning times from bottom to top in the 6-second range.

Bikes often tumbled backwards on the steep grade and this year's event was marred with a week of inclement weather and a cold front that had stalled over the Lakes Region for days. Still the event was expected to draw some 10,000 or more observers at the meet.

In 2005, Laconia reinstituted the "downtown" road race through the center of the city. The race had a history of tradition. It drew some 2,500 or more onlookers who enjoyed seeing the vintage bikes from yesteryear compete on a tortuous racecourse through downtown streets. The bikes often included the Indian, Bultaco, Triumph, BSA, Benelli, DKW, Zundapp, Matchless and a host of other modified racers that offered sidecar racing around the downtown thoroughfare, including Beacon, Church, and Main streets.

Cordoned off with hay bales, the main drag in Laconia was a fun course for riders that had run the Laconia Classic races of the past. The 1950's were popular years for many older riders in attendance in 2006, some retained the passion for road racing and *winning*.

One 1937 model Indian seemed to run like new. The bike pits were located outside the 1890's Boston and Maine train depot, a gray and red stone station with a slate roof that reminded people of the Montreal and Concord Railway history that had once hauled ice, granite, lumber, textiles and passengers to southern New Hampshire and south to Boston.

The railway station was a testimony to the days of old, woman on bicycles, with hoop skirts and parasols, the days of steam transportation and electric trolleys that ran past the stone edifice of local significance.

*   *   *

Revved bikes and mufflers caused a continuous drone day and night. In the evenings, the persistent echoes of the exhausts of hundreds of passing motorcyclists permeated the Laconia, Lakeport and Gilford geographical areas. It was a compelling reminder that hundreds of thousands of people were added that week to the 17,000 residents of Laconia proper.

Local businesses thrived with restaurants and convenience stores benefiting the most. Beer, cigarettes and fast food were the main staples of life for nine consecutive days. T-shirts that were sold from roadside stands also yielded revenues for those willing to pay a vendor fee and stand for sixteen hours under a tent. The tents were interspersed with various merchandise offerings: food, boats, bikes, trikes, choppers, leathers, trinkets, T-shirts and memorabilia.

There were antique bikes and cars ranging from '57 Chevy's to old '59-'63 Corvettes on display, motorcycles and parts from headlights to taillights of vintage models. Contests were conducted for modified and built-from-scratch bikes that were touted as "primo machines," up and down Weirs Boulevard and Lakeside Avenue. Opechee Park hosted one event.

After 83 years, most area residents found the annual events attractive and enjoyable yet there were always the dissenters who wrote "letters to the editor" to local newspapers citing the noise and physical abuse of the countryside. Some locals considered the annual event a nuisance. They either liked the black leather crowd or hated them.

Traffic was hell as well—the roads to and from Gilford / Meredith / Laconia being the worst. There was a portion of Route 106 that often became persistent "stop and go" traffic akin to old Route 3 to and from Weirs Beach.

The loud pipes, and local regulations against certain decibel levels seemed not to be enforced by authorities with many modified exhausts thundering along throughout the normally serene streets and quiet nights of the Lakes Region. The drone of exhausts reverberated off the surrounding lakes and mountains, a resounding echo of yesteryear embellished by the increased attendance and bikes of the present day. The classic sound of Harley engines was rampant everywhere.

The peaks of the Belknap and Gunstock foothills of the nearby mountains kept much of the noise localized. Each June was the same—a welcomed noise pollution of increased economy—tolerable but ever sustaining each year. It was tradition—83 glorious years strong.

Chapter 99

Over the years, the motorcycle and biker incidents, accidents and deaths had been reduced. The police and EMS services were always at the ready, stationed strategically at various points near The Weirs. This particular year, the Dartmouth / Mary Hitchcock Hospital helicopter parked at the Lakes Region General Hospital in anticipation of trauma cases that might need special emergency team services in Hanover, New Hampshire.

Normally, the chopper service was used for assisting critical care patients, premature deliveries and traumatic injuries from car crashes and industrial tragedies. It was at the ready for motorcycle-related injuries during Bike Week, those requiring specialized head, thoracic, abdominal, neural and orthopedic therapies or surgery—the proverbial broken bones and cranial insults of crashes sometimes best served at Hanover's facilities. The Dartmouth Medical School facility and staff were unsurpassed in experience anywhere north of Burlington, MA or Boston.

Bikers rarely wore protective gear from head to toe. They were playing "biker vanity roulette" since most head injuries were fatal or irreparable leaving the motorcyclist or passenger in a vegetative state. Bikers basically were willing to chance it without protective gear, often thinking bandannas and sunglasses were a barrier, absolutely the most irrational thought process by them besides the combined alcohol consumption and riding.

*   *   *

George Adams stayed in touch with daily activities by watching area TV news stations and reading local newspapers. He watched TV Channel 9 out of Manchester and read the paper on the porch of the Veteran's Home. He had been following the events of the dead girl's scenario, a mystery to the general public but still on the minds of some Rally visitors from out of town as well.

"Where the heck is Don?" he mumbled to himself from his porch. He hadn't seen him in two days and wanted to show him more pertinent journal articles that Wendell had left behind after his death.

"This here one is about the old races and the dead woman from the 50's," he grumbled to himself, sensing his own impatience and frustration. "He'll surely be interested in this."

George sat back in Wendell's old rocker. The wicker seemed to creak more now as he rolled back and forth aided by his open toed leather sandals. He watched the vendors dismantling and folding the tents in advance of Sunday's races and the end of the weekend. It was Father's Day weekend as well and George lamented that not one relative had called him to wish him well. The day, however, was not over and it was only Saturday anyway.

Occasionally, a passing pedestrian yelled up to him and wished him well. They knew he was elderly and *his home* was basically *his life*, merely existing and watching the camaraderie of bikers and their babes from year-to-year. Most well-wishers were repeat visitors from out of town and very friendly.

George cordially nodded and waved hello. He continually looked for Don Wright. He knew he had a red bike but there were many red bikes on Lakeside Avenue. Some stragglers had yet to leave the Rally at The Weirs, even on the last days. Many remained into the next week—taking extended vacation.

After an hour, George moved inside his home. It was too hot and the sun was blazing on the front porch. It was the first day of summer and the weatherman had predicted high humidity and temperatures around 90°. He grabbed himself a Cola and glass of ice when he heard a knock on the door. It was his friend, Don.

"Hey George. What'cha up too? Bored now that the kids are all goin' home?" Don laughed. "No more young ladies in skimpy outfits?"

"Well . . . I got tired of waitin' for ya ta come by," he grumbled. "Glad all the noise is leavin' town. We can get back to normal for a while—that's until the people from Boston, Lawrence and Lowell come up for the 4th."

"Yah, imagine it will pick up again with tourists over the holiday," Don added. "They help the economy," Don suggested.

"Economy, my ass," spouted George. "All they do is increase the damn traffic here."

Don looked at the old man and smiled.

"Wrong side of the bed?" Don asked. "You seem a bit miffed today."

"Was waitin' for you to come by," he mentioned, handing Don an article or two about the girl who died some decades ago. "This will give you some idea of the history," he volunteered. "It's 1955!"

"Wow. This is great. You narrowed down the year to '55! 'They never solved the crime' it says here," Don responded, with excitement. "Holy crap! She had a detailed Vincent tattoo as well. This confirms what we saw in the earlier notes. Now we have the exact year! Great job, my friend!"

"Yup," said George, heading outside to the rocker again. "Damn sun is in my eyes."

"Here. I'll sit on the railing and block it," said Don, as he read the article once again with fervor.

"There's no picture of the tattoo in the old newspaper clipping," Don said, with remorse. "Wonder if it's the same as the one that was on the dead girl this week. Vincent motorcycles had four or more logos at that time. Could have been any one of them."

"Don't know," offered Don, who was now watching the staff of the Mount Washington boat take down the beer signs on the railings. It was a clear sign that Bike Week was near over and things were getting back to normal. The Mount would be sailing again the following week, loaded with tourists.

"Where ya been anyway?" George asked Don, somewhat curious by Don's unusually long absence.

"Had work ta do for the newspaper, my friend. Can't be watchin' all this ass all of the time. I leave that to you."

George Adams laughed. That had been his preoccupation for a day or two without Don around.

"I also chased down the artist who tattooed the girl that died. Lucky happenings for me!" added Don. "The tattooist, it seems, was set up in Gilford at some campground, operating out of your basic Sears and Roebuck tent. His clients are damn lucky they didn't get hepatitis from the pasture where he was running his operation. A damn farmer's field, ya know, bacteria everywhere. The cows walk the place when the bikers aren't there."

"Really?" George responded with interest. "Bet it was the Tuttle Farm, right? They cater to these outta-towners each year . . . make some added cash for the farm. They been doin' that for years to supplement their income. Eggs and milk don't yield much money these days."

Don nodded in agreement. George was right on.

"Yah, met some "Fuzzy" Walsh guy who remembered tattooing her with the Vincent logo. Initially, he was pretty defensive. After a while, he was pretty helpful to me. Apparently, the police had chatted with him the other day as well. He was scared shitless."

"I'd be scared too," said George Adams. "If I had tattooed somebody and they died a couple days later! Damned scared!"

"I suppose you're right, George. They haven't resolved the full details of the crime yet. They concluded that she didn't drown, at least they know that much. There was no blunt trauma to the body from some assailant or accident. She did visit this tattoo guy, Fuzzy, with a "bruiser" of a guy named, Iceman. Now he's dead too."

George sat forward. "Iceman? Dead too? It's related? Saw it in the paper. Ran off the road, the damn fool . . . probably hammered."

"Yah," replied Don, rubbing his hands together. "This Iceman guy took 'Jane Doe' / 'Tammy' X to Fuzzy to have the tattoo applied . . . ya know, the *Vincent* tattoo. Now he's dead—early morning crash on Route 11 East. Sounds suspicious. He was a member of the New Jersey Rough Riders—a motorcycle club out of Jersey. The police think they are still encamped in the Lakes Region, some campground in Meredith, Moultonborough or maybe Wolfeboro."

"Hmm," replied George, deep in thought. "So this was gang related ya think, some outta-town club?" he asked. George rocked a bit and rubbed his chin with his right hand.

"Don't think they know . . . except for the link to this Iceman dude who hit a tree in the wee hours of the morning. He was dead at the scene . . . severe head trauma . . . debarked a tree like Sonny Bono. Even the Dartmouth hospital couldn't help him if they tried. He went straight to Concord for an autopsy."

"Well," added George, shaking his head with disgust, "the bastards don't wear helmets and when they *kiss* a tree, the *tree* wins. Ya see, the bike and rider moves, but the tree doesn't," he stated philosophically. "When the hell will they learn?"

Chapter 100

Don seemed engrossed in the articles and journal that George had shown him. He sat up and stared at the elderly man in the rocker.

"I've got it!" he stated emphatically.

"You got what?" replied George, smirking. "Huh?"

"The *damn* tattoo definitely killed "Jane Doe" . . . and probably killed the girl in 1955 as well."

"This guy Fuzzy killed the girl?" asked George, stopping the rocking and turning up his hearing aid.

"Probably not," stated Don Wright. "He probably knew nothing about it."

"What the hell are ya talkin' about then?" asked an antsy George Adams.

"Fuzzy told me what he told the cops . . . Iceman brought *his own ink* for the chick's tattoo . . . the *black* ink, in particular."

"So?" stated George.

"Well, the tattoo of the Vincent logo has a lot of black—the outlines and other parts, like the god and the wheel and the logo."

Don hesitated, tapping his forehead repeatedly. "I think the ink was tainted with something that might have killed the girl. The tattoo was fresh and the needle probably delivered the poison or toxic substance through her skin by way of the charcoal black color."

"You crazy, Donald Wright? Who would go to all that trouble?"

"Nope. Not crazy at all. The *Iceman* I suspect. I think she was 'shot up' with something that the Iceman had in his little bottle of ink. The question is, not so much what she died of, but *why*? What the hell did the Vincent logo have to do with it, and who the hell is she?"

Jesus," George replied, "You may have something here. What does Wendell's journal say about anything like tainted ink? Anything?"

"I'm reading it right now. Give me a moment." By now, George was looking over Don's shoulder and believing his theory.

"I think it was some sort of ritual that has to do with the history of the Vincent motorcycle. What else could it be?"

"Really?" George commented. "What ritual would be part of the Vincent bike? Murder? Sacrifice? Tradition?"

"Don't know," replied Don, while reading as fast as he could.

George pondered the possible revelation. "They *celebrate* by killing a young woman? I can't believe that."

"I haven't the faintest," Don suggested. "It's also around the time of the Harley-Davidson 100th. It was a couple years back and Iceman road a Harley chopper. None of this shit makes any sense. Damn Wendell went and died before we could solve this crime. How untimely."

"They're competing for notoriety or recognition, the two bike companies?" George asked. "Harley vs. Vincent, ya think?"

"Nah . . . don't think so," added Don. "It must have to do with the Weirs Rally and races. They are historic . . . 83 years of racing and carousing on Weirs Beach and boardwalk. I think it has more to do with the Bike Rally, than the bikes."

"Why Vincent related?" asked George. "What the hell does that have to do with it? It's an antiquated old machine that half the people here have never heard of, let alone seen . . . for Chrissake."

Don Wright stood up, grabbing the porch railing for stability. He turned toward the beach area down below. He was leaning on the wooden supports and staring at the fading crowd walking the street.

"George ol' buddy. *That's* what *you* and *me* have to figure out. The police know of Fuzzy and the Iceman, but they don't know about the possible Vincent logo relationship other than the fact that Fuzzy applied the tattoo and used Iceman's ink."

George nodded in agreement. He seemed to be staring at one woman in a revealing outfit . . . a straggler . . . and listening to Don at the same time.

"Wendell gave us clues. The coroner can analyze the tissue from the tattoo or blood and maybe find what may have killed her. That may take some time . . . the blood work. Wonder if he sampled the skin on her back during the autopsy? He surely would have taken some blood for analysis. We, on the other hand, can help solve the reason or motive of why this young lady was chosen and killed."

George stood up slowly from the rail, his knees cracking. He stared at Don and nodded three or four times.

"She was murdered."

Don replied. "Yah? That's my guess too. But *why?*"

"That's the $64,000 question," George whispered. "No one knows why."

George excused himself. He had to pee badly and Don heard the screen door slam. The spring on the door jam was too strong, startling Don in his moment of deep thought.

Chapter 101

Many of the New Jersey Rough Riders had left for home. They got an early start before the Father's Day weekend was completely over. The SuperBike race meant nothing to them on late Sunday afternoon and rain was predicted anyway. They were in New Hampshire to drink, chase some skirts and hang out at The Weirs. Each man was instructed by Ace to keep their leather jackets in their saddlebags in an effort not to draw attention by the police. They knew that the authorities would be seeking out members of the Metuchen Chapter to reconcile the bizarre fate of their fellow rider, the Iceman. Few of them had been noticed and none were subjected to any interviews in Wolfeboro, basically scattering like ants after Iceman died to avoid the police investigation.

The newspapers and TV news had linked the Iceman and his affiliation to the girl's death earlier in the week. Most of the New Jersey Rough Riders were taking alternate routes south from the Lakes Region to the Massachusetts or Vermont border.

Some elected to take a long route down the Spaulding Turnpike toward Portsmouth. Others chose to seek out a shortcut to Vermont like I-89 N and then head south on I-91 toward Northampton, Massachusetts and eventually Connecticut and New York State. That route let them escape tollbooths on I-93 south where the police were checking for New Jersey tags in an effort to garner info on how Iceman was related to the unidentified girl.

The Laconia, Wolfeboro and Gilford police were in touch with Metuchen, New Jersey authorities. The New Jersey Highway Patrol and the local cops had a long prior history with the motorcycle gang. The infractions by the bikers were minor in the past, often being cited for speeding, loud pipes and rowdiness. Parties at the clubhouse often required police surveillance and warnings to control the level of noise and activities, especially during the summer months when outdoor parties were common on the grounds of the club.

At least two Laconia police detectives were to fly to Newark and ride to Metuchen to corroborate and help coordinate the investigation of the Iceman's death and that of the unknown girl. The relationship of, and evidence that the Rough Riders' club was contributory to her demise was readily apparent to most investigators. What was now needed was the input from the New Jersey authorities that might help elucidate the real reason for Iceman's trip to New Hampshire. The motives and deadly interaction were puzzling to all concerned.

Not only was a young woman's death an issue, the fate of Iceman was more than a coincidence. Even Fuzzy Walsh had found the man bizarre, his presence and massive torso had Fuzzy fearing for his life. He tattooed what the big man wanted and did anything to appease the desires of the Iceman's agenda with "Tammy" X. Iceman had no problem paying for the tattoo in cash. He had peeled off bills from a wad of green in his front pocket, a folded lump of greenbacks a couple of inches thick.

Fuzzy thought it odd that a client would have his own ink. No one else had ever brought their own ink to his makeshift parlor in the woods and pasture. The police needed to analyze the bottle that Iceman had brought to the tent. The ink was suspect and Fuzzy was merely the conduit for injecting her with the potentially fatal fluid disguised as a tattoo . . . a Vincent icon with the god, Mercury.

The leather travel bag, which Iceman had attached on the borrowed bike stayed intact during the crash in the woods—the bottle of black ink was inside of it. The forensic bioanalytical lab in Concord would be the recipient of the vial, a potential unknown toxic substance, if in fact it were inside the container. It was.

Another independent lab in the Midwest would receive an aliquot of the same ink. Between the two labs, they hoped to compare the chemistry against known substances that were known to be toxic and potentially lethal.

Chapter 102

Suddenly, there was a break in the possible identity of the dead girl known as "Jane Doe," "Lady of the Lake" and "Tammy" X. Although her parents had allowed her to attend Bike Week to work at one of the tent venues selling T-shirts, Tamara Williams had not specified or shared much of an agenda with them about her trip or where she would be staying during the Bike Week Rally festivities.

Her parents knew she had friends near Lake Winnipesaukee and allowed her to go to Bike Week with the understanding that she was to stay with people that she knew well. She had assured them that she would be fine during the annual event. Her desire was to earn some quick, easy cash. The parents, Sue and David Williams had not heard from her but Tamara had a cell phone to stay in contact with them. She kept the phone turned off most of the time. A cell phone, however, was not recovered near any body. Was this the same Tammy?

Tamara Williams had grown up in Medford, Massachusetts just off I-93 near Boston. Her parents still lived there. Because the blonde woman who died was still unidentified, the police had no real description of the girl besides her physical appearance, a necklace and two or three tattoos.

When the parents first read in the Boston Globe of a deceased young girl at The Weirs, Tamara's mother and dad were not concerned. The young, dead woman was described as having a tattoo on her back that read the name, Vincent. The Williams family knew that their daughter did not have that particular tattoo on her body and she had no real desire to get another tattoo, her mother had remembered. Tamara had indicated that they were painful procedures, at least for her sensitive skin. Obviously, the parents were unaware that this "Tammy" had acquired a new tattoo during the extended days of Bike Week.

After not being able to reach Tamara for two or three days, the parents had left many messages on her cell phone voicemail. They began to worry when the young woman had not touched base with home. In an effort to alleviate their stress, they had contacted the Laconia police to ascertain whether the authorities could help locate their daughter. They realized that there were hundreds, if not thousands, of visitors during Rally Week.

"Can you describe your daughter, sir?" asked the patrolman on duty to the father who was concerned. "We usually fill out a form for missing persons—it helps with distribution of the data to all police units on duty."

"We're not sure that she's missing, sir . . . but we are concerned having not heard from her in days. She was supposed to work a T-shirt venue but we are not sure which one."

"Most people at the Weirs never touch base with home, sir," the cop reassured the Williams father. "We can however try and help, if you really think this is serious. Kids usually avoid home when they're here. Perhaps the phone is off."

The Williams parents talked for a moment amongst themselves. They finally agreed that it was unusual not to hear from their daughter. They decided that a report should be filed anyway, at first by phone.

"I have no problem completing the basic form for you if you answer a few questions," the officer said, cordially. "Can you describe her general appearance please?" The officer wedged the phone against his shoulder as he grabbed a pen and "missing persons form." He did not want to jump to conclusions regarding the name of the girl but in the back of his mind he feared the worst for the parents.

The father took a deep breath and closed his eyes, while thinking of his daughter's features.

"She's 21 and blonde, sir, . . . 5'7", attractive and goes by 'Blondie' or 'Tamara,'" the father commented. "She may be working at Weirs Beach—selling biker T-shirts," he repeated. That was her plan when she left home. Someone promised her a job."

The officer was quite candid. "Sir, that description fits a lot of girls this week. There are some 400,000 people here, many of them blonde, female and about that height. They are from all across the country, sir. Can you be more descriptive please?"

"She has a tattoo on her ankle and one of a cross on her shoulder."

The policeman went white. "Does she have any other tattoos, sir?" he asked with reluctance, knowing the missing girl fit the description of "Jane Doe" or "Tammy" X.

"No, sir. Not to our knowledge. We know of no other tattoos or markings, like scars, etc."

"Good . . . that's good," replied the policeman, cordially. "Has she ever gone by the name, 'Tammy?'" the policeman asked, slowly.

"Why yes . . . but only occasionally, sir. Some of her girlfriends know her by that name, but we call her Tamara and most friends do too—she was named after her grandmother, Tamara Williams, my deceased mother. She likes the formal name."

The policeman on duty placed his hand over the receiver and summoned a nearby supervisor to pick up an extension.

Captain Bennett had overheard part of the ongoing conversation, however the policeman on the phone needed to bring him up to speed on the dialogue to date. The officer alerted the Captain to the name of the family.

"Mr. Williams," he jumped in, "this is Captain Bennett of the PD in Laconia. The officer that was talking to you asked me to speak with you. Is that okay?"

"Sure," replied Mr. Williams, now apprehensive of the new person on the phone.

"I wanted to ask you when you last saw your daughter. Was it shortly before the onset of official Bike Week? The other officer here said you live in Medford, Massachusetts. When did she come north from Medford?"

"A couple of days before the actual Bike Week, I think—right, honey?" he asked his wife. "Why, Captain? Do you think someone has seen her?"

"Sir," said the Captain gingerly, "we don't wish to alarm you but there has been a tragedy up here and the unidentified person who . . . succumbed . . . this past week is a young woman who is blonde, you're daughter's height and went by the name of Tammy."

The phone went silent in Medford. The father held the phone with both hands and grappled for words to respond to the comment of the implied death and close analogy.

"Tammy?" he said, repeating the captain's words verbatim . . . "you said, Tammy?"

"Yes, sir . . . had you heard of the unidentified woman and a untimely death earlier this week?"

"Yes," came a muted reply at the other end. "I didn't equate it with my daughter or the possibility that she might be the victim but saw that a young woman had died."

"We understand the deceased to have gone by the name, Tammy," Bennett continued, "but we have yet to confirm that the person who died is a Tammy or Tamara or any other name. But the coincidence is uncanny in that you called us with a name that is similar to that of a woman with no I.D. The report in front of me also has a description of other similarities to your daughter and the deceased, but there could be any number of *Tammy's* here."

The Captain could hear the father sobbing as he tried to explain to his wife the coincidence and the potential loss of their child. They were devastated knowing that their daughter might be dead in New Hampshire and yet unidentified.

Captain Bennett gingerly and softly commented,

"Mr. Williams, I know we are dealing with the unknown here but I am requesting that you come to New Hampshire to hopefully tell us that this is *not* your child . . . we pray for that . . . to see if the deceased girl is a stranger or a relative of yours. We are hopeful that it is not you child, but without your visit, or one by another family member, we can only assume that there is a women with a similar description deceased in our Concord, New Hampshire morgue."

"I understand, Captain," he cried out in pain. "I want to rule her out. It can't be her—it just can't be."

"Either way, sir, you can help us at this point. We have no leads as to who this young woman is," the Captain pleaded. It was his only lead in the case of the unidentified woman. "Please sir," repeated the policeman. "Can you help us resolve the issue here?" There was a pause.

Silence prevailed as the father tried to catch his breath. He was beyond distraught knowing that the name and the description thus far might be his one and only daughter, Tamara. He tried to talk to the officer and also tried to allay the fears of his wife. She was seated in a wingchair, sobbing uncontrollably and fearing the worst.

"Mr. Williams . . . can we have her cell phone number? Maybe we can reach her at this end and elicit a response. If she answers, I will get right back to you . . . immediately. We *want* her to answer!"

"Sure," responded the father. "Oddly, It has her name in the numbers—TAMARA." The father then gave the Captain the remainder of the number and area code for Medford.

The father now seemed confused. He had no idea where he needed to go in New Hampshire. He knew of the towns of Concord and Laconia and spaced out on the location of the morgue that had been mentioned earlier in the conversation. His head was hurting and his stomach was upset and nauseated. "Concord, I think," the wife whispered to him.

"Where would I go, sir? Meet you in Laconia?" he asked, almost sounding composed.

"No, sir, I would ask that you go to the Coroner's Office in Concord, New Hampshire. I'll give you directions. It is not far from Exit 14, sir. Do you have a paper and pencil handy?"

"Yes, sir," he replied meekly. "Please tell me exactly where and when. I know Route 93."

Chapter 103

The police captain tried to allay the fears of the father and was saddened by the conversation with the distraught parent. He had two teenage girls himself and they were similar in stature to the dead young lady. He could not imagine losing either one of them in any tragedy like the scenario at The Weirs. *Parents were not supposed to bury their children; the children were supposed to bury their parents.*

The captain detailed the directions as explicitly as he could over the phone. Mr. Williams jotted down each and every word, repeating the directions and instructions. His hand shook and the pen made jagged words across the lined pad of paper. He needed the policeman to repeat as much of the message as he could over the telephone. The officer was happy to oblige, detailing of the roads and landmarks to focus on. They then concluded the call with some assurance that the parents from Medford could find the Coroner's Office off Hazen Drive.

"Sir, I will call the coroner, Dr. Blaisdell, and explain that you will be there today. Dr. Blaisdell's staff will also be of assistance. He is both the State Medical Examiner and Coroner for New Hampshire. Please be aware that the unidentified woman has had an autopsy. It was inconclusive as to the cause of death but further blood and tissue analyses are needed and are in progress—some tests are pending and can take days or even weeks."

"I understand," replied the distraught father. "Would dental records help you, sir?"

"Actually, a visual confirmation is feasible, Mr. Williams. The body was not harmed physically. The person was found dead on the shoreline of Lake Winnipesaukee. No overt violence or trauma to the victim was noted or reported by the coroner. Dental records would only be needed if the deceased had been dead a long time. If you wish, you may bring an X-ray from your dentist if you think it is necessary. At this point I see no reason to do so, sir."

"I won't request them then," responded the father. "If the medical examiner needs something later, we can oblige."

The father said a silent prayer hoping that dental records would never be needed or "a match" at a later date. He was optimistic that it wasn't his beloved daughter in the morgue anyway.

"I would suggest that you have someone drive you up to New Hampshire since you are emotionally distressed at the moment. I pray that it is not your Tamara," Captain Bennett said, with sincerity. The father said he would consider that option.

The officer asked one more question. "Sir, does she wear any jewelry by chance, ya know . . . especially often?"

The father sighed for a moment . . . and indicated that he had given her a gold cross and chain for Easter. The captain was distressed to hear that. She also wore two or three rings, he had said.

"Sir, this young woman also had a gold cross and chain found at the scene. I'm very sorry. That was all she had for jewelry I do believe. It was lying in the sand and close by her neck. May have broken or fallen off."

Williams did not tell his wife of the cross and chain. He went silent and then thanked the LPD officer as best he could under the circumstances. He did not want to hear any more. The father merely wanted to get on the road and see for himself the unknown person that was deceased.

"Sir," said Captain Bennett, "Tell you what. I'll meet you in Concord. I will wait there for you and hope to be of some help."

Bennett was not obliged to do that. He felt compelled to be of assistance since the case was from Laconia and he felt assured in his heart that the dead young girl was their daughter. He was also dismayed that he was about to know her real identity, an enigma to date. He still did not want to deal with grieving parents of teenagers or young adults. It hurt. From a police standpoint, it was important to resolve the outstanding mystery case. From a personal aspect, Bennett needed to be there for the Williams family and for himself—he was, after all, a compassionate person. The case needed resolution and this was their only lead to date that seemed relevant. Good or bad, it was a necessary evil for the police and for the parents.

Chapter 104

Don Wright had felt for some time, that the young lady that had died had been given something toxic or poisonous by way of the tattoo. It made perfect sense. The cops were on to that theory as well having discerned that the ink Iceman provided was most probably the culprit. No information was shared between the separate groups of people who were investigating the crime.

Because the toxic agent, which might have killed her, was unknown to authorities, and secondly, the motive for her death was questionable, Don felt compelled to contact Dr. Blaisdell at the Coroner's Office in Concord. He surmised that something in the fresh tattoo was placed into the skin by way of the needle that Fuzzy had used. The proof was now beginning to gel primarily because of the input from Fuzzy Walsh.

Don merely wanted to know if the coroner had thought about the tattoo of the Vincent logo as a route of administration of some evil substance. It remained a curiosity to Don since he was not medically trained by any stretch of the imagination. He knew that during most autopsies, the medical examiner took samples of the critical organs that sustained life—those organs included, in part, some forty plus tissues from the heart, lungs, liver, kidneys, brain, GI tract, spleen, pancreas, reproductive organs, blood vessels, and bodily fluids. *Was skin part of that evaluation?*

The tissue evaluations, gross and microscopic, often provided clues to what happened to a victim who succumbed to a drug overdose, chemical poisons or congenital effects that were of genetic origin. The pathology could be conducted by frozen tissue sections or standard formaldehyde-treated tissue embedding in a paraffin block, then treated with H&E or other stains that identified normal vs. abnormal pathological effects—cells that deviated from the norm like cancer or cirrhosis, anoxia or inflammation. The latter analytical process required tissue sections, preservation, dehydration and staining to ascertain abnormal cells. That took time and the pathological investigation required a laborious microscopic examination by a trained clinical pathologist.

On the other hand, frozen tissue sections offered a quick "look-see"—the tissue slices often performed on a chilled cryostat. They were less detailed and the morphology of the tissues had less resolution, but the procedure was used during surgical operations to confirm cancer or unknown organ samples while the patient was on the table. Cryosections could aid in probable cause death situations when general histology procedures took a lengthy period of time, sometimes many days. Analyses of blood, however, still took longer especially when the killing agent was unknown or minuscule in quantity.

*　　*　　*

"Dr. Blaisdell," Don said, "thanks for returning my call. I am doing a piece for the newspaper, which covers some of the anatomical pathology of victims of crime. I could use your input. Autopsies are an enigma to most lay people. Can you share the basics without scaring the hell otta me or the public?"

"Sure. How can I help?" Blaisdell asked. "The procedures differ with each victim. State law requires autopsies on people who die violently, yah know, knifings, gunshots, battery, some car accidents and other suspected causes of death. The idea is to methodically isolate the cause of death through the telltale clues of the bodily organs and fluids," he offered.

"The cause of some deaths are often quite obvious, hence we do not always have to do a full *post mortem*. There are distinct effects on the bodily organs that are visualized during gross observations. Others require tissue sections that reveal cells that are abnormal or damaged. Still others show evidence of harmful substances in the bodily fluids like blood, saliva, GI tract, and urine, feces or the reproductive tract. It's often painstaking but thorough, and necessary."

Don eased into the question he was really after. "What critical tissues are usually taken or sampled for evaluation, doctor? I assume that they include the major organs which you mentioned and all would be critical in determining death—do you ever deviate or modify the procedure and take other samples?"

"Yes . . . that's true, Donald, we take samples of other organs that are 'suspect.' We often remove and weigh the major organs first and examine them grossly for abnormalities—a visual exam for color, weight, size and general appearance. Other samples are just snippets of tissue from nodes, vessels and skin. For example, if the heart has failed, we need to look at the structure to see if the heart muscle is scarred or if a valve or coronary vessel has failed or shows an anomaly, something not normal in the morphology / structure. Often, we examine the arteries that supply nutrients to the heart, i.e. the coronaries. If they are blocked, we can see which part of the muscle has been deprived of oxygen or nutrition. Instead of red or pink in color, the infarct or heart attack area may be white or discolored from oxygen depletion and scar formation—a fibrous tissue."

Don was fascinated by the information but was skirting the issue he was really after.

"I was curious to know if the skin is sampled in different areas. It would seem that many causes of death might be related to skin penetration," Don stated, with curiosity.

Dr. Blaisdell thought the statement profoundly relevant and timely.

"Sure. We often can determine if a chemical enters the skin in what we call dermal absorption. Pesticides, heavy metals and other toxic agents can enter the blood through the skin, especially after extended exposure to a solvent or a topical agent that is readily absorbed in fat. There's a whole list of toxic substances that can cross the skin and enter the blood, even if applied to the surface."

Don wanted to get to the heart of the matter. "The other day I saw a man with his body covered with tattoos. From head to toe, he was proud of the artwork that he had acquired over a period of 25 years. Isn't that harmful?"

Blaisdell indicated that tattoos had been around for centuries. "Because they are usually localized in the dermis and surface, ink usually doesn't enter into the blood stream unless applied too deep or across a major vein of the arm or leg. That can happen by mistake and some people might have an allergic reaction or go into anaphylactic shock. Some pigments are home made and can be lethal."

"I read where the pigment or dye in tattoos can be made from just about anything, depending on the culture and country," Don offered.

"That's true but most tattoos are relatively safe. Toxicologists have looked at most of the *common* dyes and carriers. Some colors are made from salts of metals . . . those metals may be toxic. Somehow the body tolerates the insult," Blaisdell laughed. "I'm not sure how. We seem to insult our precious skin and organs with cigarettes, alcohol, drugs and other substances that the body would rather reject. It has a way of telling us it objects to the intrusion."

He continued.

"The liver and kidneys help rid the body of these noxious agents—that is if both organs are functioning normally. Heavy metals like lead, mercury and other substances can often settle in fat or in the bones, and are sort of permanent. The body can't remove them naturally."

Don got more specific. "Can I be candid, doctor?"

"Sure Don . . . shoot."

"I have a hunch about the dead girl from The Weirs, ya know . . . 'Tammy' X. In the newspaper, they mentioned your initial report was still in progress. Your preliminary data showed no real trauma to her body, right?" he inquired. "Might her death have been attributed to something on the *inside* . . . ingested or injected?"

"That's totally possible. I hope to solve that unknown portion of the crime. She died for a reason and we need to solve it. She was young and healthy for the most part. Of course, her medical evaluation *post mortem* is confidential and incomplete. We still don't know who she is and that's a sad scenario. She's someone's child."

He wondered where Don was going with the conversation. "Do you know something that I don't know about this case?" he asked Don. "You're out there on the street for the newspaper and could have information that could help."

"No. Not really . . . relevant to a motive, but my hunch is that she may have been injected with something that was poisonous . . . during a tattoo process. As we saw at the scene, The "Vincent tattoo" on her lower spine seemed recently applied. Is that not true?"

"Yes . . . that's true. It may have only been two or three days old by our estimates. There was swelling in the general area that suggested it was recently applied and the skin was elevated further suggesting inflammation common to new tattoo applications. Edema is one word for it. Erythema is another."

Blaisdell offered more.

"The body reacts as if a tattoo is a normal injury, ya know, like an abrasion or puncture, with the area becoming inflamed and puffed from the insult of the procedure or injury. If you pricked yourself while trimming rose bushes multiple times, you'd see inflammation and redness, right? It's kind of like that but with thousands of little punctures."

"Yes doctor, I've surely done that to myself wrestling with my garden plants and shrubs. It's not pleasant."

"Same thing, pretty much," replied the coroner. "Tattoos bleed like a puncture from a rose thorn. Some people get inebriated before undergoing the procedure, just to alleviate the pain. This can cause more bleeding. Anyway Don, the mystery continues about young 'Tammy' X."

Chapter 105

Don was ready with the next question. He felt as if he was on a roll.

"Aside from the blood that you might sample from a body, do you ever take tissue from . . . let's say . . . the tattoo area, ya know, as a possible entry of a toxic substance into the body . . . through the skin and into the blood stream?"

"Sure. Why do you ask? Are you thinking that the new tattoo that she acquired has some clues?"

"Well . . . yes. The police, I think, are on to something. I heard that through the grapevine. I would imagine that you might take some tissue from that tattoo."

Dr. Blaisdell was impressed with how astute Don was with his questions—an analytical mind for sure. Tissues that were *raised* from an inflammatory response might show deleterious bacteria or viruses that could cause someone's death. The coroner would surely want to culture the dermal layers to rule that out. He had not really thought of the tattoo site as a port of entry of a deadly chemical substance, at least not this early in the case.

"We didn't sample much of the young girl's tattoo, but come to think of it, it may be a wise thing to do—go back and recheck the site. A needle and a tattoo gun could introduce a poison or chemical into the body. It's not much different than an injection by needle in a doctor's office. Those injections are usually applied deeper than tattoo applications but you may have an idea here worth pursuing. I'm surprised that the police have not been forthright with me if they have info that is relevant. I will call the LPD."

Don was opening a can of worms, he thought. Now he was concerned for all involved.

"Doctor . . . I have this suspicion that this girl may have been "done in" by that route. The police have located a tattoo artist. Supposedly, he has been questioned on when that specific tattoo was applied."

"I've heard rumors," remarked Blaisdell, limiting his conversation to a quick answer. He knew there was a connection to the man called, Iceman.

"You've given me pause to reconsider sampling where she was tattooed. But I must run. I have a *post mortem* to complete. Please let me know if you have any other ideas that may be spurred by conversations on the street. You're out there chatting with people and I hope we can all help solve this horrific black mark on Bike Week."

Don was appreciative of his time. "Thanks, doctor. I will keep my ears open. I appreciate the pathology lesson too."

"My pleasure, Don. I hope to see you less frequently," Blaisdell offered, humorously. "Ya know . . . when I see you and your camera, it's usually bad news," he chuckled.

"True, doctor . . . very true," Don acknowledged.

*   *   *

That afternoon, Dr. Blaisdell and Captain Bennett from the LPD greeted the Williams family in Concord. To ease the burden before visiting the morgue, Blaisdell was kind enough to first show the mother and father a gold chain and cross. The response was immediate grief and a possible connection. They recognized that the jewelry was similar to their daughter's necklace, but the details on the cross they had not memorized. There was immediate confusion. It seemed to confirm their worst nightmare—their daughter Tamara was dead. The jewelry was not definitive evidence to the mother however—she appeared to be in denial. She thought the chain was much thicker on the one they had given their daughter. The type of link seemed a bit different as well. This chain was herringbone in style and Mrs. Williams seemed to remember a box link chain. She cried profusely anyway, overcome with emotion and total confusion.

Tamara's mother could not bear to see her daughter and the father followed the two men toward the coroner's lab and mortuary area, a wall of refrigerated stainless steel drawers. As many times as Bennett had been in that morbid room, it was always like the first time. He knew that a father was about to confirm that his daughter was deceased. The discomfort and anxiety of the moment was insurmountable.

"Before we open the door to the morgue, can I be of assistance to you?" asked the policeman, holding the father's arm gently at the elbow. He was concerned that Williams might faint. Williams wore a blue sport jacket, with an open-collared Oxford blue shirt and khaki pants. The policeman could not see the perspiration underneath each arm of the father. Williams was nervous and appeared weak, shuffling his feet instead of stepping in a normal gait. His face was ashen and tears welled up.

"No, thank you. I'm okay at the moment."

Blaisdell watched as the father looked around the large room, a stainless steel cadre of tables and overhead surgical lights. There were trays of instruments, similar in arrangement to a surgical suite at a hospital. The glass cabinets above the soapstone and stainless lab benches were full of disposable items—boxes of sterile gloves, gauze, disposable drapes, solutions and jars for the preservation of tissues. One bottle was clearly labeled 10% neutral buffered formalin; others included various percentages of alcohol (EtOH). A scale was nearby for the weighing of organs. It reminded the father of a simple fruit and vegetable market scale. He stared at the accessories and fell silent into a stupor. He knew he was six feet from the door and drawer with his daughter inside.

Blaisdell and a technician saw Mr. Williams stare longingly and deliberately at the surgical lights on the ceiling, as if in prayer and then refocus on the stainless steel autopsy table and smaller tables on casters that held sterile towels and medical tools, in waiting. Captain Bennett stood back for a moment

A flexible hose hung precariously near the table and was there to wash away blood and related medical waste during autopsies. It was adjacent to a vacuum downdraft system that removed the stench of death when bodies were beyond recognition and decomposed to some degree. The father seemed to be entranced by the sophisticated medical supplies, avoiding the inevitable task ahead—the mortuary drawer about to be opened. It was something that most people never wanted to see. He turned and faced the men in the room and the stainless steel wall of horror.

Chapter 106

Dr. Blaisdell walked over to the stack of refrigeration units. He looked over his shoulder as if to seek confirmation that he could proceed with the viewing. Mr. Williams nodded.

He slowly opened drawer number 7 and a chill enveloped the immediate area from the open unit. It was like a rush of a cool breeze to Mr. Williams. The father took a deep breath as Blaisdell hesitated and then pulled the marble-lined slab toward him. The body moved with ease as the slab was on rollers and a track. The noise mimicked the opening of a file drawer.

The sound of the movement was unbearable to Williams. He had an elaborate toolbox in his garage—the top-of-the-line drawer system from Sears. It made the same sound when opened and the callousness of the metal sound made the task at hand impersonal.

The body was covered in a pure white sheet. The outline was that of a woman. Only the toes were exposed. An I.D. morgue tag hung from the large toe. There was no formal name on the tag. Williams shook at the sight of the draped cadaver, a feeling like he had entered a cold storage unit without a coat. The hair on his arms stood up from the chill and the fear of the unknown. He had never done this before.

• *Was his daughter under the sheet in front of him?* His wife remained with a compassionate office assistant, in the lounge area outside the morgue. Williams held his breath and blinked repeatedly out of nervousness.

Dr. Blaisdell slowly peeled back the sheet revealing the face of the deceased girl. Captain Bennett reached for the elbow and upper arm of Williams. He was in shock and covered his face in his hands. He sobbed violently and turned away from the visual mask of death. "You can close it," he cried out. "Wait . . . let me look again, please."

He turned again and stared, leaning even closer to the girl that lay in front of him.

There was a sigh, a sense of relief and he closed his eyes.

"Oh . . . Jesus and Mary, Mother of God," he exclaimed, with tears. He looked at the coroner.

"*That* girl is not my daughter," he said, quietly. "*That* is not Tamara. Thank God." He prayed to the heavens with clasped hands. Captain Bennett stood stupefied. The silence was deafening.

Dr. Blaisdell and Captain Bennett were in shock. "Mr. Williams, please look again! Are you sure?" asked Blaisdell. "Are you really sure?"

Williams smiled ever so slightly. He was relieved and repeated the remark, "Gentlemen . . . *that* is *not* my daughter. I don't know whose beautiful daughter it is, but it is not *ours*. I pray for this girl's parents and for this girl's soul. I'm sorry . . . actually I'm not sorry," he said, honestly. "That young girl is not my child. I need to tell my wife immediately that this young woman is not Tamara."

Chapter 107

Blaisdell was aghast at the implied mismatch. He was happy that it was not the child of the Williams family but he was stymied. He and Bennett knew they were now at ground zero in the identity of the young dead woman. They had pretty much assumed that "Tammy" X was the girl from Medford, Massachusetts—Tamara Williams. The description on the phone had been a virtual *clone* of the Williams girl.

"The cross and chain?" Mr. Williams. "Was that not her cross?"

"There are many similar chains and crosses," Mr. Williams remarked. "Even if it were my daughter's chain in the lobby, that was not my daughter I just saw. I hope I have not disappointed you gentlemen, but I must tell my wife that the woman is not our child. Please let me go to her. She is agonizing out there."

Both Blaisdell and Bennett stepped aside as an assistant, who seemed to appear from nowhere, rolled the cadaver back into the cooler. The door closed like a meat locker. The sound was as cold as the "environment" in the room.

The swinging doors to the lobby opened and Williams leaned over and grasped for his anxious wife and smiled. She rose slowly from the chair, moist handkerchief in hand. They hugged tightly as he informed her of the situation. Once outside the morgue, Blaisdell approached the couple and touched their hands.

"Sir. Ma'am. There's no disappointment," remarked both men almost simultaneously. "We are pleased that your daughter Tamara is alive . . . somewhere." Bennett indicated that they would do their best to find their real daughter and have her contact home as soon as possible.

Mr. Williams constantly repeated the words to his grieving wife. "It's . . . it's not her in that room, honey . . . it's not Tamara!"

Mrs. Williams' knees buckled and both officials near her noticed the symptoms. She was fainting as all three men assisted her gently to the floor until she responded to their voices. She was lying on the rug as her husband patted her cheek. Bennett elevated her legs to get blood back to the head. Blaisdell ran for some water, thinking she might be dehydrated. Her eyes began to blink and then focus and she smacked her lips a few times, wetting them involuntarily. She seemed to respond positively as Blaisdell knelt beside her, glass of water in hand. He also held a glass capsule of ammonia to revive her, but it was not needed. She was speaking softly and staring at the ceiling.

"She'll be okay," he spoke. A receptionist asked if the EMS service was needed.

Dr. Blaisdell lifted her head gently and Mrs. Williams began to speak and answer simple questions. Dr. Blaisdell spoke quietly to her and also comforted her husband who was still in shock. The husband had just seen the deceased girl moments before, and the sad vision was clear and vivid in his mind. His wife had almost dropped like a rock and he was in a daze, totally helpless. Captain Bennett aided him to a nearby chair where he sat in a stupor for a few moments. He was given some water and seemed to regain color in his face. He knew his wife was in good hands.

In a matter of minutes, Mrs. Williams was able to ingest some water and was responsive to the coroner and other voices nearby. She thanked the people in the room for helping her, albeit she seemed disoriented from the collapse—apologizing profusely for the embarrassing moment

Once mentally recovered from the traumatic day, the Williams family exited the building and became joyous at the fact that their daughter was not the deceased young person in the morgue. Dr. Blaisdell thanked them for coming to New Hampshire and shared his appreciation of the fact that they had not lost their daughter to the tragedy.

Captain Bennett shook their hands and thanked them as well. He approached the police cruiser and stood silently in dismay knowing that "Tammy" X was still an unknown person.

In a matter of minutes, he would be on his way from Concord to Laconia. He was happy for the family from Medford, Massachusetts but also dismayed that there were no other leads to the mystery woman. They were back at square one.

Bennett chatted with the LPD home office by cell phone. He awaited the departure of the Williams family, assuring them that he would find their daughter.

Their BMW slowly left the parking lot and headed for I-93 S. Bennett left thereafter and headed north. He rubbed his forehead with one hand as he drove. He was mystified by the event. *Who in God's name was this young dead woman in the Concord morgue?*

Chapter 108

Dr. Blaisdell was miffed that the LPD had not shared some of their knowledge of the Iceman's role in the possible death of the young woman. Even Captain Bennett had not shared the fact that some "suspect tattoo ink" was in the hands of the authorities. As M.E. and coroner, he was entitled to that information, especially if a toxic chemical agent was in the ink—causing the demise of the deceased.

The preliminary report from the coroner was that the girl, "Tammy" X had shown signs of asphyxia by way of respiratory paralysis. A number of drugs however could cause such an effect, some legal and some illegal. Some muscle relaxants caused that specific clinical effect. Classically, Blaisdell knew that certain drugs from exotic plants caused that effect as well. The class of alkaloids was known to be muscle relaxants. Many originated from plants in South American countries—like Peru.

Dr. Blaisdell's report had shown some initial histology of skeletal muscle, some of which revealed relaxed muscle fibers. The intercostal muscles between the ribs showed a similar effect and it was well established that nonfunctional respiratory muscles could result in asphyxia—paralysis of the rib cage and cessation of breathing. Unusual paralytic drugs of that class often caused initial effects in the toes, eyes, ears, neck and extremities i.e. the arms and legs.

The alkaloid drugs caused that effect before the cessation of respiratory muscle function. The effect was not at the higher level of the Central Nervous System (CNS) since most chemicals of that nature didn't cross the "blood brain barrier" (BBB), a tight series of cells that kept the brain protected from chemical abuse and toxic agents.

Collaboration by the coroner, a bioanalytical lab and the police in the Lakes Region was needed. Somehow, someone wasn't updating Blaisdell.

Dr. Blaisdell phoned Bennett later that afternoon. He needed to know where the local investigation was going and if any progress had been made.

"Captain," said the coroner, cordially and forthright. "I meant to ask you while you were here. Rumor has it that some ink was found in the saddlebag of the man known as Iceman, the gentleman that I autopsied after the bike fatality. Is there possibly a relationship between that bottle of ink and the dead girl's tattoo?"

Caught off guard, Captain Bennett was initially silent and then volunteered some relevant information. He seemed embarrassed by the call.

"Yes doctor, some ink was found in his possession and we have sent it out to a lab for chemistries. I thought one of our detectives had notified you hence I had not followed up with you as yet because we had no data on the contents of the vial, other than it appeared as black ink."

"I'm sorry, Captain, but the dead woman had a recent tattoo as you know, and some newspapers are alluding to a relationship between Iceman and 'Tammy' X—they surmise that her recent tattoo may have contributed to her death. All of this is supposition of course but if the tattoo ink contained certain drugs, like the alkaloids that can cause anoxia, it might help explain some aspects of how she died. As you know, I reported possible 'death by asphyxia in the initial report—reason unknown at present.'"

"I remember that aspect of the report doctor. What's an alka . . . alkaloid?" he stammered, with trepidation.

"The alkaloids are a class of neuromuscular blockers, meaning they prevent the nerves from telling the muscles to contract. If the respiratory muscles are paralyzed, the lungs don't work and one dies of asphyxia, oxygen deprivation. The paralyzing effects can cause death."

The police captain took notes as Blaisdell explained in more detail.

"What I'm suggesting, Captain, is that if there was a drug of that nature in the ink, it may have caused her death by way of skin penetration with the tattoo needle. I am talking *intentional harm* here, perhaps murder . . . and would welcome your input on that possibility as a causative factor."

"I understand doctor. We surely wish to help in the investigation. I apologize for leaving you out in the cold. What kind of drug is an alkaloid, doctor? Is there a specific name?"

Blaisdell thought for a moment and then mentioned some strange names.

"Grieswurzel, Pareira Brava, Vigne Sauivage," was his response. "Names you don't know, most probably but drugs from the rain forest.

"What the hell are those, doctor?" Bennett reacted, with naivety.

"Curare, Captain. D-tubocurarine, a South American exotic drug from plants that cause paralysis. They are sometimes used in surgery as muscle relaxants but most people know them as the drugs in a blowgun (Pacunus) used by the Yagua Indians in Peru. They hunt for food with the plant extract.

"Jesus," said the policeman. "Are you saying that the girl may have died from a poison used in blowguns?"

"No, although that could work. My feeling is that if the tattoo ink contained an alkaloid like curare, for some strange reason, the tattooist could have innocently administered the paralytic drug and done so unknowingly. What is your lab looking for?"

"They have samples at two labs—one at the State Police lab and another at a contract lab in the Midwest. They are blue-skying it, searching for clues, for any chemical or drug. We agree that the tattoo may have been the fatal route of administration of something toxic."

"Get on the horn with the State Police and the lab out West. Tell them to look at alkaloids like curare in the ink material. My hunch is that it is in the tattoo tissue as well. I plan to remove another section of the skin at the site of the tattoo, perhaps numerous *punch biopsies* of the whole damn logo. The drug, if present, may be in the tissue and still in its original form. My blood lab can look for the drug or metabolites of the drug in the blood as well. It's a long-shot, but possible."

"Makes total sense, doctor. I will keep you better informed, I promise. I will contact our labs ASAP."

"Good, Captain. That's the way we can solve this crime. It gets more interesting each day. I am not used to such dramatic research but this autopsy has me wondering what happened to her. If we are on the right track, this could be the most bizarre death in the history of New Hampshire. It might imply a cult type of thing going on. Curare is not something one finds on the street."

"I will send some of the tissues to the histology lab in the State offices. Between the tissues, ink and bloods, there must be a common agent here that was responsible for her death," Blaisdell added.

Dr. Blaisdell was feeling more comfortable with the collaboration now. He sensed that he had caught the police with their pants down and that they were not sharing all that they knew, merely because it was a *theory* on their part. He, on the other hand, believed that they were now on the right track—thanks to Don's input.

Chapter 109

Blaisdell owed Don a debt of gratitude and planned on calling him that night in order to update him. What the police and Blaisdell did not know was that Don had another clue to the mystery—one that involved Wendell Atkins' journals and the astute knowledge of George Adams at The Weirs Veterans Home.

Wendell Atkins had, in fact, recorded history as no one else had seen—a personal perspective. Granted, it was his inherent impressions of numerous years of Bike Week activities. The relevancy of his journal notes however, to an actual crime, were slowly evolving. Had he lived through 2006, they might have solved the crime earlier. But with his death, it was now Don and George that were unnecessarily burdened with discovering the overall rationale for the strange coincidental deaths.

The information was voluminous and exasperating for both men. Don had already spent dozens of hours *working the data* and reading the journals page by page. The fruits of Don's labor would not be in vain.

Chapter 110

Dr. Blaisdell *Googled* the Internet and researched the drug, curare as best he could. He knew the basic clinical effects of the drug from his previous medical training. He clearly needed to refresh his knowledge of the clinical symptoms and drug's true origin. It was all there in front of him on the monitor.

Isolated in 1897, its use in medicine as a relaxant therapeutic was not until later—1935. Cures for curare poisoning were limited. It was only toxic if it directly entered the bloodstream. For years, the use of physostigmine was the antidote for curare poisoning in humans. Physostigmine was also used for tetanus, a paralytic effect similar in action to the effects of curare. The real utility of physostigmine was in the alleviation of *Myasthenia gravis*, an autoimmune neuromuscular disease with recurring muscle weakness and fatigue. Neostigmine and atropine were also therapeutic.

Myelos was the Greek word for muscle, and *astheneia* meant weakness. *Gravis* meant "grave or serious." The use of physostigmine was only a partial cure since the endogenous thymus gland contributed to *Myasthenia gravis* disease as well. Removal or ablation of the thymus reversed some of the adverse muscular effects of the debilitating disease.

If Blaisdell's theory was correct and the victim died of curare poisoning or some other alkaloid, someone might have been able to save her had they known the signs of the chemically induced muscle weakness. Patients could feel all of the side effects and the young woman would have probably complained to someone that she felt ill. Curare, or "woorali" to the Native Indians of South America, let the victim know they were dying, be it animal or man. Beginning with the extremities, it was clear to the person affected by the drug that something was wrong with their muscles, especially when walking and moving their arms.

Again, it was subjective at this point but Blaisdell was confidant that *an alkaloid affect* may have caused her death. If the histology and pathology of the muscles from the chest, arms, legs and digits showed an overt weakness in muscle morphology and physiology, he knew he was advancing a probable cause of death.

Because of his interest, he decided to biopsy all of those muscles on the dead girl. He had nothing to lose and the victim was still available in the morgue.

If the lab tests showed the drug in the circulation and in the tattooed tissues, the route of administration of the drug might be confirmed. All that would be left regarding the crime would be the motive for her demise and the true identity of the dead woman other than "Tammy" X, "Lady of the Lake," or "Jane Doe."

Blaisdell telephoned his assistant who was working in her office.

"Hi—If you're not busy, can you help me with some histology samples? I need to take some tissues from 'Tammy' X. I have this ingenious idea that I will explain to you in the mortuary lab."

"Sure, doctor . . . I'll meet you in the morgue," she willingly agreed. "Be there in a sec."

The doctor responded, "Good. I think I know the killing agent—it's curare-like . . . and *this* . . . was *no* accident."

Chapter 111

The State analytical chemistry laboratory was well equipped to help with the forensics needed to evaluate the relationship of the ink with a potential crime, either murder, foul play or accidental. The analytical lab contained all of the instrumentation necessary to assess the chemical structure, concentration and metabolites of biologics, toxins, toxic chemicals and the unknown pharmaceutical extracts of nature.

The preferred methods for analysis of chemicals and drugs varied with the structural chemistry of the agent and class of compounds. The coroner and others had hinted at the alkaloids as a potential causative agent, which may have been mixed in with the black ink. The Iceman had brought something unusual to the tattooist, Fuzzy Walsh. A second analytical lab in the Midwest was also looking at an aliquot of the unknown black liquid. Replicates were important when identifying the unknowns.

The objective of both labs was to qualify and quantify the ingredients of the ink, including any active chemical "peaks" that might appear as unknown ingredients, carrier excipients or active drugs. The "standards" for comparison at both labs would utilize tattoo inks provided from commercial suppliers—they were background reference materials of normal, commercially available, untainted inks. Popular manufacturers of tattoo products were happy to share the ingredients of their products with the authorities in an effort to aid the chemists in knowing what components were commonly used for tattoos. A battery of colored inks were used as a reference, black included.

In that manner, any unknown excipients or chemicals / pharmaceuticals would appear as extra "peaks" or unknown substances in the analyses by mass spectroscopy (MS), high pressure liquid chromatography (HPLC) or other infrared (IR) and ionizing methods.

Black ink, for most uses, was often carbon or charcoal-like and generally nontoxic when used properly for tattoos or for printing.

Dr. Blaisdell and Captain Bennett had informed both labs that they were looking at tissues in the pathology lab and would be sending similar samples to them for extraction of a probable alkaloid compound, curare, or a derivative. This greatly aided the focused efforts of the two chemistry labs since they could narrow down their search for therapeutics that might cause paralysis or asphyxia in the human body.

All preliminary autopsy results on the deceased woman seemed to point to weakened skeletal muscular conformations and the blood and other tissue analyses grossly showed a lack of oxygen might have contributed to her demise. More information was needed but Blaisdell had once vacationed in South America and felt that some of the poison usage for hunting in the remote jungles showed similar effects on animals sought for meat, food and clothing.

Dr. Blaisdell has studied plant extracts in his graduate research days, focusing on flora, which was therapeutic in normal dosages, but detrimental or deadly in overdoses.

Curare was only one of a class of neurotoxic drugs that he was aware of, and further knew they could affect the neuromuscular junctions and cause muscle weakness and eventual cessation of breathing. The numbing effect of that class of plant extracts or drugs could appear like alcohol poisoning, as in "drinking to excess."

It is possible that "Tammy" X merely thought she was feeling drunk when in fact it was a plant-derived drug that could also have caused those symptoms in its early stages of bodily effects. Her blood alcohol level was above average at the time of her death, but not fatal. The preliminary autopsy blood samples had been the equivalent of a few beers and the results showed that intoxication was not at abnormal levels.

The laboratory personnel at the local analytical laboratories, and at the one in the Midwest, were in touch daily. They acted in tandem as colleagues and collaborators—sharing data as needed with a common goal. Using sophisticated blood analyses methods and radioimmunoassay (RIA), they were able to analyze tissues and bloods for hormones, liver enzymes and metabolites of bodily functions. The standard techniques that applied directly to assessing the alkaloids in tissues had been elucidated and perfected many years earlier.

A gradient HPLC analysis specific for d-tubocuranine chloride in plant extracts had been perfected in 1977 by van der Maeden et. al. The suspect components were eluted from a reverse-phase column. Using a special phosphate buffer adjusted to pH 4, it allowed for distinct components of curare to be separated and identified. Attention was focused on curare poisoning in the late 1970's, when a now famous case of murder was being investigated.

On May 18, 1976, Dr. Mario E. Jascalevich was indicted for five murders. Colleagues at Riverdell Hospital in Oradell, New Jersey had suspected the doctor of murder by curare poisoning. In 1976, many articles were published about a "Doctor X."

The deaths were actually in 1965 and 1966 and a feisty court case ensued ten years later. In 1976, a judge in Bergen County Superior Court allowed for the exhumation of numerous bodies of patients that came in for routine surgeries and somehow died a few days later.

Dr. Blaisdell was familiar with the criminal case.

In 1978, a trial began to assess the data from the tissue analyses of patients. After 34 weeks of legal posturing, it became one of the *longest* trials in American history. After lengthy testimony, it was concluded that the new RIA procedure *was not specific for curare* after a ten-year duration between the deaths of patients and the analytical data of the trial. "Doctor X" was then acquitted (October 24, 1978) based on the supposition that the decaying bodily fluids and embalming fluid could alter the test results over time, making any residual curare unstable and not measurable.

The defense had stated that thin layer chromatography (TLC); HPLC, UV spectrophotometry and RIA methods had never been used before to seek out curare in embalmed, buried tissue. However, at least one exhumation of a 4-year-old girl showed curare in her lungs and liver. The method used was by mass spectroscopy. HPLC also confirmed curare in three other patients and validated that curare was present in 18 vials of "Doctor X's" locker.

In all instances, Jascalevich (Doctor X) claimed that the curare in the locker was used in animal experiments at Seton Hall Medical College, specifically for muscle relaxation studies. Dog hair and animal blood were noted on the vials in the locker and on syringes as well, further confusing the criminal case in the exhumed humans.

Was the curare used only for preclinical studies? Or were those studies a cover-up for the suspected murders of the dead patients. "Doctor X" was getting off Scott free.

Because of the famed murder trial in New Jersey, dedicated chemists modified techniques to increase the sensitivity using HPLC methods. The New Hampshire chemistry laboratory and modern bioanalytical labs felt confident in the newer techniques that isolated and identified curare in human blood and tissues. Those refined techniques were to help determine if curare-like alkaloids were anywhere in the dead girl's torso. One advantage was that there was no embalming fluid present to interfere with the fresh tissues, unlike the "Doctor X" patient cases with ten-year internments.

Blaisdell patiently awaited the input from the lab tests. He felt confident that they could solve this mystery even if "Tammy" X's true identity was never resolved.

Chapter 112

Ace remained in hiding in New Jersey. Phone calls to the New Jersey Rough Riders clubhouse went unanswered. He knew the *heat* would be on when the Iceman was returned to his home State and buried in Metuchen. Ace didn't even attend the biker's funeral out of fear that the police would seek him out. Fellow bikers that did attend the ceremony dressed in suits and ties to avoid the traditional black leather garb and motorcycle funeral parade. Plainclothes policemen attended the funeral in anticipation of grabbing Ace, the *Numero Uno Head of State*, for questioning.

The hopes of the police in New Jersey failed with Ace's conspicuous absence. The New Jersey police had few leads as to his whereabouts but knew that he would surface at some point. To coin a cliché, 'he could run, but he could not hide.'

Ace had heard that the vial of ink had disappeared after Iceman's crash. He was astute enough to assume that the police in Laconia had the saddlebags from the crashed bike, which Iceman was riding home to New Jersey. If the assumption were correct, the police would surely analyze the contents of the vial and the unknown components of the black liquid. Ace knew that Iceman's story had been all over the New Hampshire press. The boys up north had alerted him to the local newspaper Web sites in the Granite State. He could see for himself that the New Jersey club members were being sought after. He was pissed that Iceman had caused all this attention. In his mind, Ace felt that the Iceman's foibles could cause much trouble for the whole motorcycle club. Ace considered heading south for a while, either to South America or to the Bahamas.

*   *   *

Don Wright was not aware of any of Dr. Blaisdell's recent blood and tissue data. The critical samples of the young girl's body had been taken from various skin and muscle areas to help illuminate the investigation. There were indications of the presence of an alkaloid and alcohol in her system, at least in the preliminary tests. By supposition, Don had already assumed that a toxic substance had been in the ink. He was concerned that the death of the young girl was a kind of cult or ritualistic occurrence that had a long history during Bike Week—one that had not been known or resolved in the past.

"What are you on to now?" asked George Adams, observing Don staring off into space—a daydream of sorts.

"I've spent some time on the phone with the coroner in Concord, Dr. Blaisdell. He shared with me some of the details of normal autopsy procedures. I know that the girl who died was murdered. I just *know* it . . . I can feel it in my bones. They killed her somehow . . . through a tattoo. But how and why?"

Each journal seemed to have more information. He was anxious to flip the pages of earlier chronologies.

"There's no way that the police know what we know yet. They don't even know of the journals or the fact that Wendell recorded his personal history for all those years. They might find the substance that killed her through chemistry and analysis, but the identity of the girl and the motives for her elimination are probably outlined somewhere in this damn stack of notes from our friend, Wendell."

"I agree," touted George lowering himself and sitting back slowly into the wicker rocker. He groaned upon the descent.

"Was that *your* knees that I heard just then?" Don teased. George Adams nodded, yes in disgust.

Don became frustrated. He slapped the railing with his hand in protest.

"Damn you Wendell, my man! Why did you leave us hangin' like this? I need a damn beer, George. I'll be right back. I'm goin' for a six-pack and then placing my ass back down on this floor and reading this pile of shit until a clue emerges," he said, emphatically.

George just shook his head. "Patience my boy . . . patience."

In a heartbeat, Don disappeared down the steps and onto the sidewalk at The Weirs. He fired up the Ducati and headed for a local gas station / convenience store near Paugus Bay Bridge. It was less than a half-mile away and he could have walked. They surely had beer and snacks there. The Ducati made it a quick trip.

Chapter 113

It was the last night of Bike Week and The Weirs area was crowded with straggler bikers and their ladies, those that hadn't left for home yet. Each was anticipating the fireworks that were scheduled for 9 P.M. It was Father's Day and the SuperBike races had been postponed to Monday due to rain.

Bonnie, Iceman's lady for the week, sat in the wet mist by Endicott Rock and the shoreline of the Paugus Bay Channel. She stared at the passing boats and big spenders in their fancy, sleek Cigarette boats and large Sea Ray cruisers worth hundreds of thousands of dollars. Wishful thinking would not change her life—depression had set in.

They cruised at wake speed, restricting the big engines to an idle until they passed the channel buoys allowing them to open the throttles. She talked with no one but merely smoked and stared, stared and smoked. She flicked a cigarette butt into the water. She had to pee bad and sought out a nearby chemical toilet in the park. She had not eaten in hours, and when done with her biological needs, returned to her spot by the lake and rock.

Nestled within her brain were some facts that Iceman had shared with her during the short week together. The thoughts were not sexual, but casual. The facts that she contemplated related to the history of the New Jersey Rough Riders' chapter. Both Iceman's and Ace's fathers had attended the Bike Week festivities for years, albeit many years back, even decades. It was family tradition to be there each year and Iceman had shared the memories of his childhood with her. Drinking made him reflective of his past.

Bonnie knew the details of the New Jersey trips to New Hampshire that had occurred back in the 1950's and 60's. 1955 seemed to be a critical year when both Iceman and Ace's fathers had attended the Laconia Rally—their motorcycle club had just been created and touted the Teddy Roosevelt moniker of a bear and the Rough Riders name.

It was coincidental that it was the last year that Vincent motorcycles were produced, the C and D model Rapides, in December of 1955. Production of the Vincent had ended for good due to monetary struggles of the company. Oddly, The fathers of Iceman and Ace were close riding buddies and traveled everywhere, including Laconia. They rode vintage Vincent models back then, long before they switched to Harleys and Indians in the 1960's.

Iceman had confided in her after some heavy drinking and sex. He somehow felt close to her, an unusual situation for him since he had emotional ties to no one and was physically close to no one. Perhaps he knew that his life was short—the local attention that emerged about the dead girl made him paranoid as well as being on Ace's shit list. The police were chasing his colleagues around The Weirs seeking answers to a potential crime—murder and bizarre tattooing.

Iceman had the inclination that he was marked. His fellow riders had now distanced themselves from him. He sensed they were tense and secretive. He knew the signs of an internal plan. He needed to get home as soon as possible.

Bonnie was not only a great 'lay,' but a good listener. Now, after his death, all she had left to percolate was a week of memories of a close friend who had died unexpectedly. She couldn't even attend his New Jersey memorial service in fear of the club member threats to kill her.

*   *   *

Just before 9 P.M., a biker who had observed her sitting alone much of the day approached her and sat down a few feet away. The grass was wet and muddy. He wanted to make small talk with her and maybe hook up on the last night of the Rally. He had struck out all week—she was solo, it appeared.

•   "Nice night for the fireworks, eh?" he offered sarcastically. "Sky is crappy and you've been here awhile. I was a bit concerned." He could see her eyes were red.

"Really. I hadn't noticed asshole," she retorted, with a cynical smirk. "Am I in your fuckin' spot or somethin'? You like this shit weather? I'm soaked and miserable."

"Jesus, lady," he replied. "I was merely making conversation. Didn't mean to rattle your girdle, doll. I'll be goin." He began to stand when she leaned far enough to grab his arm.

"I'm sorry. I've been in a pissy mood all day and the weather sucks. It's not your fault. I've been sittin' here all day thinkin'. Please sit back down. I could use a friend and some conversation. Other guys have been hittin' on me all day, most of them ugly and gnarly."

The biker who was clean cut in blacks was not stereotypical of a club member. He belonged to no motorcycle club. He was cute, she thought, mostly dry and friendly. He managed to sit next to her and awaited her next vent or barb. *She was feisty*, he thought. He liked that.

"It's a nice night alright . . . for ducks . . . and they'll be lighting up the sky soon. I could use a drink," she added. The unknown biker, with Peter Fonda features, grabbed a flask from his leather vest and passed it to her. "Here, my lady, have a snort—on me."

"Thanks. That little pocket is convenient," she said, taking a long hard swig of the Irish Mist inside. "I needed that." She grabbed for a cigarette. He lit the end with a lighter. "You look like some actor," she offered. "Peter . . . what's his name."

"Yah. Have heard that from some folks. 'Fonda' has been suggested in the past. Wish I had that bastard's money."

"Right . . . Peter Fonda . . . cute dude."

For the first time all day she smiled. "Here," she offered cordially, "Share the wet blanket with me?" She moved over a bit and he sat on the woolen fabric of red-checked cloth. It seemed to absorb the rain like a sponge. Few portions were dry.

"What's the name?" she asked. "I mean your real name and don't fuck with me!"

"John," he replied softly. "John, from Vermont."

"That's your *real* name? I mean . . . most people here have fucked up names like 'Hangman,' 'Dumpy,' 'Bowzer' or some other crazy nickname. I've even seen the names 'Rebar' and 'The Butcher.' You come here with John? Plain ol' John?" she laughed.

He smirked in a cute and coy way and said, "Yup! Just boring . . . John! Named after my ol' man. So I'm a junior." She laughed again and took another hit from his sterling silver flask. It warmed her.

"That was my dad's flask."

"Well then, John from Vermont. That's cool. My name's Bonnie . . . 'boring, fucking Bonnie.'"

"Okay Bonnie. Why so glum? I saw you here earlier and you're still here . . . in the same ol' spot. You like boats?"

She took a breath and then commented sincerely. "Not really. I like to see how the rich people live." She hesitated . . . "My ol' man died. Bike accident here in New Hampshire, on his way home. I've just been thinkin' all day . . . all damn day."

Just then an Arial bomb went off high above them, as if Iceman protested the get-together. Bonnie jumped from the noise and John touched her arm gently.

"Jesus, honey . . . sorry . . . ya gotta be shittin' me . . . what the hell happened?"

"Don't know for sure," she cried out. "They say he went off the road in the middle of the night. Hit a fuckin' tree with no helmet . . . died on the spot." She went silent.

More fireworks erupted in tandem, offering spray-like flower blossoms, and a heart in a circle, almost in mourning. She looked up with tears flowing and then over at John. He offered her a clean doo-rag to wipe her face. Rain diluted the tears—an indistinguishable amalgam of moisture. He let her catch her breath. She resumed the conversation, whispering,

"So John, honey, what brings you here to the big Rally? Vermont is just next door right?"

"Yah . . . come here each year . . . alone. A getaway."

"Where ya stayin?" she asked while staring at the sky of lights.

"Got a cabin just up the hill above the Drive-In and across the street from where the venues are. It's a short walk. Convenient."

"Does the joint have a bed or cot?" she asked, forthright.

"A bed. Full size, no less. It's actually not bad and clean. The place was recently renovated and smells like Fabreze everywhere," he added, in support of his choice of accommodations.

She laughed.

"I rented it last year as well . . . some old lady owns three or four of them at the top of Tower Street. I got in there because someone didn't show up . . . lucked out. How about you? Where you at?"

"Nowhere man . . . nowhere tonight . . . here I guess—me and the stars and the blanket."

She grabbed for a second cigarette, having hardly smoked the first and he beat her to the match with his lighter. She took a long slow draw and exhaled even slower.

"Tonight I need a man. Have you got room? I need you."

John looked away and then directly at her and said nothing. He smiled and then looked at the sky and said, "I need you too . . . I hate fireworks. Let's ditch this gig and head up the hill." He stood and reached to help her up. She was dressed in shorts that were soaked and a tank top, both of which she had worn all day. She felt totally unattractive and dirty. He didn't care. The wet look was somehow enticing, and visually analogous to Mariah Carey in the shower. Her nipples were erect underneath the fabric, a result of the cool misty air.

"Hey, John-boy."

"Yah?"

"Your place got a warm shower or ya got some damn waterfall in the woods of 'Cow Hampshire?'" she teased, smiling. "I need to clean up."

"Sure does. Even has very hot water and soap—Lever 2000 'Boring Bonnie.' It's waitin' just for you . . . and me. I'll help with the soap and I'll *be* your towel if you want."

Bonnie smiled and grabbed his hand. They headed up the hill with what belongings she owned . . . there was nothing of value in her knapsack.

"Your hand is cold, lady."

"Yah. I know. Warm me, John-boy. I need warmth."

He leaned over and kissed her under a chrysanthemum-like burst of lights in the sky.

Chapter 114

In less than ten minutes, they were at his cabin doorway. A single light of 60 watts radiated dimly over the stoop that dripped raindrops. She looked at him and sighed, "Open the door and carry me over the threshold, please," she murmured, in a pleading fashion. "Well . . . if you're going to fuck me, I want to feel like a bride," she whispered in his ear. He was not turned off by her profanity but instead stimulated. He obliged her, with a smile and spoke nothing at all.

The sun rose early the next morning. They both had slept little, experimenting first in the shower with various sexual positions and smoking a joint or two afterwards. They awoke in each other's arms having made love most of the night. The sun's rays cast through a window and across the bed and he studied her body and face carefully. She was radiant and happy, with facial tones that were beautiful. She wasn't as *hard* as she acted.

"Night doesn't do you justice," he complimented her. "You're quite the looker and your body is perfect."

"Thank you," she responded. "You look pretty good yourself, without booze or weed."

She worked her way down from his chest to his groin and kissed him everywhere. Her lips surrounded him one more time and in short time he climaxed like it was the first time. He seemed to remain hard after the incredible ejaculation so she took advantage of the occasion and mounted him again. This time it was for her pleasure. It was past Father's Day.

"I don't know if you're a father, but belated Happy Father's Day, John-boy. He never admitted if he was a dad but kissed her tenderly. "Thanks," he responded. "You're the best present I've ever had."

"Whad'ya say we catch some races today in Loudon?" he suggested, out of the blue.

"Sure . . . I've never been to the track or a race. Always managed to stay near The Weirs and miss the real reason why some people come here . . . the races."

"Well, 'Boring Bonnie'," he joked, "I'm about to 'un-bore' you."

"Oh yah? You *bored* me pretty good all night," she mused. "A damn good *boring* job too. Ya got some drill there," she chuckled.

'Thanks. You weren't too shabby yourself," he remarked, with raised eyebrows. "You kinda drained me. I'll need water to re-hydrate."

"That was my intention from the moment you sat down next to me at the beach. I needed everything you had, and I had talked to no one all day. Good karma that you showed up."

"I'm glad I strolled by."

"Who're you kidding?" she laughed, out loud. "You had lustful intentions right from the start, you lying shit. I could see it in your eyes."

"True," he added, in confirmation. "I wanted you for sure. It was your *ass*. It's beautiful."

"Hmmn . . . Glad you liked it . . . there's more. By the way, *mentor* of racing, what time does the race start today? Thought the races were yesterday."

"Feature race isn't until later today. It was postponed because of yesterday's rain. The crowd will be lighter and people will be pissed since many people left on Father's Day. They had to go home. They hate New Hampshire when it rains. Most of the riders are too chicken to run on a wet track . . . they don't take chances even with the special tires available. Chicken shits! We have time to get there and time to spare. Let's grab some breakfast and head to Loudon after that. Okay?"

"You betcha," she said. "I haven't eaten in hours."

"Not true, my lady. Not true."

She laughed.

"Yah, know how ya feel . . . I need sustenance and nutrition myself. I'm down a quart as well. Food and some coffee would be nice."

"Can we come back tonight?" she asked, in a pleading fashion.

"For sure," he replied, with exuberance "I have this place for four more nights."

"Good . . . I have nowhere to go this week and I'd like to know you better if you want me to hang around."

John nodded to the affirmative. He'd be a fool to pass up the option.

The shower was hot and refreshing. He loaned her some shorts and a bike shirt. She wore no underwear as they headed to downtown Laconia for breakfast. After eating at Water Street Café at Fair and Water Streets, they rode south on Route 106 toward Belmont and Loudon. In fifteen minutes, they were at the racetrack entrance.

Time trials were ongoing all morning and hundreds of spectator bikes and RV's were everywhere. The track appeared dry, due in part to the jet engine-dryers mounted on maintenance trucks at the facility

There actually were race fans after all, she thought.

Her Rally experience had been "at The Weirs." She knew nothing about the races or racers that were national stars in their own right. "Boring Bonnie" was about to understand the mystique of road racing and the draw of the high-pitched engines by the popular Hondas, Kawasakis and Yamahas. The thrill was similar to NASCAR yet she had never seen the riders lean their machines into corners and scrape their leathers at the knees. She fell in love with the thrill.

Inside the track, he held her hand and escorted her up the stairs to the top row of the stands. She could see forever it seemed and they picked the first corner of the track to watch the men jockey for critical position in the pre-races. The time trials were merely indicative of what was to happen later that afternoon.

They already knew what the evening would entail. For once in her life, Bonnie didn't feel used. She gave herself freely knowing this man was someone special. She was balancing a new love with a notable annual event in New Hampshire. She had not forgotten the Iceman but she was on a new road to understanding what a *meaningful relationship* might be like—something other than sex, drugs and booze until you dropped. John was real, caring and thoughtful and Iceman wasn't. John's conversations with her after sex were compassionate and loving. She was not used to that and drank it up like a fine wine.

Chapter 115

Don Wright intensified his search of the Internet and the details in the Wendell Atkins journals that might lead to clues relevant to the woman's death. His focus was on the motive.

Nothing jumped out at him regarding the Vincent logo, the Vincent motorcycles or any noteworthy event or tradition in Wendell's journals. The 1965 riots at the Weirs shed no light on any ritual to note. There was a hint of history in the 1955 journal that elaborated on motorcycle news, in general. The predominance of American-made bikes preempted the production of some of the British and European popular names, Wendell had noted.

"Look here," Don related to George Adams. "This '55 journal that Wendell wrote cites that Vincent bikes went out of production that year. The last of two popular models ceased production—the C and D model Rapides. A week before Christmas of that year, the last Vincent emerged from the production line. Hell, that was almost 1956! It was days away and this year is 2006—fifty damn years!"

"Interesting Don, since Vincent had many other popular models. I remember the Comet, Meteor, Black Lightning and Grey Flash models—named after things in the sky. I've been reading on my own," he boasted.

"Glad you're getting involved," Don complimented him. "It's compulsive and fun."

Don read as rapidly as he could. "Says here that the logo for Vincent was cropped in the 50's to The Vincent, eliminating the HRD from the Howard Raymond Davies legacy of the 1920's."

George looked up at Don and shook his head. "What's any of this got to do with anything regarding the girl? Why would Wendell have noted this?" He scratched his forehead.

"Dunno, George . . . dunno."

The whole thing is bizarre," added George Adams. "Seems like Wendell had a reason to mention that particular bike manufacturer."

Don read voraciously, skimming for key word and articles on the Vincent. He flipped the pages of the '55 journal until one article prominently stood out.

"Eureka!" he voiced, with excitement. "This confirms what we saw earlier in undated clippings—another article! Says here that a girl was found dead at The Weirs in 1955. Holy shit. The article reads, 'Dead Girl Found Near The Mount Washington Boat.' It's more detailed than before."

"What?" reacted George, with interest, "you must be jesting."

"No crap! It's right here. A picture of the tattoo as well."

"Jesus Christ. The girl was 23. Care to see the photo of the tattoo?" Don asked.

Don smiled and showed George the page. "Bingo! It says right there! *Vincent!* On the skin . . . *Vincent!*"

According to the journal entry, the case had never been solved relevant to the dead girl in 1955. She had been found naked on the shoreline of Weirs Beach, a short distance between the Mount Washington cruise boat and the historic Endicott Rock Park.

Don drank a can of beer in celebration. He chugged 12-ounces and grabbed another one. He had already worked his way through most of the six-pack he had purchased. Two women had died at The Weirs Rally events almost 50 years apart. The end of 2005 and beginning of 2006 would have been the *fiftieth* of two similar events, complete with the tattoo and a location of death on Lake Winni.

Don now had a *link*—a new and critical link to the mysterious coincidences. What he needed to support the theory was the implication that a New Jersey motorcycle club called the Rough Riders existed back then in the mid-1950's. It did, but he was unaware of that fact as yet. If he could research that connection, he might have clues of some obscure tradition involving the New Jersey riders and the two deaths at the historic New Hampshire bike event. In essence and symbolically, *The Vincent was dead for 50 years as well.*

Don stood up from his cramped cross-legged position in front of the stacks of journals. He had more to read in the 1955 entries. Wendell had chronologically recorded the investigation of that particular year and an obscure death.

No wonder he wanted to tell the police that something similar had occurred years ago, Don thought. *Nobody would fuckin' listen to the old man the day "Tammy"*

X was discovered at the beginning of Motorcycle Week. Wendell was trying to share his knowledge of a prior event and no one gave a shit. Then he died, Don thought, with remorse. The details were buried with him. Had he lived a bit longer, the mystery would have been solved. Fortunately, his written words over the years helped connect the dots.

When Wendell died, he took other perspectives, innuendos, here-say, and fodder to his grave as well. He probably remembered more than he had written down. All of those thoughts in his brain were lost by his death in 2006.

*   *   *

Don told George he had work to do for the newspaper. Being race day, he had to shoot photos of some premiere events in Loudon. It was now midday and he needed to leave. Don grabbed the 1955 journal and took it with him.

"I'll be back this evening, most probably," he said to the elderly Adams. "You hang in there. We are on a roll and 'good ol' Wendell' is telepathically guiding us through this mysterious crime—this one apparently a *clone* of the one in 1955. See you later on."

George Adams shook his hand goodbye and settled into his wicker rocker. He watched as the last of the vendors along Lakeside Avenue loaded their gear, products and tents into their vehicles. The Bike Week festivities at The Weirs were slowly coming to a close. Another year of 400,000 transients was about to end. Bikes, babes, booze and music for 2006 would be a recent memory in the Lakes Region.

The 83rd year of the event would go down in history as a financial success, but also a tragedy, but not before George Adams added the day-by-day events into a new journal. No way was he going to halt the Wendell Atkins chronological tradition. History was history with or without the famed deaths or murders.

In a flash, Don's fire engine-red Ducati was headed south toward Loudon. His cameras were strapped across his chest. He passed the site of the Iceman's crash on Route 11 and then turned down Route 106 toward the racetrack. In ten minutes or less he would be at the site. His press pass at the ready, he was to enter the main gate for preferred media parking. He looked forward to the racing even if it was a day late due to rain. The racers were exhilarating and the opportunity for photo-ops was awesome. He had a pit pass as well—that entitled him to interview and photograph the top men in the local and national field of road racing. He longed to try his Ducati Monster on the track himself. Maybe someday, he would be lucky enough to sample the course, but at a much slower speed and controlled environment.

Chapter 116

A Vincent-HRD Owners Club (VOC) was established in 1948. It was founded and manifest itself in the UK and even Phil Vincent gave the group his support. The membership stood at 1,800 when the last Vincent was produced in 1955. That membership remains steady today even though the members had originally felt that they would only exist as long as production of the bikes was in progress. The Club is International with many "sections," 32 of which are in the UK. Another 26 sections are located around the world.

The journal, *MPH* is the Vincent Owner's Club official magazine, which often cites advertisements, stories, events and a means for communication between members.

The VOC is a major shareholder in a company, VOC Spares Co. Ltd. The Spares Company not only assists Vincent owners in selling or finding parts for Vincents of historical significance, they offer, even today, manuals and handbooks to keep the classic models on the road, and in good working order.

Because the Vincent was originally designed as a touring machine, its participation in racing was limited to land speed records (1948 at 150 MPH) and other unique events. Annual rallies are still held around the world with an International Rally event conducted every four years in any number of continents. Often, between 100 and 200 Vincent motorcycle owners come together for these events, complete with their historic machines.

Don Wright had researched the VOC on the Internet. In his search of the various logos that might lead to the implication of the Vincent Marques tattoo in the death of the woman, it was clear that the VOC membership could be a source of the Vincent history. The faithfulness of the members impressed him—many dedicated to the continuous "life" of the once famous machine, a few of which often graced the rallies in New Hampshire, Florida and South Dakota.

*   *   *

Fuzzy Walsh had spent the previous morning of Father's Day packing up his equipment and storing the tent and generator in his van. His tattoo equipment was stowed neatly in a strong box. The various inks of many colors were stored in rainbow fashion in another wooden case.

He desired to head out early having had his fill of the police inquiry, lousy weather and notoriety that *one damn tattoo* had gained him, at least with the authorities. He vowed never again to apply another Vincent logo to anyone and had resigned himself to never use someone else's ink no matter how big and strong they were.

Iceman was huge and intimidating, but Fuzzy would not relent in the future. He had no clue what contaminant was in the black liquid and if they had tried to explain how they were performing the chemical analyses on the samples, he would have never understood what the hell they were talking about anyway. HPLC techniques and other analytical methods were 'Greek' to him.

He had dropped out of school when he sixteen. The only biology or anatomy that he knew was self-taught for tattooing, or in the back seat of some old Chevy. He was aware of major muscle groups of the arms and legs and how to avoid hitting nerves and blood vessels in those muscles. That was the extent of his anatomical training except for a girl or two that taught him about the birds and bees.

"Damn nuisance," he voiced as he closed the back of the van. His neighbors had been screwin' all week in the tent next door and were still at it, completing a week of an unmitigated orgy-fest. The moaning never stopped for the bitch. Fuzzy pretty much thought that she was fakin' it anyway. No woman could 'come' that often. She was worse than the Energizer Bunny . . . one that kept her mojo "going, going, going."

Fuzzy knew that the police had his home phone and cell number. They had promised to update him on any new developments. He couldn't have cared less at this point since he was already tainted by one death that he had nothing to do with other than the fact that he had applied some ink to some girl's backside.

His next venue was at a race event in Minnesota and he couldn't wait to hit the road West.

He had no plans to return to New Hampshire in the future, even if it was a prime moneymaker for him. He was aware that he might have to come back if there was a trial against the perpetrators of the implied crime.

The police would summon him if charges were being pressed against any New Jersey Rough Riders. Fuzzy's testimony would only be needed as part of the prosecutor's case against the motorcycle club and the deceased Iceman, albeit *posthumously*.

He jumped into the front seat of the van and rolled down the window, which faced the tent of the moaners. As he got ready to start the motor and depart the pasture of fellow residents, he called out to the neighboring "sex fiends."

"Hey doll . . . how's about a BJ for the road? Ya know, for 'daddy's day?'" He was laughing as he cracked open a can of Budweiser and swilled the contents. After a moment, the girl peered through the tent door. "Fuck off, you degenerate," she exclaimed in her best voice. "I wouldn't do *you* if you were the last man on earth, pencil dick!"

"You don't know what your missin' lady-love. See ya next time if ya don't have the 'clap' and all by then. You should add your moaning to your cell phone ringer."

As he started the van, he could see her in his side view mirror pulling up her shorts and stumbling to try and come after the tattooist's van, virtually bare-ass naked. Her breasts were pendulous.

"Cop lover . . . you dirt bag," she yelled at the top of her lungs—a gruff voice in the mist. "I ain't never had no 'clap,' you dick. Thanks for bringin' the 'fuzz' to the campground, you shit head!"

He floored the van, tires spinning in the grass and dirt casting wet stones and pebbles in her direction. On a dry day, she would have been left in a cloud of dust. He heard a rock bounce off the back door of the vehicle. She had perfect aim, naked or not, and was screaming obscenities, which were not in the "spirit of the weekend"—Father's Day and all.

Fuzzy laughed all the way down the dirt entryway to Route 11. Once he entered onto the bypass, he squealed his tires on the wet pavement and headed west to Tilton and New Hampshire's I-93. "To hell with the Monday races," he grumbled.

For Fuzzy Walsh, Laconia Bike Week was over and good riddance to it as far as he was concerned. He had cleared a few grand in a short number of days, all of which was under the table and IRS free. He threw a beer can out the window as a "goodbye."

♦

Chapter 117

Don Wright returned from the NHIS racetrack and had taken all the photos that he might need for the newspaper. He had covered the featured race and took many photographs of the spectators in the crowd. They would be added to his portfolio for a future book of "faces." All the while he was at the races, his thoughts were on the subject of the journal entries of Wendell Atkins. He seemed possessed by the daunting task.

Don finally resolved himself to consider bringing the police and coroner into his personal investigation of the implied murder of "Tammy" X. He had much more to review in Wendell's other journals but felt that progress had been made toward a motive for the Rough Riders' agenda, albeit through the actions of the Iceman.

What was missing in Don's data was the fact that Iceman's and Ace's fathers had participated in earlier rallies, the same one in 1955 that touted a death that the police and coroner were not yet aware of. How would they be related?

Don decided to contact the coroner on Monday evening.

"Dr. Blaisdell, I have some information that may be relevant to your forensic evaluation of the girl from The Weirs.

"Really, Don?"

"Yes . . . you'll like this. You are probably not aware but, in years past, there was a similar episode of a dead girl during the Rally Week of 1955. The similarities of the two deaths are uncanny. I've found some research data in a personal journal from a now deceased Weirs resident. He chronicled the Bike Week events for many years, decades actually."

Blaisdell was shocked but delighted. "What do you mean, another death, Don?"

"Somewhere in the Coroner's Office in Concord is most likely a file of a similar scenario—a death at The Weirs. The year 1955 was significant to someone back then. The journals I've been reading have notes of a young woman found dead between The Mount and Endicott Rock Park during the Rally Week of that year."

"Are you sure?" asked Blaisdell, somewhat in awe of the new information. "Weird occurrence."

"Yes. An elderly resident of Lakeside Avenue kept the journals daily. Wendell Atkins was his name and he recently died. He was an acquaintance of mine and his elaborate handwritten recordings of Bike Week history have been shared with me after his death. They are voluminous."

"Tell me more, Don. This is incredible news."

"He was there the day that you examined the dead girl on the shoreline and wanted to share his memories of a past event that was apparently similar. Due to much confusion, no one paid him any mind. I was the only one who got to talk to him later. The police and your office were too involved that day."

"Jesus," stated Blaisdell, sympathetically and with remorse, "I'm sorry. I remember seeing an elderly gentleman on the stairs to the dock. Was that the man?"

"Yes. That was the same person, doctor. I followed Mr. Atkins to his home and managed to chat with him, and later obtained his written journals. What he was trying to say at the scene was important to the current crime. What is clear from what I have read to date in his records and newspaper clippings from that 1955 era, is that a similar crime went *unsolved* back then—a crime identical to the demise of "Tammy" X.

"Tell me more, please," the doctor asked. "This is incredible—what case was it?"

"Well I can help you more and point you in the right direction, but I wish to call in a 'bargaining chip.' I will share what I know if you tell me the results of your tissue and blood analyses to date, doctor. It's all tied together, I think. Confidential or not, I need to know some facts that only you might have."

"In confidence, I can share some of the pertinent info," Blaisdell offered, "but not all the details. What is it that you need to know?"

"Good . . . No problem. I'm sworn to secrecy with what you tell me."

"Listen, please," Don said, with some authority and arrogance, "the tattoos of the Vincent motorcycle logo are the key to the crime. Surely, you have heard of the vintage Vincent motorcycle?"

"Come to think of it, I have," remarked the doctor. "It was, or is, an old British machine, right?"

Don responded, "Yes. But more importantly, the logo of her recent tattoo is *that* of the famed motorcycle company and *not* the name of some boyfriend, etc. The company had three or more versions of that Vincent name as gas tank logos, some less elaborate and without the Roman icon, Mercury. The god with wings and a motorcycle wheel was the most elaborate of the designs and represented uniquely and appropriately, the 'speed' of the bike. The use of the god was intentional."

"I'm impressed with your investigative skills, Don. You seem to have solved one aspect of the unknown." Don smiled to himself at the compliment.

"As you know, the police have tied a tattoo artist and the dead biker, Iceman, to the crime as well. They have shared very little to date with the public but I will guarantee you that the bike logo, the tattoo, and the fact that a poison may have been in the ink are related. The dead girl may be the result of a cult tradition by a New Jersey motorcycle gang. They may have initiated this bizarre sacrifice in 1955, or perhaps earlier. The data I have is incomplete, but I feel that we are on the right path here in understanding what happened and why it happened."

"This is uncanny," responded the coroner. "I re-sampled some skin areas based on your prior input. The tissues from multiple sites, including the tattoo from the lower spine, indicate that the poison, curare and its metabolites were present in the most recent biological tests. This unique drug is utilized for muscle relaxation during microsurgery and was present in the blood of the girl . . . as well as in her lungs and skin tissues. She definitely was poisoned by tattooing—the *Vincent* tattoo most assuredly."

Don responded, with excitement.

"That validates what I was thinking at this end."

"The drug was not pure," remarked Blaisdell, "but the sample extracts showed other tars and gums that are traditional of curare *extracts* from plants in South America . . . the prep was so crude I'm surprised that they got it dissolved into the ink."

"Eureka!" screamed an excited Don Wright. "My premise is coming to fruition."

The doctor continued. "You surely are on the right path. I knew the symptoms of the drug class from her pathology and it was as I had suspected, the class of alkaloids, like curare. It causes breathing to stop—a paralytic effect. The girl suffocated slowly . . . it was painful for her since she would know she was dying."

"So someone in New Jersey, perhaps in the Rough Riders group, had been to South America to obtain the extract?" remarked Don, who was now pacing repeatedly with cell phone in hand.

"Could be," voiced the doctor. "It would be hard to find that extract in the United States. The drug curare, in its purest or modern day form for surgery, would not have the extra contaminants in it that the ink contained. Some bastard probably went to the rain forest to get it. Had to. I had studied the pharmacology of the raw drug during my research days and these 'peaks' in the biochemical analyses show that it is was a crude preparation in the ink.

It's something the Natives would use to capture animals for food—it's a blow dart preparation in its crudest and simplest form. A sticky tar derived right from the host plant!"

"Wow . . . we need to find out if someone in New Jersey went to South America. Perhaps the police in New Hampshire and the cops in New Jersey can provide that data. That would link key individuals from the motorcycle club down south to the death here. I can continue to work on the motive," Don volunteered.

"Awesome Don. You're incredible. Maybe you can fax me some details of the 1955 journal and case."

Don said, "Sure."

Dr. Blaisdell tried to ingest and absorb all of the information that Don had shared with him. It was pertinent to the investigation. He knew that he had his work cut out for him in terms of retrieving prior forensic data from the 1955 death at The Weirs Rally.

Don's newspaper clips were a good start but old records in the Coroner's Office related to deaths back then were probably stored in the Laconia Courthouse archives and not in Concord. Filing was a bit shoddy in the 50's. Surely, there must have been a similar autopsy and an investigation into the earlier death.

Blaisdell would pursue the records as soon as possible. He also had to contend with the existing body in the cooler. At some point, the unknown "Tammy" X required embalming and burial, somewhere. They could not keep her chilled forever and all relevant tissue and blood samples had been taken and preserved before her preservation anyway. If she were never identified, the State of New Hampshire would bury her locally, either temporarily or permanently if needed. There was a "Boot Hill" cemetery equivalent dedicated to the internment of the *unknown.*

"Once I get info from the old records of the 50's, I will be in touch, Don," Blaisdell offered. "I want to know who, where, when and why regarding the other lady that died in the 1950's. This is phenomenal. You may have helped solve more than one murder and a bizarre, traditional cult act as well. Congratulations."

"Thanks," replied Don, feeling quite impressive. "I'm glad to help and ready to share what I know with the LPD. They in turn need to bring you and me up to date on their data as well . . . they have info on Iceman, the Tattoo artist and the New Jersey Rough Riders that can impact the overall results.

Both you and I are out of the loop on where the New Jersey investigation is going but I think I know some of the reasons for a motive. Believe it or not, the fact that it's motorcycle related . . . is even more bizarre."

"I'll get what I can outta the LPD and share with you their perceptions to date," Blaisdell offered, as consolation. "I don't care if it's confidential . . . you know more than they probably do and should be in the loop. You may have to sign a confidentiality document but that's no sweat. In the end, we'll all be talking to one another . . . and with a common base."

"I can do that."

Don was curious about the curare connection. "How would the curare kill anyone if it was in ink?" he asked.

"To begin with, it wouldn't normally be thought of as a deadly agent, Don. It is not a common killing agent when used in surgery. What I suspect, however, is that the perpetrators knew that fact and were arrogant enough to think that they would not be caught. The drug can mimic common recreational drug and alcohol effects like stupor, fatigue and disorientation. The police would suspect symptoms of other commonly used drugs first—not an overdose by some obscure paralyzing agent."

Don concurred.

Blaisdell continued. "Curare in its many forms can only cause death if it enters the blood stream directly and causes the respiratory muscles to fail to work—that causes asphyxiation, which is what we saw with 'Tammy' X. It also ends up in the muscles of the arms and legs and lungs, so it's traceable. The tattoo artist may have gone too deep on some parts of the logo to enhance the coloration of the black ink. Maybe he hit a vein. He may have unknowing hit a vessel where the drug and ink entered the circulatory system. That would kill someone if the concentration of the drug were high. There was also a lot of black in that tattoo. A large amount of tainted ink was used. I suspect Iceman knew that."

Don remarked to Dr. Blaisdell that standard tattoos were normally applied in the upper layers. He had learned that from interviewing tattoo artists. In general, tattoos were not administered deep enough to circulate the ink in the body. They tended to stay localized where the artwork was being made. Blaisdell agreed and was mystified that any of the poison would enter the girl in a quantity to kill her. The facts, however, proved it was most probably the cause of her demise.

Blaisdell reminded Don that some deeper applications by amateurs could hit tissue depths not normally intended to be colored. Fuzzy may not have been totally aware of the blood supply to the lower back area. It was adjacent to the spine.

The application of many tattoos on the lower spine, like the "tramp stamp" "Tammy" X had applied could have somehow entered the lymph system or spinal fluid. It was highly unlikely, but further analyses were ongoing by Blaisdell and the State labs. The Cerebral Spinal Fluid (CSF) would be a direct connection of the poison to the ventricles of the brain. The vertical portion of the god, Mercury was right over the spine of the dead girl. Blaisdell didn't think that feasible at first since she would have been in severe pain during the process and the needle was too short to reach the CSF by common tattoo standards.

"The CSF, which we aspirated and sampled in her body also had a small amount of the drug in it. How it got there we don't know. We know the drug, curare, can't cross the Blood Brain Barrier (BBB) if it is in the normal circulation, but a direct injection into the spinal fluid or into a collateral blood vessel might cause the drug to affect the Central Nervous System (CNS), as well. It was *still* the paralyzing effect on the *chest muscles, the intercostals,* that really killed her.

I have no doubt that cessation of breathing in this girl was affected by direct action of the curare extract on those muscles between the ribs. She suffocated for sure. Her oxygen saturation in the blood was way too low. It just wasn't normal. My final report will reflect those contributory, causative effects on the death certificate."

Don appreciated the level of detail and promised to advise Blaisdell of any potential motives for the similar scenarios of 1955 and 2006. Blaisdell, by the same token, would keep Don abreast of any information from the New Jersey and LPD authorities. Both men wanted the case solved and the poor young woman identified and returned to her relatives.

Oddly, that enigma eluded the investigation to date. The Medford couple had already confirmed that the girl in the morgue was not their daughter. No one knew who the girl was and the leads to her identity had obviously died by week's end.

Chapter 118

The New Jersey authorities in Metuchen were chasing Ace and other members as best they could. Word on the street from some informants was that Ace was heading for an island off of Florida. He knew that the police would be seeking him out after the death of the Iceman. Off of Florida, could also mean the Bahamas or a United States island on the Gulf Coast. No one was sure. Some of the club members had already returned from Laconia and were holed up everywhere but at the Rough Riders' clubhouse. It was locked solid and there were no notes on the door as to anyone's whereabouts.

Oddly, the vial of ink had been a decisive clue that at least one Rough Riders member was involved in a murder investigation. Iceman was that member but the police in New Hampshire and New Jersey both felt that the death was a serious collaborative plot by many other club members. No one felt that the Iceman could have acted alone. Was he just the messenger?

Rumors in Metuchen, New Jersey were rampant that Ace frequented South America and was not in hiding in a southern state. He surely had friends to protect him south of the border.

Local kids knew that he dealt drugs on a daily basis to area teenage clients in Metuchen, Newark, the Meadowlands and as far as New York City. A few of the kids were willing to talk to the police for cash and seek anonymity or immunity from prosecution. The police had cash to pay for the information. They weren't acting cheap either when sourcing the origin of drugs and dealers involved in the Greater New Jersey area. The kids made out well if they squealed. It was unlikely that Ace would return to "ice" them. There was an APB on his head and he knew it.

*　　*　　*

Bonnie and John were enjoying the Monday after the races and official Bike Week extravaganza. They sat in The Crazy Gringo Mexican restaurant and drank some beers at the popular bar. Much of Lakeside Avenue was free of the venues and tents. One or two stragglers were removing the last of the T-shirt stands while the DPW of Laconia cleaned up the mess and trash barrels that had been left overflowing near the Drive-In and Lakeside Avenue vendor sites. The barrels were filled with bottles and cans and fast food wrappers. Few policemen were visible or were needed for special duty anymore since much of the crowd had already dissipated and the residential community was approaching its solitude again. The occasional loud bike interrupted the serene atmosphere.

Don Wright shot the last of his Bike Week photos for the newspaper.

Monday's races at NHIS had resulted in the favored rider, Scott Greenwood and his Kawasaki crashing and leaving Connecticut's Michael Martire's Kawasaki the winner of the Loudon Classic. Greenwood had already won some Saturday races and dominated the field with his prowess, but Monday was a disaster for him.

Sixteen-year-old, Shane Narbonne's Suzuki and seventeen-year-old, Shane Hudson's Yamaha had placed second, and third, respectively. Never before had *two* racers under the age of eighteen started the Classic on the front row, one newspaper had stated. Steve Giacomaro on a Suzuki, was another favorite to place high, but crashed on Monday.

Most local residents were able to reflect on the aftermath of the enormous event, and the attendees for the week. Huge revenues were generated for the local businesses. Lakeside Avenue was now open to two-way traffic and automobiles.

The TV above The Gringo bar was set on TV News 9, the Manchester station, while rock n' roll played over the table portion of the restaurant. The sounds seem to clash with one another and compete for volume. Conversations offered more confusion.

The bar area was smoke-filled as usual, a blue haze that rose toward the ceiling as the few bikers remaining drank beer and reminisced.

They weren't all that interested in the TV until a picture of the dead girl's facial profile was shown on the local news. It startled the onlookers. The police had no other recourse but to seek out the identity of the woman through the visual media. It was a last resort to seek help in the enigma.

Don Wright had stopped at The Gringo for a draft beer just as Bonnie reacted to the sight of the unknown "Jane Doe" / "Tammy" X on the TV. Don grabbed a vacant stool to the left of her seat and John was sitting to the right of her.

When a photo of Iceman, (acquired from old mug shots in New Jersey), appeared second in the sequence of TV photos, the news station alluded to his connection to the dead woman at The Weirs. Bonnie shrieked and began to sob. John attempted to console her as Don reacted to their responses. Was it fate? Fate that was to be on his side. He silently sipped his brew while listening intently to Bonnie's distress.

"John . . . oh, John," she sobbed . . . "that's the pretty girl that Iceman told me about. He was with her when she got the tattoo—that 'tramp stamp' that you just saw was *the* tattoo he told me about."

"Jesus. I'm sorry, honey . . . I'm really sorry about their deaths."

It was fortuitous that the next snapshot on TV was a close-up of the tattoo that had been applied to the girl's lower spine. It was clearly the one that Don had photographed at the crime scene. He couldn't believe his eyes. *Were the cops and the coroner actually working together on her I.D.? That would be amazing.*

"Are you sure that's the young girl?" John asked. "Why would he do in that beautiful young lady?"

Bonnie began to sob and nodded, yes. She had already consumed three or four beers and was quite vocal at this point. Don leaned toward them as best he could—her whispers to John weren't really whispers. Don couldn't resist. He finally baited her by interrupting their conversation.

"Sad that the girl died here at The Weirs, huh? Ruined the whole week for the town."

Bonnie said nothing in response to his interjection and then, leaning back against her stool, offered a comment. Her head was tilted back as if studying the ceiling of the bar.

"I knew the dude that they just showed on TV. He was a friend of mine. He died this week in an accident. I knew that the young chick had died too but never realized she was so pretty . . . such a pretty young thing." John sat listening quietly. He didn't really want her chatting with others. They could be cops or members of the Metuchen club.

Don turned toward Bonnie and Bonnie saw the two cameras around his neck. One was loaded with standard color film and the other was digital with black and white capabilities. He never missed a critical shot requiring either medium.

"You a professional photographer or somethin'? Pretty impressive hardware ya got there, lenses and all."

"Yah, I work for the local paper here in town and photograph the daily "Faces of Bike Week" shots that you might have seen in the newspaper. That is, if ya get the paper, ma'am."

"Really? Photograph me and John here, as the last people to leave this fucking joint," she suggested, laughing from inebriation. John cringed.

"I'd be glad to," remarked Don. "What's your name? I'm Don Wright."

"The name's Bonnie . . . 'Boring Bonnie,'" she joked. John disagreed with her statement. "There ain't no way this Bonnie is boring, man," he said, with a broad smile. "She's the furthest thing from boring."

Don laughed and kept the conversation moving forward.

"Sorry, Bonnie. Sad to hear of your friend's death. I had covered that accident scene for our paper—when Iceman was killed on Route 11. I'm very sorry for you that he crashed and died." She nodded, acknowledging his comment.

Chapter 119

Bonnie bowed her head and then opened up like a faucet. She felt the effects of the beer and became extremely chatty.

"He was marked!" she blurted, abruptly. "A marked man."

"What do you mean, 'marked?'" Don quizzed her carefully. "He accidentally ran off the road, right? In the early morn?"

"Like hell!" Bonnie said, tapping a cigarette on the bar. John quickly lit the Marlboro. She offered one to Don who thanked her, no.

"He was pushed—pushed off the fuckin' road by a fellow rider. The bastard crossed him. The cops don't know that."

"Pushed? What do you mean pushed? Wasn't he alone that night?"

"Nope," she replied. "He was marked for extermination by his fucking boss, a guy named Ace from the New Jersey motorcycle club that he belonged to—the Rough Riders, named after Teddy Roosevelt."

"No way," Don played along. "How da ya know that?"

"Yes, way!" she said, emphatically. "He was doomed by his so-called buddies. They put a 'hit,' on him, a 'mark' and made it look like he had gone off the road, but I damn well know better."

John cringed. She was sharing too much info.

"Jesus Christ," said Don, acting surprised. "Why would his friends 'ice' him?"

"Ya know . . . No ya don't. Ya couldn't," said Bonnie, without hesitation. "He had that chick tattooed with a bike logo, right?" She drew a long breath on the cigarette and blew smoke rings as she exhaled. Don waited with anticipation. He had always considered smoke rings a "guy" thing, not a woman thing.

"That tattoo they just showed on TV was a bike logo?" Don replied, playing dumb. "You know that for certain?"

"Sure do . . . it's the name of an old bike—*Vincent* . . . a real old bike. The gang from Jersey killed my ol' man," she cried, in pain. "He was *my* ol' man."

"You're ol' man? The Iceman dude was your boyfriend or husband?" Don asked, sounding somewhat surprised. John was sitting and staring at the TV, and feeling totally out of the loop.

John looked at Bonnie and raised his eyebrows. "Bonnie. Ya hardly knew the guy. You only met him recently. You're makin' me feel like chopped ham."

"True. I had just met him," she responded, apologizing to her new beau. "I'm sorry John-boy. I should have shut my mouth. You're my man." John smiled and kissed her cheek. "That's okay, baby," he added. "I just met ya too."

Don was trying to acquire all the information that he could. He felt compelled to pursue the lead before she clammed up. This, to him, was the hottest lead that he had in the mystery death. By chance or by serendipity, he had happened to stop by The Crazy Gringo for a beer. *Who would have thunk it?*

"Bonnie. Have you chatted with the police? I mean, they think Iceman accidentally fell asleep or something before he veered off the road."

"Sure he veered of the road," she volunteered. "He veered off the road when someone pulled up beside him and pushed his ass . . . off the road. You shitin' me? He didn't doze off. There was a fellow rider from Wolfeboro, where they were staying—he terminated him . . . or as you say, 'iced him.' I overheard other club members boasting. They were staying in Wolfeboro.

For the first time ever, Don now knew where the club members were encamped.

"What?" Don reacted to encourage more info. "Someone shoved him? There was another guy that pulled up and pushed him down that embankment? Someone from Wolfeboro?"

"Hell yes! . . . I was there when the asshole, 'compatriot' / 'faithful club member' had the balls to come back to the campground and brag about the 'deed' being done. The jerk was proud of himself. I balled all night in the Iceman's tent." Don was aghast.

"The next friggin' day they dropped me off at The Weirs. If it weren't for my current man, John here, sitting next to me, I'd still be in my two-day-old shorts and sittin' in the rain by that stupid "rock" at the other end of the street. John-boy here, saved my ass. He put me up when I had no place to go. Those rat-bastards in Wolfeboro abandoned me. Meanwhile, those 'devoted' Jersey assholes headed home by way of alternate roads to avoid the 'fuzz.'"

"Jesus, Bonnie. Didn't you tell the police about this? Your friend was murdered and they should know, right? Why not tell them?"

"Thought about it . . . really did . . . but they would kill me if the boys from Jersey found out I ratted on them. Now that I've seen the young woman that they are accused of killing, that pretty little blonde, I'm tempted to blow their cover."

John tried to quiet her and she became belligerent.

"John, honey . . . please don't hush me up. I've been holdin' some of this info inside for days and I just saw the young girl that they murdered . . . Iceman told me the deal. He was hammered and *spilled his guts* to me."

Don spoke up to quell the potential disagreement.

"Bonnie. John. Hold it. The police will protect you. You have critical information that they don't know. They don't even have the girl's name and she's dead in the Concord morgue. They could use your help. Her parents, whoever they are, could use your help. Somebody's daughter is dead and they don't even know it."

Bonnie bowed her head and wiped her eyes and nose. She knew Don was right.

Bonnie ordered three beers, one for each of them. "Another round, on me," she screamed over the TV and loud music. She pointed to each of the glasses and made a circular motion with her finger.

"Yes, ma'am. Comin' right up," Tom, the bartender responded, somewhat perturbed.

"Thanks, sweetie," she smiled at him. John went silent again. He felt that she should not get involved in *either* death. She was becoming a 'motor-mouth.' She could be targeted next, he felt. He liked Bonnie and didn't want to see her hurt or to lose her.

Don touched her hand and thanked her for the beer. He smiled at John who was extremely apprehensive as to where this conversation was going.

"He's with the paper, honey," John rebutted. "Your ass will be all over the papers. Do you want that?"

Don interjected some assurance of anonymity. "I promise not to divulge her info to the paper, but the police need to chat with her. It will help solve this mystery. I won't photograph you folks . . . not to worry. Can you at least talk to a detective that I know well? He will keep this confidential, I promise."

Bonnie looked at John and then at Don to her left. She knew Don was correct in the right course of action and she owed the Rough Riders bastards some payback. After a moment, she began to sob again. The beer had now gone from a stimulant to a depressant. It was working as most alcohol works—up, then down, way down. As she sobbed, Don consoled her in her confusion and passed her a napkin to dry her eyes. He patted her on the back gently. He said nothing more, as did John who shook his head in dismay.

They let her gather her thoughts together. The momentary silence was refreshing and the TV news was now focused on a political story. The damn New Hampshire Republicans were beating up on the Democratic governor again, and without cause. He had been the best thing to happen to New Hampshire in years.

*   *   *

John had a change of heart. "I'll help where I can," he offered. "I will stick by you, Bonnie, and through this tragedy . . . until the end. Don is right. You need to tell someone what you currently know otherwise it will haunt you forever . . . I mean, *forever!* Why let it hang over your head, doll?"

Don didn't want her to chicken out of squealing. He prodded her to accompany him to the LPD station on Fair Street in Laconia.

"I'll get the bill here," Don offered for kudos. "Bonnie, you can ride on the back of my machine and John can follow. I can call ahead and make sure that the top guy is there for you. Okay? Captain Bennett is a fair man. Chief Dalinger may also be around."

Bonnie reluctantly nodded in agreement and Don threw down two $20.00 bills on the counter for the bartender. He waved to the bartender and thanked him. "Tip here for ya, as well." Having her ride on the back of his bike, assured him that both of them would not bolt or chicken out.

In ten minutes, both bikes pulled into the police station near the center of downtown. John was unsure of where the police station was so he followed closely. Along the way, Don Wright alerted Bennett by cell phone of a breakthrough agenda. He called Dr. Blaisdell and left a voicemail as well. He was keeping his promise to the coroner.

Bonnie had clung to his waist the entire ride and whimpered on occasion. Don could feel her shaking in fear. He patted her hand on his waist along the ride. "You'll be okay, he turned and spoke." It was muffled but discernable under his helmet.

She was frightened but knew that Don and John were right by taking her there.

•   Captain Bennett welcomed her cordially. There was a much-needed break in the case.

Her testimony, even under the influence of a few beers, was astounding. She declined to have a lawyer present since she had done nothing wrong herself. For an hour or more, she spilled the beans as best she could remember. She did it for *the Iceman* and for the dead girl who was a victim of a devious and unscrupulous tradition.

Bennett hugged her when they were done with the interview. John did as well and she was to ride back to their cabin on his machine.

Don thanked her profusely and kissed her cheek before she left. John shook his hand. They departed the downtown area feeling all the better for chatting with the police. Don kept their contact information for safekeeping. He would surely need to chat with them again at some point.

He was ecstatic and now had added another piece to the puzzle. He would brief the coroner of the newfound details that were revealed by Bonnie at the police station. The case was fast closing in on the Rough Riders' agenda.

Chapter 120

After the interview with Bonnie, Don Wright was brought into the confidence of the police. It was a reward for bringing her into the LPD for questioning. Captain Bennett and the investigative team were pleased to have Don's assistance as well. They were amazed at the data he had collected since the day of the crime at The Weirs.

Between Don, the police and the coroner, the method of death was being elucidated piece by piece. Much of the forensic evidence was coming together quite rapidly in support of what Bonnie had said. Don admitted to the police that he was on the fast track of the *modus operandi*. He would be in touch as often as needed.

The gang from New Jersey may have had a prior event decades earlier that included a cult-like celebration involving another woman. Don didn't elaborate on the 1950's incident but said that a similar death had occurred decades earlier, one that most authorities may have not known about or had forgotten about by 2006. He mentioned that the coroner was chasing the files. He told Bennett and other investigators that the event was in some historical records and that he was close to identifying the bizarre motives for the killings, the relevance of the tattoo and the relationship of the Rough Riders' members to the evil event that killed the girl.

Dr. Blaisdell was happy to hear that a woman, named Bonnie, had come forward and was talking to the LPD. He now was aware that she had temporary ties to the gang, basically through the deceased Iceman. Don had left him a message that he had stumbled across someone, *by serendipity and a beer,* someone who knew the Iceman *closely*. She was his concubine of sorts. Her input might ultimately help with the dead girl's identity and the coincidence of the tattoos with tainted ink. Bonnie had actually seen the bottle of toxic fluid.

Captain Bennett thanked Don profusely and commended him on his help in the resolution of the crime. He asked Don to sign a confidentiality form so he could share relevant details to date. Don agreed to the terms and was advised of the interviews that the police had compiled from the input of Fuzzy Walsh and others.

"Your girl, Bonnie didn't hold anything back in the interview. Once she started to talk, we couldn't shut her up. She felt jilted by the club members who "iced" her boyfriend and also dumped her at the Drive-In with her limited possessions in hand. They threatened her if she said anything and we will protect her."

Don replied. "So she will be in your protective custody now?" he asked, with concern.

"Yes," was the response. "Many of the visitors have left and the New Jersey Rough Riders seem to be on the run, most likely laying low and then heading south. We don't think they will ever know she was in our facility today. How would they?"

"Hope they don't find out or find her. She'll be dead meat."

The police seemed to think that she would be okay. Nobody but the Iceman had known her full name or her place of origin. The police would not divulge to the public that she had talked to them. Their private investigation was *private*. As a potential witness, she was assured that she would only need to attend court proceedings that required her testimony and that testimony would be behind closed doors.

Don told the police that he had to leave. He had research that was in midstream. He considered it critical to the case at hand.

Bonnie and John arrived at the cabin near The Weirs. She wanted nothing other than to sleep. The police had asked her to stay in touch since they might need further testimony—especially if anyone had to go to trial over the dead girl. Bonnie agreed to all conditions. She had the protection of the police while in New Hampshire. She had no idea when she would leave the Granite State. She knew the State motto was "Live Free or Die." She wanted to live, and not be killed by some Jersey biker with a vengeance.

She was in love with John and a new life was just beginning. While she slept, he rode a few miles south to Wal-Mart and bought her a hundred dollars worth of clothes and personal hygiene items. It would be like an early Christmas for her.

*   *   *

George Adams had continued to read the journals in Don's absence. He had remembered some of the events in 1955 especially the death of a woman who had tattoos and was naked on the shore of Weirs Beach. It was the notations of Wendell Atkins that had refreshed his memory of the event. The news clippings also aided the search for information.

In essence, the information that the journals provided was limited. The case was unsolved with respect to the 1955 dead woman. It was established that she had probably fell from a passing boat and drown. The police had never completed the investigation, leaving it as an *open case* status as late as 2006.

Dr. Blaisdell would begin a detailed search of the mortuary records regarding the events of June 1955. Don alerted Blaisdell to the motorcycle week events that surrounded the woman's demise. Blaisdell knew that an M.E. had to have recorded the autopsy back then and the records with the State's investigation were filed somewhere.

Blaisdell was savvy and quickly located a file room from that era. The 1955 records were archived in a locked, musty room in the Coroner's Office, and not in Laconia as he had originally thought. With most cases *closed* from that decade of the 50's, few people even took the time to access the older files, until now. The room was dusty, dark and cobwebs inundated the corners.

Manila files and folders seemed to be piled high on top of file cabinets, in disarray. The manila folder of a "1955 Jane Doe" case was neatly filed vertically in one of the green metal file drawers. It was stored under "Motorcycle Week, Laconia—1955."

The attending coroner or M.E. at the time was a Dr. Marshall. Sadly, the victim was never identified or the reason for her death, other than purported asphyxia, attributed to drowning.

Blaisdell questioned the diagnosis of the time, since there was little proof in the file that she had drowned. There were photos of a dead blonde woman and close-ups of three or four tattoos, one of which was reminiscent of the famed "Vincent" logo.

The photography back then included a series of Polaroid shots of poor resolution, quick photos that were "convenient" at the scene of crimes. The technology was fresh and rapid, marking death for posterity. Some photos were slightly faded. Polaroid pictures often required a liquid "fixer" be applied to the photo with a special padded tool in order to preserve the photograph. Some people did not take the time to perform that step and photos faded severely or disappeared over the years. Even with the lighter colored photos, Blaisdell could see the outline of the famed Mercury figure and the motorcycle wheel and wings of the "Vincent" company.

"Jesus Christ," he voiced, with amazement. "This is an identical scenario to the current case."

He pulled up a stool and sat flipping through the files from Marshall's notes of the prior autopsy. The dim light above him was less candlepower than he needed but he was anxious to peruse all the relevant files just the same. He eventually moved to his office and reviewed the information under better circumstances—adequate light and comfort.

"The damn skin of this tattoo is raised higher than the surrounding tissue. This woman probably had the tattoo applied that specific week in 1955."

He flipped ahead to the summary report. Aside from the diagnosis of asphyxia, Blaisdell saw no reason for Dr. Marshall to cite drowning; the autopsy had shown no fluids in the respiratory tract. It was almost as if the medical examiner of that era had given up and cited drowning as the probable cause. No one would challenge him. He was the guru back then.

"Where the hell is she buried?" asked Blaisdell of himself. "Who was that woman?" He let his finger guide his eyes on each line of the paragraph in the summary conclusions. The last line said it all.

"Jane Doe 1955," a deceased ward of the State, was buried in a State-sanctioned cemetery in Concord, New Hampshire.

The State had paid for her internment. She remained unidentified and that correlation to the current case was depressing for Blaisdell.

The cemetery location was not far from the Coroner's Office and Blaisdell's facility. He jumped in his car and headed for the graveyard located off Route 3. In less than three minutes, he entered the granite gate that touted the date: 1889.

Along the way to the cemetery he considered the possibility of exhuming the body from some fifty-one years earlier. *Would it yield anything? One had to consider that the tattoo might contain an alkaloid that may have deteriorated five decades later. Did curare kill the woman in the 1955 case? Were the two cases related?* He was perplexed.

Of course they were related, he finally concluded, and he needed to exhume "Jane Doe—1955" to pursue his theory.

His car approached the top of the hill where the unknown victims and homeless were buried by the State. After walking some twenty rows, Blaisdell stopped dead in his tracks. The plain granite stone said nothing of significance or warmth:

Jane Doe—1955
Unknown Victim of Weirs Beach Drowning

Blaisdell had found another link. He now had to return home and think about his next step. Would he exhume her body? *Surely.* Would he sample any tissues that were remaining? *Yes.* Did the tattoo hold the clues? *Most probably!* There was only one answer to all. As a professional doctor and investigator, he knew the answer. *Do it and see!* If he didn't exhume the body, he would not be able to sleep from that day forward.

The following morning he filed the formal request to the State of New Hampshire's Attorney General to reopen a half-century old case and reexamine the body of "Jane Doe—1955." Blaisdell immediately called Don and the LPD to advise them of the recent breakthrough in the 1955 case, and his intensions to exhume the body.

Chapter 121

At a Holiday Inn in Freeport in the Bahamas, Ace relaxed in a lounge chair near the beach. In an instant, he was blindsided by three Bahamian police officers that approached his "space" in the high noon sun. Clothed only in a large bathing suit and covered with a coconut fragranced, oily sunscreen lotion, he was quickly apprehended before his next sip of a rum-infused Planter's Punch. A tattoo-clad biker babe lay to his right, face down on her own lounge chair, bikini top untied. She wore a thong that revealed way too much skin to some sunbathers. The police loved it, however.

When the police surprised the duo, she startled and jumped up with her arms open, revealing two pendulous breasts. It was as if someone had poured cold water on her back by surprise. Some men nearby hooted and hollered at the impressive sight.

She was pissed.

"What the fuck?" she said, startled and covering herself with her hands. "What's up here?"

One dark skinned officer, a Native Bahamian, ordered both of the sunbathers to gather their things and follow them. Ace considered for a moment trying to bolt or run for it, but his massive body was too heavy in the soft sand. The police were well-built, fit and possessed weapons—side arms. They would have overpowered Ace in a heartbeat.

The woman quickly retied her top while shouting obscenities, and both of the Americans were handcuffed and lead away to a small white police car that resembled a Fiat, the back seat a tight fit for the Iceman. Little more was said on the beach other than, "You are under arrest and desired by the American authorities. You are being deported."

"What the hell for?" asked Ace, playing innocent. "What the hell am I wanted for? I have rights to protection and a lawyer."

"You do, 'mon,' but you are in the Bahamas not in the U.S. We have our own laws."

One policeman stepped closer and stared at him. "Mon, be quiet! You are in a foreign country as a visitor, illegally it seems. You have no specific USA rights and will be sent back under the auspices of United States Customs officials at the airport. U. S. Federal Marshals are there, waiting for us to deliver you to them for the next flight to Miami—in an hour."

"Why?" Ace asked.

"'Mon.' We don't know, other than the fact that you are desired to be interviewed back home. You must be in trouble. We do not get involved in the details. We merely were asked to seek you out. The hotel and Customs had a record of your reservations and passport."

"How did you know where I was . . . I mean on the beach."

"Easy for us, 'mon.' You were described as very large, with a beard. Take a look around. Everyone on this beach is fit and tanned. They are slight and have no facial hair. You stood out like our national monument in town," he laughed. "You are pasty white, 'mon.'"

Ace smirked and the biker chick remained silent. Their interest was not in her, in particular.

A New Jersey State Police detective and numerous Customs Agents awaited the arrival of the duo at the Freeport Airport and immediately took custody of them. They were under their auspices and jurisdiction. A timely charter flight home was available and they were placed in the back of the plane prior to the general boarding of tourists whose vacations were over.

The U.S. Agents presented Ace with a warrant for his arrest—for murder and possible accessory to a murder. Ace said nothing on the flight home. Other than using the bathroom once, he remained in his seat. The 18-inch seat width was uncomfortable for him, even with the armrests elevated. The sorry bastard had flown First Class on the way down to the island chain. Not this time, he was *in the back of the bus* on this trip home with less decadence and limited attention from flight attendants.

Two hours later, after elaborate paperwork, they were back in the United States. The flight was less than three-quarters of an hour. Freeport was only sixty or so miles from the mainland of Florida.

*   *   *

The coroner in New Hampshire, the authorities at the LPD and Don Wright had been notified of the apprehension of Ace in the Bahamas.

They were exuberant. He had been implicated by Bonnie as the potential *source* of the ink that was used in the tattoo by Fuzzy Walsh—the same ink that Iceman had in his possession.

New Jersey police were able to seek him out after his disappearance from the Metuchen area. The travel records for flights pulled up Ace's real name, Carlos Hernandez—place of birth, Fontana, California—current residence, Metuchen, New Jersey.

New Jersey authorities had additional charges awaiting him, mostly drug related with local dealings in New Jersey and New York. The woman with Ace was a new member of his harem. U.S. authorities requested the help of the Bahamian authorities who gladly reciprocated and traced their visitor paperwork to the Holiday Inn on the south shore.

Don was still working on the motive and Bonnie had also shared incriminating evidence from the Iceman. It was abundantly clear to Don that the 1955 death was potentially related to the attendance of the Iceman's father during the same Bike Week Rally that year. She had implicated Ace's father as well, but until recently Don knew little of Ace's role in 2006. All he knew was that Ace was President of the Rough Riders club. Iceman was most recently 'second in command' and the apparent *messenger of doom.*

Don saw the relationships beginning to gel. There was a *tradition* that was initiated or inspired by numerous coincidences. The Rough Riders club name surely had its origin that dated back to Teddy Roosevelt. The Teddy Bear found near the deceased "Tammy" X and the fact that Bonnie was also been given a similar toy was more than a coincidence.

Historically, it was well known that the Teddy Bear and the Rough Riders military infantry were related to the popular 26th President of the United States—the famous bear having been rescued during a hunting trip in which Roosevelt was to shoot a helpless, immobilized cub for a Big Game photo-op. Teddy R. fired no shot, unlike the tumultuous Dick Cheney episode where a photo-op resulted in him shooting and injuring his duck hunting companion. Some photo-op!

*　　*　　*

The two fathers of Iceman and Ace were close friends who had attended the 1955 Rally in Laconia. They rode Vincent motorcycles to the event according to Bonnie's testimony. She had revealed much of Iceman's input during one of his binges on drugs and beer. Coincidently, the end of 1955 was the demise of the production of the Vincent motorcycle and Don suspected that that might be the link.

"Holy crap," he commented to George Adams. "This series of events can't be a coincidence." George agreed.

The newspaper clippings in Wendell's journals were helpful. He also kept all the snippets that were related to the first dead woman at The Weirs. *How is it that nothing was figured out way back then?* Don questioned.

"It took fifty more years or so to celebrate the purposed agenda of these fruitcakes," Don stated. "Somehow, the two events in late '55 and '06 were a continuation of a cult-like secret mission, left unsolved." He pondered the data.

"I suppose we would have seen more of this at the 75th or 100th Laconia Rallies, complete with more tattoos and death if it continued. I can't believe that the Rough Riders were despondent over the demise of the Vincent way back in 1955. Could that be? Why would they mark two women for death?"

"Looks that way, partner," George Adams reacted, with furrowed brow. "Makes no sense."

"That would explain the Vincent tattoo on both woman. It was probably part of the cult commemoration. How bizarre," Don added. "This is so fucked up."

"Beyond bizarre. Without Wendell's notes, how would we have known any of this?" offered George, with gratitude to his deceased friend.

"If Blaisdell finds curare or something similar in the 1955 case upon exhumation, it will be clear what the *real* cause of death was back then—a familial pattern. Blaisdell doubted accidental drowning anyway. He hopefully can get to the bottom of this mystery. My bet is that there is a toxic drug in that '55 tattoo as well, if in fact there are remains of her skin to analyze."

If she was embalmed, it might confuse the issue. The case of "Doctor X" made the analyses of those case samples questionable.

Don was hopeful that the technology had improved enough, at least bioanalytically, to solve *two* crimes, not just one.

Chapter 122

Dr. Blaisdell had, in fact, been granted permission to reopen the case. The judge didn't hesitate. Fortunately, the body had *not* been embalmed to save the State of New Hampshire some expense, but due to a virtual airtight casket and the cool temperature of the earth at six feet, the M.E. found the integrity of the body to be in amazingly good shape and well preserved. He could hardly believe the quality of the tissues to sample.

As expected, a tattoo at the base of the spine was intact, dry and accessible for multiple biopsies. Residual blood, although caked in major vessels remained for sampling. It was analyzed, along with the lungs and other tissues, seeking the presence of curare-like alkaloids that might have ended up in those areas.

In a matter of days, two labs would have the results for Blaisdell. The scientists were happy to speed up the procedures and prioritize the tests knowing that other cases might wait a day or two without compromising their forensic evaluations. Even without being positively identified, both women had yielded the greatest leads in the apparent tradition of the New Jersey Rough Riders' macabre tradition. The women were the *heroes* in this quest, but subject to an appalling scenario of death without reason.

Epilogue

A week had passed after the official Laconia Motorcycle extended week of festivities. The stragglers had had enough of the bars and drinking. The binging was over for another year. Laconia and the surrounding communities of Gilford, Lakeport, Meredith, Wolfeboro and Alton Bay were back to normal. The sound of the loud pipes had quieted with only the occasional biker remaining behind to milk the tradition one more day. Most visitors to Rally Week had to return to their jobs and homes in other States, some from as far away as California. Many of the men and women who had come to the event went home touting the phrase, "What happens at Bike week, stays at Bike Week." Cheating on their girlfriends or boyfriends was almost expected, especially when peer pressure inspired the bikers to be macho or randy.

Over the years, Bike Week had gone from a Father's Day weekend event of racing to seven to nine days of rallies, races and local events relevant to motorcycling, touring and 83 years of camaraderie. Beer, babes, bikes and sex had been the mantra each year and 2006 was no different.

Bonnie and John had stayed a few extra days at the cottage high above Tower Hill Rd. The Weirs and the nearby famed Kellerhaus, where homemade chocolate candies and ice cream was offered to tourists for over 100 years, beckoned the lovers and other tourists.

Most of their time was spent in the cabin where their relationship seemed to grow. The conversations after sex were meaningful. She desired to follow him back to Vermont and they were sorting through the details of that possible scenario. John was cautious and not one to be tied down but Bonnie was attractive to him in many ways other than lovemaking.

They needed more time to sort out the plan and both adults wanted their feelings to grow beyond lust. She had no commitments down south in the Carolinas and he had the flexibility to accommodate a new beginning for himself. John had no steady girlfriend at home.

The results of the coroner's investigation from the 1955 case matched almost identically the case in 2006. The residue of a curare like compound was detected in the tattoo and tissues of the young woman in the earlier case. The tattoo virtually matched the Vincent logo of "Tammy" X. It was located at the base of the spine. Photographs from the coroner's files, and those that Don Wright had taken in June 2006, were similar.

Black ink was predominant in both. Blaisdell reported that the girl in 1955 had curare in her blood remnants and the lungs as well. He rewrote the report with an addendum. It stated that, 'most probably, the earlier case was death by asphyxia—the confirmed poison being curare.'

Notations were made in both files, the 1955 and 2006 folders that would alert future coroners to the unidentified women virtually 50 years apart. That was noted so that someone in the Coroner's Office could take heed twenty-five years later on the 75th anniversary of the Vincent Motorcycle Company's demise, just in case something similar occurred. It was doubtful that another issue might arise in the future. Would the Rough Riders chance it? It was really the families of Ace and Iceman that had conceived the idea.

Iceman was dead and Ace had been apprehended. The Nomad and Tiny Tim were eventually arrested when a fellow sympathizer of the Iceman ratted on them. The club was in disarray.

The proceedings and murder trial of Ace and other Rough Riders who collaborated in the plot, yielded testimony from Bonnie, Fuzzy Walsh, George Adams and some Rough Riders that decided to speak on behalf of the Iceman. He did have friends after all.

The New Jersey Rough Riders Motorcycle Club became defunct or silent. Members joined other clubs in New Jersey to avoid the close scrutiny of the New Jersey and New Hampshire police.

The two women who had died in 1955 and again in 2006 remained anonymous. No one claimed them and they remain even today without names other than "Jane Doe—1955" and "Tammy X—2006." The State of New Hampshire re-interred "Jane Doe—1955" the same day.

The case was closed for now. Again, the State assumed responsibility for the reburial costs. All of the investigators including Don, George, Captain Bennett, Dr. Blaisdell and staff, as well as Bonnie and John, and unknown but compassionate local mourners attended the graveside services.

Sadly, by year's end, the elderly George Adams would also be dead from old age leaving Don Wright distraught and absorbed with the task of the transcription, summating and publishing the journals of Wendell Atkins and Adams' most recent notes. They were to be a series of books, bound and published—copies of which were offered for sale by a local Historical Society near The Weirs. The proceeds benefited local Veterans organizations, of which Wendell and George would have been proud.

*   *   *

High above the rolling cemetery, a chopped Harley sat parked near other marker stones in the graveyard. A stocky man with sunglasses, a bandanna and binoculars stood with his eyes peeled on the burial ceremonies below. A younger version of the Iceman, feature-wise, he was a dead ringer for his ol' man. The faded license plate on the rear fender read—CHILLR. The license tag was beige and that of the New Jersey DMV.

He stayed until the cemetery workers attended to the plots for the two dead women. One-half hour after the men were finished and had departed, the unknown biker walked down the hill from where his motorcycle was parked and placed two new Teddy Bears, one on each grave. The cemetery was now devoid of other visitors at 4 P.M. Fresh flower arrangements covered the two spots where they were interred.

The biker smiled at the graves for a moment and then climbed the dirt road to his Harley parked behind a large granite memorial on the hill. He fired up the loud bike and slowly rode past the deceased women stopping momentarily near their graves. He saluted the two women and then whispered in their direction,

"Adios, sweet ladies . . . sleep well," he smirked. "See ya again in another 50 years—or maybe sooner . . . 'Live Free or Die!' or . . . should I say, 'Live Freeze or Die!'"

His sarcastic laughter was *chilling*, even in the warmth of a typical mid-June in New Hampshire.

Postscript

Philip C. Vincent was born in Fulham, London on March 14th 1908. He died at Ashford Hospital on March 27th 1979. Service at South West Middlesex Crematorium April 4th. Later his ashes were interred alongside his wife Elfrida at Hordon-on-the-Hill, Essex, less than a quarter mile from High House the old Vincent family home.

Howard Raymond Davies was born in Birmingham on June 27th 1895.

He officially died twice! He was a Lt. and a pilot at Amiens in the Somme sector. His aircraft was shot down in combat by Lt. Karl Emil Schaeffer over La Coulotte, West of Avion on April 14th 1917. His obituary notice was published in the Express and Star, only for his family to eventually discover that he had been taken prisoner. He was held by the Germans for two years. He died on January 3rd 1973. His wife Ethel Maisie died two days later. A joint funeral was held at the Robin Hood Crematorium, in Solihull on Jan 8th.

Source: 10/2006

Paul Adams
Vincent HRD Owners Club.

Acknowledgements

Special thanks and love are extended to my wife and children for their patience and encouragement during the preparation of this novel. The research, writing, editing and production of a novel can take an author away from family moments that should otherwise be cherished.

I am especially indebted to my brother, Tony who introduced me to Laconia Bike Week and professional motorcycle road racing in the 1970's. The tradition of our family enjoying the annual NH gathering remains to this day.

I appreciate the expertise of close friend, Mac McLanahan, a talented professional musician and 'digital wizard' who helped with the editing of the cover photo and final cover design.

The chapters in this book were formatted in the 'style' of author, James Patterson whom this author admires. Each Chapter is purposely abbreviated in nature.

Lastly, this book is *fiction* in plot. The story is contrived and imaginary. It does however contain some actual history of the Lakes Region of NH and the "oldest motorcycle rally and races" in the country.

Additional books by the author, J. P. Polidoro, Ph.D.

Available from local bookstores (special order),
Longtailpublishing.com, Xlibris.com, BN.com, and from Ingram Books

Rapid Descent—Disaster in Boston Harbor, 2000
ISBN# 0-9677619-0-5

Project Samuel—The Quest for the Centennial Nobel Prize, 2001
ISBN# 0-9677619-1-3

Return to Raby—A New England Novel, 2003
ISBN# 0-9677619-2-1

Sniff—A Novel, 2004, Xlibris
ISBN# 1-4134-6558-7

Lavatory 101—A Bathroom Book of Knowledge. 2004, Xlibris
ISBN# 1-4134-8374-7

Brain Freeze -321° F—Saving Reggie Sanford, 2005, Xlibris
ISBN# 1-4134-9768-3

*Longtail Publishing, 176 Pleasant Street, Laconia, NH 03246